Praise for Amanda Forester's Regency romance

A Wedding in Springtime

"This entertaining novel is a diamond of the first order...the clever combination of wit, romance, and suspense strikes all the right notes."

—*Booklist*, Starred Review (a Top 10 Romance of 2013)

"Forester promises her fans a warm, humorous jaunt through Regency England—and she delivers with a cast of engaging characters and delightful intrigue."

—*RT Book Reviews*, 4 stars

"Engaging subplots involving unforgettable supporting characters make this one a must-read."

—*Publishers Weekly*, Starred Review

A Winter Wedding

"Forester's latest sparkles with charming repartee and just enough humor to spice up the romance and intrigue."

—*RT Book Reviews*, 4 stars

"A charming story infused with sensuality, suspense, and sparkle... The characters are so well drawn that they seem to step right off the page."

—*Romance Junkies*

"A scandalous romance filled with wit and warmth...a must-read."

—*Night Owl Reviews*

Also by Amanda Forester

Medieval Highlanders
The Highlander's Sword
The Highlander's Heart
True Highland Spirit
The Highlander's Bride

The Campbell Sisters Novellas
The Highland Bride's Choice
The Wrong Highland Bridegroom
The Trouble with a Highland Bride

Marriage Mart Regency
A Wedding in Springtime
A Midsummer Bride
A Winter Wedding

IF THE EARL ONLY KNEW

AMANDA FORESTER

sourcebooks
casablanca

Published by Sourcebooks Casablanca, an imprint of Sourcebooks, Inc.
P.O. Box 4410, Naperville, Illinois 60567-4410
(630) 961-3900
Fax: (630) 961-2168
www.sourcebooks.com

Printed and bound in Canada.
MBP 10 9 8 7 6 5 4 3 2 1

One for sorrow,
Two for joy,
Three for a girl,
Four for a boy,
Five for silver,
Six for gold,
Seven for a secret never to be told.
—English nursery rhyme

One

KATE STARED AT THE SINGLE MAGPIE PERCHED ON THE thick wall of Fleet Debtors' Prison. At twelve years old, she hardly needed the ill omen to know she was in peril.

Her heart beat hard within her chest and she grasped her twin brother's hand as they were forced into the stone sarcophagus of the prison. How could this be happening to her?

"Boys this way, girls that way," a pale-faced guard intoned, too bored with the plight of human misery even to look up over his desk.

"You cannot do this. I am the Earl of Darington. There has been a mistake," repeated her brother. Though tall for his age, the guards only saw him as a child and had long since stopped listening.

"Only mistake is that yer father didn't pay his debts afore he died. Now no more o' yer lies. Ye wouldn't be in debtors' prison if ye was quality or had anyone what cared fer ye." The man nodded to a sharp-faced matron, who grabbed Kate by the wrist and wrenched her away from her brother.

"No!" Kate cried, but the fierce matron pulled her through a low doorway and down a dark passage, the air growing increasingly stale and acrid with every step. The stench of years of filth and sheer wretchedness filled her lungs, causing her to gag. When they reached the very pit of hell, the woman unlocked a door and flung Kate inside.

"The girl what lived here died this morning." The matron gave her a sinister smile. "G'night, dearie."

She slammed the door shut, leaving Kate in total darkness.

"No." Kate wrapped her arms around herself to protect against the suffocating black nothingness...

❧

"No...no!" Kate awoke in a tangle of bedsheets, gasping for breath.

Someone rapped on the door of her small, spare bedroom and her twin brother appeared, leaning one shoulder on the door frame. He had grown taller in the thirteen years since their unfortunate sojourn in Fleet prison.

"Doing battle?" he asked, his face impassive.

Kate took a long, slow breath as she tried to extricate herself from the twisted bedsheets. "Just enjoying the sweet dreams of our childhood."

"That bad, eh?" Robert shook his head.

"Force of habit when we travel to London. I remember all the amusements we shared."

"Of some amusements, one can never have too little," Robert commented in a dry tone.

"True, but given today's itinerary, I fear we shall have a very amusing day, indeed."

"Saints preserve us," grumbled Robert.

"Saints?" Kate shook her head. "I doubt we shall receive any divine help today. Let us get on with our business and leave this godforsaken town."

Robert raised an eyebrow. "Has the good Lord forsaken all of London, do you think?"

Kate shrugged. "If not the whole of London, us at the very least."

Robert gave a slight nod and left the room so Kate could prepare for the day. There was no denying their visits to London had never ended well.

Lady Katherine Ashton dressed herself quickly, as was her custom. The grim remembrances of her previous visits to London dragged themselves through her mind like a macabre review. Her first visit in 1797 had resulted in being wrongfully forced into Fleet prison. Her second visit at age nineteen had ended in the dreadful accident. Now in the year 1810, at the venerable age of twenty-five, Kate faced London once more. She hoped to avoid some new tragedy, but given her history, the odds were against her.

After five years of self-imposed banishment in Gibraltar, Kate was more accustomed to helping her brother with the accounts of his business than acting like a lady. Today she would face her greatest fear—the seething pit of depravity known as London society.

Kate took a bracing breath of the cold, damp London air. It was time to face the demons of her past. Or in this case a wickedly handsome man, which was essentially the same thing.

"No, a handsome man is worse. Much worse," she muttered to herself.

She indulged herself with a quick glance in the mirror to ensure everything about her person was neat and orderly. Her brown hair was pulled back in a strict bun with not a strand out of place. Her black cotton gown was pressed sharp. Everything about her appearance was in good regulation except her eyes. She wished they were a sensible brown, but instead, they were a strange light color. She called them gray but feared they bordered on silver. Kate turned from the image without a second look and tugged on a wool coat and bonnet to protect against the December freeze.

She entered the main room, giving a nod to her brother who was dressed and waiting. She gathered her ledgers, logs, and documents. It was time to get to business.

"Our goals for the day are to free the offspring of the unfortunate masses from imprisonment and throw off the fetters of our financial bondage by facing our investors." Kate double-checked her list. It was shorter than usual, but the items were of a significant nature so she granted herself some leniency.

"Are you ready for this?" asked Robert, pulling on his worn wool greatcoat.

"Quite." Kate chose to misinterpret his meaning. "I have prepared an accounting for each one of our investors, providing details of their original investment and return."

Robert took the large ledgers from her hands. "Not what I meant."

"I shall never be ready. But let us do it anyway," she replied crisply.

They walked out of their small lodging in a working-class part of Town. Robert stopped short and stared at the modest conveyance before them with a mixture of shock and resignation. Though to the casual observer his face was not altered, Kate was well able to read the slightest change in her twin brother's expression.

"This carriage was the least expensive," Kate said, giving him an unnecessary explanation.

"Carriage?" Robert Ashton, the Earl of Darington, was doubtful.

"That's what the man called it," defended Kate. "The other options were shockingly dear." She surveyed the questionable equipage with a critical eye. What might once have been a barouche carriage was in such disrepair it more resembled a delivery wagon, and the swaybacked gray horse who contrived to pull it appeared to be on his last legs. Even if the barouche had been in good condition, the open nature of the carriage made it entirely unsuitable for the freezing weather.

"Indeed." The stern expression on her brother's face gave him the appearance of being older than his twenty-five years. He was a tall, thin man, with dark brown hair and a life of hard toil etched into the lines on his face. His eyes were as black as hers were light. Spending much of his life at sea and the last five years as the captain of the notorious *Lady Kate*, he could intimidate a hardened crew with a single raised eyebrow.

"According to my calculations"—Kate broke open one of the several large accounting ledgers—"the price of this carriage, which I obtained quite inexpensively, will cost less over our planned two-week stay in

London than hiring a hack, based on an estimation of
our routes and—"

"Yes, of course." Robert surrendered to her superior knowledge of sums. When it came to financial
management, she was the undisputed master. She had
taken them from the terrifying poverty of their youth
to their current comfortable position. Through her
careful management, every coin her brother earned
had been kept, saved, invested, and increased.

He handed her up into the conveyance without
further complaint and jumped up beside her, encouraging the poor beast of a horse to walk as best it
could through the city streets. Kate breathed deep,
but instead of the fresh scent of clean sea air she was
accustomed to from living in Gibraltar for the past
five years, her nostrils were assailed by a strong smell
of damp and coal smoke that shrouded London in a
permanent haze.

Robert snapped the reins, and they ambled along
toward the Bank of England on Threadneedle Street
where their meeting with the investors into Robert's
"shipping" business would be held. She would never
have agreed to return to London were it not for the
terms of the contract, which stated the investors would
be paid back in full at the end of five years, plus a
percentage of any profits.

Kate had developed a keen accounting for each
one of their investors, but such a meeting brought the
prospect of seeing one particular investor. A man she
never wanted to see again. Ever.

Would he be there? Would he dare come?

Lady Katherine has no beauty, no fashion, no conversation, and no accomplishments save being the sister to an earl, and an impoverished one at that. Years later, his voice still rang in her head.

It had begun innocently enough. While at university, Robert had become acquainted with Tristan Arlington, the second son of the Earl of Wynbrook, who had invited them to spend the Christmas holidays with his family. Tristan's mother had been particularly kind, and for a brief moment Kate had thought she had finally been accepted. But it was not to last.

Kate closed her eyes and remembered her fateful visit. She had heard voices coming from the open library door and stopped. She knew she ought not to eavesdrop, but she could not help pausing outside the door and listening to the conversation between Tristan and his elder brother.

"Darington might not be so bad—one can forgive lack of conversation in a gentleman—but you must admit the sister is poor company indeed," drawled Tristan's elder brother.

"Dash it, John! What a gudgeon you are," exclaimed Tristan. *"Kate's not had the advantages of feminine company is all. Their mother died bringing them into the world."*

"Perhaps, but is that any reason for Mother to sponsor her coming out with Jane this spring?"

"Why should Mother not bring out Kate with our sister?" cried Tristan. *"Quite kind of her."*

"Because it may prove an embarrassment to Mother. I do not mean to offend, but your friend's earldom was only recently created. Darington's father must have done something quite heroic in his naval career to rise from a baronet to an earl. You know how society disdains social climbers."

Social climbers!

Six years later, the words still ground like grit in her teeth. How she had hated him!

They came to a stop with a jolt and Kate opened her eyes to the intimidating sight of rising colonnades of the Bank of London. She needed to push aside the past and focus on their business. Robert handed the reins to one of the stable lads hired by the bank and received dubious looks from both the lad and passersby alike. Kate was too preoccupied with who might be waiting for them within to give their startled looks a second thought.

Her pulse pounded in her temples as they were led to a sitting room designed for meetings of the rich and the even richer. Dark mahogany paneling lined the hall, and all the furnishings from the curtains to the chairs were resplendent in rich jewel tones. Everything around her spoke of wealth and power.

Surely he would not be here. He would send his solicitor, not come in person. There was no need. She had almost convinced herself of his certain absence when they entered the room.

He was there.

The bastion of society stood warming himself by the fire, dressed impeccably in a dark blue, double-breasted suit that was tailored to perfection. She could not help but drink in his form. His broad, square shoulders revealed a powerful build, yet he had a trim waist and muscular thighs that were on the edge of indecent in his skintight buckskin breeches. With his chestnut hair, green eyes, and square jaw, he was the very definition of a handsome man.

It was him.

John Arlington, the Earl of Wynbrook.
The only man she had ever kissed.

Two

Two for joy

JOHN ARLINGTON, EARL OF WYNBROOK, WARMED HIS hands against winter's chill in the well-appointed sitting room of the Bank of England. The return of Darington and his sister was a complication in his otherwise orderly life. And for that he blamed Lady Kate.

Trouble was, he was not sure how to behave around her, which was terribly unusual. He prided himself on always knowing the correct manner of address for anyone in or out of society, but Lady Kate defied classification. She was a lady, the daughter of an earl, but hardly acted like one. Yet she was so reserved and refined, she did not *not* act like one either. It was all very confusing.

Given his conduct with Lady Kate several years ago, he had assumed an offer from him would have been expected. But then she'd disappeared and left him wondering what he was supposed to do. In truth, he had been relieved when Darington and Lady Kate had taken themselves to Gibraltar, and though it was uncharitable in the extreme, it would have been easier had they never returned.

His younger brother, Tristan, stood by the fire next to him, oblivious to any concern. "Haven't seen Dare since we graduated from Cambridge. Be good to see him again." Tristan gave him an easy smile, his eyes merry.

"I have not seen them both since…" Wynbrook's voice trailed off.

Tristan's face paled and the usual humor drained from his expression.

"Forgive me. I should not have mentioned it," said Wynbrook. No one had taken the loss from the accident harder than Tristan.

"No, we should not avoid the subject. Besides, Darington's service to us should not be forgot."

"It never will be," said Wynbrook firmly. It was one of the reasons he had invested a large sum into Darington's shipping enterprise—a shaky venture at best.

They lapsed into uncomfortable silence and Wynbrook struggled to turn the conversation, if only to put a smile back on Tristan's unusually pensive face. "I suppose Lady Kate has married by now?" He sincerely hoped so, though he did not wish to reveal his concern to Tristan. His brother was not smart, but he was clever.

"No, she is very much still available," said Tristan, the smile sneaking back to his face. "Though I should warn you, I do not believe she holds you in high esteem."

Wynbrook frowned. Lady Kate did not like him? Ladies liked him as a general rule. Come to think of it, ladies liked him as an absolute rule. And why not? He was exceedingly good company. So why her dislike?

Wynbrook could think of only one reason. It was that night. That one dreadful, glorious night.

"Do you know the reason for her dislike?" he could not help asking.

"Good sense? Excellent judge of character?" suggested Tristan with an elegant gesture of his hand.

"Spitefulness does not become you. Nor does that waistcoat. Pink? Not at all the thing, brother mine," said Wynbrook, adroitly changing the subject.

Tristan smirked. "Shocking, is it not? Took a wager I could induce the Duke of Clarence to wear this same shade of pink within the week."

"You are dreadful," said Wynbrook with a chuckle.

"Aren't I?" Tristan laughed.

They were laughing when the handful of other men in the room took to their feet. There could be only one explanation. A lady was present. Wynbrook's mouth went dry and he slowly turned toward the door. Lady Katherine stood in the doorway.

Why was she here? This was an investors meeting. Wynbrook would not have come had he thought there was any chance of meeting her. Too awkward.

Too late.

Brother and sister were dressed all in black. Their faces were thin, their mouths sullen lines. Wynbrook had met undertakers with rosier dispositions. He gave Darington a cursory glance, but his eyes remained on Katherine. She, however, did not spare him even the slightest recognition. Her eyes scanned the room, taking in the rest of the investors who circled to meet them, but stubbornly refused to meet his.

Lady Katherine's dark brown hair was pulled back

severely under a trim, serviceable bonnet. Her black gown was stark yet immaculately pressed, and once he got past the off-putting color, he had to acknowledge it did show her figure well, though she was so thin he had a sudden urge to feed her. Her face was angular, yet she had high cheekbones, giving her an almost regal air.

Her one remarkable feature had always been her eyes. They were a strange, light color, almost translucent. Those eyes radiated intelligence and glowed with the internal warmth of the workings of her mind. Despite considerable effort, he could never entirely forget those eyes. He had never seen the color on anyone else; they were hers alone.

A titter of concern passed through the investors at the impoverished appearance of Darington and his sister. Darington was a lean, tall man, with brown hair tied back at the nape of his neck in a manner common to sailors. The clothes he wore looked shockingly like homespun and gave no indication of his rank. His eyes were dark, almost black, and his expression was so stern, it made one wish to apologize for giving offense. He was an imposing man, but it was not his physical appearance that made him impressive. There was a presence to him, an aura of power that surrounded him. Wynbrook could tell this man was accustomed to being in command and had to squelch the impulse to call him "Captain."

The clear poverty of their attire did not bode well for the prospects of the investment. If their style of dress was any indication, they had not only lost the investment, but had gone down the hatches entirely.

Wynbrook had no intention of demanding repayment and instead wondered how much it would take to discharge their debts and get them back on their feet. It was not good to see them looking so poor and thin.

"Dare!" cried Tristan, breaking the awkward silence. He greeted his friend with a hearty handshake and a slap on the back. "Been too long. How are you, old man? And Lady Kate, good to see you again."

Lord Darington and his sister acknowledged him graciously, though with the distinct reserve that was their nature. Considering the bad news they were about to deliver, Wynbrook could hardly blame their grim appearance.

"Darington. It is good to see you," said Wynbrook, following his brother to greet his friends. Kate did not look at him. Not even a glance. Had he sunk so low in her estimation that he did not even register a glimpse? "Lady Katherine, you are well met." He was determined to force her to look at him.

Slowly, as if trying to find something else to look at, Kate met his gaze. Her ethereal eyes glinted, and he wondered if they reflected the pale sunlight from the window or sparkled with a light all Kate's own.

"Lord Wynbrook." She deigned to give him the smallest of curtsies.

"I assume we will be meeting the reclusive Mr. Ashton today?" Wynbrook attempted polite conversation. Darington's cousin, Mr. Ashton, had drawn up the legal paperwork for the investment. In truth, Mr. Ashton had proved himself so valuable in straightening other financial wrinkles that Wynbrook had hired the man to see to his financial welfare. It had proved rewarding, though it was odd he had never met the man in person.

Lady Kate and Darington looked at each other and some look of understanding passed between them.

"Mr. Ashton sends his regrets," said Darington.

"I see," said Wynbrook. What he saw was that the attorney who had recommended the investment and drawn up the legal paperwork for it had lost his courage when the investment turned sour and abandoned Darington to face the investors alone.

They gathered around a long table in order for Darington to report the outcome of the investment. Wynbrook expected Kate to remove herself from the meeting, but she took a seat next to her brother. There was nothing demure about her nature.

Darington stood and said only that he appreciated the support and that Mr. Ashton was unable to be present. He then turned the meeting over to his sister. Much to Wynbrook's surprise, Lady Katherine began to distribute account sheets to each investor.

"Lady Katherine will be presenting the financial information?" Wynbrook thought little of Mr. Ashton for abandoning Darington to the mercies of the angry investors, but he was shocked that Dare would put his own sister in such a position. It was cowardly in the extreme.

"I assure you, I am familiar with the financial arrangements and will be able to answer all questions," declared Kate.

"We made our agreement with Lord Darington and I feel it should be him to give the report to his investors," said Wynbrook in a soft voice. Murmurs of agreement came from the other investors. He was surprised at his defense of her, for his own feelings toward her were convoluted in a manner he only wished to avoid, and yet Lady Kate should not be made to face the wrath of the investors. If Dare failed to act, he would.

Dare began to rise, but Kate put a hand on his sleeve and he returned to his seat. "If you do not wish to hear my report, I beg you would leave." Kate spoke through gritted teeth. "For now, you are interrupting the orderly conduct of business."

Wynbrook blinked twice, taken off guard by her animosity. He had only meant to protect her. "By all means, do continue."

Lady Kate cleared her throat and paused as if daring anyone else to speak in protest. All were silent, though a discontent among the investors was quietly simmering.

"Upon our arrival in Gibraltar, it soon became apparent that shipping was not as profitable as privateering, so the *Lady Kate* set out under letters of marque from the English Crown." Kate spoke so bluntly, Wynbrook was caught off guard. He had long suspected the true nature of Dare's "business" but expected them to be more reserved in their admission.

"So you were a pirate?" asked one of the investors with a scowl as the rest rumbled with disapproval.

"Privateer," corrected Darington.

"By what right have you to change the nature of the business and put our investment at risk?" asked an older gentleman, and the grumbles among the investors grew louder.

This time, Dare did stand and people found themselves confronted with the renowned Lord Captain

Darington. He said nothing but met the eyes of each investor in turn with such a steely gaze that all conversation halted and all the investors were reduced to sullen silence. Dare slowly returned to his seat and nodded to his sister to continue.

Kate immediately got to business, spouting numbers with dizzying rapidity. Considering his expectation and his surprise to see Kate so much in command of the financial report, it took Wynbrook a moment for her words to register into coherent meaning.

He stared at the numbers in disbelief. This accounting sheet did not indicate a loss but a gain. And not modest gains but large ones. He looked at the impoverished Darington and then back at the accounting sheet, unable to reconcile the dissonance between the image before him and the numbers on the page.

"Wait, wait," interrupted Tristan, staring at his accounting sheet. "How much blunt did we make?"

"Well," said Kate, with a frown at the interruption, "what I am trying to explain is that your initial investment has seen a significant increase over the past five years. As you can see from the bottom number on your page—"

"I'm rich!" Tristan shouted with joy.

Wynbrook scanned his own sheet down to the bottom. "Is this in error?" he asked, staggered by the sum.

Kate raised an offended eyebrow. "I assure you the calculations are correct."

Wynbrook smiled sweetly at her. He had fortune enough before this morning, and now he had fortune *more* than enough. But why the poverty-stricken appearance of Dare and his sister?

Kate continued to attempt to walk the investors through each year of incomes and expenses, the additional ships, crews, and captains added to their flotilla, but no one was much concerned with how they had acquired such windfall, preferring to whisper excitedly between each other of what they were going to do with their sudden fortunes. Even the older gentleman who condemned piracy was mollified into heartily approving of privateering when it lined his own coffers. Eventually, Kate gave up trying to explain the intricacies of bringing naval prizes to the admiralty courts and fell silent, glaring at the investors as though they were recalcitrant schoolboys.

"Gentlemen, please," said Wynbrook. "Lady Katherine has the floor." He realized now he had falsely judged Darington. The man had not forced his sister to bear the brunt of the investors' ire but had allowed her the honor of giving the good news, rather than taking the credit for it himself.

"Thank you, Lord Wynbrook, but I believe this concludes our meeting and our business," said Kate crisply. "All monies owed have been made available to you in the bank. We thank you for your investment."

This news prompted the gentlemen investors to jump up to voice their appreciation and leave to claim their newfound fortune. Soon Wynbrook and Tristan were the only ones who remained with Darington and Kate.

"Now I don't have to join the regulars." Tristan was in high spirits.

"You never did," reminded Wynbrook, who had ensured that his brother, and his exacting tastes in fashion, had been adequately provided for, though it had meant reducing some of his own inheritance.

"But why are you two so shabbily attired?" asked Tristan, boldly marching into a topic of conversation where Wynbrook was cautious to tread. "Forgive me, but are you in mourning? You never mentioned it in your letters."

"No, we are not," replied Darington.

At their blank faces, Kate continued, "Force of habit. People assumed I was a widow, which made things easier."

Wynbrook stared at her. He supposed it was true that a widow had more freedom in society than an unmarried lady, but at what cost had she bought this freedom?

"Oh no, my dear, this will never do," declared Tristan. "You cannot run about London looking like…this!"

Wynbrook often felt his brother's fastidious preoccupation with clothes to be extreme, but in this case, he had to agree.

"Where are you staying?" asked Tristan. When Darington told him, Wynbrook feared Tristan might collapse of apoplexy.

"But why?" cried Tristan. "If we have made a fortune, you both must be richer than Croesus."

"We prefer to leave some monies in reserve," said Kate vaguely. "Besides, life is uncertain. One must always be prepared to take care of oneself."

"Monies in reserve?" Tristan was clearly unfamiliar with the concept. "This is nonsense. You must come stay with us!"

Wynbrook started at his brother's rash offer. Kate

stay with him under the same roof? Unthinkable! If he had any consolation, it was that Kate appeared as alarmed as he felt.

"Oh no," she said quickly. "We could not impose."

"No imposition at all," Tristan went on merrily. "You must come stay and then accompany us to the country for Jane's wedding! Did you get my most recent letter? Our sister has finally found a groom-to-be!" Tristan continued to talk excitedly to Darington. Wynbrook guessed that was why the two became friends at university—Darington rarely spoke and Tristan never stopped.

"It would be quite impossible for us to stay with you," said Kate to anyone who would listen.

"Cap'n!" A young lad banged open the door and ran into the room, followed by three bank employees.

"Sorry, my lords. We will remove him shortly," called out one of the employees, trying unsuccessfully to grab the lad.

"Leave off," commanded Darington. "This lad is in my employ."

"They need ye quick, Cap'n. Someone's broke into your quarters on the *Lady Kate*!" the boy gasped, his hands on his knees. "Hoofed it all the way here to tell ye."

"What about the men on duty?" asked Dare.

"Knocked clean out. Most o' the men on shore leave. Don't know what they took. Found the guard and saw the door busted open and ran here to tell ye. They might still be there for all I know." The lad was still gasping for breath.

"Good lad." Darington handed the boy a coin.

"Forgive me. Must leave." He gave Wynbrook and Tristan a quick nod and walked out of the room, Kate following along behind.

"Yes, of course," said Wynbrook. He and Tristan followed them down the hall and out into the large main room of the bank.

"I'll have to rent a hack. My carriage will never make it in time." Dare gave Kate a dark look.

"I'll run you down to the docks in my racing curricle—nothing faster!" declared Tristan. "John and I came down in it this morning, though it only sits two." He glanced at Wynbrook and Kate.

"I will drive Lady Kate back to their lodgings in their carriage and will take a hack back home," offered Wynbrook.

"No!" Kate said at something of a shout, causing bank patrons to turn their heads. "No," she repeated in a softer tone, ignoring the stares of those around them. "I can take the carriage back myself. Besides, I have an appointment I cannot miss."

"I would be happy to squire you to your appointment," said Wynbrook gallantly, since it was required. He had endured many trips to the milliner with his sisters; he could do it once more.

"I assure you that will not be necessary," Kate said, trying to quell his offer.

"Oh, but it is," said Tristan brightly. "Can't jaunt around London by yourself. Not done. Not done by half."

Darington paused by the front door of the bank. "Let Wynbrook take you," Dare said to Kate.

"But the errand?" A crease appeared between her eyes.

"I would be happy to oblige," said Wynbrook, wondering a bit at his eagerness. He wished to not have dealings with Lady Kate, but he could not leave her stranded when it was in his power to assist. That would be shabby in the extreme.

Dare handed Kate a large stack of papers and ledgers. "Let him help."

Before Kate could protest further, Dare and Tristan disappeared out the door and were gone.

"Allow me," said Wynbrook, reaching for the large books, but Kate held them fast.

"I am fine," she grumbled.

Wynbrook gave Kate a tight smile and motioned for her to precede him out the door held open by a footman. He had wanted to avoid Kate at all costs, and now he was obliged to squire her hither and yon. It was going to make for an interesting day.

Kate walked down the street and stopped before something that looked like a broken-down hay wagon.

"What is that?" he asked, dread creeping down his spine.

"Our carriage."

"Oh. No." *Interesting* had just taken a turn for the worse.

Three

Three for a girl

"NO. NO, NO, NO, NO. NOOOOOOO, NO, NO."
Wynbrook shook his head. He could not be seen riding
through Town in such a contraption. It was unthinkable.

Kate raised an eyebrow. "It is hardly as bad as that,"
she said, surveying the broken-down carriage and the
poor beast that was pulling it.

"You are right. It's worse than that. But I must
refrain from saying what I truly think because I am in
the presence of a lady."

"Don't let that stop you." She was glaring at him
now. Somehow it did nothing to diminish the attraction of her silver eyes.

"I do not suppose I could convince you to abandon
this...this conveyance and take some other mode of
transportation. A hack? A hobbyhorse? A wheelbar-
row?" A man could hope.

"Good day, Lord Wynbrook." Though her
face registered no emotion, her eyes snapped with
annoyance. Kate placed her books, papers, and

ledgers on the front seat and climbed adroitly up into the open carriage.

"Hold there. I have agreed to squire you about Town and so I shall." Wynbrook hoisted himself up beside her on the front carriage seat and attempted to take the reins from her hands, but she held fast.

"Lord Wynbrook, there is no need to accompany me. I know you do not want to be here, and I assure you where I am going you do not wish to go. I will wish you a good day."

"I promised your brother I would assist you and so I fear you are stuck with me." The more she tried to get rid of him, the more determined he was to stay.

She turned her steely eyes to him, her glare as sharp as a knife. "I believe in speaking plainly. I know how much you dislike my brother and myself. I confess I overheard you speaking quite candidly to your brother regarding your feelings about us the last time we were in London."

It took Wynbrook a moment to recall the conversation. In a flash, he remembered every cutting remark and was instantly ashamed of his conduct. Tristan had been right to call him an arrogant arse. There had been a time when he thought himself better than his company and utterly invincible. How quickly things had changed.

Of course, that day was not the last interaction he had shared with Lady Kate. Was she going to list their other encounter as more evidence of his crimes against her? He waited for her to continue and was met with a glare for his trouble. Were they supposed to pretend their rendezvous that night five years ago never happened? More stony silence.

Apparently so.

Wynbrook took a deep breath of the cold, damp December air. He hated apologizing, mostly because he hated the thought that his conduct was less than honorable, but in this case, an expression of regret to Lady Katherine was owed. "Please allow me to apologize for my conduct when I was young and dunderheaded. I most humbly ask your forgiveness for that day and anything else that I may have done or said that has given you offense." There, that was a blanket apology for all his misdeeds, spoken and unspoken. He should be covered now.

"If I offer absolution, will you leave me alone?" she grumbled.

"I fear nothing can release you from the obvious displeasure of having me drive you to your errand and then safely back home. I will, however, promise never to burden you with my presence in the future."

"As you wish." She sighed, accepting defeat by handing over the reins. "Remember, I warned you."

With that grim rejoinder, they were off. "C'mon there," coaxed Wynbrook, trying to increase the speed of the old, gray horse to something of a relaxed amble.

"Pickles," said Kate.

Wynbrook turned to Kate in confusion.

"The horse's name is Pickles," she clarified.

Of course it was. "C'mon there...Pickles." If he was to be humiliated, it might as well be done in grand style.

Kate stared straight ahead, clinging to her books like a shield, her back as straight as a sword. If she noticed the looks of shock and surprise from the passing carriages, she gave no indication. Wynbrook had hoped to travel the London streets without seeing anyone he knew, but instead he passed many of the elite in high society with him sitting on the driver's box of a ramshackle delivery wagon.

He greeted Mr. and Mrs. Grant, the Duke of Marchford, the Duke of Clarence, and Lord Devine with his niece, the young Miss Frances, slack jawed, her face pressed against the glass of the carriage. Wynbrook waved and smiled.

"Oh, my poor reputation," he bemoaned. It earned him a glare from the ill-tempered Kate. She continued to provide him directions, leading not toward a modiste but toward the poorer part of Town. Where could she be going?

They rolled down the London streets, the dense, coal-smoke-infused haze swirling around them. They turned down Farringdon Street and Kate told Wynbrook to pull up outside of a tall stone wall. Barred windows were built into the wall from which people called out, piteously begging for alms.

"This is Fleet Debtors' Prison," said Wynbrook. He did not like to hear the laments of the poor and was truly confused as to why Kate would bring them to such a place.

"Yes." Everything about the already-rigid Lady Katherine had grown tighter. "Understand, Robert and I have an appointment here, which I cannot miss."

"What business could you possibly have with a debtors' prison?"

"You may stay here with the cart," said Kate, not answering his question.

Wynbrook raised an eyebrow. "First, you must

think quite poorly of me to believe I would send you into Fleet alone, and second, I am gratified that you have properly defined this conveyance. It is a cart."

"Which might be stolen if no one stays with it." Kate struggled to get down from the cart with her arms full of papers.

Wynbrook jumped down and assisted her, putting his hands around her small waist to lift her easily to the ground. His hands lingered on her waist for a second longer than was absolutely necessary; for some reason, he did not want to let go. A flash of attraction surged through him, as powerful as it was unwanted. He snatched his hands away and held out his arms to offer to carry her books as if that had been his plan all along.

"I doubt even thieves would be interested in that gig," commented Wynbrook. "Here now." He tossed a coin to a heavily mufflered lad. "Watch this nag for me and there will be another farthing for you if it is still here when I return. I'll give you a half crown if you can sell it for more than a pound."

"It is not yours to sell!" cried Kate.

"Do not distress yourself. It is not worth more than a few shillings. But why are we here?" Behind his cheery bluster, Wynbrook was dismayed at her destination and could think of no reason why she would be there.

"I have business here." She walked to the arch in the stone wall and paid a coin to the turnkey. Wynbrook followed her through the gates to the large courtyard of the prison, surrounded by imposing stone walls five stories high.

"What business?" asked Wynbrook softly.

Again she did not answer but crossed the courtyard quickly, her boots crunching on the frozen ground. She climbed the few stairs to the main door and paused. Her breath came shallow and quick, and she put a hand on the wall to steady herself. Whatever this place was to her, it clearly affected her deeply.

He put a hand on her shoulder, afraid she might faint like some ladies were known to do when distressed.

"No!" she gasped and jumped away, her eyes wide with fear.

"Are you unwell?" asked Wynbrook. Despite the awkwardness between them, he felt an immediate urge to protect her. He did not know what business she had here, but he would see it done.

She blinked and the emotion drained from her face. She cleared her throat and straightened her already-straight bonnet. "I am fine. Do let us continue."

"You can wait in the carriage, if you wish, and I can see to whatever business you have," offered Wynbrook. Considering her reaction, he guessed she must know someone locked in one of these cells.

"Kind of you to call it a carriage," murmured Kate.

"You looked beset. Thought you might faint if I told you what I really thought of it." The remark earned him a twitch of her tight lips.

They walked through the door to the spare reception area. The smell of mold, filth, and human misery was overpowering.

"We have an appointment with the warden," said Kate.

"What fer?" asked a bony man behind a desk, hardly bothering to look up over his racing form.

"That is my concern and not yours," answered Kate.

"Well, I see who comes and who goes and who sees who. So ifs ye want to see anyone, ye better tell me what fer."

"We have come to show payment of debt and obtain release for some of your residents," Kate replied in a tight, clipped tone.

Wynbrook was right; she must wish to release someone known to her.

"Put the paper here," droned the man and went back to his racing schedule.

Kate dropped the stack of papers down on his desk with a thud. The guard stared. Wynbrook stared.

The guard looked up in surprise. "What's all this, now?"

"The release papers," said Kate.

"B-but how many debts ha' ye done paid?"

"We have paid the debts of every child living in Fleet and their families," said Kate with authority.

Wynbrook's jaw went slack. He couldn't help it. What was she doing?

"I'm going to need to get the warden, I am," hedged the guard.

"Indeed. Step to it then," said Wynbrook in a commanding tone, deciding it was his turn to enter the conversation.

The man scuttled off directly.

"All the children?" asked Wynbrook. He was still reeling.

"And their families," added Kate.

"It must have been very costly."

"It was," agreed Kate.

Wynbrook liked to think of himself as a generous

man, but this was beyond anything he had ever considered. Why would she do such a thing? "Do you know any of these children?"

"No. But no child should be in jail because of the poverty of their parents."

"Indeed."

"You got no right to pay all these here debts." The warden, a large man whose head rested on multiple chins, waddled his bulk toward them.

"And you have no right to charge rent and ridiculous fees to the poor souls who are forced to live here. You care not for the repayment of debt. You only wish to secure your own profit by stealing from the poor and vulnerable." Kate flushed with more emotion than Wynbrook had ever seen on her face.

"You know nothing of it!" The warden's face turned florid. "I will have to look into each one of these releases. Will take time."

"But we have court orders for their release!" cried Kate, her distress clear.

"Don't care what you think you got. Take time, it will." The warden crossed his meaty arms across his chest.

"Excellent. That will allow us time to process the claims against you," said Wynbrook, stepping forward into the fray.

"Wh-what do you mean?" asked the warden, taking careful note of Wynbrook's attire and changing his tone to be more deferential.

It was clear the warden had sized up Kate to be someone he could bully. The man changed his tune in the face of Wynbrook's multiple-caped riding coat. Wynbrook knew that people showed preference to members of society's elite, but it had never before bothered him as it did now. "Yes, we are looking into abuses of your office and the embezzlement of funds. I should not be surprised if you were required to pay back every false fine you have ever collected."

"You can't do that." The wide eyes of the warden were no longer confident.

"Do you doubt my ability to gain an audience with the Lord Mayor? I imagine paying back your ill-gotten gains would be quite a hefty sum. Would it not be ironic if you yourself ended up in the same prison you once administered?" Wynbrook tugged at his cuffs nonchalantly. He glanced up at Kate and her eyes shone, a small smile on her lips. It was his turn to catch his breath. The rare smile from Lady Kate was worth the trouble of earning it.

The warden opened and closed his mouth twice in horror. The debts were acknowledged paid.

Wynbrook and Kate retreated back to the cart, which, much to his disappointment, was still there.

"Thank you," she said with a soft glow in her eyes. It was the first time that day she had looked at him without a glare. It was strange, his reaction to that look. Maybe it was her light eyes or the memory of something that had passed between them, but tingles shot through him. His reaction was akin to a schoolboy's, which was odd in the extreme, since he was not unaccustomed to female company.

Though he was not one to brag about his exploits, he had been connected with some of the most renowned beauties, all with soft, round bodies and warm, alluring faces. Kate was nothing like them, all angles and edges, both in form and temperament. And yet she was the one he could never forget.

"I have done nothing. You deserve all the credit. I am astounded at your generosity." He was truly impressed. "Will you tell me why you did this?"

"For this," she said with a simple gesture. Families began to emerge, bewildered, from the prison, smiling, laughing, crying. It was a touching scene.

"Do they know to whom they are indebted?" he asked.

"No."

"But why—"

"Robert and I believe in giving charity. That is all."

That was clearly not all. Wynbrook clicked to Pickles, and they began to amble back down the street. One thing was evident—Wynbrook did not know the lady sitting next to him. Not in the least. Despite his initial intent to stay as far away from her as possible, he now was drawn to the mystery of Lady Katherine Ashton.

"Lady Kate, I want you to know I admire greatly what you have done."

Kate clutched the ledgers and logbooks close to her chest. "Turn left here, Lord Wynbrook. I appreciate your assistance, but I will remind you of our agreement."

"Our agreement?" His question was met with the return of the glare from Lady Kate. "Oh, yes, of course." He had agreed never to see her again. Wynbrook squinted into the stinging, cold sleet.

Just when it was getting truly interesting, time had run out on his audience with the enigmatic Kate Ashton.

❦

Captain Silas Bones sipped a glass of claret. Its annoy-ingly poor quality burned his throat. Deprivation did not suit him. "Did you get the logbooks?"

"Nay, Cap'n. Searched Darington's quarters on board, but he must have taken his logs." His wiry first mate stood before him.

"My dear man, that is simply unacceptable." Silas swirled the wine in his glass. "I would hate to think that you were disappointing me."

His first mate stood at rigid attention. "N-no, sir."

"I need those logs. I need to know what he did with the gold. Do you know why I need to know that?"

"Why, sir?"

"Because it is *my gold*!" Silas's sudden shout made his first mate jump. "Now, take some of the lads and go search his lodgings. I care not what you do to get them, but bring me back those logbooks."

"Aye, Captain." The man saluted and left.

Silas had taken a small room in a disreputable inn by the docks, the only lodging he was now able to afford thanks to being raided on the high seas by Lord Captain Darington. Silas had been sailing under the French flag as a privateer at the time, but he would make no allowance for Darington taking his ship.

Silas poured himself another glass of the inferior wine. How had it all come to this? He knew how—it was all Darington's fault. The man had taken every-thing from him. Everything.

Silas would get back his cargo, the treasure he car-ried for his father. He had to. If his father knew it had been lost...

Silas put aside the wine and pulled out a bottle of

rum, forgoing the common civility of a glass. This was what Darington had reduced him to, drinking rum from a bottle like a common sailor.

Darington may have been an excellent privateer, but Silas had something the young man did not. Darington had no idea who Silas was. The earl had no concept of how their family histories were intertwined.

Silas knew. He knew everything.

This was far from over.

Four

Four for a boy

KATE HATED IT WHEN THINGS DID NOT GO ACCORDING to plan. She had expected Wynbrook, a man so obsessed with his own self-importance he could not ride down the streets in a run-down carriage—fine, *cart*—without embarrassment, to encounter Fleet Prison with abhorrence. She had expected his delicate sensibilities to be thrown into disarray and to be met with something of a cut direct for exposing him to the underbelly of London poverty.

She glared at Wynbrook, sitting next to her on the cart as they slowly drove through the frigid streets to the lodgings she had procured with her brother. Most Londoners believed that people who did not pay their debts deserved to be in prison. She'd expected Wynbrook to feel the same. Instead, he had not only expressed admiration for her actions, but he had also helped her make it come about.

She was determined not to like him. She had every reason not to like him. It was much easier not to like him. If only he would play the role of the arrogant aristocrat, this whole encounter with him would be much easier.

Apparently, Wynbrook was determined to be difficult. Drat the man! She attempted to dispel her unsettling feelings regarding Wynbrook with a mental review of her daily list.

1. Free children from Fleet prison. *Check.*
2. Hold investors' meeting and disburse funds. *Check.*

She added another: *Meet Wynbrook for the first time since that night without doing him bodily harm or swooning at his feet.*

Check. At least for the most part.

Kate was anxious to get to her lodgings and part ways with the confusing Wynbrook, yet when they arrived, she immediately sensed something was wrong. Eyes were upon them, silent, watching, waiting for something to happen.

"Is the door usually kept open?" Wynbrook asked, pointing to the main door of house standing wide-open on a freezing day.

"No." She grabbed her ledgers and turned to jump down, but Wynbrook was already there, lifting her gently to the ground. Even in her concern, her treacherous body reacted to his hands around her waist. She pushed the disconcerting emotions aside and rushed into the boarding house, Wynbrook at her side.

The landlady was sitting on the floor with a bloody cloth to her nose, surrounded by her elderly mother and two young children. "My Lady Katherine, two men, they asked for the key to Lord Darington's room, but I didn't give it, so—"

Kate's heart wrenched to see her landlady so injured. Who had done this?

"What room?" demanded Wynbrook.

"Top of the stairs to the left."

Wynbrook dashed up the stairs three at a time, Kate following behind as fast as she could in skirts. Banging could be heard from inside their room.

"Where is it? I can't find it," said one man.

"Captain won't like it," said another.

"Quick, run! Someone's coming!"

Wynbrook barged into the room, extending an arm to keep Kate back, but it was empty, the window curtains fluttering in the wind. Kate dropped her logbooks and rushed to the window, where two men could be seen running down the alleyway. Stacked crates and other debris had been used to make a fast getaway.

"Who were they? Why…" Kate turned around in the ransacked room, stunned. It was happening again. Bad luck, every time she came to London. Cold fingers of dread snaked up her spine.

"Are you all right?" asked Wynbrook, immediately solicitous. "Here, do sit down." He righted a chair and held it out to her.

Nothing could revive her faster than the insinuation that she could not handle herself in a crisis. "I am fine," she snapped, shutting the window with a bang.

"Good, good. Well, spending a morning with you is never dull." Wynbrook leaned next to her at the window and adjusted his cravat. "Did they steal anything?"

Kate surveyed the ransacked room in dismay. Papers and articles of clothing were strewn about. Both Robert's and her sea lockers had been pried open and her precious few belongings dumped. It felt violating, but after a quick search, she could account for nothing missing. She was glad she had taken the books, her financial ledgers, and Robert's captain's logs with her, or they would have been thrown into disorder.

"What do you think they wanted?" asked Kate, grabbing her chemise from the floor. Cold fingers of dread were replaced with flashes of hot embarrassment at having her unmentionables tossed about the floor in plain sight. What could be worse than having her underclothes displayed for Wynbrook to inspect?

"Probably just thieves," said Wynbrook, picking up an item off the floor. He held up a set of stays.

Heat rushed up her neck and she snatched them from his hand. Wynbrook made no comment but his green eyes sparkled.

"But why target us directly?" Kate desperately tried to change the subject. She could not believe he had held her underthings!

"Most likely petty thieves heard an earl was lodging here and thought you would make a valuable target."

Kate's heart sank. "I never meant to put anyone at risk by choosing modest accommodations. My poor landlady."

"I am about to say something you will rarely hear me confess." Wynbrook paused and cleared his throat for effect. "Tristan was right."

"A brave admission. About everything or something in particular?"

"About almost nothing, and certainly not the shade of his waistcoat, but in the matter of your accommodations while you are in London, Tristan is right. You and Darington should stay with us."

"Aha!" Tristan walked boldly into the room in triumph, followed by Darington. "You said I was right!"

"Oh, I shall never hear the end of this." Wynbrook put a hand to his forehead.

"Right. You said I was right. Of course Dare and Kate need to stay with us. Only thing to do." Tristan looked around the room, noticing the disarray. "You have certainly loosened your housekeeping standards since I knew you at university."

"Thieves," explained Kate with the parsimony that defined her conversation. "Did you catch whomever broke into your quarters on the ship?" she asked Robert.

"No. They searched the place but took nothing. Was anything stolen here?"

"Not that I could find. Do you think it related?" asked Kate.

Robert gave a brief nod. "Must have been looking for something. Maybe they heard of how much gold was on our manifest."

"But all that is now in the bank."

Robert nodded. "Good thing, or it would have been gone."

"So you will stay with us?" pressed Tristan.

Robert met her eyes, asking her the question. She looked away from her brother in defeat. "Yes, thank you for the invitation," answered Robert.

Kate wanted to object, but what else could they do? They could not stay here, and finding new accommodations that would not put someone else at risk would be difficult and costly.

Wynbrook gave her a slow smile that did something strange to her insides. How was she going to live in the same house with such a man?

"Tristan and I will return to Wynbrook House to let our sisters know you will be staying with us. I am sure they will be delighted." Wynbrook bowed politely and left with his brother, who was still crowing in victory.

"Who did this?" Kate asked her brother when they were alone.

"I know not."

Kate shook her head. Another mystery. They still did not know the enemy who had stolen their fortune and handed them over to debtors' prison when they were young. The sad episode and lingering uncertainty had cast a pall over their lives.

Without further discussion, Robert and Kate got to packing. The fortunate part of having few belongings was that it took very little time to prepare for their departure. The room was straightened and their sea lockers packed within minutes.

Robert shouldered the sea lockers and walked down the stairs, Kate following behind. The would-be thieves should be thankful they had jumped out the window before Robert had returned. Years of hard work had made him stronger than he appeared and he was deadly in a fight.

The landlady had been moved to a chair in her modest sitting room and appeared to be recovering from the attack. Robert cast a glance at Kate and she nodded.

"We shall be staying with friends for the remainder of our time in London," said Kate to the landlady. "Please accept this payment for our stay and any trouble our presence may have caused you." She handed the landlady an envelope.

"Thank you," murmured the landlady. Then she looked at what Kate had pressed into her hand. "Bless my soul! Oh, thank you, thank you, milady. Mum, come look what the lady done gave me. Just look!"

Outside, they climbed up onto the cart and encouraged Pickles to move once more. Kate pulled her wool coat closer against the freezing wind. How was it that she was going to the one place she most wished to avoid?

Wynbrook House.

"I cannot believe we are going back there," she mumbled.

"Will you survive?" asked Robert in a tone somewhere between serious and sarcastic.

"I shall endeavor to manage. Besides, being among people of society may help you achieve your next objective."

"Which is?" asked Robert with suspicion.

"You are twenty-five now and in London. It is time for you to find a wife."

Robert stared at her aghast, his mouth slightly ajar. He tended to avoid members of the opposite sex. In truth, Kate suspected he would have rather faced a fleet of enemy ships in gale force winds than be introduced to even the most timid of ladies.

"You need to be married at some point. London seems a good place to find a bride."

Robert's dark brows lowered. "Must I do this today?"

"It would be convenient, if you could manage." To Robert's continued silence, she added, "Perhaps you could ask Tristan to introduce you to someone eligible so you can expeditiously find a bride."

"And are you also to put yourself to a matrimonial search?"

"No. I do not have the duty to reproduce that is incumbent with a title," she said smugly. Then more serious, she added, "I have lived in a man's world too long to be a fit wife. I cannot escape the stain of my past. Not ever."

"Truly? Not ever?"

They rolled slowly along in the London haze. "I will never be married," said Kate firmly. "Of that I am certain."

Five

Five for silver

WYNBROOK ENTERED HIS NEAT, ORDERLY TOWN HOUSE, still turning around in his mind the fact that Kate was coming to stay with them. Lady Kate, the one person on earth he had intended to never see again, would now be his guest. At his own invitation! As much as he wished to avoid Kate, he could not stand to see her in distress. Maybe it was his sense of honor, maybe he felt obligated to Darington, or maybe it was her strange silver eyes, but he needed to know she was safe.

"Good news!" announced Tristan as he and Wynbrook joined their younger sisters for luncheon. "Dare and his sister, Kate, are coming to stay with us and will attend Jane's wedding!"

Wynbrook watched the reaction of Jane and Ellen with some concern. The last time Darington and his sister had been invited to a wedding, it had all ended in tragedy. The room grew silent and all eyes turned to their youngest sister, Ellen. The awkward pause was broken by the footman, who announced the arrival of Lady Durant.

Their elder sister, Anne, swept into the room with an expensive swish of silk, removing her gloves with practiced elegance. "Good morning. We have much to do today to prepare for the wedding." She paused a moment, noting the tension in the room. "You are all quiet this morning. What has silenced you?"

"The Earl of Darington and Lady Katherine are in Town and have been invited to stay with us and attend Jane's wedding," said Wynbrook, gauging her response.

Anne's eyes widened and she gave a little cough. "How lovely. That will be all, Thomas, thank you." Despite being married for five years, she was at Wynbrook House as often as her own home, filling the mother role for her younger sisters, and still commanded the Wynbrook household as if she had never left.

The footman glanced at the master of the house and Wynbrook gave him a small nod. This was not the time to debate with his older sister the finer points of ordering about his servants.

As soon as the footman left the room, Anne turned on him. "Now what is this about Darington coming to the wedding?"

"Are you not pleased?" asked Tristan, oblivious to any concern.

"It is not that we are not eternally grateful for all they have done for the family." Anne glanced at Ellen, who flushed pink. No one lived with the daily reminder of the tragic incident more than Ellen.

"The accident was many years ago. I would like to see them." Ellen smiled at her older siblings. "I cannot live my life being afraid of the past." Her endorsement was all that needed to be said.

"Well then, that is settled," said Anne with resignation. Her eyes flashed at Wynbrook, and he understood her intent. This was a situation he would have to manage to reduce any awkwardness when it came to the inevitable introduction of Darington and Lady Kate into society. "Jane, call the housekeeper and have some rooms made up. Shall we go through to the drawing room? I have some fashion plates I would like to consider for the wedding."

"Shall I get your rolling chair?" Jane asked Ellen.

"Certainly not!" Wynbrook gave his youngest sister a broad smile. "Not while I am here!" He walked up to Ellen and picked her up in his arms.

"Thank you," she said cheerfully as they moved into the drawing room.

A pang of regret rippled through him as it always did when he carried Ellen about the house. Though she and Jane had escaped the accident alive, Ellen's legs had been crushed, requiring them to be amputated below the knee.

Wynbrook settled Ellen in a comfortable chair by the fire and she arranged her skirts such that no one would have guessed she was missing her lower limbs. At twenty-one years old, Ellen was in full bloom, her blond curls framing a sweet face and stunning blue eyes. She would have made quite an impression had the accident not robbed her of her future. For how could she ever enter society with no legs?

The footman entered the room and announced the Earl of Darington and Lady Katherine.

"Well, by Jove, here they are," exclaimed Tristan. "Show them in!"

"My word, 'tis worse than I feared," whispered Anne at the appearance of the morose, shabbily attired Darington twins.

Darington and his sister entered the room with considerable hesitancy. Kate surveyed the entire group of siblings with a sweep of her eyes. "Did not mean to intrude. We can return at a more convenient time."

"No intrusion. Glad you are here," declared the friendly Tristan.

"We are much obliged for your hospitality," responded Kate.

"It is good to see you again," said Anne. "Forgive me, dear, but are you in mourning?"

Kate glanced down at her black grown. "No, but I have found a black dress helpful in avoiding unwanted conversation."

"Oh, indeed…" faltered Anne.

Wynbrook feared Kate's disposition scared away more people than the funereal gown. He cleared his throat as any good English gentleman would do when caught in an awkward situation. "I am sure Darington and Lady Kate are tired from their journey. Jane, perhaps we can see our guests to their rooms."

"Oh, yes!" said Jane. "The housekeeper hopefully is done preparing your rooms. Most of the staff are back at Arlington Hall preparing for the wedding. We would be too, had not Parliament opened early, requiring Wynbrook to come to London."

"Parliament is in session this early?" asked Kate with a slight tilt to her head. Usually Parliament did not open before spring.

"Yes, to discuss the delicate situation of the health of the king," said Wynbrook.

"You mean the madness of the king. Have you not been called to attend, Dare?" asked Tristan.

"Only arrived recently," replied Robert.

"I'm glad it opened early, so you may stay with us." Tristan beamed.

"I'll get the chests," said Robert and was gone.

"I shall help," said Kate and hurried after him.

The thought of Kate carrying her own luggage had Wynbrook chasing after her into the hall. "Lady Kate," he called. She stopped and turned slowly back to him.

"You do find us shorthanded, but please do not think I mean for you to cart your own things. Thomas, please see to the lady's belongings."

The footman gave a nod and strode out the front door.

"I am perfectly capable of carrying my own kit," she argued, her hands going to her hips. She glared at him, ready for battle in her morbid gown.

"Yes, of course," he agreed, though he was willing to wager there was not another lady in all of England who would even consider carrying her own luggage.

Awkward silence settled in the hall. Kate turned and stared at a painting by a Dutch master. He had no doubt she would stare at it for hours if it meant avoiding him.

"Do you plan to stay long in London?" He was not sure whether he wished her visit to be short or long. Certainly it would be easier if it was short.

She turned to him, her strange silver eyes flashing before returning to the portrait. "We shall stay for the wedding but will leave shortly after."

"Naturally, you are welcome to stay with us as long as you wish," he said, a bit surprised at how much he meant it.

"That is kind, but we do not wish to outstay our welcome, especially as you have much to do at present. We are well able to take care of ourselves."

Wynbrook had no doubt that was true. He understood Darington and Kate had been deprived of their parents early in life, but more than that, Wynbrook realized he hardly knew Kate at all. Suddenly it became important to him to know her better. Who was this lady who would free the children of Fleet Prison and hardly blink an eye when her rooms were ransacked?

"Of course you can care for yourselves, but having friends means you do not have to do it alone."

Kate turned to him, her eyes glinting. "Are we friends, then?"

Wynbrook was once again thrown off balance. Were they friends? Was she suggesting they were more? Was she telling him they weren't?

He paused too long, the seconds ticking slowly by into eternity. But how should he answer?

"I see," said Kate at his silence. "I will find where Lady Jane has gone." She turned and stalked away, a swirl of memories in her wake.

"Friends!" called out Wynbrook to her retreating form. "I should hope we are friends." His pulse quickened and he felt as if he were a schoolboy experiencing his first attraction.

Kate paused a moment but then continued down the corridor without further comment.

Wynbrook took a deep breath at her departure. He

needed to get himself under better regulation. He was not unaccustomed to speaking with the loveliest of beauties. The fact that none ever made him feel the way she did was irrelevant.

He cleared his throat. This was all nonsense. No mere slip of a girl could affect him in such a manner. He needed to get back to his normal self. When they were next together, he would be charming and amusing and flirt shamelessly as he always did with the ladies. He would treat her the same as any lady of his acquaintance, and then she would be gone, taking all the confusing emotions with her.

At least, that was the plan.

Six

Six for gold

KATE FLOPPED DOWN ON THE BED OF THE ROOM SHE had been given, grateful for some privacy. Though their hosts had fussed and apologized for the rooms not being ready, and a maid had to scurry to put on fresh linens, Kate could find no fault in the tastefully appointed bedroom. She had to admit the feather bed, a comfort she had never allowed herself, was a delicious treat. She let go of the tension in her back and sank farther into the soft bed. It had been a momentous day and she was exhausted.

Fatigue overcame her and she succumbed to slumber. Though she longed for rest, memories she most wished to forget invaded her dreams. Images flashed before her: carriage windows coated with ice, the collapsed wooden bridge, wild-eyed horses shrieking in the frozen river, the half-submerged carriage lying on its side, one wheel slowly revolving.

"No. No!"

Kate sat bolt upright on the bed. She gasped for air,

trying to reorient herself. More nightmares. Seeing Wynbrook again made it worse. She needed to escape. It was wrong to come back, wrong to try to face the ghosts of her past. Some things were meant to be avoided forever.

She jumped up and staggered to the window, lifting the sash and opening the shutters. She needed air. The cold London air stung her lungs, but she welcomed the cold reality. It was much better than her memories.

A soft knock sounded at her door and she assumed it was her brother, checking on her again as he always did if he heard her sleep disturbed.

"Come in," she called, staring out the window. The low clouds and permanent smoky haze gave London a dusky appearance. "This is a horrible place," she muttered. "We should not have come here."

"Are you—"

"I am fine," Kate said over him, knowing what her brother would ask. "It was just another dream of the accident. More of the same revue. I had so much enjoyment living it once, it is a delight to revisit it in my dreams." She allowed the sarcasm to drip from her tone.

"The one thing I still do not understand is why the bridge did not collapse when *we* traveled over it," she continued. "Why Lord and Lady Wynbrook but not us?"

Six years ago, when Tristan had invited them to spend the holidays with his family, they had traveled from London to Arlington Hall in two coaches. The first, carrying herself, Robert, and the three eldest Arlington siblings—Anne, John, and Tristan—had passed over the frozen bridge without incident. But the second coach, carrying Lord and Lady Wynbrook along with the younger daughters, had crashed through to the frozen river below.

"Why did our coach pass in safety but not theirs?" she asked again. "Did we miss a warning sign that the bridge would collapse? Could we have rescued them faster?"

Robert had been the one to take command on that horrible day, barking orders to the coachmen to cut the horses free to keep them from dragging the coach farther into the frozen river. He was also the first to plunge into the water to rescue the occupants of the coach, followed by John and Tristan and then herself. She well remembered the frigid sting of the icy water. They were able to get everyone out, but it was too late for Lord and Lady Wynbrook.

Kate swallowed a lump in her throat, wishing she could forget how Tristan had cradled his mother's body and sobbed, how Jane had screamed in pain, or how John had sat on the cold, wet ground, overcome with shock.

"I have asked myself that same question."

Kate whirled around at the unexpected voice and stared at John Arlington, the current Lord Wynbrook.

"You are not my brother." It was an obvious statement but all she could think to say.

"True. I was helping Ellen to her room and I heard you call out. I...I thought I should assist if there was a problem." Wynbrook stood tall and formal in her bedroom. Her *bedroom*!

"Why did you not announce yourself at once? Why let me go on?" Kate demanded.

"Yes, that would have been proper," Wynbrook

hedged, looking appropriately contrite. "I do apologize, but…but no one ever speaks of the day my parents died. Jane and Ellen were so injured, they thankfully remember very little, and Tristan never speaks of it."

"I wish I could forget."

Wynbrook nodded slowly. "Everything changed that day. Everything." Wynbrook's voice was soft. On that horrible day he had become the Earl of Wynbrook. It was not how anyone had imagined his succession would occur.

Kate struggled to think of what to say. Should she offer condolences? Should she demand he leave her room?

"I am sorry that day invades your dreams." Wynbrook moved a little closer.

Kate shook her head. "I am sorry it happened at all. I cannot help but think we were bad luck to you."

Wynbrook took a few more steps forward. "No, we are indebted to you and Dare. Without your help, I do not know what would have happened."

"It was not enough." She turned to the window, a lump forming in her throat.

Wynbrook stepped up to the window beside her. "You followed us into the frozen river and pulled Ellen from the coach."

"But her injuries were so grievous…"

"She is alive because of you." Wynbrook placed his hand on hers. Heat spread up her arm and flushed through her at his touch. She should have jerked her hand away, but she did not. Instead, her eyes met his.

A quick rap on the door caused Wynbrook to

jump back in a guilty manner. Lady Jane poked her head into the room. "Hallo, Kate. Ellen and I were wondering if you wanted to join us for…tea." Her eyes widened when she noticed her brother standing beside Kate. "Is everything all right?"

"Yes, of course. Just assisting with the window." Wynbrook closed the sash in a businesslike manner. "There, now. I doubt it will bother you again." With a brisk smile, he marched from the room.

"Well!" said Jane. "He is certainly being helpful. He never helped me with my window."

"Did you mention tea?" asked Kate, hoping to change the subject.

"Oh, yes, we usually have it in Ellen's room, if you do not mind. It is difficult for her to move around a lot." Lady Jane gave her a smile. She was dressed in white with a blue sash at the high waist. She had nondescript dark blond hair and a face that was more classically handsome than pretty.

"Yes, of course." Kate followed Jane into Ellen's room.

Seated at a small round table by a tall window, Lady Ellen was bathed in the yellow afternoon light. A tea service was on the table along with those delicate little sandwiches that were the favorite of elegant ladies. Ellen smiled brightly at Kate's entrance. The bright and happy scene was so unlike her nightmares, Kate had to blink twice at the unexpected sight.

She had anticipated Ellen would live in a perpetual state of mourning for her lost legs, but instead, Ellen wore a pale lilac day dress with lace and ruffles. She had a quick smile and a cheerful disposition. Kate did not know what to make of it. Hardships should be mitigated by becoming even more pessimistic, so no tragedy could ever make you more miserable than you already were. By expecting the absolute worst out of life, Kate was immune to the sting of disappointment, for she lived it every day.

"I hope Robert and I are not imposing," said Kate, accepting a chair.

"No, not at all. I have often wished to see you, for the last time we met…" *Was the day of the accident.* Lady Ellen busied herself with the tea. "Cream and sugar?"

"Black," answered Kate. She accepted the teacup and felt she must say something and not continue to avoid the subject. "I never got a chance to tell you both how sorry I was…I *am*, for the accident," said Kate in a hushed tone.

"Thank you, but it was so many years ago. I fear it must have ruined your holiday," said Ellen.

"Ruined our holiday?" exclaimed Kate, almost spitting her tea. She stared at Ellen in disbelief. "We ruined everything for you! I wish so many times I could do it over and not have gone with you. We are bad luck. If we had not gone with you, maybe you would have taken only one carriage and perhaps the accident would never have occurred."

"Bad luck? Sheer nonsense!" Ellen clasped Kate's hand. "I remember nothing from the accident, but I understand you helped save my life. So thank you. Also, we would never have taken just one coach out of Town, so please stop blaming yourself in this absurd manner. Now have some more tea." Ellen refreshed Kate's cup.

"But your legs… I fear when I pulled you free from the coach I damaged them further. Your loss may have been my fault." Kate spoke the self-recrimination that had gnawed on her soul for the past six years.

"Kate! You saved my life. I don't have my feet, but I have a good life, a good family, and a good deal of amusement most of the time. I refuse to let you feel sorry for me or to blame yourself in any way." Ellen spoke crisply, in the manner of her older sister but with a wide smile that was all her own.

"How can you maintain such a happy attitude given everything that happened?" Kate's question was sincere.

"How can I not have a pleasant attitude? My disposition is entirely something of my own creation. Besides, I believe the good Lord can use all things— even this—for my good."

Kate shook her head, disbelieving.

"I have met many a person with all their arms and legs who are utterly miserable," continued Ellen. "Having two legs does not assure happiness, and losing your legs does not make you unhappy unless you let it. And I shall not let it. There now! Enough of such sad recollections. Have a scone."

Kate took the offering and nibbled obligingly, a bit dazed by how quickly Ellen had tossed aside the guilt that had plagued her. "Thank you."

Ellen gave her a quick nod and abruptly changed the subject. "We have written to Lady Manderlay about her ball tomorrow to see if she would extend the invitation—"

"A ball?" Kate gripped her teacup so hard the whites of her knuckles showed. Remembering the horrors of the past was one thing; a society ball was a nightmare on a whole different level.

"Yes, and the good news is that she has invited you and your brother." Jane beamed at Kate, oblivious to her distress.

"No." It was the only thing Kate could think of to say.

"It is really just a rout party. It will be a good way to introduce you and your brother," Ellen explained.

"I do not attend balls." Ever.

"But you must come," protested Jane. "I can introduce you to Sir Richard." Jane smiled at the mention of her betrothed.

"But…but I have no ball gown," said Kate, relieved to have found a way out.

"I could lend you one of mine," said Jane kindly.

Kate shook her head. "Wouldn't fit." She was right. Jane was shorter and had a more rounded figure than Kate.

Jane was stymied, but only for a moment. "Surely, you must have a gown of some other color than black."

"White," admitted Kate. She had no colors in her wardrobe, preferring a drab palette.

Jane's face relaxed back into a smile. "White muslin is acceptable for young ladies. Besides, it's only Lady Manderlay's rout party. It will be a crush, and everyone will want to meet you. John will be there, you know."

Kate stiffened at the mention of Wynbrook. "That is hardly relevant."

"When I knocked on Kate's door, what do you think I found?" Jane addressed Ellen. "It was John, helping her with the window sash!"

"Truly?" Ellen's eyebrows raised in a manner that

suggested she was taking more interest than Kate would like.

"It was simply a problem with the window. Wynbrook was passing by, heard the difficulty, and offered to help." Kate tried to quell any further speculation.

Ellen and Jane looked at each other and made humming noises with knowing grins. "John is quite the matrimonial catch," said Ellen, her eyes sparkling with mischief.

"Rubbish," said Kate. She disliked the direction the conversation had taken.

"But it's true," protested Jane, who had a tendency toward earnest literalness. "Ask anyone and they'll tell you, the Earl of Wynbrook is one of the most prized matrimonial catches in all of Britain. Any hostess would consider it an honor to have him at their party. He has good conversation, he is generally amiable, and he does not stand about, thinking himself above his company but is always ready to dance."

"And to all these fine qualities add that he's titled, handsome, and rich, and you will understand why many society mamas think it is a travesty he is unwed," said Ellen with a glint in her eye.

Kate tried to look bored yet was never more interested in a conversation. "I am surprised that he has held out so long."

"I think he does not wish to eclipse my wedding with an announcement of his own, though once I am wed, I expect we will not have to wait much longer," explained Jane.

"Has he chosen a bride, or will he simply grab whomever is closest at hand when the time comes?"

asked Kate, realizing it never occurred to her that he could have an understanding with a young lady.

"If the rumor is true," said Jane, leaning forward in a conspiratorial manner, "Lady Devine is expecting an offer for her niece shortly."

Oh.

Wynbrook was to be married.

To someone else.

"Excellent. I am glad he is accounted for," said Kate, trying not to sound as disingenuous as she felt.

"When you go to the party tomorrow, maybe you will meet her," said Jane, oblivious to any concern.

"You go with Robert," suggested Kate. A party would be a good way to introduce Robert to young women. "I would rather stay home with Ellen."

"And I would rather go to the party," returned Ellen. "So why not go?"

"And sit in my rolling chair on the side of the room to be an object of pity? No, thank you. You go and enjoy your amusements and tell me all about it. Truly, it would mean a lot to me if you would." Ellen gave her a hopeful smile.

Kate was trapped into the invitation now. Short of faking illness, Kate could not avoid the event. Besides, a ball would be a good way to introduce Robert to eligible young ladies. The sooner he found a bride, the sooner they could leave London.

Kate sighed in defeat.

⋘❦⋙

Wynbrook retreated to his study and looked over some prospectuses Mr. Ashton had prepared for him regarding his investments. Despite being a reclusive man, Mr. Ashton had proven himself to be quite valuable. When Wynbrook's father died, he had been shocked to learn his estate was not doing as well as he'd thought. Fortunately, Darington had recommended his cousin and solicitor, Mr. Ashton, who had set things to rights. The investment into Darington's ventures had paid back handsomely too.

"The girls have managed to secure an invitation for Darington and Kate to Lady Manderlay's party tomorrow night." Tristan strolled in the room, his mouth, as always, turned in something of a smirk, as if laughing at a private joke.

Whatever Tristan found humorous in that turn of events, Wynbrook did not. "So soon?"

"Unfortunately, yes. Of course they must enter society, but I so wished to *clothe* them first. Something must be done."

"Nothing we can do." Wynbrook was less concerned about their attire and more concerned about their finances. He had no concept how much it had cost to free the children of Fleet. Had they run themselves to ground with their charity? "Perhaps they have spent their fortune on other expenses."

"Not likely! Kate never wasted a farthing in all her life. She has the golden touch, to be sure, though you wouldn't know it to look at her."

"Are you certain they are flush? I witnessed a significant act of charity by them."

"The only time they are generous is when they are giving it away," commented Tristan. "But I am certain they have not gone down the hatches. Not in their nature. Hoarders of gold, they are. Which reminds me, must ask Dare about Kate."

"What about Kate?" asked Wynbrook with a sense he might not wish to know.

"Why, the amount of her dowry, of course. Already got some inquiries about her."

Wynbrook frowned. "What sort of inquiries?"

"Word has gotten out that Dare and his sister are plump in the pocket. Men will come 'round, make no mistake."

No, this would never do. "I wonder at your interference."

"And I wonder at your interest. You spent time with Lady Kate and returned to tell the tale, which already puts you ahead of most men. Shall I put out there that the lady is spoken for?"

"No, not at all!" cried Wynbrook. At Tristan's smug grin, Wynbrook realized he had risen to easy bait.

"Very well. I shall be sure to let everyone know she is firmly on the marriage market." Tristan smirked.

"You will do as you wish. I learned early that nothing can curb your tongue."

Tristan clutched at his chest. "Ah, a direct hit!"

Wynbrook cleared his throat. "Given your wild chatter, I suppose we shall have to ensure that she is protected from fortune hunters."

Tristan nodded, grim in expression but with dancing eyes. "Oh, yes, the only thing we can do."

"Well, I shall join you tomorrow night if I am able." Wynbrook rustled the papers on his desk in a random manner he hoped looked important. A glance at his brother told him the ruse was fooling no one.

"You have a good evening." Tristan gave a mock salute and left Wynbrook to glower at the door.

Wynbrook would join them tomorrow and prove to himself and Tristan and everyone else that he did not care for Kate in any meaningful way. He would be charming, flirtatious, his normal self...and he would protect Lady Kate from the scheming machinations of fortune hunters and any other man who tried to get close.

It was his responsibility since she was staying under his roof and, thus, was under his protection. It was simply his duty, nothing more.

Nothing more.

Seven

Seven for a secret never to be told

THE NEXT NIGHT, KATE WAS ESCORTED BY TRISTAN, Jane, and Robert into a large home in a fashionable part of Town. Her heart beat in her throat and her hands were balled at her sides, ready to do battle, though she knew that was not how the members of polite society wounded. No, they cut with words and destroyed with a turn of their heads. This was not a type of warfare she or Robert knew how to wage.

Kate wore a white muslin gown she had made herself, and though well-fitting and serviceable, she was keenly aware it was considerably less fashionable than the gowns of the other ladies present. The house was furnished in such an opulent style it made Kate shake her head at the elaborate waste.

"Gaudy taste. So gauche," whispered Tristan, and then raised his voice. "Oh my dear Lady Manderlay, allow me to introduce my friends!"

Introductions were made repeatedly as Kate and Robert were made acquainted to one after another of Tristan's friends. Jane disappeared with some of her friends to look for her betrothed. Kate's interest, however, was on scanning the room in search of a certain person. Perhaps Wynbrook would not come. The thought was not as reassuring as she'd expected.

She knew the moment he entered the hall. Wynbrook was a tall man, superbly dressed in a dark blue double-breasted coat, cut to perfection over his broad shoulders. His cravat and collar were snowy white, his waistcoat a golden brocade, and the crowd seemed to part before him. His eyes met hers and a slow smile spread across his lips. Her stomach fluttered in an odd way, and she was not sure if he was having some dastardly effect on her or if the evening's fish hadn't agreed with her.

"Darington, Lady Katherine, good to see you." Wynbrook greeted them with benign pleasantries but his eyes shone.

She nodded and said nothing. Robert was similarly silent. This was not their world and Kate had never felt more out of place.

"Let us introduce you to a few people, shall we?" Wynbrook gave his winning smile.

She thought she had met quite enough people with Tristan, but even more people fell into the wake of the Earl of Wynbrook, the man everyone seemed to want to greet. She thought people would be interested only in Wynbrook and Tristan, but a surprising number of people expressed an interest in becoming better acquainted with her brother and even herself.

Wynbrook, for his part, was uniformly charming and witty, words never attributed to Kate or her brother. Contrary to her expectation, Wynbrook stayed by her side, which was an embarrassment, but since he and Tristan supplied the conversation, she came to appreciate his presence. She also recognized that his attendance at their sides gave society the message of his tacit approval of them.

Lady Jane returned on the arm of her betrothed with a wide smile and high color. "Lord Darington, Lady Kate, I wish to make you acquainted with Sir Richard." Jane spoke with a bit more enthusiasm than an urbane sophisticate should muster. It was clear that Jane was quite in awe of her future husband.

Sir Richard was a distinguished man at least a decade older than Jane. He bowed before them with perfect form, yet his eyes swept over Kate with disdain. "Pleased to meet you, Lord Darington, Lady Katherine. I hope you had a pleasant journey to London." He spoke with polished condescension.

"The voyage was a difficult one. It stormed the entire way," said Kate, returning his bow with a small obligatory curtsy of her own.

"Hmmm? Indeed," said Sir Richard, looking over Kate's head. He smelled of brandy and perfume. But not Jane's perfume.

"I am glad you were able to attend tonight so you could meet my friends," said Jane, positively glowing at her future husband.

He smiled indulgently down at her. "Fortunately, my business did not take as long as I had anticipated."

There was something in his manner, some bit of a smile about his mouth, as though he was enjoying some sort of secret joke, which Kate did not like. Of course it was not unusual for her to find something to dislike about most men she met. Or most women either. She had a knack for detecting the flaws in her fellow man. It was never much appreciated, so she generally kept her musings about the foibles of others to herself. But in this case, she decided to keep a close watch on the man who was contracted to be Jane's husband.

Jane and her future husband went off to dance and he appeared to be attentive, smiling, and for the most part giving her his full attention. Only, once or twice, he made eye contact with another woman across the dance floor. There could have been a benign explanation for such behavior. But Kate, being Kate, doubted it.

The orchestra struck up a few chords, and Wynbrook turned to her with a polished smile. "Would you care to dance?" he asked politely.

"I never dance," returned Kate not quite as politely.

Wynbrook did not look at all surprised by her reply. "Never learnt, did you? Been away awhile. Understandable."

"I did not say I *could* not dance, only that I *would* not dance," clarified Kate.

"Oh no, you ought not to have said that," whispered Wynbrook, too close to her ear for comfort. "For now I will take it as a challenge to convince you to stand up with me."

Her pulse pounded loudly in the ear where Wynbrook's teasing words were whispered. Was he attempting some ill-advised flirtation? No, it was not possible. "I trust, then, that you will learn to live with disappointment," replied Kate coldly.

"Ho, ho! Such a set down," said Tristan with a

laugh. "There's a novelty for you—a young lady who doesn't fall at your feet. Good for you!"

Wynbrook ignored his brother and changed the subject. "Bit flush of company tonight for this time of the year."

"So it is. Early opening of Parliament has brought much company to London at this unseasonable time. The young ladies are out in full bloom," said Tristan with a laugh, clapping Robert on the back. "You won't escape their clutches, you know. You're an earl, no hope for it. Must take a wife, produce an heir, and all that."

Robert, who was already looking a bit stricken at having been dragged to a ball, grew a shade paler. His jaw tightened, but otherwise, he made no reply.

"I see a few mamas have broken with tradition and put out their girls early, before they are formally presented at court," continued Tristan. "Don't want the best men snagged before they even get out of the gate." He gave Robert a sidewise glance. "Of course, you know having the title puts you in the line of fire."

"Surely it can't be as bad as all that," said Kate, wanting to protect her brother from a fit of apoplexy. Robert had turned from pale to a greenish hue. Strange that he could look into the heart of a storm or the fiercest of enemies without flinching, but put him in the middle of a ballroom of teenage debutantes, and the man was likely to drop his colors and run.

"'Course it is!" countered Tristan without mercy. "Word's getting 'round there's another peer of the realm available for the taking. Sorry to put the fear in you, old man, but you are young, titled, and now have a bit of money to you. You'll find the people who didn't remember your name when you were poor now wish to be your best friend. Probably even find family members coming out of the woodwork that were never there when you were needful."

"And they say I am the cynical one," muttered Kate.

"Ah yes, but I say it in good humor, thus I am considered amusing and refreshing." Tristan gave Kate a dashing smile and was promptly commandeered by some of his friends to the card room.

"You also may find yourself sought as a matrimonial prize," Wynbrook commented to her in a benign tone, as if commenting about the weather.

Kate knew he must have been having a bit of fun at her expense. Who would ever consider her to be a bride? "You are a dreadful man." It was perhaps not the wittiest of comebacks, but it was the best she could come up with in the moment.

"I will never deny it," said Wynbrook with a laugh. He was too cheeky for his own good.

"No one would ever look to me to be a bride," she muttered, more to herself than to anyone else.

"Is that so? Then, indeed, I have poor tidings for you." His eyes sparkled with mischievous delight as he waited for Kate's response.

"I know you wish for me to demand what horrible news you have for me, but I have decided to punish you and refuse to ask." Kate turned away to watch the lovely dancing couples, remaining keenly aware of his presence beside her.

"Fine then, if you insist, I shall tell you. You also, my Lady Katherine, will be firmly on the marriage market rolls," he commented in a smug tone.

Kate wished to dismiss the concept as absurd, but even worse than it being some cruel jest was the fear that he was not joking. Did he truly believe what he said? Kate gave Wynbrook an unladylike snort. She couldn't help herself. Despite his superior knowledge of the *haut ton*, the very idea of her hand being sought was preposterous. "Have you gone mad?"

Far from being offended, Wynbrook continued. "You are a lady."

Another snort.

"You are not unattractive."

"Touched in the head, you are." She refused to accept the growing heat of her cheeks to be a blush at such a backhanded compliment.

"And you are well dowered."

Kate spun toward him. "What? There is no dowry!"

Wynbrook shrugged. "You have the scent of money about you."

"Whatever do you mean?"

Wynbrook gave her a small half smile that was so common in society's elite. "Did you think your investors whose fortunes were made would be discreet? News of your good fortune has been splashed across Town."

"But I have no dowry." It was true. Any money her father had laid aside for her had been stolen long ago.

"I fear no one will believe your brother could regain his fortune without restoring yours as well. Truth is, I can't see Dare not providing a dowry for you, especially since Tristan reminded him of the need."

"No, Robert would not do that," said Kate firmly.

Wynbrook tilted his head to the side, as if truly

confused by her denial. The more she considered the matter, the more she feared she might be wrong. Robert might consider restoring her dowry, particularly if Tristan brought it to mind.

"Dare did tell Tristan you would be amply provided for," added Wynbrook.

"What!" Kate stared at him. Robert was going to provide her an "ample" dowry? And without telling her? She looked around to confront Robert, but he had disappeared.

"Ah, I love the look of murder in your eye. Who will you do in first? Tristan or Dare?" Gone was Wynbrook's slightly bored expression; he regarded her now with singular interest.

"First one I find."

"Excellent. Can I witness?"

"Yes. No. But I'll let you help me dispose of the body if you help me find them now."

"That is an offer I can hardly refuse." Wynbrook gave her the same half smile, but this time his eyes were gleaming. "Tristan went into the back rooms to play a bit of cards and Dare followed a few minutes after, presumably to do the same."

"Robert doesn't play cards." Having once lost their entire fortune under mysterious circumstances, she had no intention of losing their hard-earned gains at the card table. If she ever discovered that Robert was gambling, she would have yet one more reason to kill her brother.

"Allow me to escort you." Wynbrook was all gallantry, and she wished to know what he was about. Had the man been drinking? He walked sure enough and did not appear foxed, but one could never be sure with an Englishman.

Kate allowed him to escort her out of the ballroom and into a parlor in which ladies and gentlemen of society's elite were winning and losing fortunes in a blink of an eye. Though she was certain Robert would not be among them, Kate was sufficiently rattled to look about the room just to make sure. It was with a certain relief that she noted that Robert was not among those addicted to chance and Tristan seemed more interested in talking than gambling.

"What now?" asked Wynbrook. "Shall you confront Tristan and demand he keep his newfound wealth a secret?"

Kate sighed. "I fear there is no hope Tristan would be able to comply with such a demand."

"Too true! I wonder where Dare has gone off to."

"Probably hiding. He has a morbid fear of young ladies."

Wynbrook laughed outright at this, causing a few people to turn their heads in surprise. One did not expect such an outburst from a bastion of society. "Come, let us find him before you induce me to sink lower in these good people's estimation. My, but you do say the oddest things."

They walked out the far door and down a quiet corridor. There were several doors along the hall, most likely leading to a variety of sitting rooms and maybe a study, library, or billiards room.

One of the doors was slightly ajar. She and Wynbrook paused a moment and exchanged a glance. They wished to find Robert, not barge in on a couple seeking a private escape. Though candlelight came from the room, no sound emerged. They pushed the door ever so slightly and peeked into the room.

"Good evening, Wynbrook, Kate," said Robert without putting down his newspaper.

"What are you doing here?" asked Kate, walking into the room with Wynbrook. She realized she still had her hand on his arm and quickly snatched it back.

Robert looked at them over his newspaper. "I thought it would be obvious. I'm reading a newspaper."

Kate rolled her eyes at him. "It is expected for you to be out there, mingling with the guests or some such rot."

"You make it sound so appealing," said Robert in a dry tone. He turned the page of his newspaper and gave no impression of a man who was about to jump up and join a ball.

Kate turned to Wynbrook in a silent appeal for help getting her brother back into the ballroom, but the man turned traitor.

"Nice hideaway you found," said Wynbrook. "What are you reading?"

"The latest on Wellington's campaign in Lisbon."

"Oh? What news?" asked Wynbrook, sitting beside Robert on the couch.

"Marshal Ney has proven an obstacle for Wellington and prevented our forces from routing the retreating French army."

"Yes, this is all very interesting, but I know you already read that article this afternoon," accused Kate.

Robert gave her a slight shrug as he handed the paper to Wynbrook, who was now more interested in the Peninsular Campaign than in her concerns with society.

"And another thing. Did you tell Tristan that I would have a dowry? An 'ample' dowry? I'm certain you would not have done such a thing without talking to me first."

"Sorry to disappoint," said Robert without a hint of apology, "but Tristan reminded me of the obligation, and I fear I must provide a dowry for you."

"Why would you do such a thing?"

Dare shrugged. "I thought you would be pleased."

"No, do you not see? By hinting at a large dowry, you have put me at risk for fortune hunters."

"I have no fear you will succumb."

"Of course not! But they will be a bother."

"Yes, there may be some truth to that." Robert did not sound at all remorseful. "But if I must face the unpleasantness of finding a marriage partner, it is probably time for you as well." Kate could only shake her head. There were reasons she could not wed. Reasons Robert should know all too well, but she could not say them before Wynbrook. Some secrets could never be told.

"Never have I heard the marital state referred to with such affection." Wynbrook chuckled. "It is marriage, not the gallows."

"I do not see you rushing to the altar," retorted Kate.

"Touché! Too true! I will divest myself from the conversation and make no further commentary. I was only here to play undertaker."

"I have a better role," said Kate. "Please take my brother back to the ball and introduce him to eligible young ladies."

"Wouldn't you rather kill me?" groaned Robert.

Wynbrook laughed again. "Come then, old man, back into the fray it is, and for you too, I fear." He held out his arm for Kate.

"No, no, you both go ahead. I need to pay a visit to the ladies' retiring room." It was the one place she could be safe.

Wynbrook began to walk with Robert out the door and looked back, giving her a scandalous wink. "Well played."

Kate left the room a few minutes after the gentlemen and was surprised to see the back of Sir Richard slipping into a room at the darkened far end of the hall. As Kate walked in the opposite direction down the hall, she passed a woman dressed in a sumptuous velvet gown of deep burgundy. The cut was low, her bosoms were high, and she floated past Kate as if fairies carried her hither and yon. Kate bit her lip as the woman swept by her. It was the same perfume she had smelled on Richard.

Kate walked through the doorway leading to the card room but stopped and peeked through the slight crack between the wall and the door. The woman entered the same room where Sir Richard had vanished.

More secrets. Now what was she going to tell Lady Jane?

Eight

KATE WEIGHED HER OPTIONS CAREFULLY. EACH ONE was fraught with unpleasantness. Trouble was, there was no clear choice. Even doing nothing, which seemed the easiest path, was not without peril. She could not imagine Jane would wish to marry someone so overtly unfaithful. Evidently the relationship, which had touched Jane's heart, was far from touching Sir Richard's. Apparently, Sir Richard had decided a connection to Lady Jane would be of benefit to him but did not feel the engagement should impede his pursuing other interests.

If she did nothing, Jane would marry him and would then be stuck living with such a husband for the rest of her life. Kate could think of no worse fate, and she rather thought Jane would not like it either. What could be worse than to fall in love with somebody who did not return your affection?

Kate knew what she must do. A few minutes later, Jane was following Kate down the hall.

"Why is it that you needed to speak with me so urgently?" asked Jane, innocent to the last.

"I do hate to do this," Kate started, wondering how to break the unpleasant news. "But I fear that Sir Richard is not worthy of you and, worse, has feigned interest only to obtain your dowry and the societal benefit of association with your family."

Jane's nose scrunched, as if smelling something distasteful. "That is a cruel thing to say, Katherine. Even for you."

Kate felt the sting of the barb but refused to comment. Jane was hurt, and hurt people said hurtful things.

"I am sorry, Lady Jane. I hope this is the right choice and you will forgive me one day." Kate swung the door open.

There was a woman's shriek, curses from Sir Richard, and the hasty grabbing of clothing. Kate gave the scrambling couple nothing but a fleeting glance. Her eyes were on Jane, for it was only Jane who mattered.

Jane's eyes were wide and her mouth had dropped open in a perfect oval. How would she respond to such unwanted insight? Would she ever speak to Kate again?

"How could you?" Jane's voice shook, though from fury or grief, it was hard to tell. Kate wasn't sure if Jane was about to dissolve into tears or strangle the life from Sir Richard. She hoped for strangulation.

"It's not what it looks like," said Richard, adjusting his pantaloons. He correctly surmised who had alerted Jane and cast Kate a murderous glare.

The woman finished adjusting herself and smoothed a hand over her hair, which had not one strand out of place—Kate could only guess she had years of practice at the art of maintaining deceptive appearances.

Indeed, had they not walked in on the activity, she would not have looked as if she had been doing anything untoward.

"Now don't get in a pet, my dear," said the woman to Jane. "You are very young yet, but even an innocent such as yourself should know how the world works. You really oughtn't go where you don't belong, for you will only see things you do not wish to see."

"I think it is past time for you to remove yourself," growled Kate.

The woman gave them a serene yet superior smile. "I shall see you next week, Sir Richard," she said over her shoulder.

Despite Jane being right there, Richard gave her a quick nod. The woman glided out of the room, her beautiful face a picture of poise and confidence. Jane, on the other hand, had gone red and her neck was turning rather blotchy. She took a deep gulp of air as if she were a fish tossed out of the water onto the cold stones of death.

Kate feared she might have to cause Richard bodily harm for this. While she could not count herself one of Jane's close confidantes, she was still a friend, and Kate had so few of them, she felt a fierce loyalty to protect her.

"She's right, you know," said Richard, straightening his cravat. "You really ought not go opening doors and sticking your pretty little nose where it doesn't belong."

"The only place I don't belong is anywhere near you," cried Jane.

Kate fought the urge to applaud Jane for standing up to him.

"Now, don't get it into that head of yours to do anything rash," said Richard with an air of contemptuous disdain. "I don't know what you expected, but this is how it is, my dear. I regret that you saw something you didn't wish to see, but I think it best that we just forget it happened. In the future, take better care to keep yourself away from places you ought not to go, and I will never mention this again after we're married."

"I do not think you quite understand, Sir Richard. There will be no marriage. There is no way that I would ever consider marrying you now." Jane ground out the words through gritted teeth.

"Don't be such a little goose. Of course we will be married. Honestly, my dear, you have no other choice. I don't wish to be ugly about it, but you force my hand. If you do not go through with the wedding, I shall sue you for breach of contract."

Jane gasped, tears springing to her eyes.

"That is most unfortunate," said Kate. "For it means that the only way for us be rid of you is to make you disappear."

Richard gave her another look of poisonous contempt. "What are you prattling on about?"

"My dear man, my brother has spent the past many years as a rather successful privateer. If need be, you would not be the first man he has had to kill."

"You cannot threaten me," demanded Richard, but Kate noted with some satisfaction that he'd gone a shade or two paler. Of course Robert would no doubt balk at killing the man outright, but Sir Richard didn't know that. If Robert thought Jane's honor had been besmirched, he could threaten the man to a duel, if Wynbrook didn't get there first. Or she could take care of the situation in her own way. Kate had no shortage of ideas for how to kill the man.

"In no way did I intend to threaten you, Sir Richard. But if you so much as whisper any scandal about Lady Jane, I swear to you that you will not be able to propagate your seed ever again. Be assured that you cannot endeavor to succeed against Lady Jane without suffering a most intimate loss. My brother and I are great friends of the Wynbrook family, and we take their care and protection very seriously. You have nothing to gain here and everything to lose. Do not ever inconvenience Jane again."

Richard's eyes bugged out from his face and a vein in his temple pulsed with anger. He opened his mouth as if to speak, but apparently thought better of it and shut it again with a snap, adjusting his cravat once more. "What lovely friends you have, my dear," he said, addressing Jane.

"Yes," said Jane, linking her arm with Kate's. "I do have the very best of friends." She turned to Kate. "Though perhaps I am not as good a judge of character as I thought, and perhaps I have not recognized who my friends truly are."

Kate was not accustomed to being appreciated and had not expected Jane to thank her for her interference. She was relieved and happily surprised Jane would still consider her a friend.

"Thank you," she said simply to Jane. They turned and walked toward the door. At the threshold, Kate looked over her shoulder to where Richard remained planted in the middle of the room, his fists balled at his sides. If ever a man was plotting revenge, it was he.

Jane's lower lip began to tremble and Kate feared she was beginning to lose the admirable pluck she had shown before Sir Richard. She needed to get Jane out of the house without anyone noticing her distress.

They found Tristan, and it only took one glance at Jane for him to spring into action. He might not have been the best choice for raiding a French frigate, but the man did know how to navigate the shoals of society safely. Within minutes, Tristan had made up a plausible excuse to their hostess, called for their coach, and collected their respective brothers.

Kate thought it best not to tell the men what had occurred until they were all safely on the way back home in the coach and out of the danger of the ballroom, to avoid such scenes as they may later come to regret. It was good she had, for at the telling of the story, Jane burst into tears and Wynbrook had to be physically restrained by Robert and Tristan to prevent him from jumping out of the carriage and running back to murder Sir Richard.

By the time they returned home, Wynbrook was still seething and poor Jane had dissolved into silent sobs. Kate immediately took Jane upstairs and deposited her with Ellen, hopeful that her sister could soothe her better than Kate's ineffectual attempts.

Kate returned downstairs to find the men in full war-room negotiations. Robert had changed into his captain's coat with a brace of pistols slung across one shoulder and his sword strapped to his side. Wynbrook and Tristan shared looks of grave concern, expressions she had rarely seen on their faces. It reminded her forcibly of the last time she and Robert had come to visit and everything had ended in tragedy. She truly was bad luck.

"There is no way around it. He must be bought off," said Wynbrook, not yet noting her presence.

"Worthless bloody bastard," said Tristan and then coughed at seeing her enter the room. "Sorry there. Didn't realize you were in the room."

"No musket?" she asked her brother, boldly walking forward.

"You're right, we need one," said Tristan with a grim smile.

"Thank you, Lady Kate, for bringing this to our attention, but we must handle it from here," said Wynbrook darkly.

"Yes, of course," said Kate, biting back a challenge to Wynbrook's belief that she was of no use in a crisis. "But you must make Sir Richard sign a contract agreeing not to sue before any payment is made." She also had come to the conclusion that risking a lawsuit was too costly, particularly for Jane's reputation, and murder was slightly too illegal, though no less than he deserved.

"You are right," agreed Wynbrook. "What we need is your cousin to draw up a document for us. You said yesterday Mr. Ashton was not available?"

Kate's pulsed increased. Mr. Ashton was not a safe topic to discuss. She exchanged a glance with her brother. "Unfortunately, he had to go out of Town to convalesce," she said at the same time her brother said, "Holiday."

At their confused looks, Kate attempted to concoct

a plausible explanation, "He is going on holiday to recuperate from a lingering illness."

Fortunately, the Arlington brothers were too focused on their sister to question the story. "Too bad. Could use a solicitor about now," said Tristan pointedly. Robert also pinned her with a singular look.

Kate knew what they wanted, but to do so might reveal herself. She hoped, nay expected, to live out her life without Wynbrook ever knowing several things, and this was one of them.

"We will need to find another solicitor. And fast," commented Wynbrook.

Use another solicitor? Kate waffled between her desire for anonymity and her need to prepare the document correctly, which meant she must do it herself.

"I do believe Ash drew up a contract for one of our officers who found himself in a similar difficulty. I have a copy of the contract and can make one for you." Kate dashed out of the room before anyone could give her words too much thought.

It took her only a brief time to compose the document. The truth that she had created the person of her cousin and had been acting as not only her brother's, but also Wynbrook's financial adviser for years under the name of Mr. Ashton, was not a discussion she wished to have, now or ever.

More secrets. She was accustomed to it.

Kate returned to the men, wondering if Wynbrook would question how the document had been created so quickly, but he seemed in no mood for debate and was only pleased to have it in hand. Kate was taken aback by the appearance of the men. Wynbrook had armed himself as well, a sword at his side, the telltale bulge of a pistol in his breast pocket. Tristan, the elite of fashion, was positively unrecognizable with a cutlass in hand.

"Are you going to speak with Sir Richard or storm the Bastille?" she asked.

"Whatever comes to mind," said Tristan cheerfully.

"The situation will be handled," said Robert.

"Don't wait up," said Wynbrook in a tone that was almost a challenge.

As if there were any chance of her going to sleep now.

Nine

KATE WANDERED ABOUT WYNBROOK HOUSE WAITING for the gentlemen to return. Ellen and Jane had gone to bed, and the servants had retired for the night. There was no question of trying to sleep, not with her brother, Tristan, and Wynbrook confronting the worst sort of man. She was not afraid any harm would come to them. Robert knew what he was about and would keep the others safe. She did have a concern that the outcome would result in one or all of them having to escape to the Continent for doing something untoward, though completely deserved, to Sir Richard. After meandering through the portrait hall, the ballroom, and the library, it was simply inevitable that Kate would find herself at the door of Wynbrook's study.

Kate entered the study, looking around her to make sure she was not seen, though she knew she was alone. She walked to the desk and held a candle up to the oak bookcase. Ledgers. Beautiful ledgers. When everything in the world was unraveling, numbers stayed the same. Numbers always added up the same way, and unlike the baffling field of human interactions, there was only one right answer.

She had always found arithmetic comforting, a convenient eccentricity. After they were orphaned at twelve, they discovered their steward had stolen everything, leading to the unfortunate incident in Fleet Prison. Arithmetic had saved her and their fortunes. She had a knack for it and for investing wisely. She had ensured they had been able to scrape by when Robert went to sea shortly after their release from prison. She managed the finances during his career in the Royal Navy and then when he resigned his commission to study at Cambridge. Even after he had turned to the more lucrative business of privateering, she had kept the books and doubled every doubloon they earned.

Kate stared at the ledgers of the Earl of Wynbrook. She was familiar with his financial holdings, since she had been advising him for years. When Wynbrook had asked Robert if he could contact Mr. Ashton for advice on a financial matter, she should have said no. Instead, she had taken up a correspondence with Wynbrook, assisting him with some financial difficulties.

At the time, she had told herself she simply wanted to help him since the loss of his parents was so new, and yet...it had been more than that. She ran her finger down the spine of the red leather ledger. She had wanted to maintain some connection with him— and if he ever found out, he would no doubt hate her for it.

She had no right. She should not be here. How could she explain if he caught her? She fingered the ledger and suddenly it was in her hands and then spread open on the desk. She breathed deeply of the seductive scent of leather binding.

She paused for a moment, but hearing nothing in the house, she scanned down the column, mentally adding and subtracting the sums in her head. She sat at the desk, dipped a quill in the ink, and corrected math errors as unobtrusively as she could.

The process brought forcibly back to mind the last time she had sat before these ledgers six years ago. It had been a few nights after the horrible accident. She had wandered the house, distressed, wanting to do something to help but not knowing what she could possibly do. She'd wandered into the study and found the financial ledger open on the desk with some glaring math errors. She had not been able to stop herself from fixing them—and then going back through the book to fix many more. She had thought she could help the family and no one would ever know.

She had been terribly wrong.

She could not stop the flood of memories that engulfed her, reminding her of things she had tried hard to forget. She was nineteen again, wracked with guilt over the horrible accident that took the lives of Lord and Lady Wynbrook.

Six years earlier, Kate had sat at the desk of old Wynbrook's study. It was the day they had laid Lady and Lord Wynbrook to rest. Kate had known she had no business entering Lord Wynbrook's study, but ledgers had always been a comfort to her. The multiple math errors she had discovered were too tempting to ignore. She had needed to do something, fix something, and what she could do was correct the books.

John's young sisters, Ellen and Jane, remained

upstairs, fighting for their lives, trying to recover from their injuries. Kate bent over her work, as if correcting math errors could heal them faster.

Suddenly, John Arlington staggered into the study in an uncharacteristic state of disrepair, his shirt open, his cravat missing. Kate was so surprised to see him in anything less than his immaculate, fashionable attire, she did not do anything to try to conceal her actions but froze before the ledger book, quill in hand.

"What are you doing?" He leaned heavily on the desk across from her, and she finally dropped the quill back into the inkwell. "This is the ledger of the Earl of Wynbrook. You have no right looking at it."

"Yes, yes, of course. I was only trying to help." Help that she had thought no one would ever see.

"What are you doing awake at this hour?"

"Couldn't sleep. I wanted to do something; I wanted to help somehow." Kate stood and walked around the desk. It was time to make a hasty retreat. "I do apologize," she murmured as she passed John.

"I don't know how to go on without him." His voice was but a whisper, his face turned away from her. She was not sure if he was speaking to her or to himself.

Kate blinked away her own emotion, his anguish wrenching at her heart. "Your parents were the best of people."

John nodded and reached one hand for the desk as if trying to hold himself up. He gulped air; the pain on his face was etched clear and deep.

"You shall survive this," Kate encouraged.

John could only shake his head, his teeth clamped tightly together.

Kate was utterly unpracticed in the art of giving comfort but could not leave him in such despair. She patted his arm, and John covered her hand with his own. She knew she should take her hand away, but it did not seem kind, and more importantly, she didn't want to.

"What am I to do?" John murmured so softly, Kate could barely hear. He took her hand in his, turning it until they were holding hands. It felt good. Right. Even though she knew they should not have been alone together at night. She had never before experienced such a war between her head and her heart.

"Forgive me. I am in no state for company." He released her hand, staggered to a settee, and collapsed onto it. Kate began to walk to the open door. It was past time to leave. Behind her on the settee came the quiet noises of a young man, hardly more than a teenager himself, trying hard not to be heard crying.

She paused for a moment, took a deep breath, closed the door, and walked back to him. She sat down awkwardly beside him as he turned his face away. She was unsure what to do but knew she could not abandon him at such a time.

"It's not your fault," she said simply.

She touched a hand to his shoulder and suddenly he turned, wrapping his arms around her, leaning his head on her shoulder. She was surprised to be engulfed by such a large, muscular man. Was this an embrace? She had never experienced one before. Unsure of her movements, she wrapped her own arms around him. She had never before been so close to a man. The strangest part was that it was not strange at all. It felt natural, comforting, though she could never remember being consoled by anyone in such a manner.

John held her tight, his shoulders shaking. She responded by holding him tighter, rubbing her hands up and down his back. She was powerfully aware of his unique, intoxicating scent. She did not generally find the smell of men appealing, but with John, she breathed deeply.

Though she was supposed to be providing solace, she found comfort in his arms. He did not blame her. He was not angry at her. She took another breath and he did the same. He was no longer trembling but moved slightly, so that his cheek rested against hers.

The stubble on his face brushed against her cheek, rough and scratchy, yet she welcomed it. Every part of her that touched him burned with a heat that went straight to her core. She had no words for this strange, new experience, and so she clung to him, waiting and willing to experience whatever came next.

Her candle on the desk guttered, leaving them in darkness. His hand touched her cheek, cupping her face, gently turning her head toward him. His lips brushed across hers, warm and soft. His lips sought hers again and kissed her hard, bringing his hand around her head to prevent her from pulling away. He need not have bothered, for she had no intention of drawing back. He deepened the kiss, demanding and anguished, tasting of sorrow and desire. His hot tears fell on her cheeks, running down her face.

Time stopped and she knew not how long they kissed—desperate, mournful, passionate. Suddenly, it was not enough. He pushed her down on the cushions, running a hand up her leg, pulling up her nightgown. She should tell him to stop. Make him stop. But she didn't wish him to stop.

What might have happened, Kate would never know. A scream had pierced the night, shocking them both back to reality. Whether it had been Jane or Ellen, she had not known, for both were suffering great pain from their injuries. John had rolled off her and staggered to his feet. A mumbled apology was all she had received before he had run out of the room.

⁓

Kate blinked, waking back from her memories into reality. She had not seen John again until they met yesterday in the bank. Over time, she had conveniently cast him in the role of the villain, but she knew he was so much more.

She was no longer the confused teenager who had met a grieving young man in the study that night. Yet when it came to John, now the Earl of Wynbrook, she was desperately unsure of herself. She was immune to the charms of men as a general rule. Lord Wynbrook was the one unfortunate exception. One dangerous exception.

The question for tonight was: Did she want to be caught again?

She turned back to the ledgers, back to her comforting number friends. They always added up the same. They never confused her. She reached for another ledger and lost herself in the allure of calculus.

"What are you doing?"

She found herself before the open ledger, an incriminating quill in her hand. Her heart began to pound. She had been caught red-handed. *Again.* Just the way part of her had known she would be.

Wynbrook stood in the doorway, alive, well, and immaculately dressed as if he had returned from the opera, not a meeting with a scoundrel. "You just can't keep yourself out of my ledgers, can you?" He raised an eyebrow, amused.

This was her chance to talk to him. This was her chance to make sense of what had passed between them six years ago. But what did she need to say? What questions did she need to ask? Staring at the impeccably dressed, undeniably handsome Lord Wynbrook, her mind went blank. Now what was she going to do?

Kate stabbed the quill back into the jar of ink and jumped up from the desk, circling around it. "I do beg your pardon. I understand this is a gross invasion of your privacy, but I just needed to correct one or two, or, well, exactly fifteen math errors. How did it go with Sir Richard?"

"Fifteen math errors? Exactly how much of my ledger did you go through?" He was not to be dissuaded.

"It would have been a disservice if I had not gone through it all. But do tell me how it went with Sir Richard. I have not been able to sleep, wondering how your interview proceeded."

"Finding you here tonight seems to bring back an old memory." Wynbrook came closer and leaned next to her against the desk.

Kate swallowed convulsively. "No, I am sure it does not."

"I rather think it does."

"I'd rather if it did not."

"Then why come here tonight and remind me?"

Kate took a breath. "An excellent question. When I have an answer, I'll be sure to let you know."

"Go ahead. I'll wait." His eyes blazed at hers as the silence stretched between them.

"I came here…" She had to think of something, but it was difficult to think standing so close to him. "I came here to extend my services to help hide the body if need be, as you offered to help me earlier this evening. Do tell me, did you leave Sir Richard in good health?"

Wynbrook raised an eyebrow. "So you came to offer mortuary services."

Kate shrugged. "I thought of it more as accessory to murder."

"Then I am sorry to disappoint but Sir Richard is alive, though perhaps not in as good health as he would wish. I must say, your brother does have a fine right hook." Wynbrook's smile was slow to build, warming places within her she would rather not acknowledge.

"Landed him a facer, did he?"

Wynbrook raised both eyebrows at her boxing cant, but answered, "Caught him in the eye. Will be quite the shiner by morning—handy too, as it will be a few days before he will be able to show his face in public."

"I cannot say I am sorry to see him injured, and it was probably wise to avoid the inconvenience of concealing a murder."

"Quite. In the end, we discussed things like reasonable gentlemen, or at least he came to see our point of view. He signed the document and took the money." Wynbrook turned to the sideboard and poured himself a glass of brandy. "I must say I resent giving the bastard a single shilling, but I cannot allow Jane's good name to be tarnished."

"It is a sad world where the villain is rewarded." Kate shook her head, thinking this might be a good time to make her escape.

Wynbrook sighed in response. He looked tired after the evening's excitement. "Please do sit, Lady Kate. If you're going to be conversing with me at this inappropriate time, we might as well make ourselves comfortable." He sat down in one of the leather chairs by the waning fire, and Kate took a seat in the chair opposite him. She knew she should not have been there at all, but there was one thing more she needed to say.

"Please let me apologize for bringing to the fore the true nature of Sir Richard on the second day I am welcomed to this house." The business with Sir Richard was just more confirmation that she was bad luck to all. "I do not like to cause everyone such distress."

Wynbrook frowned at her. "You've done nothing to apologize for. It is Sir Richard who is the villain in this scenario. I only blame myself for not seeing through his facade sooner. If I had taken better care of Jane, this never would have happened. You saw his true nature within an hour of meeting him. I blame myself for being so blind."

"It is not your fault. He appeared to be charming, at least when he wished to be, and Jane seemed quite taken with him."

"Yes, I think I was swayed by her affection. She seemed happy, his estate is an old one, and his family name is well-known. Unfortunately, I did not look closely enough at the man himself."

"It is maddening for us to blame ourselves. Perhaps we *should* lay the blame squarely with Sir Richard."

Wynbrook lifted his glass to her. "I can drink to that."

Kate felt the interview had gone as well as could be expected. She wished to say something about that night six years ago, but she could not figure out how to broach the subject. It was best to let it alone and run away.

"I shall seek my bed now." Kate stood up, ready to take flight but unable to move. Had she mentioned her bed? To him? Was he thinking what she was thinking, or was she the only wanton in the room?

Wynbrook stood slowly before her. "I bid you a good night and a pleasant evening." His voice was low and seductive, his green eyes bright with intensity.

Kate's feet finally began to move, but it was toward him, not away. She drew close before she could realize what she was doing. Now what was she to do? She must look a fool.

She gave a small curtsy to cover her mistake, and much to her surprise, he returned with a bow and caught her hand, pressing a lingering kiss on the back of her hand. He remained close, too close, and she feared he could hear her heart pound. He leaned in, and memories of their kiss surged through her mind. She tilted her face up, both of them waiting for the other. A cloud flickered across his eyes and he stepped back.

"Good night, Kate."

"Good night, John."

Kate spun and flew from the room, cognizant that they had crossed a threshold. Something between them had begun.

Ten

It had taken Lady Katherine less than forty-eight hours to utterly disrupt Wynbrook's well-ordered life. In the brief time since he'd met her again, his polished reserve had been shattered, Jane's engagement had been dissolved, and he had witnessed his affable brother threaten a man with a cutlass.

Wynbrook admitted this was not entirely Kate's fault. But certainly none of it ever would have happened had she not come to stay. Kate was a puzzle to him. He generally knew what to do with ladies but she defied every convention. She resisted pleasant overtures and repulsed flirtation even while flaunting societal rules by conversing with him alone at night in his study.

He could hardly pass her in the hall without being graced with a scowl. She seemed permanently irritated with him, and yet there had been a moment in the study the other night when only the alarm bells of self-preservation had prevented him from trying to move in for a kiss. Again.

If Kate remembered their kiss, she certainly gave

no indication. Far from the practiced flirtation he was accustomed to, she challenged him, rebuffed him, and nothing intrigued him more. Despite her barbed conversation, often at his expense, he was never more amused than when in her company. If nothing else, she certainly kept him on his toes. He only wished he knew whether behind her frequent rebuffs lay true affection or abhorrence.

Wynbrook accepted a freshly ironed newspaper from the footman, who was acting in the role of the butler while they were in Town. Wynbrook strolled into the drawing room only to find Kate, who greeted him with her customary scowl. At least she had thrown off the black and agreed to wear white, though it was hardly of the latest fashion, and her hair was pulled back in a severe twist. She was seated at one end of the room, before the card table, ledgers spread before her.

Wynbrook approached, wondering if she had once again invaded his privacy and corrected his math errors. Why had she gone to his study the other night? Was she so addicted to accounting she could not help herself? She must have wanted to be caught by him, but why? Did she remember their kisses as often as he?

"They are mine!" she defended as he approached.

"I should hope so."

Another scowl.

He was wondering what to say next when Jane wandered into the room. Since he was saved from the awkward situation and it was the first time Jane had managed to leave her room in two days, he was doubly pleased.

"Jane!" he exclaimed. "Good to see you."

Jane did not look the better for her self-imposed isolation. Her red, swollen eyes were evidence of days spent crying. Wynbrook's hands clenched. Not for the first time, he wished bodily harm on Sir Richard. Though Sir Richard was a cad and a lout, the loss of the engagement had clearly touched Jane's heart and her grief was real. Jane was miserable. Wynbrook was also miserable, witnessing her grief at the hands of the worthless Sir Richard.

Worse yet, her engagement had been greatly publicized. Everyone knew she had been about to marry Sir Richard. Anne had quietly circulated the story that the engagement had been dissolved on mutual terms. Talk had begun and everyone noted that Sir Richard had taken an impromptu trip away from London. Wynbrook had paid him enough to get him to leave London; whether it was enough to get him to stay away was another matter.

"Would you like some tea?" asked Kate, though as the hostess, it should have been Jane's place to offer.

Jane shrugged a shoulder and slumped in a chair, the very picture of misery. No one objected when Kate called for tea.

"Would you like to go for a ride today?" asked Wynbrook, trying to divert Jane's attention.

"No, thank you."

"Perhaps a book?" asked Kate.

"No, thank you."

"I know. We can go to the theatre tonight," tempted Wynbrook.

"No, thank you."

"Oh, for the love of Saint Christopher, Sir Richard

was a lout and a few other things I shan't say, since it may shock your brother. You ought not let the man affect you so," cried Kate.

Jane blinked and stared at Kate as if she were seeing her for the first time. She shook her head. "I am not upset that the engagement with Sir Richard is dissolved. He was utterly beneath my notice."

"Then what has upset you?" asked Wynbrook, confused.

"I am grieving the loss of the dream I had. It was naive. I see that now. I thought I couldn't find happiness with a boy I knew from childhood, someone like Sir Gareth. Did I ever tell you he wished to marry me years ago? I discouraged him because I thought love could only be found in someone new, someone dashing, someone exciting. I was such a fool."

"The only fool here is Sir Richard," said Kate with disgust.

Wynbrook agreed wholeheartedly, but it had little effect on Jane.

"I told Ellen I would come down for a few minutes, which I have. So now I'm going back upstairs." Jane was the picture of listless misery.

Wynbrook watched helplessly as Jane retired from the room.

"I can think of several ways to kill Sir Richard and make it look like an accident," muttered Kate.

"I know where we can hide the body where no one will ever find it," returned Wynbrook.

"Good to know."

"And I would like to know what words you thought might shock me."

Wynbrook exchanged a smirk with Kate. Their mutual dislike of Sir Richard was the one thing they agreed on, though he doubted murder was the best way to begin a courtship.

If he was interested in courting her.

Which he wasn't.

Definitely not.

"Lady Durant," intoned the footman at the door of the sitting room, doing his best impression of their stalwart butler.

Anne swept into the room, majestic as always. "Yes, yes, no need to introduce me. I think they should know their own sister."

Wynbrook was grateful for a diversion. "Anne. Good to see you."

Anne had been outraged at the situation with Jane, and they had spent many hours discussing what could be done to salvage poor Jane's reputation, but so far no one had been able to divine a solution. Today, however, Anne was in brighter spirits.

"You look well pleased," commented Wynbrook.

"I have a solution for poor Jane," she said in triumph. "Oh, good, tea has arrived."

The tea service was set, and the three of them sat down at a round table.

"Well, Anne?" queried John, teacup in hand. "If you found a solution for poor Jane, please do not keep it to yourself."

"I've just come from a conversation with the Dowager Duchess of Marchford," said Anne with the air of one sharing a great secret. "She knows an exclusive matchmaker who can help us. Apparently, this Madam X has helped other similar cases. You remember the Miss Talbot affair?"

Wynbrook shook his head. "I do not recall any such scandal."

"That's because she married Mr. Grant and it was all hushed up nicely," said Anne triumphantly. "Hopefully, Madam X will be able to do the same for our poor Jane."

"But what will this matchmaker do for poor Jane?" asked Kate, glaring at Wynbrook as if the situation were entirely his fault.

"You must realize the only way for Jane to save her reputation and her standing in society is to be married at once," said Anne, choosing a scone from the platter.

"But why must Jane have to find another fiancé?" asked Kate. "And why this concern about her reputation? She found her fiancé wanting and tossed him aside. She did nothing wrong. Why should her standing in society be in jeopardy? I do not see why this should be a tragedy for her."

John exchanged a silent but meaningful look with Anne, trying to figure out which of them would be better able to explain to Kate the workings of society. For one so clearly bright, she had little knowledge of the *haut ton*.

"It may not be fair, but Sir Richard has the law on his side. Under English law, Sir Richard can sue for breach of contract. His philandering is not considered just cause to break it off," explained Anne.

"It should be," grumbled Kate.

"I am sure it is quite unfair, now that I think of it," John said with a shrug.

"Society is cruel to women. They always take the brunt of it, which is entirely unfair." Kate's silver eyes flashed dangerously. She was ready to charge into battle. "I blame men."

The Earl of Wynbrook was not known as a coward, but neither was he a fool. Having three sisters, he knew when to agree with the womenfolk. "Quite so, quite so. Agree with everything. Good news, Anne, good news."

"I am glad you approve, for you need to speak to the Duchess of Marchford and sort out the details. These things are dearly done, I fear."

"Of course. Glad to be of service," said Wynbrook gallantly, hoping his generosity would not be overly taxed but resigned to pay whatever amount was requested.

"Good, it is settled then. I only hope this match-maker can find a replacement groom before Jane's reputation is utterly ruined."

"I still do not see why that should be," demanded Kate.

"Ta-ta, good day." Anne left in a swirl of silk, leaving John to answer the question.

Kate crossed her arms and pinned Wynbrook with a singular look from her silver eyes. She could be an imposing figure.

He cleared his throat. "Let me begin with the caveat that I agree this is wretchedly unfair." He waited for her to concede the point, for while he did not mind crossing swords with Kate, he wished it to be for a better reason than the capriciousness of society.

Kate gave a reluctant nod.

"If an engagement is dissolved, it can lead to dis-agreeable rumors that the lady was found wanting," explained Wynbrook.

"But that is unfair!"

"Indeed. Engagements are almost as difficult as marriages to dissolve. Fortunately, we had not yet signed the marriage contract; if we had, it would have been even more difficult."

"True." Kate sighed.

"You are familiar with marital law?"

"Yes, of course. No lady should enter marriage without a good lawyer."

John thought she may be jesting, but Kate's face was deadly serious.

"The marriage contract ensures that the lady has some protection; otherwise, all assets she brings to the marriage belong to her husband," continued Kate in a businesslike manner. "For example, a contract might stipulate the lady's dowry must be held in trust until any children arising from the marriage have gained majority. The marriage contract may also stipulate how much per annum she would be granted in case of her husband's death. Without a contract, a lady enters into the marriage quite unprotected."

"Precisely. If the contract had been signed, we would have had to go to court to have the thing undone. It would have been a nightmare of a scandal, and Sir Richard may have walked away with much of her dowry, for the court would not see his infidelity as reason to sever the contract."

Kate shook her head. "Of course, if it had been Sir Richard who had found Jane to be unfaithful prior to their nuptials…"

Wynbrook shook his head. "That would be a different matter entirely. I agree—these things are not fair."

"A woman should never feel trapped into marriage," Kate challenged.

"Of course not," Wynbrook agreed, though he wondered if she was still speaking of his sister.

"In truth, I do not see why any lady would wish to enter the marital state at all, since it seems only to her detriment. A lady is an equal to a gentleman in every respect, save for sometimes they have more sense."

Wynbrook was spared the trouble of responding by the timely entrance of Tristan and Robert, whom he had never been more grateful to see.

"Come, join me and my bluestocking friend for tea," John announced with the wide smile of a man who'd escaped the executioner.

Tristan and Robert joined them, and Robert helped himself to a liberal number of scones. Tristan, for his part, was positively giddy.

"What kind of waistcoat are you wearing?" Kate asked Tristan, surprising everyone at the table by commenting on fashion. Wynbrook took a glance and was shocked himself at what he saw. The waistcoat was made of simple homespun fabric.

"The latest fashion!" declared Tristan with a grin. "Gave up trying to make you and Dare fashionable by putting you in decent clothing. Decided instead to make homespun the newest thing."

Kate stared at him. "You can do that?"

"You watch me." Tristan grinned at her like a cat with a mouse under its paw. "And I spread the word that Sir Richard's cravat, which I never did like, is an abysmal failure. I now call any fashion flop a 'Sir Richard'!"

"Wynbrook House. Why did it have to be Wynbrook House?" muttered Silas Bones, his feet freezing in the slush of the London streets. He was careful to remain in the shadows outside of light cast by the gaslight.

"Don't like the house, Cap'n?" asked his second, a wiry man with a stocking cap pulled low over his brow.

"Went to Eaton with John Arlington, and now look at me, trying to break into his house. There's irony for you," said Silas in the urbane tone of a London gentleman. It would have been more effective had he not been casing a house to rob it.

"So you want we should leave?" asked the man in a hopeful tone. He would not complain to return to the warmth of the local pub.

"No. It just makes it harder is all. Darington has gotten rich off of me, and I must reclaim it." The shame of being forced to steal from the home of an old schoolmate was utterly Darington's fault. The man had taken not only his fortune, but his self-respect as well…and for that, Darington would pay.

"Watch the house while I get the others," Silas commanded. "I want to know when they come and when they go. I cannot afford to be seen."

"B-but it's cold out here!" complained the thin man.

Silas turned slowly back to the man and glared at him, his hand resting on the hilt of his sword.

The man changed his tune. "Watch the house. Aye, Captain."

Silas stalked away, his anger growing with every frozen step. This was all Darington's fault. Whatever it took, Darington's riches would be his.

Eleven

KATE WAS COUNTING THE DAYS UNTIL HER opportunity to leave the presence of Lord Wynbrook. She decided the best approach to her confusing feelings was to push them far beneath her conscious awareness and hope they would never surface again. So far, it had been a losing battle, for which she blamed Wynbrook entirely.

After her last disastrous ball, Kate was surprised when her hosts invited her to another one. She retreated to her room and considered faking a megrim. A knock on her door caused her heart to flutter. Perhaps it was Wynbrook?

Kate shook her head at her own nonsense. Of course it was not Wynbrook. "Enter!" she called, trying to gather her wits.

Her brother stalked through the door and gave her a dark look. "Not another ball," grumbled Robert.

"You were the one who wanted to stay here," Kate shot back at her brother.

"Hardly thought that meant my presence at…at…"

"A Christmas party?"

"Yes! That."

"If you could find a bride quicker, we could avoid any more of these social events once we leave Wynbrook House."

"That is your best argument for the married state yet," Robert commented dryly.

"I don't suppose," said Kate with sudden insight, "that you might be interested in Jane? They are feeling pressured into marrying her off quickly, and you already know her, so you would not have to form a new acquaintance."

"I already considered the idea, but she would not have me," said Robert with a sigh.

"She turned you down? Why?" Kate was outraged on her brother's behalf. He was worth a thousand Sir Richards at least.

"She thanked me for the offer but said something about how she wished to marry someone who was in love with her."

"Odd notion."

"Quite."

"What has love to do with marriage?" asked Kate.

Robert shrugged and retreated out the door. "Need to dress," he muttered, escaping the befuddling topic of the human heart.

A few hours later, Kate clutched her brother's sleeve as they entered the holiday ball of Mr. and Mrs. Grant alongside Wynbrook, Tristan, and Jane. Her tight grip had more to do with dragging in her brother than seeking comfort for herself. Kate thought there could be none more uncomfortable in a ballroom than Robert, but Jane was giving him a run for his money.

Anne had demanded that Jane dry her eyes and make an appearance to stave off the gossips, making Jane more miserable than ever. The matchmaker, through written instructions, had agreed with Anne and insisted Jane return to society at once to show she was not bereft (which she was) and that she was still as lively as ever (which she wasn't).

"What is he doing here?" Jane gasped, holding on to Kate's other arm with a tenacious grip and staring at the unwanted form of Sir Richard. It was indeed unfortunate that the first public appearance Jane had made since the dissolution of her engagement was also attended by the one man she least wished to see.

"I don't know, but I hope to remedy it soon," Wynbrook growled and stalked off in Sir Richard's direction. The two disappeared into a private corner, and after a few tense minutes, both emerged still alive, which Kate thought was more than Richard deserved.

"What can he be about?" asked Jane in a fearful whisper. "Do you think he has threatened to sue?"

"He would be very foolish if he did, since he has already accepted payment and signed a contract agreeing the engagement is terminated by mutual consent," said Kate. "Do not worry yourself over it, but let's go speak to Wynbrook and find out what that man is about."

She feared releasing her brother's arm would result in his disappearance, so she dragged him along. Accordingly, they walked arm in arm across the ballroom, to where Wynbrook was leaning against the wall near a potted palm, a bemused look upon his face.

"Dear brother!" said Jane, rushing forward. "What did Sir Richard say to you?"

"Has he threatened to sue?" asked Kate.

"No. It appears we will be rid of him with very little trouble," said Wynbrook. "Seems our dear Sir Richard has recognized his behavior was repugnant and will withdraw himself from the engagement without further discomfiture."

The ladies stared at him at this unexpected turn of events.

"But why this sudden change of heart?" asked Jane. "Can he honestly be trying to improve himself?"

"If I had to hazard a guess," drawled Wynbrook in a seductive manner Kate found simultaneously insufferable and appealing, "I believe our dear Sir Richard has found a new potential victim for his matrimonial pursuits."

"So you think Sir Richard wants to make peace so he can attempt to secure an engagement with some other poor soul?" asked Kate.

"Yes, though if I know our Sir Richard, the soul in question would not be poor at all," observed Wynbrook with a twinkle in his eye.

"He is the most despicable fortune hunter and should be publicly called out for his reprehensible behavior," declared Kate.

"Oh no. Pray, do not even think of doing anything of the sort." Jane clutched her arm once more.

"Jane is right, I fear," said Wynbrook, his face sobering into something of a frown "As much as I would like to make Sir Richard's life as miserable as possible, there is no way to do so without including Jane in his shame. Unfortunately, we must pretend that everything ended amicably so that Jane may find a more worthy groom as quickly as possible."

"But what about Sir Richard's next victim? Should not she and her family be warned of his treacherous fortune-hunting proclivities?" Kate protested.

"We shall have to keep an eye on him, so as to protect innocents from falling into his snare. If we know of any particular attention between him and another young lady, I can quietly go to her brother or father and put an end to the affair."

"I suppose that is the best we can do," agreed Kate reluctantly. "But I certainly feel sorry for his next victim."

More people entered the ballroom. Clearly this was a popular event. It was too many people in one place for her liking.

"This is the first event for the newly minted Mrs. Grant," explained Wynbrook. "Looks like a crush. She'll be well pleased."

Kate could not fathom how anyone would prefer to be jostled all night in a crowded room when they could be sitting peacefully by the fire reading a good book. She glanced up at her brother, who was so tense she feared he was frozen in place. The ballroom was no place for Dare.

"Ah, here is Marchford. Allow me to make the introductions!" exclaimed Wynbrook, oblivious to their misery.

The Duke of Marchford was an imposing man of dark features and aloof manner. On his arm was a plainly dressed lady in a simple white muslin gown. She was introduced as Miss Penelope Rose, the companion of the Dowager Duchess of Marchford, who, for some unknown reason, was going about the ballroom on the arm of the duke.

"Darington has just returned from years at sea,

commanding the *Lady Kate*. Came back plumper in the pocket than he left," said Wynbrook with a smile.

"You served in the Royal Navy?" asked Miss Rose politely. She had plain features, but her brown eyes sparkled with intelligence.

"Yes" was Robert's monosyllabic reply. Kate was impressed he got that much out.

"Admirable," commented Marchford, joining the conversation with his own brief reply.

"And will you begin a London season this year?" Miss Rose asked Kate.

A season? Voluntarily put herself out to market like a plucked chicken on display, hoping to go to the highest bidder? Was the woman daft? "No. I do not wish to enter society, and I certainly do not wish to be married. You will excuse me."

Kate turned on her heel and left. She hoped to find some small corner in which to hide until the travesty of the ball was over. Kate was useless at a ball. She did not dance. She did not gamble. She did not gossip. Hence, there was nothing for her to do.

Jane was asked to dance by successive young gentlemen Kate suspected to be Tristan's friends doing him a favor. It was supposed to make Jane appear happy and admired. Nothing, however, could remove the tinge of sorrow in Jane's eye.

Wynbrook naturally asked Kate to dance, and she had naturally refused. Thus, there was nothing for her to do but sit in the corner with the matrons and watch the cheerful, dancing couples float by.

Now she understood why Ellen did not wish to attend balls. There was nothing more depressing than watching other people be happy in a manner that would forever be elusive to her. She would never admit it, but it was not without a certain twinge of jealousy that she watched some of the other maidens fly as if their slippers had wings across the dance floor, expertly flirting with their utterly bewitched gentlemen companions. Their faces were bright and cheery, their conversation witty, their gowns light and shimmery, and they moved easily through the ball to the delight and admiration of all.

Kate, on the other hand, felt like a discarded lump of coal—unwanted, unnoticed, and without purpose in this room designed for the brightest ornaments of London society. The sooner her brother could find a bride and they could leave Town, the better.

After sitting alone for a while, she got up to walk in the general direction of the refreshments. She chose her time carefully after most of the others had finished their meals and returned to the ballroom, for she did not wish to be part of the chattering masses as they went to dine. She found the buffet table rather picked over, but still there was enough for a healthy supper. She found a plate and selected some bread, slices of roast beef, and a pickled egg.

She shifted her plate from one hand to the other to reach for some roasted potatoes when someone unexpectedly grabbed the plate from her hand. She turned with a start, and it was a good thing that the plate had been taken from her; otherwise, she certainly would have dropped it.

Before her was the smiling face of Sir Richard.

"My dear lady Kate," he said with a disarming smile. "Please allow me to assist you."

Kate snatched back her plate, heedless of the potato that rolled to the floor. "I do not know what you are playing at, Sir Richard, but take yourself and your games elsewhere."

"I deserve that, of course," said Sir Richard in a disarming tone. "I have not earned your society. I am most heartily ashamed of myself for my actions the other night and I am resolved to do my utmost to redeem my character in your eyes."

"I wish you would do nothing of the sort. If you are interested in redemption, I suggest you take yourself to a clergyman."

Kate turned to leave, but Sir Richard seemed unwilling to allow her to go. He swung around, blocking her exit. Short of pushing past him, which was difficult to do while holding a plate of roast beef and pickled egg, she saw she would be forced to hear whatever ridiculous thing came out of his mouth.

"I deserve that, indeed I do," said Sir Richard most contritely. If nothing else, the man was a good actor. She had wondered at Jane falling for such a man but could see for herself that he was an expert in deception.

"I only hope that you will allow me the opportunity to raise your estimation of me," continued Richard. "It is clear to me now that Lady Jane, while an excellent young lady, was not the one for me. What I need is a lady of firm character and decided moral fortitude. I am certain that if I surround myself with such admirable qualities, my character can only benefit."

Kate was unmoved. "Begone with you."

So far Sir Richard had kept his face a model of placid obsequiousness, but a flicker of irritation flashed across his features before his appeasing countenance returned. She had a strong notion he was seething beneath his polished charm. "I must insist that you allow me the honor of dining with you this evening, Lady Katherine. For truly, you should not be alone in the dining room."

"No indeed, she should not be alone, for who knows what company might appear to annoy her." The Earl of Wynbrook strolled into the dining room. Never had Kate been happier to see him.

Wynbrook's voice was calm and held his famous lazy drawl, but beneath his half-closed lids were steely eyes of firm determination. He may play the part of the bored aristocrat, but clearly he was not a man to back down from a fight.

Sir Richard took a step back, his brows furrowing at the unwelcome addition of Wynbrook. "I am glad to see that you are not unprotected here, Lady Katherine."

"No, indeed, so you may now feel free to return yourself to the ballroom with all haste." She watched with no little satisfaction as Sir Richard finally retreated from the dining room. "Thank you, Wynbrook. Your arrival is most welcome."

"I saw him going into the dining room and I feared that he had cornered his latest victim."

Tired of holding the plate before her, Kate walked a few steps to an empty table and sat down, accepting Wynbrook's assistance, though she was perfectly capable of doing the task herself. "Too bad I was the only one here. I wonder why he felt it necessary to irritate me so."

Wynbrook took a seat beside her, gazing at her with a bemused smile. "But my dear, his next target is you."

Twelve

"ME?" KATE STABBED THE PICKLED EGG WITH A vengeance. "Why would Sir Richard target me?"

Wynbrook cocked his head to the side and gave her a quizzical look. "Can you truly not think of any reason why Sir Richard would pursue you?"

"I harbor nothing for him beyond an extreme dislike, bordering on a strong desire to see him dead."

"But your dowry, my dear, would be enough to induce almost anyone to overlook these tendencies toward violence."

Kate dropped her silver fork down on her china plate with a loud clank. "Oh, hell. I forgot about that."

Wynbrook's eyebrows rose at her profanity and then lowered to form the smug look she both disliked and admired. "I fear I have upset you and that certainly was not my intent. But with a dowry as large as yours, it can be anticipated that you will have your full share of suitors."

"Dowry as large as mine?" After the incident with Jane, Kate had forgotten about the unpleasantness of the dowry. Robert had never mentioned any particular amount. "Tell me what you know," said Kate archly.

A bemused smile played on Wynbrook's lips. "I fear what I'm going to say may shock you. For the amount of your dowry that is being circulated among gentlemen in the ballroom is fifty thousand pounds."

"Nonsense!" Kate stared at him, hoping he would break into a smile or do something to suggest his words were some sort of cruel jest. He did not but leaned his elbow on the table in a lazy manner. That was the odd thing about quality—they were rigidly taught all forms of correct behavior, only to act routinely in the opposite manner.

"If you are saying this out of some perverse amusement, I beg you would stop," said Kate.

"I fear it is only too true. It seems your brother has an interest in marrying you off."

"I'm going to kill him."

"You may want to reconsider your murderous inclinations. Think about it, my dear," said Wynbrook with unruffled calm. "If he were dead, you would inherit all. I must say, that would be even worse."

"Fine then, but I will make him suffer."

"A reasonable decision. I did tell him you would be most displeased, and you would find out sooner or later, but apparently he decided not to broach the subject, not that I blame the man."

"You knew!" Kate stood, towering over him. "You knew how much he set for my dowry but you said nothing."

"Indeed, if my recollection is correct, I did just inform you." He rose also and now Kate was in the uncomfortable position of having to look up at him. She liked it better the other way around.

"Why did you not tell my brother that such an amount would make me the object of every fortune hunter in Town?"

"I think that was part of the plan. Your brother asked me what he could do to increase your odds of getting married."

"My odds? *My odds?*"

Wynbrook's smug confidence dissolved and he took a nervous step backward. "Well, that is to say—"

"Are you taking bets on whether or not I will be married?"

"No!"

"Is anyone?"

"Er…no."

"Would you tell me if there was?"

"Certainly not."

"The truth. Now!" She advanced, and Wynbrook retreated before her.

His eyes opened wide and he spoke fast. "There is a standing bet at White's regarding your nuptials, very long odds, which some completely unscrupulous men have taken. Not I. I would never. Please put the knife down."

"Oh. Right." She put the knife back on the table. She wasn't sure when she had grabbed it.

"Perhaps we should evaluate your tendency toward violence." Wynbrook blotted his forehead with a handkerchief. "I thought you were being facetious."

"Perhaps you should consider my mental stability before you put a price on my head," snapped Kate.

"Your brother simply wished to make a connection with you desirable."

Kate glared at him, and Wynbrook tugged at his waistcoat in a nervous fashion.

"More desirable than you already are," he amended quickly.

Kate stepped closer, and this time Wynbrook held his ground. The air hummed around them and she felt fully alive. "Well, now that you have helped create this disaster, you can remedy it."

"I am entirely at your service," he said in a low tone that rumbled vibrations through her.

She stepped closer. "You need to get me out of this muddle. Either I will be obliged to stay home for the remainder of my life—not an entirely unwelcome idea—or you need to start circulating the rumor that we have lost our money or at least my dowry."

"You cannot start a rumor of your own poverty without tarnishing your brother with the same brush." He was being logical again.

"Perhaps we can circulate a story that I am mentally unstable or have the pox. Yes, that's a capital idea. You can spread a rumor that I am infectious with some sort of tropical disease. That should keep them away."

"You underestimate the lengths some men will go to restore their fortunes. They would still wish to marry you, then lock you up for being mentally unstable or infectiously febrile."

"Oh, this is so unfair! I am returning to my initial inclination to do my brother bodily harm and flee to the Continent to live out my days as an expatriate."

"Before you proceed, could you tell me how his

desire to see you married is different from your desire to see him enter wedded bliss?"

Kate ground her teeth. "It is entirely different."

"How so, exactly?"

"It just is." She turned to walk away, stopped, and stomped back. "You are the most insufferable man I've ever met." She took a deep breath, trying to get her emotions under better regulation. "I just thought you should know."

"Duly noted. Though in my defense, I am generally considered good company. You, my dear, are the exception to the rule."

"Perhaps I know you better than most."

A slow, seductive smile made her toes curl inside her slippers. "Perhaps you do."

Alarm bells rang in her head. Was she fighting with the man or flirting with him? Time to flee. She turned without a word and strode toward the ballroom, poised to make her grand exit. She stopped in the arched doorway. "They are waiting for me out there. Aren't they?"

Wynbrook casually leaned a shoulder against the wall by the door. "Rumor began earlier this evening. I'm sure it has circulated to all interested parties by this time."

"What will happen when I enter the ballroom?"

"I can think of twenty gentlemen, maybe more, who will vie for your attention."

Kate sucked in a breath. "That is repugnant."

"Oh, but it gets worse. They will flatter you, fight with each other, declare their undying love for you, and generally make themselves a nuisance."

"I'm going to hurt him," she muttered.

"Who is on your murderous list this time?" asked the amused man beside her.

"My brother. Sir Richard. Every man I meet."

"You have a busy night ahead of you."

She gazed at him with cool regard. "Is there another way out of here?"

Wynbrook gave her a lazy smile. "I am well acquainted with the Grant household." He leaned forward as if to share a deep secret. "We share a tailor."

"I will give you a stay of execution tonight if you get me out of here without having to walk through that ballroom."

"I may know how to escape the gauntlet of flirtation, but I want more than a stay of execution. I'm holding out for a complete reprieve."

"Because of you, I'm in this fix. Sorry, but justice must be done. You must answer for your crimes."

"I suppose I deserve it," said Wynbrook with a shrug. "But I remain steadfast. Enter the ballroom and expect to emerge with many new friends or find it in your heart to forgive."

Kate stared out at the dancing couples. She had no desire to be pursued for her generous price tag.

"You might even be forced to dance," whispered Wynbrook maliciously in her ear.

"Never," growled Kate through gritted teeth.

"Or I can have you safe in the carriage in five minutes," continued Wynbrook in a seductive tone.

"You are no gentleman."

"No, I am a peer of the realm. Nothing could be worse."

"Finally, something we agree upon."

"What is your answer, milady?" purred Wynbrook. He knew he had her, the bastard. The right, perfect, handsome bastard.

"Fine. I grant you reprieve from being murdered in your bed tonight."

"Bed? Tonight?" asked Wynbrook. "On second thought, perhaps I should take my chances. I did not know the bedroom would be the scene of my demise."

"Too late. You are forgiven. Now get me out of here. Lord Fowler has spotted me and is coming this way."

Wynbrook bowed, an unforgivably smug smile on his face, and held out his hand. "Come with me."

Kate didn't have time to hesitate. She placed her hand in his and he broke into a run, pulling her along with him. She picked up her skirts and smiled despite herself, for she knew this was dreadfully improper, which meant she liked it exceedingly well. He led them to the wall, no window or door in sight.

"Where are you going?" she hissed. "Lord Fowler will enter the dining room at any moment."

"Here!" He touched the wall, and a door opened, a hidden passage for the servants to bring food to the dining room without walking through the main doorway.

Kate sprang into the dark passageway, heedless of the consequences. Wynbrook jumped in after her and closed the door behind him, leaving them in total darkness. It was only then that Kate decided she had been imprudent in following Wynbrook into whatever mischief he had in mind. Her grasp on appropriate behavior for unmarried females was tenuous at best, but she was reasonably certain she was not supposed to end up in a darkened servants' passageway with one of the most eligible bachelors in Britain.

For a moment, she wondered if this had been his design; perhaps he numbered among those who wished to trap her into marriage. The thought no sooner flitted into her mind than it flew out. Wynbrook had no need for her funds, as well she knew. He also had no need to entrap anyone into marriage, not the way young women hung on his every word and anything else he might dangle before them.

"I hope shutting me into the pitch-black passage was not the full extent of your plan," Kate said, whispering in case Lord Fowler was still in the dining room.

"You asked me to remove you from the ballroom and I have done so."

"I hardly think standing in the servants' passage of the house is any great improvement."

"You are particularly difficult to please, my dear."

"Indeed, I do not like to be hunted like a fox for my wealth, and I further dislike being shut into small spaces in total darkness with men I barely know. What an odd creature am I."

"But you know me quite well. So you should be happy." His voice was near, and she could smell the intoxicating scent of his cologne—or perhaps it was his own heady scent. She could not see him but she could sense his presence, his warmth. She knew if she were to reach out her hand, she would touch him. She was suddenly glad that it was dark, so he could not see the warmth that spread across her cheeks. It would certainly not do to let him know that he had any effect on her.

"Well then," she said in her most reserved tone, "since we are such old friends, let us linger here in this musty passageway for a spell. You do take me to the nicest places."

"Come along, then. I promised to have you in the carriage in five minutes and I'll show you I can be a man of my word when I put my mind to it."

"Do not tax yourself overmuch on my account."

A small sigh escaped his lips, and she smiled in the darkness at the thought that one of her barbs had finally broken through the cool exterior.

"Here, take my hand." He must have reached out his hand toward her, but of course she couldn't see it. She stepped forward, reaching out her hands, but instead of finding his fingers, she found him, running smack into his chest. The contact was so unexpected, she jumped and was surprised when he wrapped his arms around her, pulling her close. Her hands rested on the silky smooth superfine of his exquisitely cut coat. Beneath the expensive fabric, she could feel the hard physique of his muscular chest.

"Didn't mean to scare you. Are you all right?" He must have leaned down as he spoke, for his cheek brushed against hers once, twice, and remained there, their cheeks touching in the darkness. He always appeared smooth shaven, but she could feel the beginning of stubble as his cheek brushed against hers.

"Yes, I'm fine. I did not realize you were so close." She turned her head as she spoke, not away from him but toward him, her lips moving dangerously close to his.

"My fault entirely." His lips brushed ever so softly against hers as he spoke, his voice low and soft.

"Of course it is." Her lips brushed against his again. She wasn't sure if it was his fault or hers or pure accident. But no, this was no accident; this was intentional. She wanted to kiss him. She wanted to kiss him the way they had that fateful night so long ago. What was wrong with her?

She took a deep breath and stepped back, out of his embrace, instantly missing the feel of his lips on hers but knowing it was sheer madness. She didn't even like him. And she knew perfectly well he did not like her. This was just folly brought on by standing in the dark. "We should… The carriage?"

"Yes, of course," he said in a voice that didn't sound quite like his. Gone was the smug superiority, the aristocratic hauteur. He began to walk slowly, holding her hand and guiding her down the passage.

What had she got herself into now?

Thirteen

WYNBROOK WAS GOOD TO HIS WORD AND HAD KATE back into the coach in the appointed time. He sent word they were set to leave, and Robert returned immediately, ready to depart the festivities as soon as may be. He informed them that Tristan planned to stay with friends and return later by his own means.

Of Jane, no one had seen anything.

"I shall go find her. Probably anxious to leave," said Wynbrook.

Kate nodded, hoping the ball had not been too torturous for Jane.

Wynbrook left the carriage and was gone longer than she expected. She was about to return to the house to see what had become of them when the door to the coach opened and in flew someone she hardly knew.

The person looked like Jane but had a wide smile on her face. This could not be the same morose girl who had been forced to come to the dance, could it?

"Jane?" asked Kate, wondering at the transformation. "Have you taken to drink?"

Jane laughed, a happy, musical sound. "No, but I

feel as if I had been, only better. It is a beautiful night, is it not?"

"Looks like snow," muttered Kate.

"But why must we leave the ball so early?" Jane pouted.

Wynbrook climbed into the carriage and rapped the ceiling with his cane to signal the coachman to take them home. He looked almost as happy as Jane.

Kate stared at him, silently asking for an explanation.

"Jane has met an old friend, Sir Gareth. They have rekindled a friendship," explained Wynbrook with a grin.

"You seem happy to meet an old friend," observed Kate.

Jane giggled. "Yes, I am!"

"So you have recovered from Sir Richard," Kate commented.

Jane paused a moment and said judiciously, "I think I was in awe of him and was honored he chose me of all the ladies vying for his name. But in the end, I was not in love with him. How could I be? No, I do believe I am very much in love with someone else." Jane beamed at all in the carriage.

Kate thought love must be a very fickle thing if Jane could go from despondent to giddy in a matter of hours. "You are in love with someone else?" Kate repeated.

"Yes, yes, I think I always have been. Why, I mentioned Sir Gareth to you earlier today, didn't I? You see, he has never left my heart. He was something of a childhood romance, but when we grew up, I thought I needed to find someone more mature, but that was just foolishness! When Miss Rose reintroduced us tonight, I realized what a goose I had been." Jane laughed, as happy now as she had been sad a few hours earlier.

The coach took its time climbing the steep hill to Wynbrook House in the slick conditions, and when they finally arrived, Kate was more than ready to find her bed, determined not to think more on the baffling nature of love. Instead, they had not been in the house for more than a minute when the knocker sounded urgently.

"Who could that be at this hour?" asked Wynbrook, frowning.

The butler opened the door and Sir Gareth rushed in, red-cheeked from the cold and the urgency of his mission.

"Sir Gareth!" Jane ran forward and caught both his hands in her own.

"Forgive me. Terrible imposition. Couldn't wait!" Sir Gareth gulped.

"Could not wait for what, exactly?" asked Wynbrook with civility.

"I understand there was some unpleasantness with… er…a previous suitor," said Sir Gareth carefully. "Miss Rose informed me you had many suitors for your hand and would be choosing one quickly, and, well, I wished it to be me."

"Sir Gareth, what are you saying?" asked Jane, wide-eyed and breathless.

Gareth looked back and forth between Jane and Wynbrook, as if trying to determine whom he should approach first. "Forgive me, for this is most impetuous, but I lost you once and I could not live with myself if I lost you again."

"Yes?" prompted Jane. Everyone in the foyer was silent, waiting for his response.

Gareth sank to one knee. "Lady Jane Arlington, will you marry me?"

"Yes!" shouted Wynbrook, drowning out anything that Jane might have said.

Jane and Gareth were too busy sealing their engagement with a kiss to notice. Wynbrook, Kate, and Robert stepped back from the happy couple and pretended not to be aware of their obvious affection.

"That matchmaker was quite dear but worth every shilling," confided Wynbrook to Kate, well pleased with himself.

"And who is this matchmaker?" asked Kate.

"Ah, nobody knows. 'Tis the mysterious Madam X!" Wynbrook was enjoying himself a little too much.

"The contact is the Dowager Duchess of Marchford and her companion, Miss Penelope Rose," answered Robert, willing to add to the conversation when it turned to something factual.

"How would you know that?" asked Kate, suspicious.

"He asked me so he could engage her on your behalf," said Wynbrook with a teasing smirk. He was certainly in a blasted good mood.

Kate spun to confront her brother, but he had wisely sounded the retreat and was halfway up the stairs.

"You did not inform me that not only had my brother set my dowry at a ridiculous amount, but had also contacted a matchmaker!" hissed Kate, stepping close to Wynbrook to accuse him without disturbing the revoltingly happy couple before them.

"You must think me mad," whispered Wynbrook, leaning in close with a devious grin. "You already wished to put an end to my existence. Why would I give you more reason to do so?"

"I will thank you to stay out of my affairs!"

"Affairs?" He spoke the word slowly, softly into her ear, sending shivers down her spine.

Kate opened her fan with a snap. When had it gotten so hot? Jane and Gareth continued to kiss their pleasure with their new arrangement. Wynbrook was so close. She was drawn once more by his unique, intoxicating scent. All she wanted to do was turn toward him, wrap her arms around his neck, stand on her tiptoes, and…

Kate fanned herself furiously. "Should you not put a stop to that?"

"Hey there!" called Wynbrook to the amorous Jane and Gareth. "Save a little for the wedding night."

Now her thoughts turned to what happened on a wedding night. Kate spun around without another word, picked up her skirts, and ran up the stairs.

❧

Christmas was the perfect excuse. Two days after the Grant ball, Wynbrook was ready to spring his plan into action. He crouched down and spied through the crack in the door connecting the library with the drawing room. For the past two days, he had been careful to avoid Kate, recognizing he had gotten too close, but that had not stopped the conspiracy already underway. Once the crisis with Jane had been resolved, the family had turned its attention to their guests. Darington and his sister must be *clothed*.

After several clandestine meetings with the family, a plan had been devised. Wynbrook did not exactly approve of his current methods, spying through the crack of the door, but there was no way he was going to miss this.

"I have a present for you." Tristan entered the drawing room where Kate and Darington were enjoying a quiet winter afternoon. Actually, it was more than quiet; it was dead silent. Did Dare and Kate communicate telepathically, since they were twins? Never had he seen two people more reticent.

Tristan held up a hatbox. He had been nominated to present the offerings since he could get away with more than most. Besides, if Kate realized Wynbrook was behind the gifts, she would never accept them.

"I have no need for a hat," said Kate, returning to her book.

"It's not for you," Tristan said with a smug look and handed the box to Darington.

Dare opened the box and pulled out a sharp blue bonnet. "Not sure what to say." He turned the lady's headgear around to study it from all angles.

"Say nothing yet. There's more!" Tristan beamed at the twins as no fewer than four deliverymen entered the room, carrying boxes of various shapes and sizes.

Dare opened a box and stood to hold up a pristine white gown. "I'm rather backward when it comes to fashion, but I doubt it will fit."

Wynbrook had to suppress a laugh. Dare did have a dry wit.

"Try this instead," said Tristan with a sly grin. He handed him another box and inside Darington found a dark blue dinner jacket. Without a word, Dare shrugged off the one he wore and pulled on the new one. It was perfect. Their tailor, who they kept a great secret, was an absolute wizard to so finely cut a coat without formally measuring the man.

"We cannot accept such gifts," said Kate, rising, her light eyes glinting. She was beautiful when irritated, which, given her temperament, meant Wynbrook had ample opportunity to admire her beauty.

"So sorry. I have no gifts for you," said Tristan with a dazzling smile. "These all are for Dare. Merry Christmas, old man!"

"Christmas?" asked Dare.

"Yes, Christmas. Now, don't tell me you don't know it's Christmas Eve."

Dare and his sister looked blankly at Tristan.

"Yule log? Mistletoe? Holly and ivy?" Tristan pointed around the room at the tasteful decorations for the season.

Dare and Kate looked around as if noting the decor for the first time. Wynbrook shook his head. What life of deprivation had these two led?

"Christmas!" cried Tristan, utterly outraged. "They must have Christmas even in Gibraltar."

"Yes, we attended church," said Kate.

"Yes, very good. But the presents! What about the presents? And the feast!"

More blank looks.

"It is a good thing my mother is already in her grave, or she would drop dead at the two of you!" exclaimed Tristan. "Here now, let us begin to make up for lost time." He shoved another box into Dare's hands.

"Don't know as I can accept all these. Must have cost quite a bit of blunt," said Dare.

"'Course it did! I ain't cheap, you know! But fortunately, I invested wisely and can well afford it." Tristan winked at Kate.

Dare tried to hand the box back, but Tristan refused. "You are new to this, so I will try not to take offense, but it is a great insult to refuse a gift!"

"But—"

"But nothing! You have given me far more than anything I could ever repay. Please, please, let me see you dressed as you should be. I beg you! It would be a great gift to me, you know. Ah, the time! Must dash. We are all engaged for the Devine Christmas gala tonight. They light up a tree, you know!" Tristan flew from the room, leaving the two of them in the room filled with boxes.

Wynbrook held his breath, waiting to see if they would accept their gifts. Everyone knew Kate had a morbid addiction to thrift, but would she accept a gift?

Dare moved about a bit in his new jacket. "Bit tighter than I'm used to. Guess I'll get used to it."

"You are not considering keeping these things. They must go back!" demanded Kate.

"You heard Tristan. He'd be insulted. Besides, I like it. You would look nice in this." Dare handed her the gown.

"Tristan said they were all for you."

"Not my size."

Kate shook her head.

"Kate," said her brother softly, causing Wynbrook to lean forward, trying to catch his words. Wynbrook really should go. If Kate caught him, she might strangle him with the ribbons of her new bonnet, but he could not tear himself away. He needed to see if she would accept it. Besides, one of his legs seemed to be falling asleep from maintaining the uncomfortable crouch too long.

"Tristan and his family have been exceedingly kind. Must not cause embarrassment by wearing work clothes to their fancy goings-on." Dare gathered up several parcels and left her with the new gown in her hands.

Kate took a deep breath and held the gown up as if weighing its worth. It was one that Wynbrook had particularly chosen for her, and he leaned forward further to gauge her reaction. It was a simple gown, expertly crafted of fine ivory silk. It was designed with clean lines and an overdress of exquisite lace, giving it a fine appearance of understated elegance. Jane and Anne had wished for ribbons and flounces, but Wynbrook vetoed the suggestion, insisting Kate's gowns be consistent with her taste: simple and without frills or fuss.

Kate moved toward the window and Wynbrook shifted position again to see her through the crack in the door. He started to lose his balance, overcorrected, and fell down on his backside.

He tried to scramble up, but pins and needles shot through his right leg and he flopped down once more with a thud. Kate was going to kill him! He dove behind his desk, hoping he would not be spotted. Eavesdropping on the interchange had sounded like a much better idea when he had not thought he was going to be caught.

The door burst open, and Wynbrook froze, hiding under his own desk like a child. What was the matter with him?

"Hello?" asked Kate.

He said nothing. How could he explain crouching

under his desk? He listened carefully but he heard nothing. Finally, the door creaked shut again.

With a sigh, he dragged himself to his feet only to find himself face-to-face with an irritated Lady Katherine. Her eyes flashed, but this time it filled him with dread.

"Ah, there's my quill," he said, trying desperately to cover the awkward moment. "Hullo, Kate. Didn't see you."

"You!" she accused. "You were spying on me."

"Me?" When in doubt, deny, deny, deny.

"Explain yourself! Why were you spying on me?"

"An excellent question. When I have an answer, I'll be sure to let you know," said Wynbrook, repeating her words when he'd caught her in his study.

"Go ahead. I'll wait." Kate folded her arms across her chest.

"I seem to think I have had this conversation before."

The faintest of smiles flitted across her face. "It does seem vaguely familiar."

"I'll forget about the study if you forget about this."

"Deal!" She turned and stalked out of the room, pausing in the doorway. "And thank you," she said in a voice so faint he could hardly hear.

"My pleasure," he responded, because truly, it was.

Fourteen

SHE WAS OUT OF EXCUSES. KATE HAD ALWAYS maintained that her reason for not buying expensive clothing was to avoid the cost. Truth was, that was only part of it. She wore her plain gowns because it kept people away. It gave her distance. She knew she was not skilled in social arts, so she simply avoided playing the game.

Wynbrook offered an arm to escort her into the Devine Christmas gala. Her feelings toward him were so convoluted, she did not know what to think. She was glad for the presence of Jane, Tristan, and her brother—the first two at least kept up the conversation.

Kate held on to her wool coat with a firm grip. Footmen were coming to take people's wraps, but she did not wish to give hers up. Her black gown had been her armor. Her plain white gown had made her invisible. The new gown she wore now made her feel naked.

The footman held out a hand, and she paused. Could she get away with wearing her coat all night? She took a deep breath. This was no time for cowardice. It was just a gown, nothing more. It was

Christmas Eve, and despite the fact that Christmas had never been much of a holiday to her, she could give Tristan this gift of wearing something he appreciated.

With a brisk tug, she handed over the coat. She glanced down at her silk ball gown, sparkling with a shimmering overdress of exquisite lace that gleamed in the candlelight. Truth was, she liked the gown.

She could not help but glance at Wynbrook. If he laughed at her, she would feign sickness and go home. Was it too late to consider the ague?

Wynbrook was all smiles, greeting people and escorting her with the utmost chivalry. He glanced at her and did a double take, turning to her and staring, openmouthed.

Alarmed, she put a hand over her chest. "Is there something wrong?"

"No! No, you look…you look lovely. Quite lovely."

"Thank you." She could breathe again, but Wynbrook appeared to be having some difficulty with the task, coughing and clearing his throat.

Despite his current breathing troubles, Wynbrook always cut a fine figure. He wore a dark green tailcoat and a gleaming silver waistcoat, which, as always, showcased his broad shoulders and trim waist. The green of the coat brought out the green of his eyes, and they sparkled at her with amusement and not a small measure of mischief.

He escorted her into the main ballroom, and she paused a moment to take in the splendor of the room. Glass icicles hung down from the chandeliers with small candles inside, lighting the wondrous crystal. Fresh holly was festively displayed, with red velvet ribbons tied around the bundles. Most impressive was the tree—a huge evergreen prominently located and lit with hundreds of candles and trimmed with red bows. The effect was enchanting if slightly frightening, but most dangerous of all were the numerous sprays of mistletoe hanging in different locations, waiting to catch unsuspecting guests in romantic encounters.

"I thought this talk of lighting a tree inside the house was all a hum," she admitted.

"Apparently, this is a Germanic tradition. Comes from her side of the family," said Wynbrook. "I think Tristan and his set only come each year to see if something will catch on fire."

"Does that happen?"

"Occasionally."

Kate scanned the room, looking for potential hazards of open flame and hanging mistletoe, not sure which would be worse.

"Let us greet our hosts." Wynbrook directed her to the reception line, and they were duly introduced to Lord and Lady Devine, and their niece, Miss Frances. Kate's heart felt a bit squeezed as she was introduced to Miss Frances, the girl Wynbrook's sisters predicted him to wed.

"Ah, Wynbrook, so glad you could make it to our little festive soiree." Lady Devine beamed at him. "Of course you are familiar with our precious niece."

"Yes, of course, how are you this evening?" Wynbrook gave Miss Frances a bow.

Frances was a cherub-faced girl, just emerging from the nursery into society. She giggled and returned the bow with a curtsy of her own. Instantly, Kate knew

Frances would simply not do as a bride for Wynbrook. The girl was too young and too pretty.

"My niece is ever so fond of dancing," hinted Lady Devine.

"Then she must save me the first dance!" cried Wynbrook. As if on cue, the orchestra began to warm up their instruments, and Wynbrook offered his other arm to the young Miss Frances.

Kate had to bite her lip to prevent herself from voicing protest.

"I do beg your pardon, Lady Kate," Wynbrook said to her. "But I am well aware of your abhorrence to dance."

"Yes, indeed," she said and snatched back her hand from his arm.

She watched from the shadows of the ballroom as Wynbrook and Frances stepped into the flickering candlelight in the middle of the room to await the beginning of the dance. Kate had to remind herself that she did not care in the least that Wynbrook was dancing with another lady. Of course he would dance with other ladies. He could dance with every lady present, and she wouldn't care a whit.

"Do they not make a handsome couple?" asked Jane.

"The handsomest I ever saw," said Kate through gritted teeth.

"I do expect them to announce soon after our wedding."

"I wish you both many felicitations," said Kate, almost choking on the words.

Sir Gareth walked toward them with a wide smile. Jane returned it, beaming at him.

"Gareth, you are well met this evening," said Jane with a becoming pink blush and a girlish giggle.

Kate felt free to roll her eyes, for no one was paying her any heed. "The music is about to begin. Why do not the two of you dance?"

Sir Gareth glanced over at her as if startled to see her there. His eyes were only for Jane.

"I should not like to leave you by yourself," said Jane, hesitating.

Kate realized that her brother and Tristan had long since abandoned them—Tristan with his friends, and Robert no doubt to find somewhere to hide. "Go on, I—"

"All right then!" Jane and Gareth joined the dance floor before Kate had finished her sentence.

"I am accustomed to being alone," Kate finished to no one in particular. Kate watched for a moment, wondering what it would be like to be in love as Jane and Gareth so clearly were. Of course, that would never happen to her. No, she had lost the chance of happiness long ago.

Wynbrook and Miss Frances spun into view and she watched them dance effortlessly across the floor, swirling with the other beautiful elite of society. An emptiness echoed within her heart. She had never been more certain she had no place in this life.

Across the dance floor, Kate spied the person of Miss Rose, the companion to the Dowager Duchess of Marchford and the contact for the notorious matchmaker, Madam X. Yet as Kate considered the matter, it was Miss Rose who had reintroduced Jane and Sir Gareth and Miss Rose whose comment had induced Sir Gareth to spontaneously propose.

This was no innocent intermediary. Kate highly suspected Miss Rose of being the infamous Madam X herself. Kate needed to put an end to any thoughts of matchmaking. Putting herself on the marriage market would only end in humiliation. Kate would have none of it.

Keeping to the edges of the ballroom, Kate made her way toward the suspected matchmaker. Miss Rose had worn a simple frock the last time Kate had met her, but this evening, much like herself, Miss Rose had been transformed by wearing a lovely emerald ball gown. Kate wondered if Rose's people had similarly disapproved of her wardrobe.

"I understand my brother has contacted you regarding my matrimonial prospects," said Kate, bluntly initiating the conversation.

"Perhaps we should find a quiet corner? I believe the balcony boasts a fine view of Town," suggested Miss Rose with the raise of an eyebrow.

"I am agreed."

Miss Rose led Kate to a side balcony. It was not snowing at the moment, but the snow on the ground lightened the entire view of the streets before them. Though the chill air was refreshing after the heat of the crowded ballroom, it was soon going to be uncomfortably cold.

"Your brother did make an inquiry with Madame X to find you a suitable match," began Miss Rose in her calm, direct manner.

"I do not mean any offense, but I have absolutely no inclination to marry. In truth, I am quite set against it," said Kate.

"Is there something in the institution that offends you?" She did not appear at all surprised at Kate's declaration against marriage.

"The prospect of handing over my money, my future, my very freedom to a man of any sort makes me ill. No, I shall never marry; on this fact, I am entirely resigned."

"I shall relay your feelings to Madame X," said Miss Rose, the picture of serenity.

"I thought you were Madame X." In truth, Kate was sure of it. The more she considered the matter, it was clear Miss Rose was responsible for bringing Sir Gareth and Jane together.

"Whyever would you think such a thing?" Miss Rose did look surprised this time.

Kate shrugged. She had no need to unmask Miss Rose as Madam X; she simply wished to stop her match-making interference. "Truly, it makes no difference to me. Either you are Madam X or you are in her employ; either way, I would like to redirect your efforts."

"In what way?"

"I have no need or inclination to wed, but my brother must marry. He has a title and no other living family to take his place. If he dies, the title dies with him."

"I see. So you would like Madame X to find your brother a wife instead of you a husband."

"Yes. I am glad you are of a quick understanding."

"Any particular guidelines in terms of the type of young lady who would be best suited for your brother?"

Kate considered the question. She decided to invent something that would not only help Robert find a bride, but also demonstrate to Miss Rose that

Kate herself was not a candidate for matrimony. "She must be of a serious nature, not vibrant or chatty. She must be able to bear children, though I suppose it may be difficult to determine this beforehand. Perhaps a young widow with children, though Robert would not care to have children underfoot, particularly if they were not his. Perhaps a lady who had conceived children but they had died, but not from illness; we do not need sickly brats."

Miss Rose blanched, a reaction that had nothing to do with the outside chill. "So the perfect wife for your brother would be a silent, serious woman who had not only lost her husband but her children as well?"

"Yes! Perfect!" Kate smiled to herself. That should keep the matchmaker away.

After a weighty pause, Miss Rose said, "I shall pass this on, but you must understand, there may not be many young widows whose children have also passed away."

"Yes, well, tell Madame X to do her best. If you cannot find these characteristics, just go for someone pretty. But no one who will speak insistently, I beg you, or I may be forced to cut out her tongue myself." Kate was only half jesting with this comment.

"Perhaps we should return to the party so we do not freeze," suggested Miss Rose, her grim face telling Kate that her mission to redirect the matchmaker away from herself had been successful. Kate smiled at the retreating form of Miss Rose. If that hadn't scared her off, nothing would.

It was the end of the set and Jane walked up, flushed from dancing, smiling on the arm of Sir Gareth. "Are you having fun, Lady Kate?"

Kate was saved from having to make some reply by the emergence of a footman. "Excuse me, my lady," said the footman, addressing Kate. "I have been requested to inform you that the Earl of Darington is on the balcony off of the blue sitting room and is requesting your presence."

Kate's heart sank. She knew that Robert was uncomfortable in these settings, but so far he had managed to hold his own. Perhaps it had finally gotten too much for the man. "Thank you. I will attend him directly."

"Would you like me to go with you?" asked Jane. "I do hope he is not unwell."

"He is most likely shy around company. Go and enjoy your dance. I will see to him."

Jane did not need more convincing and, within an instant, was arm in arm with Sir Gareth, being led back to the dance floor, a radiant smile on her face.

After a bit of trial and error, Kate located the door to the blue sitting room. It was quite out of the way, down a corridor and past the dining area and the salons set apart for gaming. She was not surprised; Robert *would* choose the most out-of-the-way location to hide from society. She was feeling a bit overwhelmed herself, particularly wearing her new gown, and welcomed the chance to have a reprieve from the critical eyes of society.

True to its name, the blue sitting room had a distinct blue motif, with floral blue wallpaper and a settee of light blue velvet. No one was in the room, and it was barely lit with only a few candles on the wall sconces. Robert had certainly found a remote place to hide. Blue brocade drapes hung on the other side of the room, which she guessed hid a door to the balcony. Did her brother feel the need to retreat so far as to stand out in the cold? Perhaps he was ill?

Concern putting a spring in her step, she slipped past the curtain and opened the French doors to the balcony.

"Robert?" She stepped outside into the frosty air, her breath visible in the cold night.

The doors behind her shut with an ominous click. She spun to face Sir Richard, who regarded her with a devious glint in his eye.

"What are you doing here? Where is my brother?" demanded Kate, wondering if Sir Richard had chased her brother away.

"Last time we were together, I did not feel we had enough time to truly get to know one another. I know you have little regard for me, but I must insist that you give me the opportunity to rise in your estimation."

"You arranged for me to be here? Is this some sort of trap?" Kate wrapped her arms around herself against the cold.

"I prefer to see it as an opportunity to kindle a new friendship."

"This time you've gone too far." Kate marched to the door, but Sir Richard held fast and would not let her past. "Stand aside, now!"

"Oh, such bad manners. You shall have to learn to control your temper, my dear," chided Sir Richard in a superior tone.

"Let me pass," growled Kate, her heart beginning to beat a bit faster. What was this man playing at? Why was he trying to prevent her from leaving the balcony?

"Let us be completely frank, shall we? I was initially engaged to Lady Jane. You ruined it. My financial situation at the moment requires me to have a large sum at my disposal in the very near future, or I shall be forced to flee to the Continent."

"Enjoy France," said Kate without a hint of sympathy.

"I have no intention of leaving. Since you were the one to cause my current dilemma, it is only fitting that you should provide the solution or, more to the point, your dowry."

"If you think I would marry you under any circumstances, you are very much mistaken." Kate took a step to the right, but he anticipated and blocked her. She stepped to the left and he did the same. It was most annoying.

"Soon, you shall have no choice. We shall be discovered together on this balcony in a compromising position, and you will be forced to marry me." He said this with such cold, calculating certainty that Kate, who had not felt the remotest bit of fear, now experienced a frozen sliver of dread creep down her spine.

"Let. Me. Go." Her hands balled into fists at her side.

"You are mine," he said with a snarl and grabbed her arms, pinning them to her sides and pulling her toward him. Anger, hot and raging, seethed within her. She slammed her knee up, causing her attacker to howl in pain as he clutched himself, bending over at the waist. She struck the heel of her hand into his nose and was rewarded with a satisfying crunch.

He fell to the ground, blood spurting from his nose. "You broke my nose! Oh, ow, ow, you broke my nose."

Kate straightened her skirts and looked down at him with contempt. "Do not ever let me see you again, or your nose will be the least of your worries."

"Kate! What happened here? Are you all right?" Wynbrook burst through the door.

"Yes, I am well. Only Sir Richard here attempted to trap me into marriage."

"He did what?" roared Wynbrook, grabbing the man by the lapels of his jacket and dragging him to his feet. Kate had never seen Wynbrook more enraged. Was he going to do the man bodily harm?

"His attempts at seduction did not end well, unfortunately for him," said Kate. "I do despise the man, but I would hate for you to have to answer awkward questions because you were forced to kill him. Do let us just leave him be. But how is it that you knew where to find me?"

Wynbrook scowled, but let Richard fall back to the ground. "Jane told me you had been directed to the blue room to meet your brother, a curious thing because I knew Dare had retreated to the library. I was immediately suspicious and it seems I should have been."

"This is what comes from telling my brother to set my dowry at a ridiculous amount."

"Please, let us not quarrel about that again. Your brother is only trying to protect you and provide you what you are worth. No one intended for you to be molested at a private ball."

"I know he was trying to help," conceded Kate.

"A pox on both of you," sputtered Richard, struggling to regain his feet.

"What shall we do with this wastrel?" asked Kate.

From the room beyond, they could hear voices of people entering the blue sitting room, though the heavy brocade curtain kept them hidden for the moment. "I saw Lady Kate and Sir Richard sneak away here, I know I did. Far be it from me to turn a blind eye to such goings-on," said a lady's voice.

"I wish he weren't here," whispered Kate, motioning toward the seething form of Sir Richard.

He still held his nose with one hand, the blood continuing to drip down onto his snowy-white cravat. He held on to the stone balcony wall for support. "You broke my nose, you little bitch."

Wynbrook said not a word but strolled directly over to Sir Richard and, with one good shove, knocked him clean off the balcony.

"Oh!" gasped Kate. "I told you not to kill him, though he did deserve it." She ran over to the balcony wall and looked over. Sir Richard lay on a bushy hedge one floor below.

"Ow," howled Sir Richard. "You ruined my best dinner jacket."

"Sorry to disappoint, but he does not appear to be dead," drawled Wynbrook.

"There! I told you we would find them here." The woman Kate had seen before with Sir Richard swept back the curtain with supreme confidence, only to have her countenance twist into one of shock. "But where is Sir Richard?"

"Sir Richard is so deep in his cups he fell off the balcony," said Wynbrook with a slow drawl. "Lady Katherine and I heard his plaintive cries and came to the balcony to see if we could render assistance. I fear someone may have to drive the poor sod home, for he is in no condition for public viewing. Quick now, somebody go down to the gardens and retrieve him from the rhododendron."

Kate had to flick open her fan to hide a smile. "I suppose there is going to be quite a stir about this."

"Fire!" someone shouted from inside the house. "Everyone outside!"

"Gracious! Has the tree lit up?" asked Kate as Wynbrook ushered her to the nearest exit. Everyone poured out of the house with tales of explosions and fire and possibly an exploding tree.

With shouts of "Make way!" several footmen and a few young gentlemen ran the sizzling tree out of the house and dumped it unceremoniously into the snow of the front lawn.

"Best Christmas party ever!" shouted Tristan in high spirits.

"Was anyone hurt?" asked Wynbrook.

"No, no, just a good deal of smoke. What fun!" answered Tristan.

Wynbrook ran back inside the ballroom to help escort out some of the elder attendees of the party. Kate followed to do the same and was not surprised to be passed by Robert, who was carrying out a portly matron who had apparently fainted at the excitement.

Kate was never one to run from danger. She took the arm of an elderly gentleman to help him outside and felt she had her feet under her again. Evacuating people from a fire was something she understood how to do.

After everyone had been escorted to safety, it took a bit to collect their wraps from the harried butler who was attempting to serve the crush of people standing on the front lawn. No one appeared injured, and the fire had apparently been put out in time.

"At least no one will remember the Sir Richard affair," commented Wynbrook.

"True," said Kate with a smile.

"Merry Christmas, Kate," said Wynbrook.

"A happy Christmas to you too," answered Kate, realizing that the only parts of the evening she had appreciated were those in the company of Wynbrook, even if they were also the moments of disaster. She had enjoyed it because she was able to face it all at Wynbrook's side.

Too bad he was intended for someone else.

Fifteen

KATE HAD A PROBLEM.

It was Christmas.

The time of year some people gave gifts. She had never participated in such activities, but it seemed clear the Arlington family was among those people who did. They had graciously opened their home to her and her brother, sponsored them in society, *and* given them both entire wardrobes.

Gifts in return were required.

But what could she possibly give? The shops were all closed and she would not know what to buy even if they had been open.

She rummaged through the sea locker that held all her worldly belongings, wondering if somewhere in her meager belongings, gifts could be found. She pulled out her ledgers, precious only to herself, and her homemade clothes, rejected soundly by everyone in the house. Those things would not do. She removed her traveling desk, so beaten and worn it could be appreciated only by the one who used it. She tossed aside a stack of unopened letters tied in string from their godfather, General Roberts. He had not been there to help when they needed him, so why should they acknowledge him now? She had considered tossing the letters into the fire but somehow could never bring herself to do it. Instead, she kept each one and tied them together, unopened.

At the bottom of the chest, she removed an old hatbox tied in ribbon. She had not looked in the box for a long time, for it held memories, and memories and she did not get along. She slowly untied the ribbon and opened the lid. These were her treasures, the things she had taken with her to school before her father passed, and a few things she had picked up along the way.

She spread them out on her bed and made her selections, wrapping them carefully in parchment paper and sealing them with wax. The gifts to the ladies of the house would be from her, and the gifts to Wynbrook and Tristan she signed from Robert. Satisfied that everything was correct and proper, she placed her remaining items back in the tattered hatbox.

She left her gifts on the bed, to be easily retrieved when the time was right. In respect to the holiday, Wynbrook had given the servants the day off. Some of them visited family if they were local in London, and others retreated to the servants' quarters for a celebration of their own. A cold supper had been prepared in advance for the family to enjoy, and afterward, the family gathered around the fire in the sitting room.

Seated comfortably in an armchair, Kate had the ridiculous notion to lean back and relax. She would never actually do such a thing, but the temptation proved to her how comfortable she was feeling within this family group.

The family was seated around the fire in a cozy half circle. Robert was next to her, then Jane, then Tristan, Ellen in her rolling chair, and across from Kate was Wynbrook, John Arlington himself, looking comfortable yet daring with the firelight glinting in his eyes. Perhaps he was even more dangerous when he was relaxed, for he appeared even more handsome in repose. Truly, the man was not safe. Not for her.

"Now for the best part," said Tristan with a gleam in his eye.

Kate thought it must be the presents, but instead, he knelt by the fire with a bag of sifted sugar, some bottles of flavorings, and a pan. He mixed sugar and lemon juice and began to bring it to a boil over the fire.

"Do you remember doing this at Cambridge?" asked Tristan with a grin.

Indeed she did. Fondly. Tristan often would come to their lodgings with an armful of fixings for sugar drops, and the three of them—Kate, Robert, and Tristan—would eat sweets and study into the cold winter nights. Or at least, she and Robert would study while Tristan made the sweets. She prepared more than one paper for the fun-loving Tristan. She enjoyed reading his books and doing his work. Had she been able, she would have enjoyed attending university. Technically, Tristan had graduated with a degree in the law, but it was Kate who had benefitted the most from his education.

"Ah, I haven't done this since I left the nursery!" Wynbrook exclaimed, and to her surprise, he joined his brother, kneeling by the fire to make the candy. When the mixture was almost at a boil, they removed it from the fire and began to swirl silver wire around the edges to form a lemon drop, and then plunked it down onto a tin plate to cool.

"Do you remember trying to hide the candy from Nanny Forman?" Tristan told the tale, and soon, all the Arlington family was laughing. Robert even formed something close to a smile. It was quite a night.

"Is it time for presents?" asked Jane with a happy smile.

"Yes, indeed!" Wynbrook cried and reached into his breast pocket to retrieve envelopes for his siblings. "Open them! These gifts were too large to wrap in boxes, so I made a few notes."

"Oh!" cried Jane. "A new feather bed! Thank you!"

"The set of bays I was admiring at Tatt's?" Tristan sprang to his feet and jumped up and down in a most unsophisticated manner. "Thank you!"

"Just do not kill yourself," admonished Wynbrook.

"I shall try, for you. Ah, but what a way to go." Tristan's grin was infectious.

"Oh, John, a new pony cart?" Ellen's face was radiant.

"So you can decide where you want to go," said Wynbrook. "I had this pony especially trained for you to be able to handle."

"That is so thoughtful. Thank you!" Ellen grinned at her elder brother with a tear of joy in her eye.

Kate wanted to cry too but for different reasons. Her gifts were shabby indeed compared to those from the master of the house. Ellen, Jane, and Tristan now exchanged gifts, all thoughtful, expensive, and time-consuming. The girls gave handmade embroidered items that must have taken them months to complete. Tristan gave a fancy watch fob to Wynbrook and lovely jewel necklaces to the girls. Of course, Robert and Kate had already received gifts, but they still received embroidered handkerchiefs.

Throughout the merriment, Kate felt herself sinking into her chair. She would have dropped through the floor into the kitchen if possible. Robert gave her a raised eyebrow. She had mentioned at dinner that she had gifts for the Arlington family, but how could she give her poor offerings now?

"We also have something for each of you," said Kate in a hesitant tone. "I shall just go to my room to fetch them." She grabbed a candle and left the room on light feet. She had a new plan. She would run up to the room and prepare envelopes for each of them, writing in some large gift. Her original items would be stuffed back in her sea locker and never considered again.

She dashed up the stairs, determined to work quickly to avoid detection. She reached the floor where her bedroom was located and came to a dead stop. Her door was ajar and a shaft of light emanated from it. What was this? The servants had the day off and all the family was downstairs. She pressed herself to the wall and blew out her candle.

Slowly she crept forward. Through the crack in the door she saw two men in silhouette, rummaging through her sea locker. Without making a noise, she removed the knife she kept strapped to her calf. One man grabbed her ledger and ripped out some of the pages.

Kate gasped. *He ripped her ledger!*

Before she could think, she jumped into the

doorway, brandishing the knife, screaming, "Thieves! Unhand those papers, you bastards!"

The men spun, but with scarves wrapped around their faces, she could not identify who they were.

"Dammit!" shouted one of the men. The other dropped the papers and ran into one of the conjoining bedrooms.

"Get back here! It's just a girl!" demanded the man, but his friend was in fast flight, the banging of the door in the next room a clear indicator that the man had escaped out into the corridor. The remaining thief grabbed the papers and bolted after his friend.

"Robert, John, come help! Thieves!" she screamed. She ran out the bedroom door, knowing the man had only one way out, determined to head him off. She ran to the open side bedroom door and banged it shut just as the thief was trying to make his exit.

"Ow, my nose," he shouted, along with a foul curse.

Kate had been on ships too often to be affected by language, no matter how offensive. She wrenched the door back open and grabbed the pages out of the stunned man's hand.

He grasped the wrist of her hand that held the knife and twisted hard until the blade fell. "You give those back, you little—"

"Kate, what is—" Wynbrook appeared at the top of the stairs and let out an unholy shout of rage. He ran screaming down the hall, his face twisted into utter fury, with Robert right behind him.

The man wisely turned tail and ran. Kate clutched the papers to her chest and slumped against the wall in relief. Her brother raced by her without a word, running after the would-be thief who had disappeared down the servants' stairwell.

Wynbrook was by her side in a flash, wrapping his arms around her. She was definitely not the fainting type, but just for a moment, she leaned back into the warmth of the Earl of Wynbrook.

And it felt good.

"Are you well? Were you hurt?" asked Wynbrook. "Here, let us get you back to your room," he continued without waiting for a reply. Before she knew it, he had picked her up in his arms, carrying her easily into her bedroom, now in cluttered disarray.

"I am well. Do put me down. I am fine." The words were spoken without the bite that would have naturally accompanied them. She did not mind being carried about by him, though she knew she really ought to object.

Wynbrook set her gently on her bed and then sat himself beside her, ignoring any shred of propriety. "This is infamy! That a man could be robbed in his own home on Christmas Day, it is the very peak of villainy itself!"

Kate had never seen Wynbrook so enraged. Not even when he was plotting the demise of Sir Richard had his color heightened so. "It is well now. I have my pages," said Kate, setting a hand on his shoulder, trying to comfort him.

"If anything had happened to you..." He did not finish the sentence but shook his head with gritted teeth.

Kate patted his shoulder again, wondering if his concern would be the same for anyone or if it related to her specifically. Whether from the excitement of the foiled burglary or the man sitting so close to her, her heart skipped along merrily.

"Did they steal anything?" asked John. It was impossible for her to think of him as Wynbrook when he sat so close.

"I do not know." Kate stood and began to gather the things that been tossed about the room. Her hatbox had been dumped unceremoniously on the floor and she knelt down to retrieve her things. John came beside her to help, and she raced to get her belongings back in the box before he could see. She felt naked before him, her life splashed across the floor.

"Were these your parents?" he asked, picking up a set of miniatures and replacing them in their box.

Kate only nodded.

"You have your mother's eyes."

Kate gazed at her mother, the woman she had never known. "She died bringing Robert and me into the world. My father was gone at sea much of our early years, serving as a captain and then an admiral in the Royal Navy."

"I understand he was raised from a barony to an earldom for services rendered to the Crown."

Kate looked up sharply, wary for any tone of condescension, but she noted none. "Yes. He discovered a traitor in a Captain Harcourt, who had for the love of money put a flotilla of ships in danger, one of which carried several of the royal princes. My father exposed the plot and saved them from death or capture."

"He was a brave man, your father."

"I wish I had known him better. He returned

nearly blind from a gunpowder flash that afflicted his eyes. He was sick for a while before he finally passed."

"I am sorry to hear it. What ailed him?" John asked gently.

Kate paused. "I do not know. After he died, we returned and discovered our fortune had been stolen and we were left deeply in debt."

John frowned. "Your fortune stolen? Who did that?"

Kate sighed. "We never could find the culprit. It is one thing about my past I wish I knew."

John put a hand on her shoulder, and his comfort warmed her soul. His eyes met hers, and their gazes held as the clock quietly ticked out the seconds. As if catching himself, he removed his hand and let it come to rest on the nearest object.

"Is this your brother's?" asked John, picking up the glazed medal with a white ribbon, edged in blue.

Kate stared at the medal dangling from his hand and said nothing.

"What action was this from?" asked Wynbrook, turning the medal over to read the inscription.

"The Battle of the Nile," she responded, her throat dry. She had a sudden impulse to tell him, to confess the things she had shut away in the box.

"Got away." Robert barged into the room, his expression one of disgust. "Rummaged through my room too but took nothing. It does not appear they searched through any other room. Did they get anything?"

"No," said Kate, swooping the medal out of Wynbrook's hand and stuffing the remaining items back into the hatbox. "Ripped pages from my ledger though. Why are they targeting us?" An old apprehension crept back up her spine.

Robert came to inspect the pages that had been torn. "The accounts of our latest prizes."

"Maybe they are looking for an accounting of your treasures." Wynbrook stood and offered her his hand in gallant fashion.

Kate stared at the proffered hand longer than was the social norm before accepting it gingerly.

"First the attempt on the *Lady Kate*, then our lodging house, and now this. Don't like it by half," growled Robert.

"I suppose the news of your immense fortune has made wicked men bold in trying to claim some for their own. Have you buried any of it anywhere? A secret map perhaps?" asked Wynbrook, his charm returning, though Kate would not soon forget the real flesh-and-blood man beneath the polished exterior.

"Bury the gold and forsake the interest? I should say not!" declared Kate, brushing out her skirts.

"You remind me of your cousin," said Wynbrook mildly. Kate stared at him, but there did not seem to be any hidden meaning. "He is a master with investments."

"Quite," said Robert without a trace of emotion. He looked at Wynbrook and then back to her. "I shall check on Tristan and the ladies." He turned and left directly.

Kate was aware she had been left alone in her bedroom with the Earl of Wynbrook. Left alone by her own brother, mind you. Kate glanced at Wynbrook to see if he had noticed the breach in protocol, but his eyes had fallen onto the packages on the bed.

"I believe I have found what you came to claim."

John gave her a cheery smile. "At least they did not make off with my Christmas present."

"Oh, no, those are…those are just small tokens. Nothing really." She watched in agony as he picked up the one she had labeled for him. "I just wrapped some shells for the girls, and some homespun I made for Tristan, since he seemed to like it so. 'Tis nothing, truly."

"May I?" Wynbrook held his parcel in hand.

"If you must." Kate almost couldn't bear to watch.

He opened it slowly, as if savoring the process of opening a sealed package. It was agonizing but also strangely seductive, watching his nimble fingers work. The paper fell away. He stared at the object and a smile slowly spread on his face.

"It is only a blank ledger book for when you need another," she said miserably. Why had she thought it appropriate?

"Oh, I know what this is." He held the blank ledger book close to his chest. "A remembrance of our times balancing accounts." He gave her a seductive smile that brought forcibly to mind the times those lips had been pressed on hers. "I shall treasure it always."

❧

Captain Silas Bones glowered into his ale. He had been so close! Damnable luck to have Lady Kate come up the stairs at that time. A few minutes more and he would have been out of the house.

A gentleman slid into the seat across from him in the dark corner of the working-class pub. By the look of his bruises and two black eyes, it appeared the man's nose had recently been broken.

"Do I know you?" asked Silas, his hand instinctively on the pistol in the pocket of his greatcoat.

"No, but I know you, Silas. You were at Eton, no?" said the gentleman with a smirk.

He had been recognized. "Who are you? What do you want?"

"I am Sir Richard. I have been watching Wynbrook House, looking for a way to repay them for this." He motioned to his face. "I watched what you tried to do and how you failed."

"Piss off."

"No, you misunderstand me. I am certain you intend to make trouble for Darington and his sister; thus, I only wish to help."

"Help how?"

"I have information. I know where they are going, how they will get there."

Silas shrugged, feigning nonchalance. "So tell me."

"First, we discuss the price."

So it was like that. "Fine, let us step outside," suggested Silas. He got up, remembering his social graces, and led Sir Richard out the back way, to a dark alleyway.

"Now about my price—" Sir Richard stopped speaking abruptly as Silas shoved his pistol into Richard's face.

"I would like to make a bargain with you," said Captain Bones mildly. "But you see, I find myself a bit embarrassed of funds. What could I possibly give you in return for your valuable information?"

"Don't kill me," pleaded Sir Richard.

"Not kill you? Well, I suppose I could do that. Would that satisfy you?"

"Y-yes, yes. Wynbrook and family will be traveling soon to Arlington Hall. I can give you the address. I know the posting houses. I know the routes."

"Keep talking," said Silas with a smile.

Sixteen

"ARE YOU SURE YOU WANT ME TO STAND UP WITH you?" Kate was certain that Jane would change her mind if she only thought about it more carefully.

The week after Christmas had gone smoothly enough. Wedding clothes and all the things apparently needed to complete the bride's trousseau were collected. Jane and Gareth had been celebrated at an engagement ball, and society quickly moved on to juicier gossip. Kate saw Wynbrook often, though always in company and always much engaged in managing his sister's upcoming nuptials.

Security in the house had been increased. Robert had taken to patrolling the grounds with a rifle on his shoulder and a sword strapped to his side until he'd terrified more than one caller come to pay respects to the bride, and the ladies of the house had politely asked him to desist. In any event, the entire party decamped to Arlington Hall, their country estate, and the concerns of brazen London thieves were pushed aside.

Kate was beginning to enjoy spending time with

Jane and Ellen, and apparently the feeling was mutual. The unfortunate part of this was that Jane asked Kate to be one of her bridesmaids—an honor Kate would have been happy to forgo. Why would anyone want her to be on display at their wedding? It defied explanation. And the gown that Jane had chosen defied something else entirely.

"Of course I want you here with me," said Jane, smiling radiantly as Anne fixed a wreath of flowers on her head. It was the morning of her wedding and Jane was as beautiful as only a bride could be. "If it wasn't for you, I would be marrying that wretch Sir Richard, not my true love."

"But…" Kate struggled to come up with some reason why she could not perform the requested office. "Surely there are others more deserving of the honor than myself."

Jane gazed at her reflection in the looking glass and smiled at the pretty picture that she indeed was. "I cannot wait to be wed!" She punctuated this statement by floating about the room in a dizzying, blissful haze. She had the coloring and the demeanor to make her chosen color for her wedding gown—a pale-pink blush—appear positively glowing.

Not trusting Kate's questionable fashion sense, Jane had firmly offered to select the gown Kate wore to the ceremony. The chosen color was a deep shade of pink. Not blush, not salmon, not crimson, but pink. Pure, unadulterated pink.

"Do you not like this shade?" asked Jane, gesturing to the vision of pinkness. "I know it is a bit bold, but the color looked to me like love."

"Love" was not a word Kate would have chosen. In truth, the only words that came to mind were not those she could utter before a lady. She contented herself with a long-suffering sigh. While Kate could never be accused of being on the right side of fashion, even she knew that with her coloring, such a shocking pink gown on her was nothing short of a travesty.

Kate took a deep breath. She'd been asked to do many difficult things in her life. But somehow those paled in comparison to the bright pink monstrosity. Yet none could accuse her of cowardice and so she dressed herself in the bright pink gown, trying to avert her eyes.

She thought the worst was done, but then lady's maids appeared, wielding curling irons straight from the fire. Kate took a gulp and remained perfectly still for fear of being branded. The maids merrily chatted with each other while holding burning instruments of torture a mere whisper from her skin. Finally, they deemed her torment complete by placing a wreath of pink flowers on her head. Kate did not need to look in the glass to know she looked a fool.

It was time to leave, so Kate went downstairs to inform the rest of the party the bride was ready. She scrunched her nose at the odd feeling of wearing this new gown. The previous gowns she wore had not been quite so tight, nor had they required such rigid stays to hold everything in place. Despite wearing multiple layers underneath, the silk-satin gown did not rustle in a familiar way but rather slinked noiselessly and glossy smooth. If she ever were to commit a crime, satin would be the right choice for her attire.

"My word! Lady Kate?" The Earl of Wynbrook

stared at her from the bottom of the stairs. He was impeccably dressed in a double-breasted gray tailcoat, but his eyebrows were raised almost to his hairline.

Kate stopped abruptly in the middle of the stairs, wondering briefly if it was too late to turn and run. There was no hope for it, so Kate cleared her throat and continued her descent. "Lady Jane is dressed and ready for the ceremony to commence," she said, hoping to direct his thoughts to the activity at hand.

"You are looking very…" Wynbrook was not to be diverted from her unusual appearance.

"Prepared for the ceremony to begin?" she asked, hoping to turn the conversation away from her attire.

Wynbrook shook his head, the look of amazement still clear on his face.

"Delighted to be witnessing your sister's wedding?" It was a futile attempt, but Kate thought she would give it one last try.

"No… You are looking so…"

"Pink," she groaned.

"Yes! Pink. I've never before seen you look so… so…pink."

"Your sister chose the gown."

"I have no doubt she did."

"I advised against it."

"I am certain you did."

Kate reached the bottom of the stairs but remained on the bottom step so as to look Wynbrook in the eye. "You do not appreciate your sister's choice in palette."

"On the contrary, I am finding her choice quite—"

"Don't you dare say 'amusing,'" Kate threatened. One could only take so much.

"Would not dream of it." He spoke the words with solemnity, but his eyes were dancing. In truth, he had lovely green eyes, especially when they were full of merriment.

Kate cleared her throat and looked over his shoulder to the hallway beyond. It was most awkward to be standing next to the Earl of Wynbrook, wearing a shockingly bright gown. She had a sudden urge to wrap herself up in a shawl—a very large, very black shawl.

"You look very bright," said Wynbrook in a halting cadence, as if filtering his words to find something palatable.

Kate glared at him, willing him not to say anything more.

"And very, very pink." Wynbrook succumbed to the obvious.

"We have established I'm wearing pink."

"It bears repeating."

"We shall have to disagree on that score," grumbled Kate.

"You do look quite—"

"Pink. I know. Please let them know they are about to bring Lady Jane downstairs." Kate walked past him, trying not to look as if she were fleeing for her life. It was going to be a long day. A very long, very pink day.

❧

Wynbrook stared after the retreating form of Lady Katherine in frank admiration. He had been utterly surprised to see Kate in such an unusual state of attire. He never thought he would see the day when Kate, whom he was willing to bet had never added a single ribbon of adornment to her hair, would wear such a bright color.

The grumbling demeanor aside, Kate was quite lovely. Her hair had been dressed in curls and the gown was designed in the current fashion, with a high waistline, a sculpted bodice, and a wispy skirt floating down the length of her body. Not every lady could wear this new fashion—it took a thin, statuesque figure to display the gown to best advantage. This was easily achieved by Kate, and so unconsciously done that it only added to her beauty.

Wynbrook paused. Beauty? Over the past few weeks, his admiration for her figure had increased to the point where he had to admit she was a handsome lady, but in the formfitting silk-satin, she became something more. She was a seductive siren, daring him to follow her onto the shoals…and follow her he would.

Wynbrook shook his head to dispel such thoughts and proceeded into the courtyard. Anne had taken control of deciding who would ride in what carriage and in what order, and Wynbrook was perfectly content to let her manage those details. Despite the nervous energy that had taken hold of Jane and his other sisters, Wynbrook was perfectly at ease. His middle sister would be married; social disaster had been averted; all was right in his world.

Wynbrook was to play the role of his father in the ceremony and so was ushered into their best carriage with Jane alone. It was a sobering moment, realizing he had taken his father's place. He experienced the familiar ache of wishing his parents had not left this earth so soon. It should have been his father standing beside Jane today, and one look at the tears glistening in Jane's eyes told him that she also felt his absence. It was every girl's right to have her father proudly walk her down the aisle at her wedding. He handed Jane a handkerchief.

"You look very well," he said, trying to redirect Jane's thoughts to a happier topic.

"Thank you," whispered Jane in a shaky voice.

Wynbrook did not know how to address the issue of their missing father, so he tried again at redirection. "You are marrying the right lad, you know. Glad it worked out the way it did."

"Yes." This gained him a smile, though she dabbed her eyes once more.

"Father would have approved."

Jane turned to him, her eyes wide. "Do you think so?"

"Yes, of course he would. And Mum would have loved him."

"Oh, I hope they would have. I fear I have lost a bit of confidence in my own judgment of character."

"No need for that," he reassured her, clenching his hands at the thought of Sir Richard. "You chose the right man in the end."

"Thanks to Lady Kate. I shudder to think what would have happened if she had not opened my eyes to Sir Richard's true nature."

"Yes, we all are indebted to her." The carriage rattled on for a moment before he added, "You put her in pink."

Jane gave him a guilty smile and hid a giggle behind her hand. "I did, didn't I? I suppose that was unkind." But she said it with a laugh.

"She is bearing it with the demeanor of a prisoner being led to a firing squad," drawled Wynbrook.

Jane laughed outright. "I fear it was most unkind of me to repay her kindness in such a manner. I thought only to brighten her for the wedding, but I could see this morning she did not care for it. By that point it was too late to change. What was I to do?"

"No, no, do not feel sorry one jot. I have rarely enjoyed anything more than seeing Kate in that lovely shade of pink. Reminds me of a cat you girls had when you were young and dressed it up as a baby."

Jane laughed again. "Poor Muffin. She was a very long-suffering cat."

"I swear Kate has the same look in her eye."

They both laughed.

The wedding progressed as weddings should and Kate, the long-suffering, stood bravely before the assembly in her shocking shade of pink. If her demeanor resembled something more appropriate to a funeral than a wedding, at least she performed her required office honorably and did not run screaming from the church.

After the wedding, Anne took over the arrangements for traveling back to Arlington Hall for the wedding breakfast. Naturally, the bride and groom would ride together, and the remaining wedding guests were ushered into different carriages, leaving Kate and Wynbrook to ride the relatively short distance together. Wynbrook was initially pleased, though one glance at Kate told him the feeling was not mutual.

Kate climbed into the carriage, ignoring the offered

hand of the coachman. She swung herself up easily into the carriage and settled onto the red squabs. The red velvet clashed garishly with the bright pink of her gown, making it appear even more gaudy and unnatural.

Wynbrook climbed in after her only to be received by a most unwelcome glare.

"Why do you not ride with your sisters?" demanded Kate. "I'm sure they would be glad of your company."

"I cannot speak to the pleasure they may or may not have in my presence, but I will say that Anne has directed me to escort you in this carriage, and when it comes to wedding arrangements, I dare not oppose her in any way." He thought that would be the end of any debate on the subject and was surprised that she pursued the matter.

"But the wedding is over. Now you should be able to ride with whomever you wish."

"The wedding over? My dear girl, now comes the wedding breakfast, followed by the wedding tea and the wedding dinner, followed by the wedding card game, the wedding supper, and finally, the wedding bedchamber. I may not know much about any of this, but I do know that on the day of the nuptials, everything has the word 'wedding' in front of it and even the most benign activity takes on the significance of a high and holy moment. I have learned to stand where I'm directed, smile when instructed, and do what I'm told." He rapped on the ceiling to let the coachman know they were ready to leave whenever it was appropriate in the procession.

Kate sighed loudly, so loudly that it resembled more of a growl.

Wynbrook attempted polite conversation. "I believe it was a successful wedding."

"Yes, the intended bride and groom were married at the end of the ceremony, thus a successful conclusion to the event." Kate had not a shred of romance in her.

"Yes, indeed, but I was considering the whole manner in which they were wed. The bride was appropriately blissful, the groom was stoic, the church was packed, and the bridesmaids were fashionably attired."

Kate glared at him with such venom he shifted a bit farther away from her on the velvet squabs, though he already sat across from her.

"This gown is not fashionable; it is fatal. I fear if I am forced to wear this thing for one moment more I shall scream or spontaneously combust or go mad."

"It is perhaps not a typical color palette for you." Wynbrook chose each word carefully, making sure he did not laugh openly at her, so she had no reason to wrap one of those ridiculous pink ribbons around his throat.

"It is *pink*." She spat the word as if it were poison on her tongue.

"So very pink." He could not keep the mirth from bubbling past his lips. She was utterly outraged, and the comparison with Muffin the cat was too great to suppress his laughter.

"That's it. I cannot stand to be in this gown. I must change now."

"It will not take too long to get back to the house. I am certain my sister would understand if you changed into some other frock once you arrived." He tried valiantly to contain his amusement at her discomfort.

"No, I must change now. You are laughing at me with every second I am in this hideous gown. I cannot abide it one second longer." She leaned over and hiked up the hem of her dress, grabbing a small dagger strapped to her calf. Wynbrook could only stare. What was she going to do? He feared for a moment that she might do him harm, though he made no effort to defend himself. Fortunately, her target was not him but rather the offending garment. In a quick movement, she reached around to her back with the knife, slicing through the ties of her gown.

"What are you doing?" Wynbrook cried, lurching across the carriage to grab her arms. Interesting how he moved quickly when he thought she might do herself harm but not at all when he considered his own safety in jeopardy.

"Let me go," demanded Kate.

"Not while you're holding that dagger. You are not yourself." Or maybe she was exactly like herself—he didn't rightly know.

Kate offered the dagger to him, raising one eyebrow. "Here, take it. I'm finished with it now."

Wynbrook released her but sat beside her carefully. "Finished with what?"

"Avert your eyes." Kate did not wait to see if he did or did not comply, which he did not. She stood in the coach as it rolled down the rough country road, stooping a bit so as not to bump her head. With one swift motion, she reached down, grabbed the hem of the offending pink gown, and pulled it up over her head, tossing it to the opposite seat in the carriage where it slumped down on the velvet seat like a vanquished foe.

If her gown was off of her, what was she wearing? His gaze shot back to her. She smoothed her hands down one of her new, gauzy white gowns made of the lightest, most ethereal fabric. It was so light and formfitting, she had managed to wear it under the pink gown.

She sat back down, folding her hands before her prim and proper, yet the gown was so sheer he could almost see through to her petticoats. Little wonder she could wear it under the pink silk; it was barely there. It was nothing more than the latest fashion, clearly one his sisters had chosen for her, but his jaw went slack.

Struggling, he finally formed words. "You wore that under your gown?"

"Yes," said Kate simply, looking decidedly more comfortable though infinitely more desirable. He was not laughing now.

"I cannot believe you...you just took your gown off in front of me," stammered Wynbrook.

Kate regarded him with an expression similar to one of his tutors when he was slow with his sums, the look of resigned patience with the intellectually feeble. "First, I did tell you to avert your eyes. Second, I agreed to wear that travesty for the wedding and not one moment longer. So I have now removed it. It was no different from removing a coat since, as you see, I am fully clothed. You saw nothing."

What he saw was that Kate had removed her gown before him. What she had underneath was irrelevant, since his imagination supplied the rest. It was going to be a long night, and he feared Lady Kate would be prominent in his dreams.

"Yes, yes, of course." It was the only thing he could think of to say.

"You can return my dagger to me now," Kate demanded, holding out an empty palm.

He should have withheld it from her on principle, but a rebellious side of him wondered if she had the knife maybe she would remove another layer of clothing. He handed the dagger back to her. She accepted the dagger and leaned down, pulling up her skirts once more to reveal a shapely ankle. But she did not stop there and pulled her skirts even farther to reveal the sheath strapped to her calf. She replaced the dagger, dropped her skirts, and sat up tall, folding her hands in her lap as if nothing out of the ordinary had occurred.

The carriage ground to a halt and the unwanted pink silk garment slid into a bright heap on the floor of the carriage. Wynbrook realized their time together was over. His mind spun, trying to comprehend what had just occurred. Had he truly witnessed her removing her gown in front of him? The pink puddle at his feet seemed to indicate it was true.

Kate alighted from the carriage, accepting the hand of the coachman. If the man noticed the change in attire, he had the self-control to not say a word.

At least with Kate, life would never be dull.

Seventeen

WYNBROOK FOLLOWED KATE INTO THE HOUSE LIKE A moth following a flame. She was not at all the lady for him, he felt compelled to remind himself. Everyone expected him to make an offer to Miss Frances, though in truth he'd never had much interest in the match. Frances was a perfectly pleasant girl, from a well-known family, and she would make a socially acceptable countess.

Kate, on the other hand, would make a terrible countess. Her brusque manner had none of the inviting social grace of his mother. No, she simply would not do. Besides, even if he did ask for her hand in marriage, she would most definitely turn him down flat.

Wynbrook realized with a start that he was considering Lady Kate as his future bride. Had he lost his mind?

"John!" Tristan appeared with a bemused smile. "So lost in your thoughts you can't even acknowledge your brother?"

"Sorry. Woolgathering."

"Left your mind behind?"

"Somewhere with the pink frock," muttered John.

"Kate changed quickly," Tristan commented with a laugh.

"You have no idea."

"Be cryptic if you like, but the guests are beginning to return for the wedding breakfast. You might want to be present since you are our host!" Tristan left him with a smile.

"Yes, yes, of course," mumbled Wynbrook, his eyes still on Lady Kate. She and her brother had taken up defendable positions in a corner of the room, near an exit. Though he needed to attend to his responsibilities, he could not tear his gaze away from Kate. The formfitting gown hugged her curves, which had increased with the past few weeks of good food. In truth, Kate's appearance had improved dramatically once she had lost the look of haunted deprivation and gained more rounded edges. She was looking very fine indeed.

"Lord Wynbrook!"

Wynbrook was startled for the second time in a handful of minutes into recognizing he was not paying the slightest attention to anyone around him save Lady Kate.

"Lord and Lady Devine," he said quickly. "And Miss Frances. I am so glad you were able to come to the wedding." Wynbrook greeted the couple and their young niece, who was expected to make a brilliant entrance into society, if not move directly into marriage. A marriage in which he was supposed to play the role of groom.

Admiral Lord Devine and his wife were very kind people who had been friends of his family since well before John had been born. Their niece was very pretty and exactly the sort of young, biddable girl he should be marrying. Yet, as he glanced again at Lady Kate, he knew he could never marry Miss Frances.

"We would not miss dear Jane's special day for anything. It was a moving ceremony," said Lady Devine.

"Yes, quite," said Wynbrook. He had not paid the least bit of attention other than to ensure the marriage was good and legal.

"I think it is a very good thing for young people to be married. Do you not agree?" she added, giving him a pointed look followed by a smile at her niece.

Wynbrook cleared his throat. "Yes. I have heard some people approve of the marital state."

"I do believe now that Jane is wed, you also shall consider taking a bride."

"Now, my dear," Admiral Devine gently chastised. "Do not badger the man about getting married."

"Oh, but I must!" cried Lady Devine with a charming smile. "Lady Wynbrook was my dearest friend and I know she would have John in thumbscrews by now for being still unwed. I am only doing my duty to speak for his poor mama."

John laughed, for everything Lady Devine said was true. His mother had begun plotting his wedding from the moment he'd turned eighteen. "I accept the chastisement on behalf of my mother. I am sure she would be pleased to know you are carrying out her wishes."

"Well played, my boy." Admiral Devine laughed and gave John a hearty slap on the back. "Only do take care." He leaned in to give a little friendly advice. "Nothing like a wedding to turn a lady's head to marriage."

Wynbrook took the warning to heart. As invited guests began to arrive for the wedding breakfast, all he could see were determined mamas with their unmarried daughters. And here he was an unmarried earl. It was a travesty so great, they all were determined to remedy the situation, with Wynbrook being the prize catch of the day.

He soon found himself surrounded by eligible females—tall ones, short ones, plump ones, skinny ones. All he needed to do—nay, was *expected* to do—was pick one. He could have no further excuse. It was considered nothing short of criminal that he had not chosen a bride already.

He looked over to Kate for some sort of sympathy, for he knew she would be standing alone amidst the crowd, but he could not find her. Instead, there was a crowd of young gentlemen surrounding the spot where he had seen her last. He looked closer and realized she was in the middle of the feeding frenzy.

His heart began to pound. How dare they surround her like vultures? They were only after her money, the opportunist knaves. He was marching toward the group before he realized what he was doing. Kate would not like to be smothered by fortune hunters. The gentlemen parted before him and he found Kate, but not as he was accustomed to seeing her.

This Kate was regal, aristocratic, and in command. With a start, he realized the men might not be swarming around her for her money but for her beauty. Those surrounding Kate were not base fortune hunters but his friends, many of whom he knew had no need for an heiress. It was even worse than he'd thought. They were here not for her money, but for the lady herself.

Her ethereal eyes flashed, and he knew he must say something since he had barged his way over in a great state. Where was her brother, anyway?

"Lady Kate, forgive me, but your brother wishes to see you in the drawing room."

She raised an eyebrow but laid a hand on his sleeve and allowed him to escort her out of the hall. "My brother is in the privy," she whispered to him when they were out of the dining room and beyond hearing of the guests.

"Oh, well, I guessed you would not like to be swarmed so came to save you."

"I was not in need of rescuing," she said staunchly.

"Forgive me for misreading the situation." He led her into an empty drawing room and shut the door behind them. It was a relief to be outside the room where he felt hard-pressed to make some young lady an offer, and it was even better to separate Kate from her would-be suitors.

Kate sat tentatively on a chair, not quite looking at him but not quite avoiding him either. "Do you think those men were merely fortune hunters?"

"You are well dowered," he insinuated, though his conscience pricked him to say it.

"I wonder that you would invite such gentlemen to your sister's wedding." She looked at him directly, a gaze he was not equal to return.

"I… that is to say…they might not all be seeking a rich wife."

"Then why would they seek my company?"

Wynbrook was now the one staring at the art on the walls. "Well now…very nice in your new Town togs. Polite to be receptive to our guests." He stumbled over his words.

"I see," she said, but said no more, remaining curiously quiet.

He wondered what precisely she saw. He knew she would not be right for any of those men who swarmed around her. He knew it in the very marrow of his bones.

"Have you…" He cleared his throat. "Have you any thought towards marriage?"

"Marriage is an institution designed to subjugate women and rob them of their resources and basic freedoms. A woman's dowry should be her resource to dispose of how she pleases, not held in trust until such time as she weds and then handed over wholesale to her husband."

"Yes, yes, I quite agree," said Wynbrook, heartily relieved that she was not considering any of the young bucks who had swarmed around her as candidates for a groom.

"Then why did you encourage your sister to enter into the institution?"

"Well, I…" He had stepped in it again. He really needed to be more careful when he spoke with his Kate. *His* Kate?

Fortunately, the drawing room door opened and Darington walked in, stopping a moment and frowning at the two of them before shutting the door behind him. Wynbrook realized he had been caught alone in a closed room with the sister of a lord. Had circumstances been different, he might have been called upon to make an offer. He had no fear of this but still felt the need to explain.

"Your sister was being crowded by a bevy of admirers so I helped to facilitate a rescue," said Wynbrook as justification for being found alone in a room with Kate.

"I was fine," muttered Kate.

"You here to escape company as well?" asked Wynbrook.

"Lot of young ladies," said Dare, clearly uncomfortable with the female company.

"I am afraid there are. But we must be brave, can't avoid them forever. Have you found a bride yet, old man?"

"None that would have me," muttered Dare.

"He offered for Penelope Rose," explained Kate.

"The new Duchess of Marchford? Unfortunate. But do not despair, plenty of fish in the proverbial sea. I fear I must return to the guests. Brotherly duty and all." Wynbrook walked to the door, secretly hoping Dare and his sister would remain safely in the drawing room—where no young men could find her.

"Rather be fishing for actual fish," commented Dare.

"True, indeed. Many times in society, I'm not sure if I am the hook or the bait."

The corner of Dare's mouth twitched up a fraction, the closest thing to laughing Wynbrook had seen.

"Perhaps we shall remain bachelors forever and you can teach me how to sail," said Wynbrook.

Darington nodded. "Happy to have you on board."

Wynbrook opened the door, and they stepped out into the hall where some of the guests had congregated, chatting in small groups. "Perhaps you will allow me the honor of taking command of the *Lady Kate*," said Wynbrook, thinking perhaps he would make an escape to a life at sea.

"No," said Dare flatly.

"No? You would deny me the *Lady Kate*?"

"She is a tempestuous lady, needs a firm hand. Not for the young and inexperienced," said Darington in all seriousness.

Wynbrook realized the man did not jest about his ship. "Is there anything I could do to prove my worth?"

They walked back into the dining room as Darington shook his head. "Sorry, for you have been good to us. But the *Lady Kate* is not for you."

❧

Captain Silas Bones pulled up his collar against the cold. It was a bright January day, the sun glinting off the pristine snow, but bitterly cold. He looked down on Arlington Hall with resignation. He had used the information from Sir Richard to follow Wynbrook and Darington, but they had kept in tight company and had not given him the opportunity to attack. More and more people arrived at Arlington Hall.

"No hope for it now," he said. "Might as well go back to the inn."

His men, four in all, stamped their feet in the snow behind him. He had been so close to getting his hands on the ledgers. Where was all the gold? Had it all gone to the bank? Wouldn't have been his choice, but was it theirs?

"Your father will be sailing into Portsmouth soon,"

said a large man with massive forearms. "What are you going to tell him about his cargo?"

Silas ground his teeth. After their failed attempt, Wynbrook had posted footmen as guards and barred the doors. Silas had hoped he would have more of a chance when they parted for the country estate, but now the country was crawling with gentry.

"What do you propose we do? Show up at the door and pretend to be wedding guests?" growled Silas. Had things been different, he might have been one of those guests. But that was forever barred to him. And Darington was to blame.

"Captain will be mad as fire if you don't have his money."

"I know very well the character of my father! Now, unless you would like to return to him and report on your failure, I suggest you shut your mouth and do what you're told." Silas glared at the large man.

"Aye, sir," said the big man.

"Wait here. Tell us when they depart," said Silas, leaving his detractor to cool his opposition in the freezing temperatures. In a flash, he made a decision. If he couldn't be a thief, he might as well go for kidnapping and ransom instead. "I am done trying to find the ledgers. Time to go for Lady Kate."

Silas sighed again as he trudged back to his modest inn. From a wedding guest to a thief to the abductor of young maidens. It was a long way down and he had the feeling he was not done falling.

Eighteen

MEN ATTENDED HER IN A MANNER KATE FOUND strange, bordering on the bizarre. It was one thing for those she knew were in desperate financial straits (Tristan was an impeccable source of gossip), but there were also a few who did not have need of an heiress, which baffled her. Why would they wish to spend time in her company? And why was Wynbrook glaring at them from across the room?

It was a good wedding by all accounts. The bride was glowing and the groom was bursting with pride. Everyone wished the happy couple well, and they were surrounded by a chorus of happy voices. It was a new beginning for them…and an end for her and Robert.

When the pianoforte was brought out in the evening for some spontaneous dancing among the happy crowd, Kate and Robert retreated to the library. Dancing was not going to happen. Not ever.

"How long do you wish to visit with the family after Jane and Gareth leave tomorrow?" asked Robert.

Kate did not wish to leave, yet she knew she must.

Wynbrook was meant for another. There was no reason to stay. "We can leave tomorrow as well," she said.

"Back to London or to Portsmouth, to return to Gibraltar?"

Kate sighed in defeat. She had hoped Robert would find a bride, but he seemed more reluctant than ever. "We might as well return to Gibraltar." Kate did not say "home," for Gibraltar would never be that. Truth was, they had no home. Robert would go back to sea and she back to her ledgers. Though they honestly had no need for more financial gain, she did not know what else to do. Ironic that they had regained their fortune to take their place in society only to discover they no longer belonged.

"I thought I might find the two of you hiding in here," said Wynbrook, entering the library. "Came to tell you cake is being served."

"Cake?" asked Robert, always interested in good food.

"What is this about Gibraltar?" asked Wynbrook.

"We will be leaving tomorrow to go back to Portsmouth and then Gibraltar," said Kate in a matter-of-fact tone.

Wynbrook stared at her like a puppy that had just been kicked. He blinked and his cool reserve returned. "So soon? I'm sure we expected you to stay awhile at least."

"We have already encroached on your hospitality long enough. We have completed the tasks we set for ourselves, concluded our business with our investors, and wished Jane well at her wedding. We should return to our business now and allow you to return to yours."

"But what of your mission to find Dare a bride?"

Kate shrugged. "Seems a hopeless case."

"Yes," said Wynbrook without emotion. "Yes, I understand. I wish you a safe journey." He turned to leave and paused by the door. "Too bad you will not be here longer, for I've made a tangle of my accounts, can't make sense of them. Thought you could help. Oh well. I'm sure it can be sorted out somehow." He gave a quick smile and left.

Kate watched him leave. Was that all the good-bye she was going to get? A lump formed in her throat. If this was all the farewell she could hope to receive, then she did not care that she was leaving either. In fact, she was glad to leave. The sooner the better!

Several hours later, after the house had gone to sleep, Kate lay awake thinking of Wynbrook's words about the difficulty with his accounts. How could she leave with it uncorrected? It would bother her forever. With a sigh, Kate grabbed a wrap, shoved her feet into slippers, and padded down to Wynbrook's study. A "tangle of the accounts"? He would "sort it out"? She had no confidence in his ability. At least she could set things to rights before she left. Besides, this was as clear an invitation to correct his books as she was going to get.

The ledger lay open on the desk, beckoning her to fix it. Kate sat down before the ledger, brushing her long, brown hair out of the way and beginning her work. Strange how six years ago she was in the same place, doing the same thing, and here she was again, just like last time. Just like a few weeks ago too. In truth, it did seem a bit too coincidental. Her suspicion grew.

"Wynbrook?" she called out.

John emerged from behind the drapes in the

shadows and strolled forward, still immaculately dressed as he had been all day. "I knew you could not resist correcting my ledger."

"You lured me here!" cried Kate, feeling at a distinct disadvantage for being clothed in only a night-gown and wrap, while he looked like he'd stepped off the pages of a fashion plate.

"Yes," replied Wynbrook, completely unremorseful. He stepped closer, the light from her candle casting him in a rosy hue. "Other ladies might be tempted with wine or jewels, but your head is turned by the prospect of solving math equations."

"It is more the thought of your errors not being corrected," growled Kate.

"It is a worthy concern, for I am not the most attentive when it comes to my sums."

"Yes, I can see that." Kate made a final notation on the ledger. "What I do not see is why you would wish me here, especially considering your future bride lies sleeping upstairs."

"My future bride?"

"Do not play coy. Everyone speaks of your connection with the Devine family." Kate was not one to mince words.

"Ah yes, I have heard the rumors too. Hate to be disobliging to anyone, but I fear there is no truth in the tale."

Kate's heart tapped faster in her chest. "Truly? That is to say, please tell me what you wish to discuss." Kate used her most businesslike tone to cover the hope that surged through her.

Wynbrook cleared his throat and motioned for her

to sit in a chair beside the waning embers of the fire. He took the chair opposite her and Kate waited in silence.

"The last time you left was so sudden, I did not have the chance to say good-bye. This time, I wanted to be able to express my gratitude for your service to my family."

Kate gave him a short nod. "Duly noted." She knew this was not the reason he had wished to see her alone.

"I was surprised to hear you are leaving so soon," commented Wynbrook.

"Our business is concluded, our investors paid. There is no reason to trespass on your hospitality any further." She attempted to keep her face neutral.

Wynbrook gave her a quick nod. "Then there is only one more thing to discuss." He cleared his throat. "The kiss."

Kate was so surprised, she gaped at him. "Whatever do you mean?"

"The night before you left six years ago—"

"Was terribly difficult for you," said Kate, attempting to change the subject. "You had suffered a grievous loss. I am sure your recollections of that time are hazy at best." She was giving him a way out. *Take it.*

"No, it will not do," said Wynbrook after a moment's pause. "I must beg your forgiveness for such inexcusable behavior."

"Nonsense. You were sick with grief. If anyone took advantage, it was me," said Kate.

"Do not be absurd. My behavior that night was unconscionable. As a gentleman, I cannot abide it."

"But you have already told me you are no gentleman."

John gave her a slow smile. "Very true. If anyone had seen my behavior, an offer of marriage would have been expected."

"But no one did see it."

"You could have told your brother. I would not have denied it. In truth, I do not know many young ladies who would not have confessed what happened, knowing the outcome would be a wedding."

"If you think I would trap you or any man into marriage, you are very much mistaken."

"Yes. You are unique in that." He gazed at her with frank admiration in his eyes, bringing to the fore all the difficult emotions she had worked so diligently to repress.

"I have no desire for a proposal." Was she telling him or reminding herself?

"I do not blame you for holding me in low regard. The only thing worse than kissing you when you were under the protection of my own house was to do the thing badly. I fear my kiss was poorly executed, and for that, I apologize."

"It was not… That is to say…I would not have said it was poorly done," she faltered.

"So you liked the kiss?" He sounded sincere, but his eyes blazed with mischief.

"You are incorrigible. If you would excuse me." Kate stood. It was past time to make her escape.

John stood as well. "Forgive me, please. It is not my intention to cause discomfort, truly. Is there anything I can do to make amends?"

"For one thing, it is hardly fair to have a conversation with me in such dishabille and you fully clothed."

"You are beautiful as always, but I grant you the point." He shrugged out of his formfitting jacket.

"Lose the cravat," she demanded.

He untied it with a flourish, tossing it aside with the jacket. The waistcoat followed.

"And unbutton the shirt," said Kate slowly, feeling powerful and very, very naughty. It was delicious.

"As you wish." John undid the three buttons at the top of his shirt, revealing a glimpse of a perfect, muscular, chiseled chest.

Kate swallowed on a dry throat. When had it got so unbearably hot? She was playing with fire. It would not end well. Nothing following this moment could be good for her. She should leave.

But she didn't.

They stared at each other in the near darkness. What would happen next?

"If anyone were to catch us having a tête-à-tête together at this time of night, particularly in this state of undress, we should surely be forced to marry. We should retire to our separate bedchambers." There, she had said the right thing.

"You give sensible advice," he agreed.

But neither moved.

"Since you are leaving tomorrow," began John, "and I know not when I might see you again, I feel compelled to confess that though I am not unfamiliar with feminine charms, your kiss is the only one that haunts my memory."

"Why is that?" Her pulse skipped in a merry dance.

"I do not know. I believe you are the only one who can help me."

Kate stared at him, fearing it was some cruel jest. He remained earnest, and she feared even more that he was sincere. Truth be told, Kate had given more than enough thought to that kiss as well, but she reasoned it was because it was her first and only. If John also thought often of the kiss, what did it mean?

"How many other debutantes have you gone about kissing?" asked Kate, getting down to the practicality of his request.

"None! Save you," he amended.

"Then who have you been kissing?"

He shifted and looked away, answering her with false carelessness. "Truth be told, none of late. But in my younger, wilder years there were young widows, the unhappily married, professional courtesans, the typical fodder for a disreputable lad, but I recall none the way I remember you."

"Then you have your answer. You have had connections with others who want something from you. They wish for your money, your body, or your name. Their kiss is currency."

He turned back to face her. "And yours was a gift. Given freely." John stood a small step closer, a half smile of wonder on his face. "Thank you."

They stood in silence staring at each other. This was her last chance to have any interaction with the man who haunted her dreams and she could think of nothing to say. "You say the kiss was a poor one?" Had she said that out loud?

"One of my worst."

It seemed a shame that if one kiss would haunt her dreams forever that it not even be his best. If she was to cling to one memory of a kiss for the rest of her lonely, celibate life, should she not at least taste what the man could truly offer?

"I am willing to attempt the process again, and you can judge whether or not my performance is improved." He was so somber and matter-of-fact, she almost missed the fact that he had offered to kiss her again.

That will not be necessary. Those were the words she should say, but somehow they were stuck in her throat. *Kiss me!* were the words she wanted to say, but she held that in check as well.

"In truth, I should beg your indulgence to give you a corrective kiss," he suggested slyly.

"A corrective kiss?"

"Yes, one to correct the memory of the poor one I gave earlier."

"You are asking to repeat the kiss?"

"Yes." John smiled a smile Kate bet few women could resist. "As a favor to me." He stepped forward. "Lady Kate, may I give you a *proper* kiss?"

Her heart pounded its acceptance of the proposal. Yet there was nothing proper in his request. This was the truth from which she was running. This was why she had demonized Wynbrook in her mind. She was madly, wildly infatuated with him. Now here he was, alone with her at night. This was her last chance to live out the dream.

"As you wish," she acquiesced, but she felt powerful in the acceptance.

He stepped slowly forward, placing his arms around her, taking his time with every movement. He drew her closer, but she did not care for the agonizing slowness of his actions and wrapped her arms around him.

He tilted his head down and brushed his lips against hers, sending shock waves down her spine. She could not wait for him and stood on tiptoes to press her lips to his. He drew her in closer, holding her tight down the length of him. He deepened the kiss, and she feared she would melt into the floor. She'd had no concept of the powerful emotions that could be aroused from the joining of their lips and the intimate dance that followed.

Finally, he broke the kiss, only because of the need for air. Kate gasped herself, tingling in places she hardly knew existed.

"Marry me," he whispered, touching his forehead to her own.

Nothing could have restored sense to her more than those words, which were like a slap across her face. She stepped back. "Fortunately, as I have said before, I am not one to trap a man into marriage, so such an offer is unnecessary."

He took a breath. He was still the same man but somehow a bit deflated. "Yes, quite true."

"I hope this time we may part friends," said Kate, unsure what had just happened but feeling bereft from the loss of something she could not quite name.

"Yes. Friends."

Kate sped from the room, wiping the tears from her eyes. She had been a fool to play with fire. She thought the worst thing in the world would be never experiencing what she wanted more than anything in the world.

She was wrong.

The worst thing was being offered everything she ever wanted and walking away with nothing.

Nineteen

IT WAS TIME TO MAKE HER ESCAPE. KATE WAS
determined to sneak out of the house early, but their
hired coach was late in arriving, leaving her to pace
in the entryway with her sea locker packed and ready
to go.

As for her purchased carriage, Robert had vetoed
the idea of driving it to Arlington Hall as likely to be
fatal to Pickles. In the end, the "carriage" had been
sold for scrap and Kate had arranged with the stables
at King's Cross to gently care for Pickles—an arrangement that was costing her far more than simply renting
a decent coach would have been. This left her waiting
for the hired carriage, her anxiety growing with each
passing minute.

She had done it again—she had kissed John. *Lord
Wynbrook*, she mentally corrected. It was a wonderful,
proper kiss. But one that should be the end of their
association. She needed to make her escape. She could
not face him in the light of day.

The happy chatter of voices struck a discordant chord
in her ear. Footmen began to carry luggage down the

stairs and past her, out the door. Guests were beginning to make their way down the stairs as well. Not only had she been unsuccessful in avoiding company, but now she appeared to be caught up in a mass exodus.

"Hullo, Kate!" Tristan tripped down the stairs, impeccably dressed as always. "Leaving soon? So will we all it appears!"

"You are all leaving?"

"Those eminent members of Parliament in our midst have been called back. Governmental crisis!" he said with a gleam of excitement.

"Robert?" Kate called.

He emerged from a nearby sitting room, missive in hand. "King's mad. Going to make Prince George regent."

"And that requires your presence?"

"The House of Lords have been respectfully recalled." Lord Wynbrook, the man who had kissed her *properly*, strolled down the mahogany stairs, looking much more handsome than ought to be legal. The only crisis she could see was that her escape had been thwarted.

"I trust you and Dare will continue to stay with us at Wynbrook House, since now we are all headed to London." He gave her a knowing smile, which she might have been able to forgive had it not been accompanied by a scandalous wink. Wretched man! He knew she could not fly into a temper with the host of witnesses now making its way down the stairs.

"Brilliant." Kate was thoroughly displeased.

After an agonizing time waiting in the foyer with Lord Wynbrook, the coachman finally arrived to announce their carriage was ready. They spent much of the day rolling along in a line, heading back to

London. Her only solace was that she was alone with Robert in the hired coach.

Until the wheel fell off.

"This is officially the worst day of my life!" Kate hissed to Robert as the Wynbrook coach slowed to a stop behind their broken carriage.

John and Tristan jumped out, while Ellen waved to them from the window.

"Horrible luck, old man," said Tristan in good humor. "Fortunately, we are here to render aid."

"Yes, do come with us. Plenty of room," said Wynbrook with a smile that could not be contained.

Before Kate could think of a valid reason why it would not work, Robert had assented to the plan, and their luggage was duly transported to the Wynbrook coach. She decided if she must ride with Wynbrook in the coach, at least she would make sure she was not seated across from him, forced to look at his smug face for the next six hours.

As it turned out, she was seated next to him, which was infinitely worse. Robert and Tristan rode backward, with herself and Ellen riding forward, and of course John, happy as a lark, in between them. She could not even tell him to move over so that his side was not touching hers without inviting unwanted attention to her discomfort.

"Do you have an idea for a replacement?" asked Tristan, prattling on about the need to replace the elderly rector for Arlington Hall, utterly oblivious to her distress. Perhaps she always looked miserable such that he could not tell the difference between general and specific discomfiture.

"No, I do not have a candidate for the living, though I am certain it should not be difficult to fill. Always something to manage when one owns an estate, eh, Dare?" Wynbrook addressed him in a friendly manner.

Robert nodded. "Need to find new tenants for Greystone."

"You rent out your country estate?" queried Wynbrook.

Robert nodded again. They had not set foot in their countryseat since their father had died there. At first, they needed the rent, but now neither wanted to return. Too many bad remembrances.

They rolled up on a public inn for refreshment and a change of horses. They were not alone in the idea, and several other familiar carriages of the wedding guests could be seen outside. Kate alighted from the coach and immediately sought the privy, needing to get away from her present company. Afterward, she wandered about the yard, not wanting to return to the inn. She could not think of anything more uncomfortable than to make mindless small talk over a cold lunch with Wynbrook and his family.

She was lured into a pretty spot of wilderness beside the inn and wandered into the trees, breathing deep of the fresh pine scent. Her feet were cold in the snow, but she had no desire to return.

Wynbrook. How was she ever going to get him off her mind? He had kissed her. Offered for her hand. Of course it was only because he felt some obligation and knew she would say no. But what if she had said yes?

She sat on a boulder and closed her eyes, indulging

her imagination. What would it be like to be the Countess of Wynbrook? She would be at his side. Sleep in his bed. Manage his estate. Sleep in his bed. Be expected to live in society. Sleep in his bed. Face hateful gossips who would observe she made a wretched countess. And yet…she would sleep in his bed.

Her attention was drawn by a sudden silence in the woods. No birds chirped. Even the rustling of leaves in the gentle breeze stilled. It was as if the whole of the forest had collectively taken a breath, waiting for something to happen.

A crunch of footsteps in the snow behind her got her attention. Was Wynbrook or her brother coming out to find her? The footsteps moved slowly, as if trying not to be heard. Not her brother. Another crunch to her left. Two someones were sneaking up on her. Every nerve, every fiber was now alert, ready, but she kept her eyes closed, not wanting to give away her wariness, which was her only advantage.

She slowly leaned down and reached for her knife. The footsteps rushed toward her and she sprang up, swinging around, knife in hand. The surprised man attempted to stop, slid on the slick ground, and fell into the boulder.

"Get her!" yelled someone and two more men advanced upon her, all wearing mufflers around their faces to hide their identities.

She had no idea who they were or what they wanted, but she would not go down without a fight. The first man grabbed at her and she slashed his arm, causing the big man to howl in pain.

She spun and kicked the legs out from the other

man, who fell to the ground. She slashed at the first man who had regained his feet, backing him away. She needed to get back to the inn. The click of a pistol stayed her.

She turned to see a fourth man, similarly wrapped in a muffler, pointing a pistol at her head.

"Drop it," he commanded with authority.

She was not going to win this one. She dropped the knife.

"You're coming with us," said the man.

Kate screamed before they could get on the gag. She struggled, but they had surrounded her, tying her hands before her and holding her fast on each side.

"Get her into the coach, quick now!" They half carried, half dragged her a short distance to the road and bundled her into a coach.

"Kate!" Robert yelled at her from a distance.

Kate lay crumpled in a heap on the floor of the carriage. She kept her eyes mostly closed, feigning unconsciousness. Her brother had seen her. He would come. There was nothing she could do now to fight off four armed men, so it was best to lie still and wait for a better opportunity—specifically, when Robert made his move.

"Captain should be pleased," said one of the men. Though the curtains of the coach were drawn, their mufflers remained in place, masking their faces. Their voices were unfamiliar to Kate. She scanned a mental list of people who might hold grudges against her or Robert and found, quite to her displeasure, that being in the business of taking the worldly goods of other people meant one did amass a large number of enemies.

But who would have the audacity to attack

them here in England? Robert had a well-deserved reputation for ferocity on the high seas, but he had never attacked a British vessel, and these were clearly Englishmen. Could some French captain have hired these thugs? But for what purpose? If someone was seeking revenge, why keep her alive?

"How much do you think we'll get for her?" asked one of her assailants. She stared at his brass hobnail boots through half-closed eyes. One of the nails had come loose and was sticking up through the leather.

"Enough. Don't you worry none about that," answered a man with large forearms.

Ransom. They planned to hold her for ransom. At least they would not kill her. Probably. The thought did little to soothe her strained nerves, and she wished Robert would hurry up and rescue her. Whoever these men were, she did not wish to find out what they had planned. The carriage sped along the road, jostling her from side to side. She was going to be good and bruised before the day was out.

She heard the approaching galloping horse before they did. Of course, she was listening for it. It approached closer, riding hard. It was Robert; it must be. He needed these men to be distracted.

She rose suddenly and slammed her tied fists down on the crotch of the nearest man. He howled in pain. She swung her arms around, connecting with the man on the other side, hitting him in the eye.

The other two men jumped on her, holding her down. The particularly large one raised a massive fist to slam into her head. It would have knocked her into unconsciousness had his fist actually connected.

Fortunately, Robert crashed feetfirst through the window of the coach, knocking the man off of her. Several men reached for their pistols, but Robert leveled his and shot at one man, who cried out and dropped his weapon. Gunpowder and smoke filled the carriage.

Another shot rang out, but it missed Robert and he grabbed the discharged pistol with his left hand and tossed it out the broken window before punching the man in the nose with his right.

Kate yanked down her gag. "Robert, watch out—"

A third shot cracked sharply, hurting her ears in the confined space. Blood spattered on the coach wall, and Robert slid to the floor, clutching at his side.

"No!" screamed Kate.

"Lie still or I'll kill you!" threatened one of the abductors.

Robert met her eyes. Even injured, he had not given up. He looked up quickly at the carriage door latch and back at her. The carriage jostled and Robert used the motion to move his feet, so that they were flat almost against her. In a flash, she knew what he was thinking. She shook her head ever so slightly, but Robert narrowed his eyes and glared at her, resolute.

She had to do this. Yet if she did, her brother would be left behind. And if she didn't, they would both be abducted. She gritted her teeth. This was her only hope. She steeled herself for the impact and quickly reached up, pulling hard on the latch.

"Hey!" shouted one of their assailants, grabbing for her. The door clicked open and Robert kicked her hard, pushing her out of the carriage and onto the frozen road. She tucked her chin and rolled with the impact. She expected it would hurt, and it did, but this was not the time to nurse her wounds; she needed to get away and find help.

She staggered to her feet and yelled for help, spinning around to see if there was anyone who could render them assistance. Unfortunately, the road was now deserted.

The carriage continued to roll forward, then came to a stop with a jolt. Men were shouting inside the carriage and she had no doubt that Robert was making as much trouble for them as he could. Wounded as he was, she doubted that he could overcome four men. A man jumped from the carriage and staggered toward her.

She turned and ran with all her might, though it was difficult with her hands bound before her. Her heart beat wildly in her chest from the exertion and raw fear. She ran down the road and saw the posting house in the distance like a beacon of hope. Could she reach it before she was caught?

Behind her, the man was running awkwardly after her. Maybe she had a chance to reach the inn before him. The road curved, but going through the forest was a more direct path, so she took it, hoping to outrun him. She rushed into the trees and looked behind her. He was not to be seen. Perhaps he was going to head her off by running down the road. Or maybe he would suddenly appear from behind one of the many trees.

Wynbrook. She needed him.

She sprinted to the inn, jumping over downed tree limbs and sliding over the icy rocks. She fell twice but got up and kept running. Kate ran until she feared her lungs would burst and then she ran some more. Finally, she emerged at the edge of the wood by the inn. She paused before entering the clearing next to the public house. Where was the man who had been chasing her?

She panted for breath, her lungs screaming in pain. She had never run so hard. Where was her knife? She had dropped it somewhere close. She scanned the snowy ground, her breath steaming from her lips. The knife glinted in the snow and she pounced on it.

Footsteps came up behind her and she jumped up, lunging at her attacker.

The man in the large greatcoat turned toward her and she skittered to a halt.

"Wynbrook!"

Twenty

"KATE?" A STARTLED WYNBROOK DROPPED THE BOOK from his hand.

Kate aborted her attack, lost her footing, and fell right into his arms.

"What has happened?" asked Wynbrook.

"Robert has been taken. Quick! There is no time to lose," she panted.

"Good heavens, Kate. Are you all right? My word, are you bound?"

Kate realized that though she held her knife with both hands, her wrists were still bound. "They have Robert in a coach. They grabbed me first to hold me for ransom. Robert caught up with them and managed to push me out of the carriage, but he was shot, and somewhere there is a man who is following me. We must catch them. We must catch them now!"

"Hold still, let me free you." John grabbed the knife from her hands and cut through the bonds on her wrists. She rubbed her wrists, which were raw from the effort of trying to loose them herself. He picked up the book and dropped it and the knife into one of his greatcoat pockets.

"The man, we must get him." She turned and would have run from the clearing except for a strong hand on her shoulder that held her fast.

"My goodness, Kate, you are bloodied and bruised. Let me help you."

Kate's legs buckled under the slight pressure and she collapsed into his arms. "But, Robert... The man..."

"I will see to it." He carried her to the clearing, and for just a moment, she rested her head against his shoulder. Despite all that was happening, he had a certain confident calm about him that made her feel things would somehow be set to rights. She took a deep breath to revive herself and motioned for Wynbrook to put her down. This was no time to lose her nerve. Taking a careful look around, she could see nothing but the Wynbrook coach being readied to go.

"Come, we must go after them." Kate ran for the coach with Wynbrook at her side. "I left them stopped down the road. If we hurry, we might overtake them."

"Where is the coachman?" Wynbrook asked the stable lad who was holding the heads of the horses, their breath visible in the crisp cold.

"Gone in for a pint," replied the lad.

"No time!" Kate urged.

"I'll take this for a spell," Wynbrook said to the baffled stable hand as he took the reins.

The stable lad shrugged. "Your coach, m'lord."

"You stay here," Wynbrook directed Kate, climbing up to the coachman's seat.

"You don't even know which coach you are looking for without me," said Kate, climbing up after him.

Wynbrook sighed through gritted teeth and slapped the reins to get the horses moving. They rolled out of the yard and onto the road.

"John?" cried Tristan, emerging from the inn. "John! Kate! Where are you going?"

"Trouble with Robert. Must run!" cried John and urged the horses to gallop down the road.

"Trouble? What trouble?" called Tristan, but there was no time to stop and explain.

"I don't know how long they stopped. Might still be waiting," said Kate, rubbing her elbow where it ached from her fall. Now that she was sitting, she took a mental check of her person.

"You are hurt. You should not be out here," said John, squinting into the stinging cold as they galloped down the road. "Do we need to stop to attend you?"

Kate was hurting in several places but not bleeding profusely and she doubted anything was broken. "No, I am all right. It is not much longer. If we are quick, we might overtake them. I just wish I knew where the man who was chasing me is now. Wait, stop!"

On the side of the road lay the crumpled form of a man in a black wool coat. Wynbrook pulled up short and Kate jumped down from the coach. She crept up slowly, cautious of an ambush.

"Is that the man who was following you?" asked Wynbrook beside her.

"Not sure."

Wynbrook rolled the man over. The man's

glassy eyes stared unseeing toward the sky. "Dead." Wynbrook looked back at her.

"It must have been the man Robert shot."

Kate wondered if Wynbrook, who was accustomed to the finer things in life, would be able to manage such a shocking turn. He had the presence of mind to unwrap the man's muffler, revealing his face.

"Do you know this man? Do you know any reason why he would have attacked you or Dare?"

Kate shook her head. "We must follow the coach." She turned and ran back to their coach, the horses pawing at the frozen ground.

"We cannot leave a dead man on the side of the road," said Wynbrook.

"We must go after Robert or his will be the next body we find. He was shot!"

Wynbrook covered the man as best he could with the muffler and joined Kate on the driver's box of the coach. Wynbrook took control of the horses and sped along the frozen ground as fast as possible.

Kate wondered what they were going to do if they caught up with the coach. Even with one man dead, there were still three left in the coach, plus the driver. As if reading her mind, Wynbrook reached behind him and lifted up a brass-barreled coaching blunderbuss. "Do you know how to use this?" he asked.

"Yes." She took the gun.

"Careful." He released the catch and a sharp blade sprang from the tip of the barrel. "It's spring-loaded." He grabbed one for himself as well. Clearly the Wynbrook coach was prepared for highwaymen.

"Nice." Kate was impressed. Far from being

unhinged by events, Wynbrook was as collected as ever, taking on this new challenge as calmly as he entered a society ballroom. She couldn't help but be a little more attracted to him. A handsome man was nice. A handsome man holding a brass-barreled pistol with a spring-loaded bayonet was even better.

"Here we are. This is where I left Robert in the coach," said Kate, getting back to the task at hand.

The coach was gone, leaving deep ruts in the snow. She quickly looked on both sides of the road to see if he had been dumped there. It was clear, no bodies in sight. She took a breath, wondering how long she had held it.

"They must have driven on," said Kate, fear gnawing at her heart.

"Then so shall we," said Wynbrook. He put a gloved hand on her arm. "Do not worry. We'll find him."

Kate nodded and Wynbrook snapped the whip to get the horses moving at a fast clip. Wynbrook was a competent horseman, she was pleased to discover, and she soon put complete faith in his driving ability. He would catch up with them. He must.

"Do you know who these men are or where they were going?" asked Wynbrook.

"No. But they said something about a captain."

"Sea captain or army captain?" asked Wynbrook.

Kate shook her head, miserable for not knowing their enemy. "I do not know."

"We shall find him," Wynbrook said, trying to encourage her.

Clouds rolled in and the afternoon darkened as it grew closer to night. Still they did not overtake the coach. They came to a turnpike as it began to snow.

"We are looking for a dark blue coach with a broken right-side window," said Kate. "Maybe the man here has seen them."

Wynbrook asked the toll collector whether he had seen the coach they sought, providing a few extra shillings for the information. They were rewarded with confirmation that such a coach had recently passed.

Kate's heart soared. They were on the right track. "Was there anything unusual about the occupants?" she asked. "Was anyone sick or hurt?"

The man stared at her and she realized it was an odd question. "No, milady. Nothing odd. Just the coachman and the three men inside."

"Three men?" Kate choked. "Just three? Are you sure?"

"Three was all I could see," said the man, removing his hat and scratching a bald head that somehow matched his short stature.

"Thank you," said Wynbrook, driving on in the direction the man had indicated. They said nothing for a few minutes. What had they done to Robert after she had escaped? Was he even still alive?

"Dare is a formidable opponent. I would not want to be the man who attempted to subdue him," said Wynbrook in a confident tone.

"He fought them after he pushed me out of the carriage. What if they…"

"He's strong and tough—stronger and tougher than any English gentleman has a right to be. I cannot begin to imagine all the many battles he has faced. He has survived till now and I believe he will survive this as well."

"But the man said he saw only three in the coach."

"From his vantage on the ground, he would be looking up at the persons in the coach. If your brother was tied and lying on the floor, he would not have been seen."

"Yes, yes, you are right," said Kate with renewed determination. He was alive; she just knew it. If he were dead, she would feel it somehow.

Wynbrook navigated as swiftly as possible to the next turnpike. Yet at this next turnpike, they had no luck. No coach of their description had passed. Wynbrook turned the horses and coach around in fine form and had them flying back down the road in no time. They must have taken the wrong fork in the road. They corrected themselves and flew to the next turnpike.

At the next turnpike, they were rewarded with the information that they were on the right road. The coach with the broken window had passed not an hour before. At the next crossroads, they again had disappointing news. No coach.

By now darkness had fallen and they had to light the coach lanterns. Kate was frozen through and desperately wished to stop to warm herself but knew they must push on.

"Tristan must be utterly confused," said John. "I have done him a bad turn leaving him and Ellen at that humble inn."

"At least they can stay there tonight out of the wind and snow," called Kate over the biting wind that blew snow sharply into her eyes. She pulled her collar up even farther, disappearing into her coat like a turtle.

"Oh no!" cried Wynbrook.

"What is it?" asked Kate, looking around, fear

pulsing through her veins. Did he spy Robert by the side of the road?

"Tristan's chest. We have it in the coach."

"He will have to spend the night without a change of clothes?" asked Kate.

"He might have to borrow sleeping garments from the landlord."

Kate covered her mouth, holding back untimely mirth. Tristan without his wardrobe was unthinkable. "Oh, he's going to kill you."

"I think you might be right."

They followed the tracks in the snow until they turned to ruts, making it impossible to tell who had passed by recently. The weather also deteriorated, and Wynbrook was forced to slow down to travel safely.

"They will be forced to go slowly as well," said Wynbrook. "Why don't you sit in the carriage and warm yourself? I will keep watch and let you know if I see anything."

"No. Good to keep more than one set of eyes on the road," she said through chattering teeth. What she didn't say was that she was keeping watch for anything by the side of the road that might be the form of her brother. If she sped past her brother in the night, she would never forgive herself.

It had stopped snowing, which was good, though the temperature seemed to drop even lower, which was not. They pushed through and made it to the next turnpike, asking the man if the carriage had passed. This man appeared to go about his work with his eyes closed. He did not know about any blue coach with a broken window, but Kate was of the opinion that he had not opened his eyes for any passing travelers. He did murmur sleepily that a coach had passed by relatively recently. He was less helpful in identifying which way the coach had gone.

The road out of the turnpike branched into several directions, a few leading in various ways down to the coast. Both roads showed signs of travel and it was impossible in the dark to tell which ruts had been made more recently than others.

"Lady's choice," said Wynbrook.

Kate sighed. If she chose wrong, it could mean the death of her brother, her only family. She did not frequently turn to prayer, but she did so then. If ever she needed divine intervention, it was at that moment. A sliver of the moon emerged from behind a cloud and shone over one of the paths. She pointed toward it and Wynbrook snapped the ribbons.

She only hoped they would be in time to save Robert.

❦

Silas Bones sat in the private room of the inn, sipping his sherry. He had everything prepared for his guest, the Lady Katherine. Food was laid on the table, a fire was in the hearth, and an unscrupulous landlord had been given a hefty bribe to see nothing.

Three of his men shuffled into the room, holding their caps in their hands and looking sheepish. Something was wrong.

"Did you not get her?" asked Silas.

"Aye, we did," said one.

"But we lost her," said another, staring at the floor.

"You lost her?" Silas rose to his feet.

"But we got Darington."

"You kidnapped Darington instead? What is wrong with you idiots?"

His men all began to talk at once, saying it wasn't their fault, blaming Kate and Darington for resisting her abduction, and informing him that one of their number had been shot dead.

"Silence! You are utter fools." Silas had heard enough.

"You want us to bring Darington here?" asked one man.

Bring Darington to his little scene of seduction? He had planned to enjoy the company of his captive while he waited for the ransom to be paid. "Are you daft? No. You take Darington to Portsmouth and tell my father what happened. Maybe somehow we can make this work."

"Aye-aye, Cap'n," said a lanky lad, sitting down at the table and gazing at his supper with a hungry eye.

"Good, then you can get on the road now." Silas held up his hand to silence complaint. These men needed to be taught to fight a little harder.

"But it's cold," complained the big man.

Silas made no return reply but glared at the men until they all shuffled out of the room. His father was not going to be happy with this turn of events.

He shuddered at the thought.

Twenty-one

THE PIT IN KATE'S STOMACH GREW AS THE LIGHT faded. It was late and she was beginning to despair. She had hoped against hope that somehow they would be able to find her brother before night fell. It was clear now that hope was in vain.

She pretended for a while that it was only twilight, but soon she had to admit they were in complete darkness. The brief reprieve they'd had from the weather lapsed, and the snow fell hard and wet. Kate would have preferred fluffy white flakes, but this was heavy and thick. She was cold, she was wet, and they could hardly see the road before them. They could run over the body of her brother without seeing it.

After their initial successes with the toll collectors at the turnpikes, they had not found any further word of the broken coach. Her brother's abductors could have continued down the main road or taken any number of side roads to one of the many towns or hamlets or country houses that dotted the landscape. In truth, her brother could be anywhere.

Wynbrook slowed the horses to a walk, further straining her already taut nerves.

"We cannot tarry. We must move faster." Though move faster to where, she could not say.

"The horses are blown."

She knew that. But still she needed to press on; they must find her brother. "We must get a change at the next posting house."

Wynbrook said nothing for a moment. He adjusted the ribbons in his gloved hands. "It is late. And we are alone together."

"What has that got to do with anything?" she snapped. She did not want to hear about propriety when her brother's life was at risk.

"You must be aware that if we arrive together at this hour at a posting house—"

"We will simply tell them that we are a married couple or make up whatever story you choose."

"Unfortunately, I have traveled these roads frequently and I am known in many of the posting houses."

"Then go to a posting house in which you are not known. Or go to one that you are. I care not. I cannot do nothing when my brother's very life hangs in the balance. If my reputation is ruined, it is no great loss. I was not particularly fond of society anyway."

Wynbrook was quiet for another moment, and Kate suspected he was once again going to say something she did not want to hear. "Even with fresh horses, we don't know where we are going."

"We will continue to move on and ask at the different tolls and posting houses until we find someone who has seen the carriage we seek."

"The men at the tolls generally work in shifts. By now, the night watch will have taken over. If the coach passed by before their watch started, asking them will do no good."

Kate shook her head even as she began to tremble with the cold. "We cannot stop searching for him. What would you do if one of your sisters had been abducted?"

"I would do the same as you. And I imagine that if you were with me, you would probably be the one giving me this same advice, as unwanted as I know it is."

He was right. She wished it was not true, but he was right. Roads crisscrossed across the landscape, and her brother's captors could have taken any turn along the way. Without good direction, they could lose the trail and travel miles from where they needed to be. It would be reasonable to stop until daylight and begin the search again. Reasonable, but the thought of stopping, of giving up, of abandoning Robert to his fate, sliced through her heart like a knife.

"We'll find him," said Wynbrook, doing an impressive job of sounding confident. "He is experienced in handling himself in difficult situations. I fear more for the lives of his abductors than for him. I have no doubt when we finally find him, he will be sitting in the office of the magistrate calmly describing how he disposed of each and every one of his abductors."

"I would like to think so," said Kate with much less confidence. Robert could be a formidable foe and would not hesitate to act if given the chance. But he was injured, and she did not know how grave his wound may be. "I will never give up on my brother." If she had to search down every road of Britain and ask at every estate and farmhouse and crofter's hut in all of the British Isles, she would never stop searching until she found him. Robert would do no less for her, and she could not consider life without him.

"Of course not. But there is very little we can do for him tonight."

The slushy snow began falling harder, and she had long ago lost the feeling in her fingers and toes. Wynbrook was right. They needed to find shelter.

"All right. Let us stop for the night," she said through chattering teeth.

"We are coming up on a town now. I generally stay at the inn on the town square, but I believe on the outskirts there is another posting house by the name of the Prancing Cow."

"Prancing Cow? What kind of name is that?"

"I have no idea. Perhaps the Prancing Pony was already taken. Or perhaps the host has a peculiar sense of humor. In any event, it is not a place I frequent, as the clientele are a bit rough, but we would be unknown."

"Would we be able to get a change of horses?"

"I should rather let the horses rest and take the same ones in the morning than try our luck with whatever nags they may have."

They pulled into the inn of the Prancing Cow, but no stable lad ran out to meet them. Though light shone through the cracks of the shuttered windows of the inn, it did not seem a place inviting to strangers. Wynbrook was right when he said this was not a place he was likely to frequent. Even Kate, who had much lower standards when it came to amenities, disliked the general disregard to duty.

"Forgive me, my dear. It seems I must go rouse our host." Wynbrook handed Kate the ribbons. "A thousand pardons to leave you here in this inclement weather, but if you could hold the horses for but a moment, I will try to find a stable hand."

Kate gave him a quick nod and tried to hide a shiver. The wet snow had soaked through her bonnet and dripped down the back of her neck. She was damp and quite cold. Where was Robert now? Was he badly injured? She was so deep in thought that she did not notice the man approach the coach until a hand grabbed her ankle.

She jumped back and instinctively kicked the man, landing the heel of her boot on his shoulder. The horses spooked at her sudden movement and pranced forward, causing her to have to pull up the reins and give a low command to be still once more. It was difficult to manage the ribbons with her frozen hands.

"I like me a girl with some fight. You're a comely wench, you are." The man staggered, and even a few feet away, she could smell the stench of liquor on his breath. He gave her a grin, revealing two missing front teeth. Kate reflected that this was likely due to his unfortunate habit of grabbing people by the ankle as they sat in carriages, leaving him vulnerable to being kicked in the head.

Kate refused to look at him and hoped he would go away.

"You staying here, luv? I have a nice room. Just me an' me girl. We could use more companies like you. You look like you got a lot of fight in ya. I like me a wench with some fight. Makes it more sporting like."

Nothing could make his speech more repulsive than the fact that he swung himself up onto the coach and sat down beside her, his thigh pressing against hers.

"Get down, you filthy bastard," she yelled. Suddenly, the man flew backward off the coach box, landing on his face in the mud.

"Are you all right? Did he harm you in any way?" Wynbrook's expression was one of alarm.

"No, just surprised me is all." Once again, she was impressed by the quick thinking of the Earl of Wynbrook.

A stable lad had been found, and he took the heads of the horses, allowing Kate to release the ribbons. Wynbrook jumped down from the carriage and took the opportunity to lift her from the box and set her on the ground. Even when her feet were securely on the ground, he left an arm around her, protecting her against any and all offenders.

Once inside, Kate wanted to breathe a sigh of relief, but the faces of her fellow travelers were no friendlier and only slightly less inebriated than the drunk outside. A man with a red face who must have been the innkeeper greeted them with a suspicious scowl. "We don't get no quality here. You want to go to the inn on the green in town, you do."

"Yes, I am sure you are correct," said Wynbrook, his pleasant tone returned. "But the weather was so inclement I promised to stop at the next posting house I saw. Too cold to go on, you understand, for the lady."

"Very well then," said the innkeeper with as little hospitality as possible.

A woman Kate guessed to be the landlord's wife

stepped up with an equally disagreeable frown, crossing her arms over her ample bosom. "We only got the
one room left. Who are you, anyways?"

"Mr. White, if you please. Glad to make your
acquaintance." It was perhaps the least sincere thing
Wynbrook had ever said, yet he delivered the line
with a pleasant countenance.

"And the lady here. She be your wife or your
sister?" asked the landlord's wife with suspicion.

Both Kate and Wynbrook spoke at the same
time. "Wife."

Twenty-two

IT WAS WITHOUT QUESTION THAT KATE AND Wynbrook preferred to avoid the common room. A short time later and a few more coins than Kate thought necessary, Kate found herself in a small, private parlor sitting across from Wynbrook at a lop-sided table with a greasy tablecloth. The roaring fire, provided for a few more coins, and the surprisingly appetizing fare were a welcome relief. The food was simple but flavorful, the bread was still warm from the oven, and the hearty stew amply filled her growling stomach. She would have enjoyed it more, however, if her mind had not constantly been focused on her concern for her brother.

"I'm sure he will be fine," said Wynbrook, under-standing her silent worry. He put the finishing touches on a letter to Tristan.

She nodded her head, for anything else was too awful to consider. Her brother was all she had left. She had faced the possibility of losing him before, but she had been unprepared for it today.

"I knew every time he sailed off, especially with his

work as a privateer, that there was a chance I might not ever see him again. But this is different. We were not supposed to be in mortal danger traveling through the English countryside. We were unprepared." It was the worst thing one could ever be.

"Do not blame yourself. You could not have predicted such an occurrence." Wynbrook sanded and sealed his letter. "Tristan is going to find a way to repay me for this, you can be sure of that."

"I am sorry I got you into this mess." She prided herself on being prepared, organized, and resourceful, but despite her best intentions, they now found themselves facing some unknown threat by some unknown adversary. Even worse, she had dragged her friends into her troubles.

"Not at all. Everyone needs a little adventure," said Wynbrook kindly.

This was one adventure she would have gladly missed. She stared into the fire as it started to wane. She was not afraid of action; she rather preferred to be able to do something. At least in war on the high seas, you had a known enemy. There was an honor to it, two ships blasting at one another. "I want to do something. I feel I have let Robert down by not coming to his aid. How can I be of help to him if I cannot even find him?"

Kate pressed her fingers to her temples. Her head was starting to throb.

"It has been a very long and difficult day," said Wynbrook. "Let us get some sleep."

"How can I sleep when Robert is out there somewhere, possibly bleeding to death? I must do something."

Wynbrook reached across the table and took both her hands in his. "Earlier today, you prayed for guidance. Perhaps we can pray now for protection for Dare and his swift return to us."

Kate shook her head. Given her unfortunate history, she was of the opinion that the Lord was unconcerned for her welfare. "I am not much for prayers. I do not believe I am or have ever been in His good graces."

"Perhaps God allows trials so that we will turn to him."

"That's just cruel."

Wynbrook squeezed her hands. "Before the accident that killed my parents, I thought I was invincible. I suppose I may have been a bit arrogant."

A bit? Kate said nothing but raised an eyebrow.

"After they died so suddenly, I was lost. I remembered the prayers of my mother and made them my own. It gave me a peace I could never have found relying on myself." Wynbrook took a deep breath and blew it out slowly, looking up in thought. "I still miss my parents, but I hope I am a better man for having experienced what I did."

Kate stared at Wynbrook. This was not the polished facade he showed the world; this was real, raw, and intimate. "You are a better man."

Wynbrook met her eyes, and their gazes locked together. She leaned toward him, unable to stop herself. She wanted… No! She pulled back and turned away. "I mean, you were a pretty arrogant arse to start with."

Wynbrook laughed. "I will not deny it."

"Would you pray we find Robert?" said Kate, quickly changing the subject. She could not reject any opportunity to find help. Perhaps Wynbrook's prayers would be better received than her own.

"Of course." He lifted up a prayer for Robert, and Kate prayed along with him. It seemed asking for a miracle was their best chance.

"Thank you," she said when he was finished.

"He will be all right. This is Dare, you know."

Kate nodded, the aches and pains of a difficult day catching up with her. There was nothing she could do now, and allowing herself to become exhausted would do her brother no good.

"We should rest a few hours before beginning the search again," she said, resigned to giving up for the evening.

Wynbrook nodded. "Go up to the room and I will find the landlord to post this letter. You may be concerned for your brother, but I am more worried over the wrath of Tristan!" He smiled at her and Kate could not help but return it. Somehow, Wynbrook gave her courage that all would be well. She needed to cling to this hope.

He held open the small parlor door for her, and she went upstairs to the room they had taken for the night. The room was small, though clean. Their luggage had been brought up, leaving little space for the occupants. One glance revealed a problem. There was just one bed.

One bed.

❧

Wynbrook let out a long sigh once Kate had left the room. His day had certainly taken a turn into the unbelievable. He was the Earl of Wynbrook. Such things did not happen to him. Yet here he was in a questionable inn, with a young lady to whom he was not married, on a search for the villainous abductors of the Earl of Darington.

How had his day gone so wrong?

He reviewed his options. He felt the need to inform the local magistrate of such evil doings but he could not quite overcome the obstacle of informing the authorities without revealing Kate's involvement. He was not sure if he could be of any help to Lord Darington, but he could at least protect the man's sister. If Dare had been there at that moment, he was sure that Kate would have been foremost on his mind.

Wynbrook well understood the looks of derision thrown his way upon entering the humble inn. Quality did not frequent this establishment. If a man with no less than seven riding capes on his greatcoat came looking for lodging with a young female in tow, one could be sure they were up to no good. The only fortunate thing was that Kate seemed not to notice. She was so consumed with worry over the fate of her brother, she did not concern herself with her own reputation.

No, her place in society was going to be his concern. He leaned a shoulder on the edge of the doorway and pondered what needed to be done. No matter what angle he looked at it, there was no way to inform the magistrate without involving Kate and that must be avoided at all costs. Besides, what could the local magistrate serving the location of the original kidnapping do? The men who had captured Darington had presumably moved into someone else's jurisdiction, but whose? These local law enforcers had no assets to search the country looking for stolen aristocrats.

The only force with the ability to do that would be the Bow Street Runners and they were back in London. By the time Kate and Wynbrook made their way back to London to inform the Runners of the crime committed, the men who abducted Robert could be anywhere.

No, there was nothing to do but stay the course, search for Robert, and keep Kate out of anyone's notice as best he could. When this was over, he would have to attend to another serious issue.

He broke the seal on his letter to Tristan and reviewed the contents. It read like the lurid novels he secretly enjoyed. He had briefly explained what happened and gave instructions how to notify the authorities of the corpse left on the side of the road, had it not already been discovered.

Wynbrook took up the quill and paused. Was he really going to do this? Lady Katherine was simply the most amazing, most unusual lady he had ever met. They were totally unsuited for each other, and yet, the thought of her with anyone else made his blood boil. Somehow, when looking at them separately, they were wrong for each other, but together, they worked. He added one last instruction to the letter.

Go to Doctors' Commons. Buy a special license.

Wynbrook stared at the words, letting their meaning set in. He was asking his brother to obtain a marriage license. Surprisingly, he was not at all displeased with this turn of events. How he could bring the thing about was another matter.

He resealed the letter and called for the landlord to post it. Unfortunately, the landlady came instead, giving him a withering frown.

"Do not think I don't know what you're up to," she said accusingly. "This is a Christian inn!"

"My wife and I are happy to hear it," said Wynbrook mildly, wishing he was dealing with the husband and not the wife.

"Wife? Ha!" she snorted with derision.

"If you would see this letter posted, I would be most grateful."

The woman folded her arms over a generous bosom. "I'll be no party to such goings-on."

"I assure you there is nothing nefarious in this letter. Please allow me to pay to have it special delivered tonight." He handed the woman a generous sum.

Her eyes widened at the amount and he could see the internal struggle being worked out in her mind. "Fine then." She snatched the money and the letter from his hand. "But you won't so easily bribe your way past Saint Peter at the heavenly gates!"

Wynbrook gave her a winning smile. He did hope Saint Peter would take his side in the affair. His duty discharged, he walked up the narrow stairs to the bedrooms. Whatever happened next, perhaps it would be best if Saint Peter turned a blind eye.

Twenty-three

KATE WAS NOT SURE HOW LONG SHE STOOD THERE, staring at the single bed, trying to figure out what to do. She was still standing there when Wynbrook joined her a few minutes later. Kate's eyes trailed from the large figure of the Earl of Wynbrook to the small bed provided. Neither of them spoke. Kate might not be well versed in all the intricacies of societal rules and all appropriate manners and graces, but even a simpleton would know that she should not be alone with Wynbrook in a roadside inn—sharing a bed! Her heart began to pound.

"If you feel you will be comfortable here, I will bed down in the stable," said Wynbrook nobly. "Be sure to lock the door behind me when I leave." He turned to the door but Kate stopped him.

"Will it not seem odd to our host if you sleep in the stable?" It was a reasonable question, but Kate had a nagging suspicion that she was raising objections to his departure for not quite the right reasons.

"I doubt anything we do would redeem our reputation in the eyes of our host," Wynbrook commented with a weary sigh.

Kate was alone with the one man whose kiss, *proper* kiss, she could never get out of her mind. This was quite possibly the worst thing that ever had happened to her. Or the best. She couldn't decide which.

Wynbrook put his hand on the latch and paused. "Damn thing doesn't even have a lock." He turned once more and looked around the room as if he could magically find a separate bedchamber by the power of his sheer will. There was no hope for it and the room remained as small as ever.

"There's only one bed," said Kate, feeling the ridiculous need to point out the obvious.

"Yes, indeed," snapped Wynbrook, still looking about for that magical separate bedchamber to appear. "I have no issue in going out to sleep in whatever stable accommodations they might have. Whatever the hosts may think, they will keep their mouths shut for the right amount of blunt, but I do not wish to leave you alone and unprotected in such an establishment. The door has no lock, and it seems not quite the gentlemanly thing to do to leave you."

It was also not quite a gentlemanly thing to do to sleep together in the same room, but Kate did not say it out loud. "I am certain I will be fine. Do not trouble yourself on my account." Too late on that score. She was fair enough to admit that Wynbrook had done nothing all day but trouble himself on her account. The only reason he was in this fix was because of her.

Why had she turned to him for help in the first place? She could have looked for a magistrate or applied for assistance elsewhere. Of course there was none as close at hand as Wynbrook, but she had not even considered anyone else. Despite his polished airs, she knew she could rely on him to provide instant assistance, which he had. But now…now they were in a bit of a jam.

Wynbrook shook his head. "I cannot leave you here by yourself. Particularly not after your drunk admirer made such advances. I would not be able to sleep for worry."

"You should get some rest. I shall stay up and watch the door."

"You must have a very low opinion of me if you think that I would agree to that suggestion. You are the one who holds a greater need for sleep. You rest, and I will watch the door." Wynbrook opened his portmanteau and took out the coach guns.

"You packed them?"

"But of course."

Her admiration for him rose higher. "The plain truth is, we both need sleep if we are going to be able to have the fortitude to continue the search for my brother tomorrow." She took a wooden chair and wedged the back of it under the latch, preventing anyone from opening the door. "Let us both get sleep."

Though she spoke in a calm and rational manner, or at least that was her intent, her heart skipped along at a rapid pace. Had she just suggested that she sleep in the same bed as the Earl of Wynbrook? She must be mad.

Wynbrook gazed at her for a moment, saying nothing, though his eyes were smoldering. Of course, Kate had just showed him how to secure the door without a lock. If he was serious about bedding down in some cold, wet stable, he could certainly take the opportunity to do so. Would he leave her now? Wynbrook seemed to be considering the matter. He turned his attention to the door, then the narrow bed, and back to her.

"As always, you have made a logical and sensible suggestion." Though his words were distant, his tone was warm and inviting. She had never before been called logical and sensible in such an alluring manner.

"We should remain dressed, to maintain propriety." Somehow she managed to say the words without laughing outright. It did not matter if she wore ten gowns; propriety had been lost a long time ago. Besides, any number of skirts could be lifted. Her cheeks warmed at the traitorous thought. What was wrong with her?

It was all due to the night before. The night of their *proper* kiss. Had it only been a day ago? She had intended—they both had intended—it to be a farewell between two people who were supposed never to see each other again. Now here she was, not twenty-four hours later, shut up with him in a tiny bedroom.

"We should, though, remove our damp clothing. To avoid illness." Again it was not the words he spoke but how he said them, his smoky green eyes warm and inviting. She did not need to change her clothes to get warm; she was hot already.

"Yes, that would be sensible." She removed her wet wool coat and hung it on a peg. He did the same with his greatcoat and hung it next to hers. Something about their coats hanging next to each other seemed so domestic, so right.

"Please do change your clothing and I shall avert my eyes," she said briskly, determined to focus on the business at hand. She sat on the bed and covered her face with her hands.

"As you wish."

Kate's heart rate sped to an alarming rate as she listened to his movements. She strained to hear every little sound. Two thuds on the floor must have been his Hessian boots. Some rustling must have been his double-breasted riding coat followed by his waistcoat. A long slick sound must have been him removing his cravat. She recalled the sound from the night before.

She was glad her face was covered by her hands for she feared the heat in her cheeks would be noticeable. She was surprised at her own reaction. When did she become such a wanton? Was that rustling his shirt or his buckskin breeches? Those buckskins he wore were practically painted on. It was positively, deliciously indecent. What was he doing now?

She didn't mean to. It just sort of happened that she accidently, ever so slightly, opened her eyes just a smidge and—oh my! The glorious form of his naked backside filled her view. She was not entirely unfamiliar with the male form. She had sailed the seas with her brother from time to time and thought she had seen just about everything on the male specimen there was to see. She was wrong.

Wynbrook was, quite frankly, the most perfect, most handsome man who had ever lived. And he looked even better from the back.

"No peeking," he said playfully.

She squeezed her eyes tight. Did he know? How could he know? There was no way he could know. Could he?

"As if I would wish to see your bare arse," she retorted.

"How did you know I was bare arsed?" he asked with a slow drawl.

"Hurry up and clothe yourself," said Kate, much flustered. "I am cold and damp, waiting for you." She was burning so hot she was surprised there wasn't steam rising from her wool traveling gown.

"How much clothing is required to meet your approval?" asked John.

She opened her eyes. He stood before her in nothing but a pair of fresh buckskins so skintight they left very little to the imagination. He was utterly, completely, ravishingly naked from the waist up, revealing a perfectly chiseled muscular chest.

She sucked in air, trying to breathe before the image of the perfect man.

"Hullo, I do believe you're peeking."

"It is your fault if I am!" she cried, standing up to defend herself.

"If?" He grinned at her.

"Entirely your fault!"

"Really? Enlighten me as to my crimes."

"You entrapped me to come into the study, luring me with the prospect of correcting math errors."

"Guilty as charged, I fear." He appeared smug, not contrite.

"Then you...you...kissed me! *Properly!*"

"Inexcusable." The smug, overconfident grin faded a bit, and he added with a touch of anxiety, "You did not give an opinion of which kiss was the better. Was last night much improved?"

"Would I be peeking at your bare arse if it wasn't?"

John burst out laughing. Kate stared at him, too shocked by what she had just said to make further comment.

"Oh, Kate," he finally said when he could speak. "I do adore you."

"Would you adore me enough to put on a shirt?" she grumbled. There was only so much of the perfect male form she could take, even if he was laughing at her.

He grabbed a nightshirt and pulled it over his head. "Acceptable?"

"Barely," she grumbled. "Now close your eyes so I might divest myself of this wet gown."

"I shall do you one better and turn around so that even if my eyes accidently open, I shall not violate your person, like other people I shall have charity not to mention have done." He gave her a smirk and turned toward the corner of the wall.

She sat back down on the edge of the bed and fumbled with the laces of her boots. Curious, she had never noticed an ineptitude in the ability to remove her own shoes before that moment. Finally able to remove her recalcitrant footwear, she unstrapped the sheath for her knife. Not much good it had done her. She tossed it on the bed.

She paused at her stockings but decided to remove them. They were wet and she would do better tomorrow without sleeping with wet feet. She hung the wet stockings over the angled seat, so that they could dry by morning. She turned back toward the bed and found that Wynbrook was still standing obediently in the corner.

"I feel like I am being punished for being a naughty boy," he said.

"You have been a naughty boy."

"I know."

It was time to remove her gown. Unfortunately, with her new formfitting gowns, she needed help to get in or out of them. She tried to maneuver her arms behind her back in order to undo the buttons. She managed to undo a few at the top of the gown, but beyond that it was impossible. She tried to remove it without unbuttoning, and that too was impossible. She either had to cut herself free, as she had with the pink monstrosity, or she was trapped in the gown.

"Wynbrook?"

"Yes?" He turned around quickly, an expectant look falling a little to see she had only removed her footwear.

He appeared so eager she changed tack. "Where is my dagger? I need to put it back where it belongs." She pointed to the leather sheath on the bed.

He paused a moment before answering. "It's in my coat pocket."

She fished out the long blade and shoved it back in the sheath. He watched intently.

"Do you always carry the knife?"

"Yes."

"Why? If you do not mind my asking."

"To keep me safe from things like this happening. You see how well it worked." She sighed, the memories of her abduction flooding back. "This was all my fault. I should have been more careful."

"Nonsense! Had you any idea anyone would try to attack you?"

"No. Not here. But I should not have wandered off

into the woods. I simply wished for a little quiet and to avoid you." She gave a humorless laugh. "That plan didn't work so well either."

"Do not blame yourself."

"But I do. If I had better defended myself I would not have been dragged to the carriage and Robert would not be in danger."

"No one could have predicted that four armed men would have abducted you. Come now, you are human, not a soothsayer."

He sounded the voice of reason and it was a relief to hear someone speak against the self-recrimination she felt. "I suppose you are right."

"Of course I am right. I am glad to hear you finally admit it! Now get out of your damp things and let's get some sleep."

"I'm stuck."

"I beg your pardon?"

"I'm stuck in the gown."

He gave her a wide smile. "You need assistance? I am happy to oblige." He walked toward her, and she turned so he could give his attention to her back.

"But first I need to request something from you," he murmured seductively.

Wretched man. "Name your price." She should be angry—she certainly sounded angry—but her body hummed with intensity from his standing so close.

"Call me John."

"What?"

"If I am to undress you, call me John."

"John," she growled.

"We'll work on your tone at a later point."

"Just get me out of this dress before I catch my death of cold."

He worked quickly, and it was clear her gown was not the first lady's garment he had removed. The thought of him with another woman made her ill. She sighed. It had been a long day and she needed sleep.

Finally the buttons and ties had been undone enough for her to remove the damp gown and petticoats. John obligingly returned to the corner and Kate opened her trunk to grab a nightgown. She slipped on a nightgown, slippers, and a wrap. She crammed a wool cap on her head for good measure against the cold, though she doubted she could be anything but unbearably hot with Wynbrook in the room.

When she gave the word, he turned and gave her a smile. "I see we have chosen comfort over fashion. Very good."

"You are always quick with your little insults," she said, even though she had chosen the stocking cap with the idea of making herself look as unappealing as possible.

"No, no, I do apologize." He was immediately contrite. "I did not mean to insult. I am only slightly nervous and it may appear as disregard."

"You, nervous?" The thought was impossible.

"Yes, of course. I thought last night was the last time I would ever see you, so I indulged myself and allowed things to get a bit out of hand. Now that we are again together, I am not sure how to proceed."

Kate stared at him. He had quickly and honestly spoken of the things she was trying to ignore, even in her own mind. "I'm sure we both let things get out of hand last night."

"I do not regret it." He stepped closer to her. There was not much distance between them in the first place.

"Nor do I," said Kate in a voice even she could barely hear.

They stood there in their nightclothes, unsure of how to proceed.

"May I kiss you good night?" he asked.

"Properly?" she could not help but ask.

"If you like."

She did like. More than she should. One tiny step forward was all that was needed and she was warm and safe in his arms. She relaxed into the embrace and he kissed the top of her head. She soaked up his warmth, his strength, his assurance her brother would be all right. She needed this confidence to go on and not collapse from worry.

"He will be fine," said John, giving her a small squeeze. She wished she shared his confidence.

"What if he—"

He kissed her, soft and gentle, comforting and warm. She relaxed into him, the tension floating away.

"He'll be fine," he said when their lips finally parted. He drew her closer into his embrace, and for one glorious minute, she believed.

But minutes, even glorious ones, do come to an end, and she pulled away, realizing she should not indulge in temptation. "We should sleep. I want to be on the road before sunrise."

"Yes, we should catch a few hours of rest."

"I suggest that one of us sleeps under the bed linens

and the other on top. That way there could be no..."
She stopped mid-sentence, not wanting to commit to
words where her mind had just gone.

"Yes, we would not want there to be any..." His
voice was low and trailed off, which only increased her
thoughts on the forbidden subject.

He was raising her temperature again. After a few
awkward moments, she climbed into bed under the
top sheet, while he lay on top of the sheet, and the
blanket covered them both. The bed was an old one
and had a decided dip in the center. No matter how
much she tried to pull herself away, she slid back to
the hole in the middle, as did he.

"I cannot keep myself away from you," he chuckled.

"I seem to be suffering the same malady. The uni-
verse is against me."

"Hmm, I was thinking just the opposite."

She turned so her back was to him and he did the
same, their backs touching, separated only by a thin
linen sheet. Not much to keep them apart.

"John?" she asked.

He turned and put an arm around her, cuddling
around her and making her feel warm and protected.
She had never slept this close to another human being.
It was utterly foreign to her, and she liked it. She
closed her eyes and breathed deep.

"Thank you."

Twenty-four

KATE WOKE EARLY, ARMS AND LEGS ENTANGLED WITH the Earl of Wynbrook. She had apparently rolled over in the night and was now sprawled over him like a harlot. He breathed peacefully, still asleep. She needed to disentangle herself without him waking to find her all over him.

She tried to move slowly, lifting her head from his chest and her thigh from his—*oh my goodness!* She tried to ease away gently, but he moved slightly and brought his arm down over her, holding her fast.

"You are awake, aren't you?" she accused.

"Very, very much so." He opened one eye and grinned at her.

"You are incorrigible."

"I am not the one sprawled over you like—"

"Yes! Thank you. Enough of this nonsense. We need to be on the road." Kate flew from the bed, pushed the chair out of the way, and opened the door. "You there!" she addressed a scullery maid, who jumped at being so accosted. "We need another room where my husband can dress, a maid sent to my room to assist me, and a meal packed in a bucket for our trip. Have the stable master hitch up our coach and four. There's a half crown in it for you if all this can be accomplished in less than fifteen minutes."

"Yes, ma'am! Yer husband can use this room here, just finished cleaning it. I'll run to tell cook and the stable master and come back to be yer abigail!" The girl dropped her bucket and flew down the hall.

"You certainly found a way to motivate the staff," said Wynbrook.

"We leave in fifteen minutes!" demanded Kate.

"Yes, ma'am!"

They rolled out of the stable yard of the Prancing Cow in fourteen minutes flat. The sun was shining brightly over a pristine white blanket of snow, the glare bright in her eyes, but after the storm of the night before, she welcomed it. It was impossible to feel discouraged on such a crisp, glorious day. They were close to Robert. She could feel it.

They asked at every turnpike, posting house, and roadside inn they came to for signs of the coach with the broken window. Finally, they came across a matron and proprietor of a posting house who had seen the broken carriage.

"Yes, I seen such a coach. Bad people. What did you say you wanted with them?"

"The owners stole something of great value to us," Wynbrook said carefully.

"What makes you say they were bad people?" asked Kate.

"Traveling late, demanding whiskey, paid only half

their tab. One of them clean drunk on the floor of the coach."

Kate pressed her hands together. Could that have been Robert? "How many of them entered the house did you say?"

"Four gentlemen, and I use the term loosely, came in last evening and I still am owed for the bar tab."

Wynbrook produced a few shillings from his pocket. "Where did they go?"

The landlady pointed the direction, and they were following the trail again moments later.

"It must have been Robert on the floor of the coach," said Kate.

"Good news is we know where he was and can follow their movements."

"Why would they all leave him? They must not have feared he would get away. You don't think he is—"

"No!" said Wynbrook forcefully. "If he had died, they surely would have dumped the body."

It was grim comfort, but she clung to it, since it was all she had. Still, Wynbrook was right about one thing—at least they had found their trail and were following it again. "It seems they are making a direct line to the coast in the direction of Portsmouth. Since they mentioned a captain, I think that is our most likely destination."

"To Portsmouth it is." Wynbrook flicked the ribbons and set the horses flying.

They traveled for the better part of the day, stopping occasionally to ask if anyone had seen the coach with the broken window. No one had. Of course, Kate reminded herself, if the coach were traveling at night, no one would have seen it.

With time on her hands and nothing to do but watch the road and hope to find them, her mind went over and over the events of the past day. She was going to drive herself mad if she didn't think of something else.

"Do you enjoy reading?" she asked, remembering that when Wynbrook had found her in the woods, he had been carrying a book.

"Yes, quite. Admirable way to engage the mind."

"What were you reading yesterday?"

"Yesterday?" His voice hedged a bit.

"Yes. You had a book in your hand."

"Don't know. So much has happened since then. Seems an age ago."

"Yes, but you dropped the book in your pocket. It must still be there."

"Must have fallen out, I fear."

"You didn't even look," said Kate, sure she was onto some mystery and not about to let it go.

"Don't want to."

"What was the book?"

Wynbrook said nothing.

"I could search your person myself."

"Oh yes, please, let's do that. Much better idea."

"John! What book were you reading?"

"Would you believe a commentary on modern warfare?"

"Not now."

John sighed and pulled a book out of his great-coat pocket.

"*The Captain's Curse*? Isn't that one of those new horrid novels that ladies are warned against reading?"

"Oh, that explains it. I thought I was reading a history of war," said John, urging the horses faster as if it could somehow turn the course of the conversation.

"You were reading a tawdry novel!" declared Kate, enjoying herself.

Wynbrook refused to look at her, but his lips were tight and his hands were not quite as relaxed holding the ribbons. "It was my sisters'," he grumbled. "I was only reading it to…determine if it was suitable reading material for them."

"That is quite admirable of you," said Kate.

"Yes, it is."

"And what have you determined is the value of such a book? Will you be allowing them to read it?"

"Now that I have read a bit, I *know* it is not suitable for my sisters."

"Then why did you have it in hand when I saw you in the woods?" asked Kate sweetly.

Wynbrook turned to her with a glare. "If you must know the truth, I did start to read it because I was concerned it wasn't suitable reading material, which it most definitely is *not*. The trouble is the story is quite diverting and now I must finish the tale. If you hadn't so rudely interrupted me, I would have found out how Miss Prudence escapes from the castle tower with treacherous Captain Hemlock stomping his peg leg up the stone stairs after her."

"Oh! Now I know why you were in the woods. I thought you had come to look for me, but you were just stealing away to read your lurid novel without anyone seeing you!" Kate accused.

"It is not *lurid*."

Kate could not stifle a smile. "Captain Hemlock? Peg leg?"

"Fine, laugh if you wish. It is the most riveting tale. Of course this real adventure makes the book pale in comparison."

"Oh, I do not know about that. We haven't been attacked by a man with a peg leg."

"Yet," said Wynbrook ominously.

❧

They passed the greater part of the day companionably enough, though Kate was constantly on edge. She scanned the road, the carriages they passed, and the people they came across for anything that might give them a clue as to her brother's whereabouts.

Wynbrook slowed as they passed through a small hamlet near the coast.

"Look!" Kate cried, not quite believing it was true.

Wynbrook stopped the coach in front of a carriage house. Inside an open door was a blue coach with a broken window. "Is that it?" asked Wynbrook.

"Only one way to know for sure." Kate jumped down without waiting for any sort of assistance. She looked around, unsure if masked men would jump out from the bushes or from behind the hitching posts. Seeing none, she continued in a cautious manner toward the carriage house.

She glanced behind her to note Wynbrook glaring at her for going ahead without him. He called for assistance from the carriage house but could not leave the coach box without someone holding the horses.

She glanced around once more, but other than a

stable lad who was mucking out a stall, not paying any mind, no one was about. She walked up to the carriage on light feet and peered through the broken window into the carriage. No one was there. She wasn't sure what she had expected—perhaps to find her brother lying there, but of course, that was not to be.

"Is it the one?" asked Wynbrook, who had managed to get the attention of the stable lad to hold the horses so he could jump down from the coach.

"Yes." She looked closer in the coach and a chill shot through her. There was a large bloodstain on the floor of the coach. "John," she gasped. More she could not say because her heart was beating in her throat.

"I see it," he said grimly. "You there," he said, hailing the stable lad. "Where is the man who brought in this carriage?"

The young man shrugged. "Don't reckon I know. Stable master would know more."

"And where is he?"

The lad shrugged once again. "Pub, I reckon."

"Thank you," said Wynbrook. "We shall rest the horses here a bit. See them fed and watered, there's a good lad." Wynbrook tossed the boy a coin, and the lad became much friendlier, doffing his cap to them with a smile.

They made their way quickly to the closest pub and soon found the stable master, a ruddy man with good humor well on his way to having that humor enhanced by liberal amounts of ale. After a short interview, they left the pub without much more information than that three men had arrived, looking a bit worse for wear, according to the stable master. Any attempt to get descriptions of the men was greeted with failure.

Kate left the pub frustrated. "What now?" Before Wynbrook could answer, a young lady walked up to them. She was a beautiful girl, with blue eyes and golden hair that fell in ringlets, perfectly framing her sweet face. She had a full figure, bordering on plump, and despite wearing a modest, white muslin gown, her bosom defied its stays and quivered at the top of her bodice with every step. Kate had never considered describing anyone as looking angelic, but this girl did.

On instinct, Kate glanced behind her to see who the girl was walking toward, because clearly such a creature could have nothing to say to her. Surprisingly, the young lady walked directly up to Kate and leaned close to her as if they were intimates.

"Are you Lady Kate?" she asked.

Kate glanced over at Wynbrook, but he looked as astounded as she was. "I am. Who might you be?"

"I am Emma St. James," she said with a pretty smile. "Your brother has been anxious to find you."

Twenty-five

KATE FOLLOWED MISS ST. JAMES ACROSS THE NARROW street to the Green Man Inn. She wondered if it could be some sort of trap. Could the sweet creature be working with the men who abducted her and her brother? It did not seem possible, but she had learned not to trust in appearances. She glanced back at Wynbrook; his hand was in the large pocket of his carriage coat, no doubt holding the coach gun she knew was there. It was a reassuring thing to know the man was cognizant enough of their situation to be wary.

If Miss St. James was leading them into a trap, it was very nicely done. She beamed at everyone she met, bestowing her radiant smile on them as she entered the inn and led them up the stairs to the guest rooms. She was halfway up the stairs when she suddenly turned around, the smile gone from her eyes.

"Into the taproom," she whispered urgently.

Kate heard footsteps coming from above and was practically shoved by the determined Miss St. James back down the stairs and into the taproom. Kate guessed Robert's abductors must be coming down the stairs. She wanted to get a glimpse of these men, but of course, if she waited to see them, they could also see her. And they knew exactly who she was.

Wynbrook sent her a glance, silently asking her if this was the moment to make a stand, but she shook her head. There was too much she did not know and did not want to make a move if it might put her brother in danger. Besides, Miss St. James didn't look like much of a fighter. Kate waited in the taproom, just out of sight of the men. Wynbrook and Miss St. James stood next to her, quiet and still.

"Maybe he's dead," grunted one of the men as he walked past the taproom door.

"Maybe he is. Been shot, lost some blood. But we can't trust a man to die when he ought to," replied another.

"Better hope he's not dead," said a growly voice. "Bones wants him alive and he won't take kindly to this."

"We got to find him, that's what. Either alive or we bring in his corpse, but we can't go back without a body."

Their voices trailed away. Kate's little group remained in the empty taproom for a minute longer until they were sure the men had left the inn.

"Is my brother well?" asked Kate.

Miss St. James gave her a bracing smile and continued to lead them quickly up the stairs. She led them down the hall and opened a door, welcoming Kate inside.

"Robert!" Kate raced across the room to her brother, who was propped up in the bed. Though she was not particularly prone toward demonstrative shows of affection, she figured the past few days had allowed her some leniency and gave her brother a warm hug.

"Kate, good to see you. Ow! Easy there."

"Do be careful, Lady Kate," said Miss St. James, coming up behind them. "You might rip out the stitches."

"Stitches? Where were you shot? Are you all right? How did you get away?" Kate was nothing but questions, and demanding ones at that.

"Your brother was shot in the side and lost some blood. Fortunately, it missed any major organ or he would not still be with us," said Miss St. James matter-of-factly. "Please, sir, shut the door if you would and bolt it." She directed this comment toward Wynbrook, who was standing by the open doorway.

Wynbrook quickly complied and strolled forward to clasp Robert's hand. "Good to see you, old man. I say, but you've looked better. But still, to see you this side of heaven is a good thing. Shot, were you?"

"Not as bad as it sounds," said Robert.

Kate noted that he did not get up off of the bed, and he was, to her very great surprise, naked, at least from the waist up. He was pale, his face even thinner than normal, but he was alive, and for that she was incredibly grateful.

She glanced around the room, noting it was a larger and nicer one than she had experienced the night before. A young teenage girl stood, wide-eyed, in the corner.

"Let us all sit and make ourselves comfortable," said Miss St. James in a friendly voice. "Let me introduce my maid, Sally Winters. She has necessarily been privy to these events."

"Yes, and allow me to make known to you John Arlington, Earl of Wynbrook," said Kate.

"Pleasure to meet you, Miss St. James," said Wynbrook, and Kate felt a rush of hot jealousy flow through her. A pleasure, was it? Never mind that it was a common social response. She did not want him to say the word "pleasure" to anyone save herself.

"Likewise. I am certainly glad to have met you both. Now, Dare and I will tell you our side of the story, and then you must tell us how you came to be here too."

Dare? Kate did not miss that this young lady was calling her brother by his common nickname. They must have become good friends fast. If he were anything less than critically injured, she would have been suspicious.

"Please do tell us what has happened," Kate said, and found something to sit on as directed.

"After Kate escaped," began Robert, "I made myself difficult to give you time to run. Not quite myself, being shot, I got struck on the head. When I came to, I was rattling around on the floor of the carriage. Head bad. Side bad. May have passed out. Woke again when the carriage stopped at night. Two men got out, leaving only one in the coach. They seemed occupied moving something from the road, so I figured it was time to part company.

"I grabbed the knife from the knave's boot and gave him a bit for what I had got. Jumped from the coach and saw those bastards had pushed an overturned carriage from the road and were robbing its occupants." Robert paused for a moment to cough and catch his breath.

"Indeed, the whole scene was quite terrifying," said Miss St. James in a voice that indicated that terrifying was not an altogether bad thing, at least according to her mind. "I was on my way to Portsmouth when my coach must have taken a curve too fast and overturned. I can tell you it was quite surprising and rather unnerving to find oneself suddenly sitting on the side of a carriage instead of on the seat where one belongs. My maid and I managed to climb out and retrieve our trunks. The hired coachman could not right the carriage on his own, so he rode ahead with the horses to get help.

"Another carriage came upon us, and I thought at first that we were to be rescued, but the men jumped out and instead of helping, they pushed the carriage deeper into the gully and proceeded to rob us at gunpoint. That is when Lord Darington arrived."

Miss St. James's eyes shone with clear admiration, and she rose to her feet to give the story a dramatic rendition, acting out the scene with great enthusiasm. "He rushed forward like a hero of old and grabbed one of the robbers and held a knife to his throat, demanding the other men drop their pistols. But the other robber, without a blessed thought for the safety of his friend, shot at Darington and hit his own comrade. The robber Dare held dropped dead to the ground, but Dare caught the pistol as the man fell and fired, shooting at the other robber. The man turned to flee, staggered a few steps, and dropped to the ground. I thought he was dead, but later we realized he was not, so he must have fainted dead away.

"A third robber rushed at Dare with a knife, but

Dare dodged at the last second, tripping him and knocking him to the ground, where he moaned and lay still. It was the most amazing display I had ever seen."

Kate stared at Miss St. James, who was clearly delighting in such a dramatic if slightly romanticized tale.

Emma St. James cleared her throat and returned to her seat. "Poor Darington was in a dreadful state. Having used his last strength in the fight, he was barely able to stand. I knew I must get him out of there before those base robbers regained consciousness."

"Dreadful state?" asked Kate. "How badly were you wounded?" She glared at her brother accusingly.

Robert sighed and struggled to sit up. Miss St. James was immediately at his side, helping him up. Kate and Wynbrook exchanged a glance. If it were not for her brother's obvious ill health, she would have been quite suspicious. Of course, this was Robert, and she knew more than anyone how terrified he was of young ladies. Yet he did not appear unduly frightened with Miss St. James assisting him, touching his bare arms to help him up. No, he appeared quite comfortable with her presence, if one looked past the grimace of pain from his injury.

Robert pushed down the sheet and revealed a bandage on his right side, a few inches above his hip bone. He lifted it, revealing several stitches and a large, purple bruise.

"Robert," said Kate in a half whisper.

"He was lucky—a clean in and out. I just cleansed the wound and stitched him up!" Miss St. James spoke as if she had trussed up a goose, not provided medical care to an unknown man.

"You did? *You* stitched his wound, Miss St. James?" Kate stared at her in disbelief. The young lady before her looked like she was ready for her presentation at court, not conducting surgery.

"Oh, please, call me Emma. My father was a gentleman physician, and I fear I followed him everywhere he went. He trained me to be his assistant. But, of course, that was when it was just the two of us. My mother died when I was young, so I fear my father treated me like a son, for he did not know any better." The curvy bastion of femininity looked nothing like a son, and Kate doubted she ever had.

"If you were able to help my brother, then I am glad for it." Kate inspected the wound with a critical eye. She had seen her share of wounds and had even been called upon once to stitch up a gash on the arm of the boatswain when she sailed with her brother. She'd never forgotten the ordeal, and she bet the boatswain never had either, since she had cast up her accounts on him during the process. Twice.

Robert's wound appeared to be clean and the stitches tiny, straight, and true. Much better than anything she had ever done.

"You must forgive that Darington does not have a shirt at the moment. The wound bled a bit, and I fear I ripped the shirt to shreds, using it during my tending. It was important to clean the wound thoroughly, for I find it helps to prevent it from festering."

"Emma has been very helpful," said Robert with genuine admiration.

Emma? Well now, they were on intimate terms. She glanced again at Wynbrook, whose eyebrows rose considerably. Once again, she would have questioned romantic involvement, but her brother was clearly wounded and Emma's maid stood silently watching in the corner.

"But what of the men who abducted you?" asked Wynbrook.

"Unfortunate circumstance, they came to the same inn as we," said Robert.

"It was a dreadful walk to the inn, I must say," said Emma, who was clearly enjoying the memory. "We never knew when we would be set upon by robbers again, and Darington was so weak he could barely walk. I gave us up for dead several times, but somehow we made it through. We took a room at the first inn we found, which I'm sure is what those awful robbers did too.

"Dare warned me not to use our real names, and so we have registered here under the name of Mr. and Mrs. Anders. I said my husband was dreadful ill, and they have left us alone ever since. We were quite despairing when we discovered our enemies had moved in down the hall. But now you have come, so we can make our escape!" Emma smiled brightly.

"But how did you know it was me?" queried Kate, though she was beginning to believe Emma could do anything she wished with a flip of her golden ringlets.

"Dare saw you from the window and asked me to fetch you. He said it would be dreadfully dangerous, so of course I went to collect you straightaway."

"Of course you did," said Kate.

"But how have you come to be here?" asked Robert. "How did you find me?"

"Your sister has dragged me up one frozen, ice-caked road and down the other. I am certain that if we had not found you here, she would have knocked on every door and searched through the hedgerows until she did," drawled Wynbrook.

"After I was pushed from the coach, I ran back to the inn and found Wynbrook outside. We rushed after you in the coach, hoping to overtake you quickly, but it was not to be," said Kate, leaving out the part where they had slept in the same bed. "Fortunately, we got a few good leads and eventually they led us here."

"Well now, we have all had such adventures! Sally, could you go down and bring us all up a good cup of tea?" asked Emma.

Sally grumbled and left the room.

"Forgive my maid. She has a low opinion of adventures."

"I'm not sure I don't share her opinion," said Kate. "But I am so glad that my brother met you and that you had the wherewithal to know what to do in a crisis." Her praise was entirely sincere. She hated to think of what would have happened to her brother had Emma not been there.

"I do hope I was a help to your brother. Truly a doctor does not do much more than patch things up a bit. It's the patient who does all the healing. Dare has shown great forbearance and has been delightful company." Emma gave the room a brilliant smile.

So charming was she that Kate was almost inclined to believe her, but she knew that her brother could never be called delightful company. Most people considered him taciturn at best. Of course, Kate knew he was not foul-tempered but mainly shy. Considering everything, Kate was rather surprised Robert had been able to utter a word.

"Forgive me for breaking up this touching moment," said Wynbrook, "but I feel compelled to remind you that your adversaries remain at large. Shall we involve the local magistrate?"

"Yes, that is just what I thought to do as well," said Emma in her perpetually cheery voice. "Unfortunately, when I attempted to alert the local magistrate, I found the robbers had got there first and blamed the entire event on Darington, including the death of one of their number. The authorities are now on the hunt for him."

"We need to set the record straight," said Wynbrook.

"No," said Robert in a soft but firm voice. "I fear as soon as our presence is revealed, our friends shall make short work of us. We need to get Emma out of danger."

"We have been trying to think of a place to retreat where Dare can regain his strength. I fear he is not yet strong enough to fight them at this point, though I will say he is a fast healer," said Emma with a warm smile.

"Actually, we may not be far from Greystone," said Kate, surprised the suggestion would emerge from her lips. Greystone Hall. A place that haunted her memories. A place to which she never wished to return.

"Greystone?" asked Emma. "Is it a nearby village? Have you friends or relatives who can help?"

"Greystone Hall is our..." Robert paused as if not sure what word came next. "Home."

Twenty-six

KATE STARED OUT THE WINDOW OF THE INN AT THE growing gloom. The sun had set and the sky had lost its battle against the encroaching darkness, turning from brilliant orange to dusky blue then muted gray, and finally fading into black. Even as night fell, it was not without its little beacons of hope, the stars twinkling white. As the darkness grew, so did the number of the sparkling lights spread out haphazardly across the dark night sky. It was strange to think that those faraway stars were always there, but it took the coming of the night to see them.

Four sharp raps at the door broke her reverie. It was the appointed signal. Emma's maid roused herself to answer the door.

"It's done," said Wynbrook in apparent high spirits as he entered the room.

The maid looked suspiciously back and forth in the hallway before closing the door and locking it tight.

"Here are some clothes to make you decent." He tossed a bundle onto Robert's bed.

"It is fortunate you have arrived with my clothing."

"Fortunate for you but think of poor Tristan, whose portmanteau I still have in the coach."

"He will track you down."

"Yes, I'm sure of it!" said Wynbrook with a laugh.

"Are they hitching up the coach?" asked Kate.

"Yes. I'll bring it 'round as soon as the company is ready to depart and drive you to Greystone myself. Safer not to engage a coachman, who could tell the wrong people where we have gone. I also had the distinct impression we may need to deny ever being here." He gave Robert a knowing glance. Of course, it would never do to have the general public know Darington and Emma had spent the night together, even with his gunshot wound and her maid present.

"Thank you, Lord Wynbrook. You are very conscientious." Emma gazed up prettily at Wynbrook and batted ridiculously long eyelashes at him in a manner that made Kate's blood run cold.

"I even asked them to warm a brick for you so you might ride in comfort," said Wynbrook with a winning smile.

"We have no time for such frivolity. This is hardly the time to think about enjoying oneself," said Kate severely.

"Oh yes, one should never think of comforts when one is in mortal danger," agreed Wynbrook dryly. "For one runs the risk of enjoying the last few moments of one's life. I cannot think of anything more tragic than to arrive at the gates of heaven with a smile on my face."

Emma laughed out loud and dazzled the company with such a radiant smile that Kate bit her own tongue before she said something reminiscent of an outraged sailor, rather than a lady of society.

"If we are to leave this place, we should go now," said Robert in a humorless tone. Though she doubted anyone else in the room noticed, Kate knew Robert also was not pleased by any hint of flirtation between Emma and Wynbrook.

Kate had to admit, Wynbrook and Emma would be a good match for each other. Both were of pleasant dispositions, and had easy smiles and comfortable manners. Wynbrook was terribly handsome, and Emma was bright, merry, and undeniably lovely. They would make a nice couple and produce adorable little children.

Fortunately, she didn't care about such things. It made no difference to her what he did with his spare time. If he wanted to marry a girl who looked like an angel and had a bosom that quivered with every step, it was entirely his affair. She didn't care in the least.

"Lord Wynbrook, maybe we should go prepare the carriage and bring it around to the inn while Miss St. James and her maid ready Robert for travel," said Kate. She was just trying to be efficient and logical; the fact that she recommended Wynbrook to remain with her and away from Emma was completely coincidental.

Despite some anxious moments, particularly since they did not know where their attackers were, they all made it into the coach. Darington managed with some slight assistance to make it down the stairs on his own power but collapsed onto the velvet squabs as soon as he entered the coach.

Kate did not like to see her brother injured, though he seemed in competent hands. Emma did not reveal any anxiety regarding the eventual recovery of her patient, which helped Kate to be more at ease—at least when it came to her brother. Traveling to Greystone Hall was another matter entirely.

The mere thought of returning to Greystone filled her with foreboding. She had not returned since her father had died. The place represented all the misery of her childhood. She had never wanted to return.

After several hours of jarringly rugged terrain, they turned down a drive that, no matter how long she had been away, Kate would never forget. The carriage began to climb, winding its way up to the top of the bluffs where Greystone Hall held dominion, over-looking the ocean. They turned a tight corner, and the imposing house came into view, a yellow moon hanging low behind it.

Greystone Hall stretched five stories high and, true to its name, was made of gray stone. At night, however, it was a monstrous black tower. The tower dominated the scraggly bushes and windswept trees that dotted the landscape along the bluff overlooking the coastline.

"My, but that is a striking hall," said Emma, leaning next to her to see out the window. "This is your home?"

Home? It was a long time since she'd thought of Greystone Hall as home. "This is where we were born and we spent the first few years of our life here. We have not been back since our father died thirteen years ago."

"Thirteen years?" asked Emma. "But then, you haven't been back since you were children. Is this not your countryseat?"

"It has been more financially advantageous for us to rent the property." Kate did not mention that it had been the only way to try to overcome the immense debt they found themselves in once orphaned. "We've had a series of respectable families who have lived here, though it is vacant at the moment. We have kept the house fully staffed, as we expect our land agent to find a new tenant soon."

"How fortunate it is that your home is staffed, as if it was waiting for you to return." Emma smiled brightly at the prospect.

Fortunate? It would not have been the word Kate chose. She did not even bother trying to return Emma's smile.

They pulled into the dark drive, a knot tightening in Kate's stomach. She was not sure whether she was more concerned for her brother, who was clearly pained by the journey, or wounded by the memories that flooded back as they pulled slowly into the shadow of the great house cast by the bright moon.

"It is certainly quite a large house," commented Emma with clear determination to be cheery.

"Yes, it is a very large house." So large that Kate would never be free of the ghosts that haunted it.

The carriage rolled to a stop, and a moment later, Wynbrook opened the carriage door and helped the occupants out. "I trust I found the right place," said Wynbrook through chattering teeth.

"Oh, you must be chilled through," said Emma sympathetically. "What you need is a good bowl of wine punch."

"Make that rum punch and I think you've about got it."

Kate glared at Wynbrook and Emma. Yes, they

would be very happy together. She, on the other hand, would never be free of the legacy of Greystone. She steeled herself to face the beast of a house. This was not so much a house as a mortuary. This was where her mother had died. This was where her father had died. She had no interest in having it be the final resting place of herself or Robert.

There was no one to greet the carriage, of course. At this hour, no one in the house could be expected to be awake. Wynbrook assisted Robert out of the carriage, who, between the pain and medication Emma had given him, was unsteady on his feet.

"Let us rouse the staff," said Kate, wondering what sort of reception they would receive. To suddenly appear in the middle of the night without one word of advance warning was inconsiderate, even if one was going to one's own house, but it could not be helped.

"Yes," agreed Wynbrook. "I've hitched the horses to a post, but they should not be standing outside long."

Kate walked boldly up to the door and rapped loudly on the dark wood. They waited for a while but heard nothing. "I fear the servants' quarters are not close to the front door and they were expecting no one this evening," muttered Kate.

She banged on the door several times more before she finally heard footsteps. The door opened a crack. The butler, with his white wig askew and hastily donned robe, stood next to the housekeeper with her wide eyes and quilted robe.

"Who goes there?" demanded the butler.

"It is I, Lady Katherine, with my brother the Earl

of Darington, master of this house. Quick, man, let us in at once, for it is dreadful cold."

The man at the door stared in surprise, then stepped back, opening the door wide enough to allow entrance, closing the door quickly behind them to keep out the cold. "Lord Darington?"

"We had no word that the master was coming," said the housekeeper, much suspicious.

"Yes, Mrs. Brooke, you would not have, for we did not know we were driving here ourselves until earlier this day." Kate quickly recalled the names of her staff. "Thank you, Mr. Foster," she said, handing the butler her wool coat and bonnet.

Kate had considered the story she would tell on the drive here, and now came time for her performance.

"There's been a terrible accident," she began. "We were traveling to Portsmouth and our coach was overcome by robbers. Lord Darington defended us bravely and scared them off, but he was shot in the process."

"Oh my stars and garters." Mrs. Brooke gasped, staring at Darington who was being held up by Wynbrook. "I can see he is not well. I shall call for the doctor at once."

"I do not believe that is necessary. He has already been seen by a capable physician, but we were not in a place where we could stay comfortably and we judged that we must bring him back to Greystone as quickly as possible so he can recuperate."

"Oh, my dear. Such goings-on." Mrs. Brooke looked from Robert to Kate to the others, clearly unsure how to proceed.

Kate quickly took command. "Send a groom to

take care of the coach and horses, for they should not be standing out in the cold. Please prepare rooms for myself and my brother, and our friends, the Earl of Wynbrook, and Miss Emma St. James. Miss St. James is traveling with her maid, Sally Winters."

"At once, milady," said Mr. Foster with a bow.

"Thank you, Mr. Foster. And if a bowl of punch"—she glanced at Wynbrook—"rum punch could be brought to the drawing room where we shall rest until all is provided for, it would be much appreciated. It has been tremendously cold and we are all chilled to the bone. My brother in particular needs his spirits revived."

"Yes, milady. At once, milady." Mrs. Brooke had always seemed through her letters and various correspondence to be an efficient, clearheaded sort of woman. Kate was glad to find that this impression was not false, for after she had recovered from her initial suspicion and shock, Mrs. Brooke brought the household to action at once. Fires were laid in the grates, beds were turned down, maids and footmen appeared to take care of every need, and, most gratifying, warm punch and biscuits were provided as a welcome reprieve from the chill.

Despite all the excitement of the past few days and the discomfort she felt on entering the house, Kate had difficulty keeping her eyes open over her punch, and she noted the others were no better. They soon all retired to their respective bedrooms.

Once she had seen to Robert's care, ensuring that he was safe, Kate retired to her bed, which had been deliciously heated with a warming pan. Allowing herself to relax, she realized how tired and sore she was. The excitement of the past several days had afforded her very little rest. In spite of the nagging concerns she felt for all the turmoil in her life, she fell quickly into a deep and abiding sleep.

Twenty-seven

WYNBROOK AWOKE TO A BRIGHT JANUARY DAY WITH the knowledge that he needed to speak to Lord Darington. He had been much too long in the company of the man's sister to do otherwise. He generally found Darington to be a decent sort of man, but he also could be imposing, with a hint of danger to him. Wynbrook was well aware that even the most rational of men could become irate if his sister's reputation was at stake.

Wynbrook rapped gently on the door of Darington's bedroom, not wanting to wake the man, especially considering he was still recovering. A voice from the other side bade him enter at once. Wynbrook turned the knob and entered the room, finding Dare sitting up in bed, looking pale but better than he had the night before.

"Feeling better, I hope?" asked Wynbrook.

"Feel like I was shot," said Dare. "I expect you've come to talk about Kate."

The man certainly did not waste time with pleasantries. "Yes, I thought we should have a discussion."

"Help me up, will you? What I have to say can't be said rightly when I'm not even wearing my trousers."

"Is the invalid allowed to leave his bed?"

"If the invalid can do so without being caught in the act." Darington attempted to stand up and grimaced in pain.

Wynbrook was about to ask if it was a good idea but held his tongue. From the determined look on the man's face, he would not be dissuaded, and Wynbrook did not wish to irritate him.

Wynbrook called for a footman to play the office of valet and, once his friend was dressed, helped Dare downstairs. On the way, Dare asked the butler to call for the local magistrate, a different man in that part of the country from the man Miss St. James had tried to approach, so they could report the incident of the robbers.

"That should be an interesting conversation," Wynbrook commented.

Dare merely nodded as he made his way slowly into the main drawing room, where he practically collapsed onto the settee. The drawing room was sparely furnished, with nothing more than two chairs, a settee, and a few side tables. There were no decorations of any sort or personalized touches that made a house a home.

"Now tell me what you wish to say about my sister," said Dare grimly.

"You are aware she asked me to help find you and we have been on the road together for some two days in the process," said Wynbrook with some anxiety as to how this conversation would progress.

"Yes, and I also know how you met with her in the study the night before we left Arlington Hall." Dare met his gaze evenly, his tone and facial expression revealing nothing.

Wynbrook felt his blood run cold. How much did Dare know? "Kate told you?"

"No. But it is my responsibility to look out for her. I am wondering what you think your responsibility is to my sister."

"An offer of marriage will be forthcoming, if you approve."

"It is not my approval you need concern yourself with. Kate won't like it. There are things you ought to know about her, but they are not for me to tell."

Wynbrook waited for a moment, hoping Dare would continue, but the grim man said no more, leaving Wynbrook to wonder what secrets Kate hid.

"Things about her past?" asked Wynbrook, hoping he could prompt Dare to be a bit more forthcoming.

"Yes, things in her past that still affect her. Kate is unlike any other lady you will ever meet."

"I am well aware," said Wynbrook.

"I understand there may be some attraction between you. I also understand that you have performed admirably in protecting my sister and the lives of Miss St. James and myself. I want you to know that I do not hold you obliged to make an offer of marriage. If you wish to walk away, please do so with my thanks for services rendered to my family."

"Thank you, but I do not choose to walk away. In truth, my wish to marry your sister goes far beyond any sense of obligation."

"In that case, I need your word as a peer of the realm that if you make such an offer to Kate, you will not rescind the offer once you know her history more fully."

A sense of foreboding hung heavy in the stark drawing room. Wynbrook wondered what horrible secrets lay in Kate's past that would cause her brother to make such a statement. Wynbrook paused a moment to consider if there was anything about Kate that would change the way he felt about her.

"You have my word, my offer of marriage will stand firm. There is nothing about her past that would dissuade me."

"I hope you have the fortitude to match your words with action." Dare gave him a look so severe and so solemn, Wynbrook had to fight the urge to stand to his feet and snap the man a smart salute.

Wynbrook was saved from one difficult conversation by the arrival of the magistrate, which was fraught with its own difficulties. Darington began relating a version of the tale told by Lady Kate to the servants, while Wynbrook called on the butler to bring some tea and biscuits, noting in a friendly manner that it was cold outside and the magistrate must have come in a great hurry to arrive so soon.

The magistrate informed them he had been on his way to visit friends in Brighton and the messenger had caught up with him on the road. It seemed prudent to come at once, so as to know whether or not his planned visit needed to be postponed. Dare soon related the facts such as he felt fit to be shared, and Wynbrook regaled the man with cheerful banter.

If the man began to ask questions down a dangerous line of reasoning, Wynbrook made sure the man was offered more food and artfully changed the subject. He found the man was an avid fisherman, and they talked of hooks and baits and the best places to ply one's craft.

As the magistrate prepared to leave, he reassured Wynbrook and Darington that he would set his fellow magistrate straight regarding the true nature of the crimes and begin to look for the men responsible. The magistrate was in quite good humor and felt confident enough that the highwaymen would soon be apprehended.

"Well played," said Dare after the man left.

"And you as well," said Wynbrook. "Do you think the magistrate's men will be able to apprehend them?"

Dare slowly shook his head. "They seemed too crafty to stay in one place long. I guessed they had tried to hold Kate for ransom, but they never asked me for money or even took my watch."

"Did you ask them why they had abducted you?"

"No. I was either unconscious or pretending to be, waiting to escape. I hoped they would talk freely and I would learn more that way, but other than going to meet a captain, I learned nothing more."

A mystery to solve and a marriage to propose. Wynbrook had quite the full schedule ahead of him.

Twenty-eight

KATE WOKE WITH ONE THOUGHT.

He would leave.

Now that Robert had been found, there was no need for Wynbrook to stay and every reason for him to go. She should have been pleased at the outcome, and of course she was. Robert had been found alive and it appeared he would make a full recovery. Only a few days ago, she'd feared her brother was lying dead in a hedgerow, so this was the best possible outcome.

Looking out her window at the sparkling reflection of the sun on the ocean, she was strangely disappointed to see the adventure end and wondered at her own reaction. Was she so used to excitement and danger that living without left her strangely flat? It was odd that she had never felt this way when Robert had left her in Gibraltar. On the contrary, she had enjoyed the quiet time to herself, even when Robert had been gone for months.

Even in her isolation, she had never felt this sense of disappointment. Perhaps it was because her time with Wynbrook was finally coming to a close. The truth rattled, unwanted, around in her brain. She fought against it, but even she had to acknowledge that she had enjoyed his company and had come to trust him.

Kate sighed and rang for help getting dressed. She chose a simple but becoming white muslin and allowed the maid to dress her hair a bit more around her face than her usual severe bun. She could not possibly be dressing for Wynbrook. No, not possible.

Kate took a moment to wander through the house, taking stock of its condition. The rooms were barely furnished with the basic necessities. No knickknacks or personal touches decorated the rooms. Not even a throw rug on the floor cheered the spaces. Kate disliked clutter, but even she found the space sterile and uninviting. The house had a rather vacant and forlorn feel.

Kate entered the sitting room and found Wynbrook and her brother already there. Wynbrook and her brother had each taken one of the chairs, her brother ensconced with a stack of newspapers. With her entrance, they both rose briefly until she settled herself on the settee, but only Wynbrook spoke. "Good morn to you, Lady Kate. You look well this morning."

"Thank you," she replied, trying very hard not to be delighted in his compliment. She thought she was looking quite tolerable until Miss St. James waltzed into the room.

Emma entered the room looking as fresh as a daisy. Kate had heard the expression before, but until she met Miss St. James, she had not known what it meant. With blond ringlets framing her face, sparkling blue eyes, and a perfect peaches-and-cream complexion,

Emma did in truth remind Kate something of a daisy. She had a quaint little rosebud mouth with rose-colored lips to match. Her simple muslin frock was fresh and snowy white. She was several inches shorter than Kate and decidedly plumper, with a generous bosom and rounded hips. Overall, she looked like a girl who had stepped out of a portrait, more perfection than an actual real human being.

Her brother had barely glanced at her when Kate entered, but for Miss St. James, the paper was laid aside and he vaulted to his feet, though it clearly pained him to do so. Kate glanced at Wynbrook to see if he also had fallen under the spell of the deliciously ripe Emma St. James, but he was looking at Robert with amusement in his eye. Kate turned back to Miss St. James with more charity in her heart.

"Miss St. James, so good to see you this morning. I trust you had a pleasant night. Here, please sit." Robert motioned for her to take his own seat and then, without dropping his eyes from her face, sat in the seat across from her without realizing that he had just usurped Wynbrook's chair.

Wynbrook only smiled at this and joined Kate on the settee. Kate scooted herself all the way over to the side in order to prevent any of *her* touching any of *him*, yet still his thigh brushed up against the fabric of her gown. Of course it was not inappropriate but she could not help but glance more than once at that strip of fabric that rested along his thigh.

"What brings you on your journey, Miss St. James?" Kate asked Emma to distract herself from sitting so close to Wynbrook.

"Oh, I have embarked on a remarkable journey," said Emma with a wide-eyed smile. "My stepmother has arranged for me to marry a man in America. I know it seems a bit unusual to wed someone you've never met, but he and his family were close friends with my stepmother's family and he is quite a respectable man. I also confess an interest in seeing parts of the world that are foreign to me and cannot wait to see what the American shores might look like. It all seems a very great adventure, though my journey has already been so exciting, I am not sure if America will be any more thrilling than this."

"I have sailed to the Americas and other territories many times for trade," said Dare.

"Oh! You must tell me everything you know, so I can be prepared for all the fun I will have on my arrival."

"But what if you don't like this man you are supposed to marry?" Kate was never one to avoid pointing out the obvious even if it was an unwelcome grounding from flights of fancy.

"I am sure that will not be a problem. If we decide we are not compatible, then I will simply return home with my maid."

Kate said nothing more, and the line in Robert's brow deepened significantly. Kate feared Emma may be in more trouble than she imagined if she decided against the marriage. Kate was not sure how to broach the subject with her though, and in the end, it was really none of her concern. It was only that Kate felt a sense of obligation to Miss St. James since she had helped to save her brother's life.

There was a slight pause while everyone in the

room shared concerned glances for Miss St. James's well-being, save the lady herself, who seemed quite at ease and unaccountably happy.

"I do not suppose I could trouble you for a look at one of your newspapers?" she asked Robert, who immediately handed her the entire stack, including the one he was reading.

"Thank you! I am so glad to catch up with my reading. I have not been able to get the *Times* for several days since I began my travels." She donned gloves to keep the ink from staining her hands.

"You enjoy reading the paper? Capital," praised Wynbrook. Kate also thought it admirable for her to read the paper, though was not pleased to have Wynbrook point it out.

"Not really," said Emma with a smile. "I mainly read for the society pages."

"I also enjoy glancing at them from time to time," said Wynbrook with a playful banter. "Mostly, of course, to see if I am listed."

Kate rolled her eyes at such an abominably arrogant thing to say, though she suspected that the words were only spoken to tease. Determined not to rise to such easy bait, Kate addressed Emma instead. "You enjoy the gossip columns?" Once again, Kate was surprised that a woman who had clearly been trained in medicine and could keep a cool head in times of crisis would be amused by such trivial societal pursuits.

"Oh yes, I confess I do. I've never been to London, and so I enjoy reading about the intrigues of the society ladies and gentlemen," said Emma with infectious excitement. "Of course, it's the closest I will ever come to London. In truth, it reads like one of my stepmother's novels. I cannot wait to open the page and find out what happened next. With all this excitement, I am a few days behind in my reading. I believe I shall begin three days ago."

"That was the day of my sister's wedding. Lady Jane to Sir Gareth. I hope it was mentioned. It would please my other sister, Anne," said Wynbrook.

"Let me see." Emma bowed her golden head before the newspaper, her eyes gleaming. "Oh yes, here it is, the wedding of Lady Jane. They say the bride looked radiant and the wedding attracted all the notables of society."

"Ah, my sister will like that," said Wynbrook.

"Since Lord Wynbrook is eager to make an appearance in the pages, do tell us if he has been identified." Kate gave Wynbrook one of her biggest smiles.

"Let me see," said Miss St. James from behind her newspaper, missing the sarcasm in Kate's tone. "Why yes, I do believe he may be. *All may not be entirely well for Lord W in his own quest for matrimony, for Lord D has refused Lord W's offer, saying he would never relinquish his sister to him. Will Lord W ever find a bride? We know many a matron who would be happy to supply her daughter for such a prize!*"

Miss St. James looked up over her paper, her smile fading as she noted the look of confusion on the faces of her new friends. "Oh!" Emma turned to Kate, her mouth a perfect oval. "Were they speaking of you?"

"I hope not," grumbled Kate. "But what is this nonsense of you talking to Wynbrook about me?" she demanded of Robert. Had he truly tried to scare Wynbrook away from her?

Wynbrook and her brother exchanged equally blank faces. Finally, Wynbrook blinked in sudden recognition. "I know. The conversation we had about sailing away from society when we were speaking of your ship. You said you would never relinquish her to my hands."

"Oh, the *Lady Kate*." Robert shook his head.

"Your ship is called the *Lady Kate*?" asked Miss St. James. "That is unfortunate."

Kate, Robert, and Wynbrook all exchanged a similar glance. It was indeed most unfortunate.

"Shall I continue reading?" Emma asked.

"There won't be any mention of us the next day," said Wynbrook with confidence.

"But I believe there is," said Emma, her head behind the newsprint. "*On the return to London, Lord W was seen riding away from Town with the sister of Lord D. No one has seen either of them since. Could the two lovebirds be making a run for Scotland with the brother in pursuit? We leave it to your fertile minds.*"

Kate's heart stopped beating for a moment. Someone had seen them. She'd been so worried about her brother, she had not thought for one instant about the repercussions of being seen leaving in a coach with Lord Wynbrook. Robert's mouth was a thin, firm line. The humor had drained from Wynbrook's face. Silence pervaded the sitting room.

Miss St. James took up the next paper and they all waited for her to read it. Later, Kate would wonder why Emma had to be the one to read the column, but somehow it was she, the only one whose life did not depend on the few sentences written, who was the neutral party to read out their fate.

Miss St. James cleared her throat. "*Lord W, along with Lord D and his sister, remain missing. Though a shocking elopement can be the only explanation, Lord W's family remain strangely silent. Of course, who can blame them?*"

Emma gave Kate a sympathetic smile. She was a kind executioner.

"Anne will ring a peal over my head," muttered Wynbrook, putting his head in his hands.

"This is nonsense," said Kate in a voice that did not quite seem her own. "We simply need to tell people that…" She paused but could not quite think of what story they could tell. The truth was the stuff of those ridiculous lurid novels, even without the peg leg. Who would possibly believe them?

"We shall tell people we planned to meet Darington on our journey," said Wynbrook, straightening his spine. "We then traveled together to your home, where we were married."

"Married?" Kate glanced around the room, silently pleading her case to all present. "Surely there can be no cause for anything so extreme."

Silence once again reigned in the sitting room. Miss St. James sat pretty as a picture, her hands clasped demurely in her lap.

"Robert?" Kate barely mouthed the word.

Robert's face was grim. He directed his comments to Wynbrook. "I should not wish to entrap you into any arrangement you would not otherwise choose. You have done us a great service. More from you is not required or expected."

"Thank you, my friend, but there is nothing else that can be done. We shall be married as soon as may be."

"Do not talk about me in such a manner!" demanded Kate. "I am not a commodity to be exchanged in the public market. Wynbrook, your scruples do you credit, but you have provided me with great assistance and I shall never demand a proposal from you because of it. There will be no wedding."

"As much as I dislike to disagree with a lady, I fear I must disappoint you," drawled Wynbrook. He had overcome his initial shock and now appeared as he always did—confident with an aura of unruffled calm and a slight element of humor, as if mildly amused by the tragedy unfolding before him.

"I have been seen running off with the sister of a peer of the realm," continued Wynbrook. "It is an offense only a wedding can rectify, and even that may not be enough for high sticklers to propriety."

"No!" Kate was adamant. She would not be cornered into marriage, nor would she allow Wynbrook to be trapped. It was not fair to either of them, no matter what her personal desires may be. "You are a lord and a gentleman, and I shall not allow you to be forced into marriage because of a few idle words in a gossip column. No one who was in possession of all the facts could possibly feel that your willingness to assist us in our time of need should be rewarded by matrimonial entrapment."

Kate met Emma's eye hoping to find support. Instead, Emma gave her a sympathetic half smile. "I fear that society can be quite unforgiving," said Emma. "Having read the gossip columns for many years, I can tell you that these things are unlikely to be quickly forgotten. In a case such as this, I feel Lord Wynbrook has indeed done the honorable thing."

Wynbrook and Miss St. James exchanged smiles, only furthering Kate's ill humor.

"I do apologize," said Kate, having difficulties in meeting Wynbrook's eye. "But I am forced to be disagreeable in this matter. I simply will not allow you to propose marriage simply to protect my reputation."

"It is not only your reputation that will suffer." Wynbrook turned so that she could no longer avoid him, and she was drawn into the strange warmth of his green eyes. "According to the papers, I have abducted the sister of a peer the realm. If I do not return married to said young lady, I will find my society lacking. No decent person will speak to me. My own sisters will be forced to cut the acquaintance."

She was outvoted. Wynbrook, Miss St. James, even her own brother felt that she should marry the Earl of Wynbrook, one of the biggest matrimonial prizes in all of Britain. Kate swallowed convulsively. Her world had just slid sideways. This could not possibly be happening. Everyone was silent in the room.

"I think I should attend to some of my correspondence," said Emma with a tight smile. She gave Kate one last sympathetic glance before leaving the room.

Both men stood at her exit. Wynbrook sat down once more beside Kate, but Robert lingered on his feet. He gave the unhappy couple a brief nod and then headed for the door. "Good luck," he said in a voice so soft Kate was not sure if it was intended for herself or for Wynbrook.

The door closed behind him with an ominous click. Silence once more fell upon the room, suffocating her with its vast emptiness. She sat beside

Wynbrook, yet they might have been sitting at opposite ends of the empty room for how much distance she felt between them.

"So I gather you are not pleased with the prospect of becoming my wife." Wynbrook stretched his long legs out before him and reclined against the back of the settee in a most relaxed manner. He was positively lounging.

"How is it that you are so much at your ease?" demanded Kate, spearing him with what she hoped was a piercing look. He did not seem at all distressed.

"If we are to wed, it would not be inappropriate to make ourselves comfortable around each other."

"If I were to be comfortable, I would have to remove this damned new set of stays," grumbled Kate.

Wynbrook's eyebrows shot up. "I invite you to do so. Most passionately."

Kate scowled at him and changed the subject away from the topic of her undergarments. "You are showing a decided lack of surprise at this turn of events."

"I confess, I had decided a proposal from me would need to be forthcoming. My only disappointment is the papers anticipated my pronouncement. I was trying to decide how best to broach the subject and now I no longer have to strain myself to devise the perfect plan."

"Why should you need to propose? There is no need, I assure you."

"I kissed you."

Kate felt as if he had sucked all the air from her lungs. She opened and closed her mouth, not able to speak. Not able to breathe. He mentioned the kiss. She had hoped he would never speak of it.

"Several times, actually," Wynbrook continued. "Once might be forgivable, but repeatedly? And of course I will not even mention our sleeping arrangements of two nights ago. No, a proposal is required."

"There were extenuating circumstances," Kate insisted, still trying to remember how to breathe. "It was simply a case of being thrust together." Her mouth went dry at the recognition of the words that had just fallen out of her mouth. "It could have happened to anyone," she added quickly.

Wynbrook stubbornly shook his head. "If the situation had been reversed and Dare had come to me for help to find you, I would not have—"

"Yes, yes, you need not be ridiculous."

"The truth is I kissed you." He looked back and forth as if checking to make sure the room was indeed empty and moved closer to her in a conspiratorial manner. "And I have the lingering impression that you kissed me in return." He leaned closer so that he was whispering in her ear, his breath warm on her skin. "And what is worse, I enjoyed it, and I believe you enjoyed it too. In truth, I would like to kiss you right now."

Kate turned to tell him to stop whispering tempting words in her ear, but she turned toward him, not away, and now her lips were dangerously close to his. She froze, unsure what she wanted to do, but Wynbrook was not so undecided and quickly closed the gap, pressing his lips to hers.

Kate's arms wound around Wynbrook of their own accord and he returned the embrace, pulling her close to him and deepening the kiss.

When their lips finally parted, Kate took a ragged breath. What was she doing? How could she let him kiss her again? "I...I confess a small attraction between us."

"Nothing between us is small," interrupted Wynbrook.

"But it does not change anything." She stood up and took a step back. "It cannot change anything."

Wynbrook rose to his feet, the smug, satisfied look fading from his face. "Whatever do you mean? That kiss changes everything."

"No, no, it cannot. There are things about me you do not know. Things that make it impossible for me to wed." Kate took another step back and cast a furtive glance at the door. "I am sorry, truly I am, but I cannot marry you. It is simply impossible." She turned and ran from the room.

Twenty-nine

KATE SAT IN THE WINDOW SEAT OF HER ROOM AND stared out onto the ocean, the sunlight casting sparkles along the churning waves. The rhythmic roar of the ocean was comforting and familiar in a world turned upside down. Wynbrook wished to marry her.

Marry her.

But of course, that could never be.

A soft knock at the door interrupted her thoughts. She paused a moment, not sure she was up to another round with Wynbrook, or her brother, for that matter. "Who is it?"

"It's me, Emma."

"What do you want?"

A perpetually cheerful face popped in the doorway. "Talk? I brought tea and pastries."

"I am really not in the mood for conversation."

"Just tea then," said Emma, carrying in a tea service.

Kate wanted to tell her to go away, but the smell of the cook's scones and the rumble of her stomach over-ruled her pride. Perhaps a good cup of tea was exactly what she needed. Emma placed the tea service on a small table and carried the table over to the window seat, so Kate would not need to move.

Emma poured the tea and offered the scone, sitting next to her on the window seat and sipping on her own cup.

"This is a lovely view," she commented.

"Yes," agreed Kate. She had forgotten how much she enjoyed watching the waves from her high perch in Greystone Hall.

"I know we only just met, but it seemed to me that perhaps you would like someone to talk to or just someone to be a friend. I hope you know I would like to be that friend." Emma gave her an encouraging smile.

Despite being annoyingly perfect, it was hard to dislike Emma St. James. It would have been like kicking a puppy. It just felt wrong.

"Thank you," said Kate, taking another sip of tea. "You have been very kind to our family."

"Forgive me, for I know it is none of my concern, but I see the way Lord Wynbrook looks at you and you at him. Why are you opposed to marriage?"

"I do not wish to marry someone out of obligation."

"I am sorry I read those gossip columns. They always seemed to be about faraway people in society. People who were not real. Now I see the true damage gossip can cause, and I am ashamed of myself for being a party to it."

"'Tis hardly your fault."

"Nor is it yours for what was written," returned Emma. "I would hate to see anyone throw away a chance at happiness because of a few idle words."

Kate shook her head. "You do not understand. I

can never marry anyone. I have seen things…done things. Marriage is not possible for me."

Emma gave her a sympathetic look and passed the jam. "I believe our hardships produce in us the fortitude to triumph over our challenges. For as it is written in Romans 5:3–5, *We glory in tribulations also: knowing that tribulation worketh patience; And patience, experience; and experience, hope: And hope maketh not ashamed; because the love of God is shed abroad in our hearts by the Holy Ghost which is given unto us.*"

"Sorry, but I do not care to glory in my tribulations. And I think patience is an entirely overrated character trait."

"But what of hope?" asked Emma with an infectious smile. "It seems you could use some. What of the love of God being poured into your heart? I believe our hardships are actually blessings in disguise."

Kate snorted. Blessings in disguise? What kind of tea was this girl drinking? She was about to retort that it was easy to glorify sufferings if you never had any, but she stopped a moment before the words left her lips. Perhaps Emma was more familiar with tribulations than one would initially guess. "Why are you sailing to America to get married? Have you hardships that led to the choice?"

Emma's countenance turned almost guilty, as if caught at something she wished to remain hidden. "I was very close to my father. My mother died when I was young, and it was just him and me. When I got older, he thought I needed a mother figure in my life, to help me and bring me out in society. I believe when he married my stepmother, he was thinking mostly of me. Unfortunately, he died, leaving me with her and her son."

Emma's smile faded and an uncharacteristic frown settled on her somber face. "They wished for me to sign over my inheritance to him, saying he could manage the estate better than I. When I refused, they demanded I marry him."

"That is horrible!" exclaimed Kate.

"I confess, I was not pleased. Then they hit upon the idea that I could wed a man in America."

"But do you not see they are just trying to get their hands on your inheritance?"

"Yes, of course. But I do not mind going to America. I think it will be a grand adventure. Why, I've had such a diverting time so far."

"I would not call this diverting."

"I have met such nice people."

"But, Emma, they are essentially robbing you of your inheritance. You cannot let them do that." Kate spoke passionately from experience.

"My happiness is more important than my inheritance, is it not? Besides, maybe someday I will return. Or maybe someday I will not. Either way, I am free of a situation that was deeply unpleasant, and I have the opportunity to travel and see wonderful new places." Emma's eyes sparkled. "Truly, I would not miss this adventure for a thousand country homes."

Kate sipped her tea. Maybe whatever Emma was drinking would inflict her with a similar joy without regard to circumstance. Give Emma her due—at least she was happy.

"So will you at least try?" asked Emma.

"Try what? I am not going to America in search of a husband."

"No, but maybe you could walk to the drawing room?"

"If Wynbrook knew me, knew the whole story, he would not have proposed."

"Why do you not test your theory and see if it's true? Tell him the truth."

"What if he rejects me?"

"What if he doesn't?" Emma gave Kate a sweet smile, picked up the tea tray, and skipped out of the room, which honestly was rather hard to do while holding a tea tray.

Kate stared after her. Who was that girl?

She did not have long to wait before there was another knock on her door. It was her brother.

"You should not be out of bed," she chastised, jumping up to help him into a chair.

"Cannot lie about," he grumbled.

"You certainly can. How else do you think you will recover?"

He shrugged. "Talked to the magistrate. Told him the version you told the staff. They are out looking for the men who did it. Wish I could go myself."

"Don't even think it. You can hardly stand."

"Do what I have to. Hopefully, I don't have to." Robert sat back in his chair and closed his eyes. He was paler than usual, and Kate did not care to see it. He was always so invincible, seeing him vulnerable was not welcome.

"You should see Emma. She has scones. And jam," Kate added.

A rarely seen smile lit Robert's face though his eyes remained closed. "I know. She brought me some."

"She is a good person."

Robert opened his eyes. "The best."

"She thinks I should talk to Wynbrook."

"So do I."

"Is that why you are here?"

Robert nodded. "Know you don't want to be married. Know the reasons why too. Think you should give Wynbrook a chance."

"And if he should reject me?"

"He won't. Better not, anyways. Even if he does, you won't be in any different place than you are now."

"Yes, I would. If I reveal my secrets to a man who rejects me, then I have been scorned and thrown aside, discarded like so much rubbish."

Robert paused a moment and gave her an appraising look. "You like him, don't you?"

"Yes." Her voice was small. She sat back down at the window and pulled her knees up to rest her chin on them. The ocean swirled below her in a constant yet unpredictable motion.

"Talking involves risk. Fortunately, my sister is no coward." Robert struggled up out of the chair and walked stiffly out the door, shutting it behind him.

He was wrong. She was scared beyond reason.

Thirty

WYNBROOK FINISHED A LETTER TO TRISTAN AND another to Anne. He was certain they would not be pleased with him. To have such vulgar gossip about the family in the *Times* was anathema to Anne. He hoped Tristan would soon arrive with the license. Considering he still held the man's suitcase, he had no doubt Tristan would travel with all due haste.

While he was fearful his family was irritated at him, he was certain Kate was more so. He wondered what could be so horrible that he would not wish to marry her. Was she a Napoleonic spy? Did she have a love child hidden in Gibraltar? Twin love children?

A quiet rustle at the door caught his attention and the object of his musing stepped tentatively into the room. Kate paused, hesitant and unsure, quite at odds with her usual direct manner. She glanced at the door as if ready to make a run for it at any moment. He stood up slowly, afraid any sudden movement would make her take flight.

"Hello," he said.

"Good day," she returned.

Silence.

"Have you had tea?" he asked, trying to stick to benign topics.

"Yes. Emma brought it. Though I suppose as hostess I should have poured it." She shook her head as if mentally chiding herself. "You see what a wretched countess I would make."

"Come, please sit. It has been a difficult day." He smiled and hoped she would sit next to him on the settee. She chose a chair as far from him as possible.

"Emma and Robert think I should be married. To you," she added, just in case he could possibly be confused on this point.

"Excellent. I'm glad to know I have allies."

"They think I should let you know why I cannot be wed, so you can decide."

"About that. I have decided to accept your twelve children born out of wedlock and adopt them as my own."

"What?" She was aghast.

"Your love children. I am trying to imagine what would be so horrible I would not wish to wed you. Illegitimate offspring was the best I could come up with. There aren't actually twelve, are there?" He was a little anxious.

"There aren't any!"

Wynbrook let out a breath, more relieved than he wished her to know. "Well now, that's a relief, because making up a story to cover all twelve would take more imagination than I've got." Wynbrook hoped to make her smile but Kate was not having it.

"What would make you think that I would...that I would have...that I would do that?"

"Nothing. Only you have skulked in here like you have a horrible secret and I have been racking my poor brain to figure out what it might be."

"I will have you know my virtue, such as it is, is quite intact," she said primly. "Though yours is not the first bare arse I've ever seen."

"Well, now you have me intrigued. Please come and tell me the whole story. I have a feeling it will make a good tale. Is there a captain with a peg leg in it?"

"No. Well, actually I have met a captain with a peg leg, but he was married with twelve children."

"I knew somewhere there were twelve brats!"

Kate gave a reluctant smile and he was gratified to finally break through her icy reserve. If ever he did win her heart, her devotion would be worth the effort, for it was not easily bestowed.

"Now come sit next to me and tell me your tale. I promise not to bite…unless you ask me to."

"You are incorrigible." Her tone was disapproving, but she did sit next to him.

Wynbrook said nothing, hoping his silence would make her feel more inclined to share.

Kate took a deep breath and began to speak, staring straight ahead of her, never once glancing at him. "When we were twelve, we were called home from boarding school for our father's funeral and found the house had been gutted. We were told our father had left us deeply in debt, though we knew that could not be possible. It was clear any money we had and any valuables we owned besides the estates themselves had been stripped from us. What was not clear was who had done it or why."

Wynbrook covered one of her hands with his in a silent gesture of compassion. She took a breath and continued.

"We were informed by the steward that we needed to travel to London to see our godfather and legal guardian, General Roberts, a friend of our father's. We made the journey, but when we arrived, we were informed that our guardian was too busy to attend to us. We were quite alone in the world."

"Too busy? Unforgiveable! Was there no one else? None to whom you could turn?" Wynbrook could not remember a time when he did not have a multitude of friends and relations. He also had lost his parents but had been immediately surrounded by family. How could Kate, at only twelve years, be left so unprotected in the world?

Kate shook her head. "We have no other living family. We were told we were paupers due to our debts. The steward handed us over to some rough men who deposited us in debtors' prison." She turned away so he could not see her face.

"Debtors' prison?" He was certain he must not have heard right. "But you are members of the peerage. That cannot be."

"I assure you it can be if you have no friends and those around you deny who you are. The prison guards were told we were the children of a dead merchant who had not paid his debts and that we were habitual liars and to pay no heed to anything we said."

"Oh, Kate. Now I understand why you set free all the children of Fleet." It was all starting to make sense.

"Yes. It was a memorable experience."

Wynbrook squeezed her hand. "I cannot believe such a thing could happen."

Kate kept her face turned from his. "We were fortunate. We were only there a week."

"A week!"

"Some people live much of their lives in prison."

"But you should not have been there at all!" he growled. It was wrong, so very wrong. "Where is this bastard steward? I cannot believe he could get away with this." He was ready to take the man to task himself.

"The steward is dead. After we escaped Fleet, we found the man murdered."

"Murdered!"

"Clearly someone ensured he would not be able to talk."

"So if someone killed the steward, then he was merely the pawn of a larger player."

"Yes, exactly so."

"And you never found out who did this to you?" he demanded. One hand lay gently on Kate's but the other was clenched at his side.

"To this day, we do not know."

"But how did you escape?" he asked, still incensed that his precious Kate would be so mistreated.

"One of Robert's teachers, a rather unconventional fellow, had been let go from his post and followed us to London, I think in the hopes of gaining a position as a tutor. Instead, he discovered our plight and paid enough of a bribe to secure our release."

"This cannot be. It cannot happen," said John, unable to get past the unfairness of it all.

She finally turned to him with sympathy in her

eyes. She patted his hand as if trying to comfort him. He needed to pull himself together. He was supposed to be consoling her.

"After we left the prison," continued Kate in her most businesslike air, "we found ourselves in a tenuous position. We were only twelve years old and obviously had not reached majority. The steward had been murdered, and we were fearful whoever came after him would come after us next."

"What did you do? You must've been terrified. Had you no one to protect you?" John was on the edge of his seat.

"I suppose this is a rather lurid tale. All I need is a peg-legged captain and I could pen the next popular novel." Kate gave him a weak smile.

For once, Wynbrook did not feel like making light of the conversation. He was too angry at the injustice done to her to see any humor in the story. "I fear I cannot laugh at any story in which you are hurt."

A softness crept into Kate's light eyes and she continued her story. "Our best course seemed to be to take our well-being into our own hands. We both agreed that, though young, we could hardly do worse caring for ourselves than anyone else had. So we went to court to gain Robert's majority."

"At the age of twelve?" Wynbrook was incredulous.

"It does seem young now, but we did not know what else to do. We were helped in this regard by our tutor. He was the only one we could trust."

A spark of humor shone in her eyes, and Robert guessed this was one part of the tale she recalled in a positive light. "I fear what I have to tell you does not reflect well on myself or Robert. I would remind you that we were twelve years old and in desperate straits."

"Yes, of course. Please do go on. I can't imagine how you survived this." He squeezed her hand and realized she was holding his. He did not recall how it had come to be, but he was glad for it.

Kate gave him a brief nod to acknowledge his comment. "Our tutor snuck in to the courthouse and found an application for a young man to reach his majority and I made a replica for Robert."

"You created the legal papers?" He was impressed.

"Yes, and I purposely made the hand barely legible."

"But still," John argued, "even if you smudged the papers, no one looking at a twelve-year-old boy could think he was full grown."

"True. That is why we stole the judge's spectacles the night before the hearing." Kate grinned.

John laughed. "Incredible! This is much better than my novel, I must say."

Kate made a guilty sort of chortle he had never heard from her before. "I confess, we even drew on something of a mustache for Robert before we went before the judge. Fortunately, Dare has always been tall for his age. It all seems quite fantastic now, but it did work. The judge must have assumed Robert to be close to being of age and issued a ruling giving him majority. The first thing we did was to change bank accounts. We hired a new steward and gave him instructions to sell off anything we could to pay off debts, which were indeed substantial. A land agent was engaged to take over the management of the house. Until yesterday, we had never returned."

It all explained so much. Her generous gift to release the residents of Fleet prison. The desperate clinging to every farthing. The general distrust of people. The isolation and betrayal she had endured certainly did not make for an inviting personality. Still, she had a warm heart and was fiercely loyal to those she loved.

But would she ever love him?

"We realized that even with strict economy, it would take a while before we had even two farthings to rub together," Kate continued her story. "We also were desirous to leave London, and returning to Greystone was not an option. In the end, there are only a few occupations open to a gentleman of Robert's age and position."

"He joined the navy," said Wynbrook. It was all starting to make sense.

"Yes. Our tutor was brought on board the ship to instruct the young gentlemen."

"But what did you do? Did you return to school?"

"I would have liked to, but we had not the funds, and we still did not know what had happened or who had gone out of their way to cause us such pain. Perhaps it was cowardly, but I feared remaining in England by myself without Robert there, and besides, where was I to go?"

"That is sensible. I would not have allowed my sisters to go off to school in a similar situation. Who knows what could've happened to you alone and unprotected?"

"Yes. But I fear that there were very few options open to us, and I am certain we chose one you would never have done for your sisters."

"What did you do?" he asked softly, almost fearing

the answer. This was no doubt why Kate felt she could not ever marry him.

Kate shook her head. "It is too terrible."

"It is your story, your past, and so whatever it is, we can face it together."

The doubt in her eyes was clear. "I hope you mean that."

He hoped he did too.

Thirty-one

KATE CLEARED HER THROAT, TRYING TO FORM THE words she needed to say. She looked away, unwilling to watch Wynbrook's reaction. Whatever was blossoming between her and Wynbrook, this revelation would kill it. Kate kept her eyes straight ahead, looking out the window to the bright orange sunset. The day was over and so too was this potential life with Wynbrook. She was watching it come to an end. Or possibly she was killing it with her bare hands.

"I decided that since Robert was joining the navy, if I wished to remain with him, I must join too."

Kate paused to allow her words and their meaning to be understood. She did not want to watch as Wynbrook began to understand that she had been ruined beyond all hope of redemption, yet she could not help but turn to him. At first, his face remained impassive, a slight frown on his brows. Then understanding dawned, his eyes widened and his lips parted but he said nothing. He squeezed her hand again and it gave her the courage to continue.

"I cut my hair. I quickly reworked some of Robert's

clothes to fit me. I did not tell him my plans until I had completed the disguise, then presented myself to him and our tutor."

His voice came in a hoarse whisper. "He let you…"

"No, he told me I would not go, could not go. He was working on some agreement with a girls' seminary to accept me then and be paid later, but his request was denied. Perhaps we were young and did not know all our options, but to this day I am not sure what else we could have done. We did not know whom to trust. And Robert feared for my safety if he left me unprotected."

"Oh, Kate, I wish we had known you then. We could have protected you. I would have…" His voice trailed off. "And to think I said such horrible things about you and Dare that day before the accident. How can you ever forgive me? I was such an unmitigated arse." The pain was clear in his eyes.

"Yes, you were," Kate agreed. "But you have more than made up for your uncharitable words. Indeed, Robert and I are quite in your debt."

Wynbrook shifted closer to her. "But how did you manage? How…?"

"Robert introduced me as his cousin, Ashton. I was young and thin and looked for all the world like a lad. I worked as a cabin boy and ran powder to the gunners during engagements."

His eyes opened wide. "Engagements? You were in battle?"

"Yes, I served under Lord Nelson in the Battle of the Nile."

His eyes flashed with sudden understanding. "The medal I found, it was yours, not your brother's. Oh, my sweet girl." He suddenly embraced her, wrapping her in his warm, strong arms. She was stunned, utterly speechless. This was not the reaction she had anticipated. Hesitantly, she rested her cheek upon his shoulder.

"So you see why it is that I cannot marry you. I cannot marry anyone." Her voice was muffled from his shoulder.

He released her from his embrace but held her at arm's length, his hands on her shoulders. He frowned at her until sudden realization dawned on his face. "Wait, *cousin* Ashton? Not the Mr. Ashton who has been serving as my solicitor for the past six years."

"Er…yes." She had hoped he would not make the connection.

Wynbrook stood up and began to pace the room. It was a lot to take in all at once. "So let me get this straight. You were defrauded of your inheritance, sent to debtors' prison, served in the Royal Navy, fought in the Battle of the Nile, and for the past six years have been acting as my financial adviser and solicitor."

"So you see why I am not fit to be your wife. Or anyone's wife." She felt quite small having her faults laid out before her so succinctly. She clasped her hands together in her lap so tightly her knuckles turned white.

"And Tristan knew this!" he cried, saving the worst offense for last.

"Some of it," she confessed.

"I always wondered how Tristan managed to graduate Cambridge with a degree in law. You helped him!"

"A bit." And by "a bit," she meant quite a lot.

Wynbrook shook his head. "It would be a thing he would do."

"I enjoyed learning, and it allowed us to manage our affairs better."

He shook his head. "Unbelievable."

"Yes. Quite. I will leave you in peace." It was past time to make her exit. The best she could hope for now was to withdraw with whatever dignity she had left. She stood to leave, but Wynbrook caught her up in his arms.

"I am sorry to have alarmed you with my reaction. It is just such an amazing story, though now I understand why you are as you are. I thank you for telling me. Most ladies would have taken the offer and never shared their past."

"I am not most ladies," said Kate stiffly. "Now please unhand me."

"Sorry, my dear, but my offer still stands." He released her from his embrace but held both her hands in his, smiling down at her.

She could not believe her ears. Her jaw dropped and she could do nothing to keep from gaping at him. "After all I just told you, you still wish to marry me?"

"Yes, indeed. Only when we are wed, I will expect you to perform the office of financial adviser gratis. Save me several pounds a year." He grinned at her.

He must be mad. She was sure of it. "The purpose of this revelation is to explain why I cannot marry you."

"So you keep saying," drawled Wynbrook. "But I still refuse to see why that is so."

"I spent a year of my life masquerading as a cabin boy. What if your society friends were to discover this fact?"

"I should laugh in their faces. What a ridiculous story. Too fantastic to believe." He snapped his fingers as if it were nothing to bring about, and she had to admit the daughter of an earl working as a cabin boy aboard an English Navy ship was too far-fetched, even for society.

"But…" Kate was at a loss for words.

"The thing we really must do is find whoever did this dastardly deed to you and Dare in the first place. Do you think your abductors and your old enemy may be connected?"

"I…I don't know."

"Well, it's past time we found out. Have you interviewed the staff who worked here at the time?"

"Some inquiries have been made, but no one knows anything. We have let go all the staff that worked here when we were young, not knowing whom to trust. I do not believe anyone is still alive who might be able to help us."

"Have you asked your current housekeeper?"

"Well…no. But she was not employed here then. Of what help could she be?"

"A competent housekeeper knows all," he said with confidence. He rang the bell and asked the footman to request the presence of the housekeeper.

"I do not see how she could help," said Kate when the footman had gone to fetch Mrs. Brooke. She was feeling rather unsteady at his acceptance of her secrets and his immediate jumping in to investigate her greatest mystery.

"You never know until you ask," said Wynbrook. "We need to put to rest the ghosts from your past so we can move on," he said kindly.

"We? There is no we. These are *my* ghosts. Do not trouble yourself."

The conversation was cut short by the arrival of the housekeeper. Wynbrook motioned for her to ask, and

Kate relented, knowing there was nothing the new housekeeper could reveal on this matter.

"Mrs. Brooke," said Kate, "I am looking for information on how the house was run before your time. Do you know any of the staff who worked before you who might still be around?"

"There's Mrs. Hennings, the housekeeper."

"But I thought she committed…that she took her own life," Kate stammered. This had been the information she had received.

"She tried. But she survived, or what's left of her. She lives with her daughter, Mrs. Saunders, in the village."

"Thank you, Mrs. Brooke," said Kate. She stared at Wynbrook when the housekeeper turned to leave. She could not believe that after all these years, she finally had a clue as to someone who had been present when her father died.

It was getting late and darkness had crept up slowly, so any adventure would have to wait until the morrow. "So would you like to have a chat with your old housekeeper tomorrow?" he asked.

"Yes!"

"And now will you marry me?"

"No."

Wynbrook shrugged. "Can't blame me for trying. Your refusal does not sound quite as adamant, and in that, I take hope."

❦

Silas Bones did not relish returning to his father empty-handed. After his men had first lost Lady Katherine and then misplaced Lord Darington, he had

joined them in the fruitless search for the missing earl. They had asked around, greased the palms of many individuals, but the only thing he had discovered was that a gentleman and a lady had taken some interest in his men's coach but had driven off a short time later.

He could only guess that either Darington had died somewhere in the hedgerows or he had been spirited away by the mysterious couple in the coach. Silas returned to Portsmouth without any sense of haste. His men he had sent ahead, with the hope his father would burn out his fury on them. Captain Harcourt was known for many things, but patience, forgiveness, and understanding were not any of them.

Silas walked down the docks toward his father's frigate, the *Kestrel*. Moored next to the *Kestrel* was the *Lady Kate*, the Earl of Darington's ship. He wondered what Darington would think if he knew his enemy was so close at hand.

With leaden feet, Silas climbed aboard the *Kestrel*. His two companions were slumped over on the main deck, still bound to the mast where they had been whipped. The memory of his own punishments flooded back. He spared them no more than a glance. They knew the risks of disappointing Captain Harcourt.

He found his father enjoying his port and cigar after what had surely been a fine meal. His brows lowered when Silas entered.

"You lost my cargo," he began, his voice deceptively soft.

"Aye, sir."

"You lost my cargo to Darington." His voice began to rise.

"Aye, sir." Silas braced himself for the onslaught.

Harcourt bounded to his feet and rounded the table to stand inches from Silas as he screamed in his face. "You lost my cargo, my treasure, my money, to the son of the man who stripped me of my rank, my title, my *everything*. You worthless, spineless idiot. I am repulsed by your inept presence. I should keelhaul you until you are sliced into chum and feed you to the sharks like the rubbish you are!" Harcourt cursed further and Silas said nothing.

In a flash, Harcourt struck him across the face. Silas took it on the jaw, remained standing, and said nothing in response. He had failed his father. He deserved rough treatment.

Cursing more, his father rummaged through some papers on a side desk of the captain's quarters. He turned back and thrust a piece of parchment at him. "Fortunately, I prepared one last trick on the first Earl of Darington, just in case his brats ever troubled me. You take care of this. Don't return to me until you have Lady Katherine's dowry."

"What's this?" Silas took the parchment.

His father gave him a sinister smile. "Your marriage contract."

Silas opened the parchment and read through it quickly, stunned by the contents. "A marriage contract between myself and Lady Katherine? You want me to marry her?"

"I don't care what you do to her. Just get me the fifty thousand pounds." His father pounded the table with a menacing thud. "Do not fail me again."

Thirty-two

THE NEXT DAY, KATE AND WYNBROOK PLANNED TO interview the former housekeeper. When Robert was informed the old housekeeper, long thought dead, was still alive, he insisted on coming along. In the end, they all decided to take an excursion to the village, Wynbrook driving them in an old carriage they had found in the barn. Kate was a little unsure if Emma should accompany them, but her brother seemed to appreciate her presence and Kate did not object.

Emma had the presence of mind to pack a basket of goodies to be given to their old housekeeper, which seemed a decent rationale for their visit. Gray clouds hung low in the sky, but it was at least dry when they drove the five miles down to the village, nestled around a cove by the ocean.

The modest fishing village was comprised mainly of small, white houses, closely clustered near each other, as if huddling together for protection against the elements. Robert knocked on the door of a humble cottage and shifted his weight from one leg to the other. Though he said nothing, Kate had no doubt his wound was hurting him, and she hoped he was not pushing himself too hard to do the interview.

For herself, the tension of meeting their old housekeeper made her very bones ache from holding herself so rigid. What did the woman know? Was she complicit in some of the evil plot against them? Would she even talk to them at all?

The door opened to reveal a plump, middle-aged woman wiping her hands on her apron. Upon seeing the quality at her doorstep, her eyebrows rose significantly, and she gave them a curtsy. "How can I help you?"

"We are here to see Mrs. Hennings." Robert handed the woman his card, which she obediently took from him. She glanced at it, but no flicker of recognition crossed her face and Kate doubted that the woman could read.

"Me mother is ill, sir. She sees no one." The confusion and distress on the woman's face was clear.

"Lord Darington and Lady Katherine have brought some gifts for your table. May we come in?" asked Emma sweetly, holding up the basket.

"Yes, yes, of course!" She opened the door wide and ushered them in, her face reddening for having kept such persons waiting on her stoop. She showed them into a small sitting room with a low ceiling, forcing both Wynbrook and Robert to duck their heads as they entered the room. Several wide-eyed, openmouthed children stared at them from the corner of the room, which Kate could tell was the main room for the household, serving as the sitting room, dining room, and anything-else-that-needed-to-be-done room. The woman made a quick gesture, and the children vanished without a sound. "Please, do make yourselves comfortable."

The woman glanced around at the threadbare but comfortable furnishings, a frown on her face as if doubting very much that the notable persons before her could find much comfort in her humble room. Kate was not at all unnerved by the humble furnishings and found herself a chair. Robert motioned for the woman to sit, which she did obediently, and they all followed, making the small room seem to shrink with their presence. The woman's eyes were wide at the uncommon courtesy afforded to her by Lord Darington and his friends.

"Please allow us to introduce ourselves," said Emma with ease and charm. "This is the Earl of Wynbrook, I am Miss Emma St. James, and you have already met Lord Darington and his sister."

"How do you do?" said the woman automatically.

"Forgive our intrusion," said Kate, trying her best to mimic Emma's grace in the awkward situation. "We should have visited before this time, but we were of the understanding your mother was no longer living."

Kate was attempting civility, but the woman's eyes grew even wider and her face turned pale. She did not respond nor did she seem capable of speech. Kate exchanged a glance with Wynbrook.

"May we have the honor of knowing your name, madam?" Wynbrook asked.

The woman started, as if shocked back into reality. "I'm Mrs. Saunders, Mrs. Hennings's daughter."

"And did your mother work at our estate as a housekeeper?" asked Kate.

"Aye, she did, milady. Until…"

"Until what?" asked Kate with growing suspicion that here in this shabby room lay the secrets to understanding what had happened in their past.

"Well, I suppose you have a right to know if anyone does. Me mother worked there till the creditors came and took everything. She was let go but was never the same. She even…" Mrs. Saunders held her hands before her on her lap tightly and took a breath before continuing. "She tried to take her life. She spent ten years in the sanatorium. She rarely speaks now and I take care of her. She is not a well woman."

Disappointment washed over Kate. They had finally found someone who might have been able to shed light on what had happened only to find she was an invalid. "Forgive me, for this must be a difficult subject, but do you know why she wished to die? Was she mentally unstable?"

"No!" Mrs. Saunders shouted. "Forgive me, but my mother is a good, Christian woman. She would never have tried to kill herself."

"Then how do you explain her actions?" asked Kate gently.

"I cannot," said the woman miserably, pushing aside the strand of brown hair that had fallen into her eyes. "I don't know what caused her to do something so out of her character. She never speaks of it or what happened in that house."

Greystone Hall had claimed another victim.

Kate wasn't sure what to do next. Clearly, the poison that had afflicted Greystone had affected more than just her family. But if she was ever to find out what had happened, she needed to speak to someone who remembered those sad times.

"Maybe Lord Darington and his sister could be permitted to see her?" asked Wynbrook. His tone was gentle and sympathetic.

Mrs. Saunders appeared to be wrestling internally with some dilemma. She bit her lower lip and looked furtively at her guests.

"We do not wish to upset her, but I remember her as a kind woman when I was a girl, at a time when there was little kindness about me. I should like to give her my regards." Kate wished to at least be able to set eyes on the housekeeper, even if they would not be able to glean any helpful information.

"All right then," relented Mrs. Saunders. "I just worry for her, you understand, after all she's been through."

"I understand," said Kate, though she also understood that this may be her only chance to ask the housekeeper any questions.

The housekeeper's daughter led them to a small back room in which a frail, gray-haired woman sat in a chair, looking out the window, her wrinkled face illuminated in the gray light of the cloudy day. "Mama? I've brought you some visitors."

Kate stepped closer to her old housekeeper, trying to see the woman she remembered. The Mrs. Hennings of her memory was a stout woman with rosy cheeks and a long braid of light brown hair worn pinned around her head.

Vaguely, Kate remembered getting caught by Mrs. Hennings trying to sneak an extra sticky bun. She and her brother had expected the worst, since their governess was quick with the switch, but Mrs. Hennings had merely laughed at their antics and allowed them to eat their ill-gotten gains.

The woman before Kate hardly resembled the Mrs. Hennings she remembered. Gone were the plump, rosy cheeks and the easy affection she had shown them.

"Mrs. Hennings?" Kate stepped up closer, moving into her view. "I do not know if you will remember me."

Slowly, the frail woman turned from the window to Kate. Her eyes widened, and she put a shaky hand to her chest. "My Lady Darington," she gasped. She attempted to rise to her feet, her hands and legs shaking.

"No, please do not rise for me. It is me, Katherine. Lady Darington's daughter."

"My Lady Darington. How well you look. Have you recovered from your illness? We were so worried." The woman's crackling voice sank Kate's hopes of gaining any more information. The woman thought she was her mother. Clearly her mind had been addled by whatever had happened.

"Yes, I am well now, thank you." Kate tried to think of a way to try to have the woman remember what had happened, but she didn't know if the woman's mind could tolerate the memory. Her daughter, Mrs. Saunders, stood nearby twisting a bit of her skirt in her hands, and would no doubt jump forward if she thought her mother was in any danger.

"You are the housekeeper at Greystone?" asked Robert, playing along with the woman's delusion.

"Yes, yes, I have worked for the Darington family for years now." The woman gave them a small smile, which appeared to crack her face into even more wrinkles.

Her daughter put a hand to her heart, whispering, "I have not seen her smile in years."

"And do you enjoy your work, madam?" continued Robert in a conversational tone.

"Yes, the family is very good to me." The smile faded and a cloud passed over her countenance. "A shame the master is ill."

"Do you know what makes him ill?" asked Kate. It was one of her many questions. Why had her father lingered in illness and died so young?

"No," the old woman whispered, but her eyes were wide and wild. "So many bottles. I didn't know." She grabbed Kate's hand and held it with a surprisingly strong, icy grasp. "I swear to you, I didn't know."

"Didn't know what?" asked Kate.

"I didn't know!" Mrs. Hennings cried. "Forgive me, Lady Darington, for what them bastards did to your husband and your sweet babes. I swear I didn't know."

"It is all right, Mum, of course you didn't know." Her daughter rushed to her side to comfort her, but Mrs. Hennings would not let Kate's hand out of her grasp.

"What is this about?" asked Kate, wincing at the tight grip of the old woman.

"I know not," said the daughter. "Forgive me, but I think you should leave. Me mum is not well, as you can see."

Kate nodded reluctantly. "Mrs. Hennings, I'll take my leave now."

Mrs. Hennings released Kate's hands and began to cry into the shoulder of her daughter. What could have happened to cause such grief and pain?

"Mrs. Hennings," said Kate, and waited for the

woman to quiet herself, though the old woman's face remained buried in her daughter's shoulder. "It is I, Lady Darington. I do not wish you to blame yourself. All is forgiven. I wish you a peaceful rest."

Mrs. Hennings looked up, her face twisted in anguish. Slowly, her features relaxed and she took a deep breath. She sat up in her chair and gazed at Katherine as if seeing her for the first time. "Ah, Lady Kate. You always was a kindly child."

Kate held her breath, realizing that Mrs. Hennings had recognized her for the first time.

"I've been waiting to hear those words a long time. A long time." Mrs. Hennings took a deep breath. "At least there is someone to care for you and the young master. I made sure of that. How is General Roberts, dear?"

He was an unfeeling cad who could not be bothered to help them when they needed it most. However, Kate did not wish to distress her more, so she gave a forced smile, saying, "He is well, thank you."

"Good, good," said Mrs. Hennings, bobbing her head.

"Mrs. Hennings, there is something I must ask you," said Kate, ignoring the flash of warning from the daughter. "Of course no one blames you for any of what occurred, but we feel that those who were responsible for it may be trying to cause trouble again. Do you know who these people might be?"

"No, no." The old housekeeper's eyes grew wide again. "I cannot say. Never. Never."

She knew something, and Kate needed to find out what.

Her daughter, however, was looking increasingly worried. "I think it might be time for—"

"Tea!" declared Emma, joining the conversation with a brilliant smile. "What an excellent suggestion. Come, Mrs. Saunders, let us let these old friends enjoy their reminiscences."

"Yes, I have it on good authority they packed some delicious items in that basket. Let's open it up and find out!" Wynbrook held out an arm to usher her out of the room.

"But, my mother—"

"Will be in good hands, and I'm sure will do better for a spot of tea. How do you prepare yours, Mrs. Saunders?" Emma asked politely. Between her and Wynbrook, Mrs. Saunders was escorted out of the room, leaving Kate and Robert to interview their old housekeeper. Wynbrook turned back to her and mouthed the words *good luck*.

She smiled back at him. Truly, the man could be helpful when he set his mind to it.

"Mrs. Hennings," said Kate when they were alone in the room, "I fear Darington and I may come to peril if we do not know who our enemy is."

Mrs. Hennings gritted her teeth but slowly nodded her head. "You should know, you should know. I hope you shall not think too badly of me."

"Never, especially if you would help us now."

Mrs. Hennings sat taller in her chair and closed her eyes as if going back in time and watching the events as they occurred. "Your mother died bringing you into the world, poor dears. At first, I feared you two may not make it, for you were so small, but your father loved you dearly. I think it was his love what saved you."

Unexpected tears sprang to Kate's eyes with that small piece of information. She had few memories of her father. He had been gone much of their young childhood, and when he'd finally returned, he was nearly blind. "Go on," she said roughly.

"Lord Darington's eyes were never good after a flash of gunpowder nearly blinded him in the war. But soon he began to become ill. We sent for the doctor, of course, and there were pills and bloodletting and draughts to be given. I always made sure he received everything the doctor told us to do. His steward insisted on sending for a doctor he knew from London, saying that he would be better than our old country practitioner. I don't know about that, for it seemed he only got worse.

"After you two were sent on to school, strange things started happening. At first, pieces of silverware would come up missing, and then one day, it was all gone, just gone. I reported it, of course, to the butler, but he told me not to worry. The next day he was gone. I never saw him again." She began to wring her hands.

"Do not fret. You did all you could," soothed Kate, not wanting her to stop her tale.

"Yes, I did, but what was I to do? More and more things went missing. Finally, the steward told me that the earl was in dire financial straits and the things must be sold to pay his debts. Most of the staff was let go and we shut up most of the house. I was glad you and Robert were off at school, and I hoped Lord Darington would recover and be able to set things to rights. The doctor came more frequently and stayed with us for a while with his teenage son. By this time, practically everything that wasn't nailed down was sold. I was starting to look for a new position, you understand, not knowing how much longer they could afford to pay me. In truth, towards the end, I had not received my pay in over four months."

"You are a good woman, Mrs. Hennings, to continue to serve my father so."

Mrs. Hennings became more agitated, wringing her hands. She did not look at Kate but stared once more out of the window. Fortunately, she continued her tale.

"Then came the night his lordship passed away." Her voice was strained. "I had just posted the letters, informing your schools of the earl's passing and requesting that you and your brother return home at once. It was late and I wished for some tea to steady my nerves, so I went down to the kitchen to prepare it. I heard voices. It was the doctor, berating the cook, saying 'You gave him too much' and 'I didn't want him to die yet.'"

"He didn't want my father to die *yet*?" asked Kate.

"Aye, that's what he said. I thought it strange too and turned to leave, but he must have heard me, for the next thing I knew, he was beside me on the stairs. 'You ought not be eavesdropping on conversations,' he told me. 'I would hate to have you repeat anything you heard and have anything happen to your sweet children.'"

"Your children?" asked Kate.

"Aye, I was so afeared, but I went to the steward and reported to him what happened and my fears over the well-being of my children and you two as well. I hoped all would be well, but the doctor confronted me the next day with…" She began to sob and shake.

"Do not fret." Kate tried to comfort the woman, who appeared as if she might shake herself apart.

The old housekeeper wrapped her arms around herself, as if to keep her together. "That demon doctor, if he ever was such, grabbed my arm and said he knew I had told the steward. He handed me a golden curl from my baby daughter's head and said if I opened my mouth again, none of my children would never wake to see the morn." The housekeeper brushed the tears away with the back of her hand. "I was so afraid. I knew if he thought I would tell anyone, he would kill all my babes. I thought if I were dead, my children would be safe. So I…I…"

"Oh, Mama!" cried her daughter, running into the room, while Emma and Wynbrook stood behind her. "You were trying to protect us? Why did you never tell us?" They embraced each other tightly, and Kate felt tears in her own eyes.

Wynbrook handed her a handkerchief. She took it and blotted her eyes. "I do not suppose you know the name of this evil doctor?" asked Kate.

"He went by the name of Dr. Bones, but I am certain that was not his real name. He was in his midthirties perhaps, a muscular man, with black hair and gray eyes that squinted when he talked."

Kate took a deep breath and blew it out. Wynbrook's warm hand rested on her shoulder, comforting and strong. It was a lot to take in. Something evil had infected their house, in the form of a nefarious doctor.

And her father, her poor father, had been murdered—poisoned. She did not say anything until she was surer of her voice. "I wish there were a way to know who this man was or why he did something so horrible."

"I do not know why," said Mrs. Hennings with a sniff, "but I might know his name."

Kate held her breath.

"The doctor, he stayed at Greystone before his lordship passed and I did his laundry. In one of his coats, I found a letter."

"Did it have a name?" whispered Kate. It was the loudest sound she could make.

"Captain Harcourt."

Thirty-three

"CAPTAIN HARCOURT?" ASKED WYNBROOK WHEN they were back outside the cottage. "The Captain Harcourt whom your father exposed as a traitor?"

Kate nodded her head, her stomach too tied in knots to answer. Harcourt was alive? Impossible. Yet it explained everything.

"Oh my stars!" gasped Emma.

"They went to arrest Harcourt for treason, but the ship taking him back to England was lost at sea. He and all souls aboard were presumed dead," said Dare in a voice like gravel.

"That is why we have been so cursed. He came back to effect his revenge. Evil, hateful man!" Kate was so angry she could have spit. Robert had a glint of murder in his eye.

"At least you finally know the truth of what happened," said Wynbrook.

"Yes. Thank you for suggesting we talk to the housekeeper," said Kate, pacing back and forth. She needed to do something with the pent-up emotion she felt.

"Perhaps you would like to walk back to the

house?" suggested Wynbrook, correctly guessing her need to do something active, preferably attacking Captain Harcourt but a walk would do.

"Yes, that would be good. It would be good indeed."

Robert put a hand on her shoulder, his eyes silently asking his question.

"Yes, I am all right. Just angry," she said.

"It is good to know, for now something can be done." His tone was ominous.

Robert handed Emma into the carriage and drove off, leaving Wynbrook and Kate to walk home. She set off at a fast clip, walking along the beach for a while before the trail turned inland. She had walked the path many times as a girl and much remained the same.

Wynbrook said nothing but kept pace with her, a silent comfort. Her father had been murdered. Murdered!

"I cannot believe it!" she finally cried out. "I want to murder that man myself!"

"If you mean Harcourt, I believe your brother will take care of the matter. Do you think he is behind your recent attack?"

"If he discovered we had made a fortune, he would certainly try to come back and destroy our lives once more. Vicious beast!"

Their path turned to a low bluff overlooking the ocean, and Kate paused to look out over the restless waves. The wind was brisk and biting, stinging her face. Wynbrook put an arm around her, drawing her close, comforting her.

"I hope the revelations today can help put to rest some of the difficult memories of your past," said Wynbrook.

"I fear my past will always afflict me."

"Indeed, I hope not. I would like to see us happy after such pain and trial."

Us? Kate sighed. When would he ever understand that there was no *us*? "Your persistence does you credit, but my answer to your question is still no. Nothing revealed today changes that," said Kate severely.

"Still refusing to marry me? My pride may at some point be hurt by your refusals."

"Wouldn't you rather marry Emma St. James?" asked Kate, voicing the streak of jealousy that had taken hold.

"Why would I wish to do that?"

"Why wouldn't you? She's pretty, smart, cheerful, kind, and has a host of other redeeming attributes I will never have. She can stitch up a wound with one hand and serve you tea with the other. Hell, *I* want to marry Emma St. James."

Wynbrook laughed. "Then we are both doomed to disappointment, for I will wed none but you."

"But…why?" Kate was exasperated. "Why not marry someone more like you?"

"If I wanted to marry some chit accustomed to society, I would have done it by now. I have been hunted as a matrimonial prize for years, though I know you will think me vain for saying it. I know the talk about Lord Devine's niece and myself. But no one makes me feel so…so alive as you."

They continued on the path back to Greystone Hall, the waves foaming and roaring beside them. A storm was coming. A storm was also raging in her heart as she tried to express why she could not be a fit wife yet all the while longing she could say yes.

"You have no idea what I've seen. When the

ships came into port, they ran the bumboats to ferry women to the ship. Most of the crew wasn't allowed to leave, so the women got brought aboard. Some were girlfriends or wives, but many others were there for a sailor to pay her coin for a go at her. I have seen things I ought not have seen."

"I am so sorry this has happened to you. But I think you are amazingly brave. I would be honored to have such a wife."

"But..." Kate stared at him. Had he not just heard what she had said? "I'm ruined!"

"You are still a maiden, you say?"

Kate nodded.

"Then you are not ruined."

"But in London, a lady can be ruined for taking a walk down the street by herself or being caught in conversation with a man without a chaperone. Do you know how many times I've been alone with a man, or a group of them for that matter? By London standards, I am a hopeless case."

"But we are not using London standards. Forgive me, but you do not understand the nature of being ruined. You can do whatever you want to as long as nobody catches you. Yes, you had a most unconventional education, but the point is no one knows but me. Thus, you are not ruined."

He frowned a little as he considered what he had just said. "Or at least, you weren't. When someone caught you leaving with me in the coach, an elopement was assumed. If you return to London unwed, you would not be welcomed back into society. We must both be married—to each other—to avoid censure."

"So you're telling me that I can spend a year on a navy vessel, surrounded by men with not a chaperone in sight, and still my reputation could be intact as long as nobody knew?"

"Yes, quite."

"Though when my brother is kidnapped and I try to rescue him with an old friend, my reputation is in tatters. Am I understanding this correctly?"

"Yes, I do believe you are getting the gist of this." He grinned at her, the wind playing with his light brown hair.

"That is ridiculous! This makes no sense."

"True," said Wynbrook, utterly nonplussed.

Kate paused to look out over the ocean. The sky was gray with clouds that hung heavy with rain, threatening to unleash at any moment, and the ocean below them was dark and grumbling.

"Can you not see that everything I have experienced makes me unfit?" She had believed it for so many years, it was hard to let go of a long-held truth.

"Perhaps everything you experienced has given you the strength and the ability to face your challenges."

"Have you been talking to Miss St. James? She said something similar. Some verse about tribulations causing perseverance causing experience causing hope or some such."

"I tell you the truth. When you told me Dare was abducted, my first thought was to find a magistrate or travel on to find the Bow Street Runners. If you were not there, I would not have raced off to find him myself. You knew what to do because you have been in crises before and were not afraid to respond."

"You think so?" asked Kate, barely audible over the rush of the wind around them. It was a strange thought that the very experiences that she felt made her unacceptable had actually given her the ability to help her family.

"If we had not left immediately and stuck with the chase, who knows how long Miss St. James and Dare would have been able to hold out without being discovered. You did that. No prim society miss would have been able to do the same. You saved your brother's life."

Kate said nothing, stunned by this new perspective of herself. Her past was not a millstone around her neck; it was valuable experience that gave her unique capabilities. They walked on in silence as she considered this new possibility.

A flock of magpies flew overhead, looking for shelter from the oncoming storm. She tried to count them as they flew, reciting an old nursery rhyme about the fortune-telling magpies. "*One for sorrow, Two for joy, Three for a girl, Four for a boy, Five for silver, Six for gold, Seven for a secret never to be told.*"

"Do not stop there," said Wynbrook.

"I beg your pardon?"

"The rest of the rhyme."

"There is no more."

"Oh, but there is. *Eight bring wishing, Nine bring kissing, Ten the love my own heart's missing!*"

"You are making that up!" she accused.

"Indeed, I am not." He laughed. He paused at the top of the bluff, looking over the tempestuous sea, and she stood beside him. "Kate, I wish to marry you. The more you reveal of yourself, the more I admire you. But if your heart is truly against me, please tell me now. I wish to save both our reputations, but I do not wish to make us both unhappy for the rest of our lives. Better to live on the Continent than to see you miserable." He smiled brightly, but there was tension to it.

There it was. He would not pursue her any longer if she would only tell him that she had no romantic interest in him. It was easy. All she had to do was agree and the whole affair would be settled. Of course, she would never again be allowed to enter society, which would not do her brother any good, but she could return to Gibraltar and live out the rest of her life the way she had always planned, masquerading as a widow, managing the business from there. Everything would return to the way it was. All she had to do was agree.

"I shall return to Gibraltar." It was all she could say, and even then she could not look at him. She could not look at him and lie.

"So our kisses, you did not care for them?" His voice sounded slightly strangled.

"I... That is to say..." What was she going to say to him?

A slow smile returned to his lips and a mischievous glint came to his smoky-green eyes. "So you want to kiss me."

She should have known he would never let her go that easily. She turned away from him, taking a turn at looking at the scenery. At first glance, it was nothing more than a blustery gray day, but it had wild beauty of its own. The wind tugged at her bonnet, pulling strands of hair free from the tight knot of her bun. "I think it best to forget any such behavior…connection…between us." She struggled to find the right word and knew she had failed miserably.

"Connection?" Leave it to that man to pounce on the one word she wished she had not said. He moved closer to her. She could not see his face for she kept the brim of her bonnet low.

Taking a chance, she raised the brim ever so slightly, turning her head just enough to catch a glimpse of him through the corner of her eye. He was an insufferably handsome man, with a square jaw to match his square shoulders. If he had any consideration for her, he would not dress to such perfection nor would he choose garments that hugged his body, revealing his muscular form.

"It seems you are a bit unsure," he commented in a casual tone. "Perhaps if we try again, we can determine whether an actual connection between us exists."

"Try again?" asked Kate, turning her head a little more so that she could see him fully. She should not have asked, but she could not help herself.

"The kiss," said Wynbrook simply, as if it were a matter of offering a cup of tea. "If you are not sure if you find me appealing or repulsive, I suggest we attempt to kiss once more to determine your true feelings in the matter. It would seem a logical course." Though his tone was benign, his eyes gleamed with impish mischief.

Kate swallowed hard. What was she to say to this?

"Besides, I would like to know the truth. Did you or did you not enjoy kissing me?"

Kate stared at him like a rabbit caught in a snare. "I was not unaffected by the kiss."

"Not unaffected?"

She cleared her throat. "It was…nice."

"Nice? No, I beg you, anything but nice. Tell me it was awful, tell me it was vile, tell me you would rather kiss a codfish, but please, do not placate me with 'nice.'"

"Nice is…nice," she protested.

"No, nice is not nice. Nice is getting a scarf from your aunt for Christmas. Nice is a hug from your sister. My kisses cannot possibly be nice."

A smile crept onto her face. "I cannot deny your kisses were nice, for they were quite good."

"Good is better. But I still feel you are lacking a certain finesse when it comes to describing the experience of the kiss. It is, after all, important that the record be clear on this matter so we can move on, knowing exactly the state of affairs."

Kate narrowed her eyes at him. "You want to kiss me again, don't you?"

"Yes, yes I do. I'd like to do it again and again, and tomorrow and the day after that and the day after that. In truth, I'd like to kiss you every day of your life."

"If you hope to trap me into marriage—"

"My dear, we've already been trapped into marriage. Now come here and let's make the best of it."

He reached out to her, and she could not resist being gently drawn into his arms. He softly put a hand on her shoulder and ran it around her back, moving in closer. He brushed his lips against hers and heat flushed her cheeks, sending tingles down her spine. He paused a moment, retreating an inch. She could feel the heat of his breath on her skin and waited for his next move, but he did not make it. Instead, he held still, gorgeous and inviting. She should deny him, deny herself, but she could not.

She pressed forward, meeting his lips with hers, running a hand around from his cheek to the back of his neck. His lips were warm and inviting, and she could not resist initiating the kiss. He did not disappoint and returned her kiss with a gentle power. Excitement coursed through her veins and she pressed closer, wanting more of him. Suddenly, alarm bells rang in her head and she pulled back with a start.

She gasped for breath. "I cannot do this."

"Forgive me, but it seems very much that you can, and more to the point, you just did."

"I concede that I enjoy kissing you."

"A fine concession."

"But to be married, more would be expected."

A delicious grin spread across his face. "Yes, indeed."

"But what if I cannot do more? I cannot tolerate the thought that my body would no longer be my own." She began to stride toward Greystone again with him by her side, his long legs easily keeping up with her furious pace.

A brisk wind blew against her face, the cold like tiny needles on her skin. Yet she turned her face more to the chilling gusts. She knew she needed to speak the hidden truths that would forever bar her from any relationship with the man beside her. Despite being insistent that no union between them could ever exist, she found herself hesitant, standing on the brink of the abyss of love lost.

"When I joined the Navy in disguise, I always had a fear that I would be discovered. I saw the way those men treated women. I feared if they found out, I could be hurt. I could be assaulted. I learned to be wary, to protect myself." She cleared her throat. She had never confided this fear to anyone. "I fear I could not be a wife to you or to anyone because the thought of belonging to someone, of losing control over my own physical being... I cannot abide it."

Thunder grumbled in the distance and rain began to fall lightly.

"You did not seem uncomfortable when we slept together at the inn."

"I kept my knife under my pillow."

Wynbrook paled. "I see. Rather glad I did not know it. I do recall waking up to your being rather friendly."

Despite the cold wind and rain chilling her face, heat rose to her cheeks. She had hoped he would forget the incident. "It is different if I am the one to initiate."

"Well then, it's simple. You may initiate." He gave her a cheeky grin, though there was concern in his eyes.

"And what if you had to wait?"

"I would wait."

"What if I could never tolerate it?" She turned and looked at him squarely. "Marriage is like slavery for women. All my money, all my possessions, my very body would belong to my husband. I have defended myself for so long and enjoyed complete freedom, I do not know if I could ever abide it."

"I would never force you to my bed. Not ever." Wynbrook was firm and she believed him.

"Are you prepared to live in chastity for the rest of your life?"

Wynbrook frowned but said nothing.

"Or would you take up a mistress?"

He shook his head.

"But you would. And I would be miserable. And you would be miserable. Do you not see why we should not wed? Why I should never wed anyone?"

"What I see is a beautiful lady who deserves more than to be alone for the rest of her life." Wynbrook held out his hand to her. He did not demand. He simply asked. Tentatively, she took it. His gloved fingers closed around hers, warm and protective. "I know what I feel when I kiss you. When we kiss each other. I have never felt anything like it. A connection like that does not happen every day. I will trust in us."

Kate had to blink back tears. No one had ever said anything so kind, so compassionate to her. "You still wish to marry me?"

Wynbrook slowly dropped to one knee before her on the cold, wet ground. "Lady Kate. I am honored you have chosen to reveal yourself to me. The more I learn of you, the more my admiration for you grows. Would you do me the honor of becoming my wife?"

Something within her cracked open, like something that had long been frozen beginning to thaw. She had been utterly convinced if Wynbrook knew the truth, he would run away. She had misjudged him.

"Kate." Wynbrook spoke her name reverently. "Will you marry me?"

There was nothing else she could say.

"Yes."

Thirty-four

Eight bring wishing

THE HEAVENS OPENED UP AND IT BEGAN TO POUR down rain. Wynbrook stood up and their lips met, hot and passionate, the cold rain running in rivulets down their faces, blending together as they pressed together, unable to get close enough. A sudden flash blinded her for a moment, and Wynbrook held her tight as thunder cracked above them.

"Come, let us run for the house before we are struck down," yelled Wynbrook over the increasing roar of the wind and waves.

Fortunately, the tall outline of Greystone Hall was in sight and they ran for it, hand in hand. The rain and wind whipped about them, stirring up the mud at their feet. Kate was certain they would look a splattered mess when they finally arrived, but she cared not. She grinned into the storm, the kind words of John, her future husband, ringing in her ears. As they reached the edge of Greystone and made their way around the corner of the building to the front door, she thought she saw a shadowy figure standing by some low brush by the side of the house.

She stopped and turned back, but the figure was gone.

"What is it?" asked John.

"Thought I saw someone."

"Come on. Let us go inside or we'll both catch our deaths." He pulled her along to the door.

Outside the door was a large, muddy puddle. She paused, not wanting to wade through and completely ruin her boots. To her surprise, John lifted her up into his arms and carried her across the mud to the house.

Mrs. Brooke rushed up, her face a picture of concern as they entered the house. "What is this, now? Has milady hurt herself?"

"No, no, I am fine," reassured Kate. "Only wet is all and avoiding the mud, thanks to Lord Wynbrook. Thank you. I am sure I can manage from here." Despite the chill of her soaking wet clothes, her face burned. Instead of setting her down, John proceeded to carry her up the stairs as if she weighed nothing at all. "Put me down. You're making a scene," she hissed at him.

John appeared not to hear her, or at least he did not listen to her, for he continued to carry her up to her bedroom. Finally, he set her down on a chair. Mrs. Brooke bustled in after him.

"Quick, Mrs. Brooke, get hot water and send for her maid. Lady Kate will be needing a hot bath immediately," said Wynbrook, taking command.

"Yes, my lord." Mrs. Brooke bobbed a curtsy and left the room.

Kate wished to argue with him, but a hot bath did sound rather good.

"We need to get you out of these wet things." John began fumbling with the buttons of her coat, but she swatted his hands away.

"The maid will tend me. You need to care for yourself, for you are just as wet and twice as muddy."

John looked down at his own coat, recognizing for the first time that he was sopping wet.

"You're puddling," Kate accused, for he was creating a muddy mess from water dripping off his coat and boots.

"Good thing I left my valet behind. He would suffer apoplexy to see me now." He grinned at her. She grinned at him. Suddenly, they were kissing again.

"Ahem," said Mrs. Brooke sternly, standing in the open doorway.

"Ah, Mrs. Brooke. Please also send up a hot bath for Lord Wynbrook, for he will be needing one as well," said Kate.

"Very good," Mrs. Brooke said in a voice laced with disapproval.

"Please do take care of Lady Kate," said John. "We can't have the future Lady Wynbrook catching cold."

"Oh! Oh, indeed not. Now I understand." Mrs. Brooke was all smiles.

≈

The next day, Kate awoke with a strange sense of calm. She had lived with the uncertainty of their enemy for most of her life. Now that she finally knew, it was like being able to breathe fully after living with a weight pressed down on her chest. Not that the truth was easy to hear, but at least she knew who her enemy was.

And who her friends were.

Some thoughts of Wynbrook made her smile and others made her blush. She expected to feel panicked at the thought of giving away her freedoms to another human being, but instead, she felt a giddy excitement at becoming his wife. Very strange.

A soft rap at the door brought her brother, already fully and somberly dressed.

"Hello, Robert," she said and sat in the window seat, inviting him to sit beside her. "Well, now we know."

"Now we know," he agreed.

"Do you think the robbers and the kidnappers are in league with Captain Harcourt?"

"Don't know, but I can think of none other who would wish us more harm. We'll know no peace until he is brought to justice or dead."

Kate looked out the frosted window at the white-capped breakers of the ocean. "You are going after him."

"Yes."

"But your injury. Are you well?"

Robert shrugged in a noncommittal manner. "Well enough. I must go."

"I know you must. Please do be careful."

"Always. I wish I could be here to see you wed. I'm glad you decided on Wynbrook. He's a good man."

She gave her brother a small smile. "What of Emma?"

Emotion flickered across his face. "She is an extraordinary girl."

"And adorable."

The faintest of smiles hovered about his lips. "And adorable. But engaged to another."

"But—"

"And it would not be safe to involve her with me until Captain Harcourt and his men are found."

She knew it was true. If they would not stop at abducting her to get to her brother, they would certainly not stop at attacking Emma as well. "When will you leave?"

"This morning. I will drive Emma and her maid down with me. Her ship leaves soon."

"Be safe and return to me." It was what she always said when he sailed off to sea.

"Stay well and remember me."

❧

"As your solicitor, I do not recommend you sign it." Kate handed Wynbrook the marriage contract she had prepared. She asked if he would meet her before breakfast in the study to review the document she had prepared.

"Why not?" he asked, quill in hand.

"It is a rather bad deal for you. It allows you no access to my dowry, which will be available for me to spend as I see fit during my lifetime and then put in trust to be given in equal portions to any of the children our union should create."

"I have no problem with it," said John and began to sign the paper.

"But wait!" cried Kate, putting a hand on his sleeve to stay his hand. "You will get nothing from the union. None of the dowry, which by law should be yours. This is a bad deal. As your solicitor, I strongly urge you not to sign it."

John smiled at her and signed the paper. "I am not

marrying you for your money, nor am I concerned that you will spend a ha'penny in a frivolous manner. I am marrying you for you. Nothing more is needed."

Kate was filled with a warm glow and floated to the breakfast room with the others. After breakfast, she and Wynbrook saw Robert and Emma off on their journey. Robert made a somber figure in his dark blue wool naval coat, while Emma was a bright flower in a cape of scarlet.

"Thank you so much for your hospitality. I have had a marvelous time," gushed Emma.

"It is we who need to thank you, for you saved the life of my brother," said Kate.

"And he saved me from robbers, so you see, we all have been of service to each other. I wish you and Lord Wynbrook every happiness in the world."

"And I wish the same for you," returned Kate. "Please do write and let me know how you like America. If you need anything at all, including passage back to England, please do not hesitate to apply to us for help."

"I will do that. You are the very best of people, Lady Kate. I am so glad to have met you. This is a verse for your wedding." Emma pressed a piece of paper in her hand.

With a flurry of excitement, smiles, and waves, Emma left the house, followed by the more somber Darington.

"What is the verse?" asked John when they had left.

"It is Second Corinthians 5:17—*Therefore if anyone be in Christ, she is a new creature: old things are passed away; behold, all things are become new.*"

John tilted his head to one side. "She?"

"I think Emma took some liberties with the verse."

John shrugged. "All things become new. I like it."

"Yes. I like it too," said Kate, feeling the verse had aptly captured her feelings of the moment. Everything seemed fresh and new.

John held out his arm with a smile. "Shall we go talk with the rector?"

Thirty-five

Nine bring kissing

HE KISSED HER BEFORE THEY LEFT ON THEIR ERRAND. He kissed her once they arrived at the local parish church. He kissed her after they had found the elderly rector who agreed to marry them on the next day, providing a special license could be procured. He stopped the carriage once, maybe twice on the way back to Greystone to kiss her some more.

And the worst thing was, she enjoyed it. She was a willing partner in all these small crimes of passion. Or maybe, since they were engaged, they were not considered crimes at all.

In the few moments when she was not kissing Wynbrook or thinking about kissing Wynbrook, Kate wondered how he was going to get a special license by the next morning. He did not seem concerned, so she left it to him to figure out.

When they arrived back at Greystone Hall, they found Tristan, Anne, and Ellen waiting for them.

"Hallo, Brother! Well, you have had an adventure!

Where is my portmanteau? I am quite cross at you for riding off with it!" Tristan greeted him with a warm embrace and a slug on the arm.

"I knew it would bring you 'round on the double." John laughed.

Kate stood a bit apart, not sure what her reception would be from his family. Did they fault her for the salacious gossip in the *Times*? She would not blame them if they did.

"Ah, the blushing bride!" Tristan came up to her and gave her a big hug, then realized what he was doing and adjusted his cravat. "So pleased you'll be one of the family. Now that you are to be my sister, my world is complete. When is the wedding? Tomorrow! Well then, you'll be needing this." He handed John the special license.

"You must have had confidence to request the license even before I agreed to marry you," exclaimed Kate.

"Oh, he asked for it ages ago. First day you left," declared Tristan.

"Did you?" Kate raised an eyebrow at her husband-to-be.

"It occurred to me when we were at the inn that a proposal from me would be forthcoming," said John with a smile.

Kate smiled back. He *had* decided to propose before he read the gossip column in the newspaper. Her grin widened.

"Come through to the drawing room, where Anne and Ellen have taken up residence in your absence. Anne has called for tea and will be running your household by sunset if you are not careful," warned Tristan.

Kate was most concerned about meeting Anne, but her reception was warm.

"Well, there you are! I am so glad to hear Lord Darington is alive. Welcome to the family, Kate. I had an inkling you were made for John. He needs a strong hand to keep him in line and I think you shall do nicely!"

"Anne!" chastised John.

They all sat down to tea and told the various sides of the story. Wynbrook, with permission from Kate, told them the story of her father's death and Captain Harcourt, which made Anne pat her hand in a motherly fashion and Ellen cry. Kate's history with the Royal Navy was not made public.

Anne was most concerned about restoring their reputations and with the details of the wedding and the wedding breakfast. When she heard Kate had not thought about the menu, she immediately had a discussion with Mrs. Brooke.

Ellen called her over and Kate sat beside her. "I cannot believe you and Dare were abducted! Have you no idea who these men were?" asked Ellen, clearly riveted by the tale.

"We guess they may have something to do with Captain Harcourt, but as to their individual identities, I do not know. They kept their faces covered, so all I know is that one man has a poor cobbler who put a brass hobnail through the top leather of his boots."

"I do like a good adventure, but this is too much!" exclaimed Ellen. "Though if this gave you a little push in John's direction, I am glad for it for I am so glad you will be marrying John. I hope you will not mind if I live with you from time to time. I can also stay with my sisters."

"Certainly not!" cried Kate. "You are mine to keep. I will not hear of you leaving your home. Unless you wish to go visiting for a while," she amended, trying to be welcoming to Ellen, not her jailer.

Ellen grasped both her hands in hers. "Thank you. I shall love having you for my sister!"

Eventually, everyone had dinner and went off to bed, as the prospect of an early wedding was promised. Despite all the joyful chatter and well wishes, Kate lay awake in bed, her mind too full to sleep.

Gone was the ease she had experienced earlier in the day. Old fears returned in the night, and instead of feeling like a new creation, she fell prey to old worries and concerns. Kate read over the contract again. This was what it came down to. She was legally giving herself to another person, to John Arlington, Earl of Wynbrook.

Though her feelings toward him were decidedly positive, her feelings toward becoming someone's property were equally negative. He could choose where and when she went. He could demand admittance to her bedchamber, deny access to any children they might have, or beat her senseless, and the law would still be on his side.

She did not think he would act in such a manner, but he could, and the thought sickened her. Could she really give this kind of power to any one man? She had tried to give herself as much freedom in the marriage contract as possible, but the truth was, once they were married, Wynbrook had rights to her body. In fact, the law required that she surrender her body to him once they were wed, and she had no recourse to deny him her own physical being.

Kate crawled out of the comfortable bed, wrapped herself in a dressing gown, and began to pace, her feet cold on the wooden floorboards. How could she do this? How could she enter into a relationship that demanded of her the most intimate aspects of her being? She flopped down on the window seat and pressed her forehead against the cold, wet pane of glass. It was a relief to her heated brow.

She had spent so many years protecting her physical being, ensuring no one could touch her. Now with the stroke of a pen and a few vows, she was supposed to be on her back without further complaint. No, it could not be. She could not so suddenly give up the one thing she'd been protecting all these years.

And yet…the prospect of Wynbrook kissing her, caressing her, left her more breathless in anticipation than filled with dread. She did not wish to enflame his pride further by admitting it, but she desired him desperately. It was no use to try to deny it to herself when every fiber of her being yearned to be held in his arms. She was not sure what to name this sickness, this insipid weakness, but she knew her body would make no complaints to sharing his bed.

Kate remembered the strange sensations that arose within her every time they kissed. If she was honest, every kiss awakened in her a new desire, a desire for something more…much more. She had told Wynbrook she was not ready for the kind of physical intimacy shared by man and wife, but that was not true. Her body was on fire for it.

If only she could be with John on her terms, without the impending sense of doom that marital obligation stirred within her. She recalled the comfort she had found in his arms the night at the inn and the way her body had responded to his, the spark of passion he had lit within her. Even in the cold of the room, her cheeks flushed hot with thoughts of all she had long tried to deny.

Tomorrow night, she would be John's bride. Would they share a bed their first night? It was no doubt customary to do so. The marriage was not considered valid until consummated, but then everything they shared would be obligatory. They would be together because they had to, they were required to, not because they wanted to. If she waited until after the wedding, it would be too late.

This was her last night. Her last night to make choices for her own body, choices that were hers and hers alone. This was her last night of freedom.

What would she do with it?

Thirty-six

Ten the love my own heart's missing!

WYNBROOK ALWAYS IMAGINED THE NIGHT BEFORE HIS wedding would be spent in some sort of drunken carousing prior to settling down to married life. Tonight, however, he found himself in an isolated house, snuggled warm and cozy in his bed, a copy of *The Captain's Curse* in hand. With all the excitement, he had not yet been able to figure out how the heroine escaped the crazed peg-legged captain. Considering Kate's opinion of married life, he figured he may be doing a lot of reading in bed and he might as well get used to it. If he was to have no romance in his life, at least he could read about those who did.

He was just getting to a particularly nail-biting moment with the cursing captain knocking three times on the door of the tower room of the distraught heroine when a knock on the door of his own room shocked him back to reality. He looked up from his book, momentarily confused. Had someone locked him in his room and was coming to ravish him senseless?

"Enter," he called, willing to take the risk. To his surprise, Kate entered the room, looking around furtively to ensure there was no one else present, and then barred the door behind her. Perhaps he was being locked in his room after all.

"Is something wrong?" he asked.

She walked up holding a candle, her silver eyes glinting in the candlelight. She was dressed in a simple wrap, her long brown hair falling in thick waves around her. Truly, she looked more faerie than human. He would not have been surprised if she'd sprouted wings and flew around the room.

"I cannot go through with it." Her strange, light eyes filled with unshed tears.

Wynbrook's heart dropped. He was afraid something like this would happen. "What is wrong?"

"I fear we are too different to suit. I think too much of you to let you do something I know will make you miserable for all your life." She placed her candlestick on the nightstand and sat down on the edge of the bed beside him. For a girl trying to give him the heave-ho, she certainly had a friendly way of doing it.

"You think so well of me that you do not wish to marry me?" he repeated. Given how skittish she was about marriage, he was not surprised she was having second thoughts.

"Yes." Kate shifted on the bed, moving closer. Her thick, brown hair pooled around her and he longed to touch it.

"Never mind the institution of marriage. I thought we had established that you did not look upon kissing me with utter abhorrence."

The corner of her mouth twitched. "True."

"Let me understand this correctly. You enjoy being with me, you think well of me, you are attracted to me and enjoy our kisses. Thus, you have come to the conclusion to dissolve the engagement?" He was beginning to enjoy himself. But then, he always enjoyed himself when he was with Kate, and never more than when they matched wits.

"I think the only reason I could enjoy kissing you is because we were *not* married," she said with exasperation.

"I beg your pardon?" He had lost her train of thought entirely, but never had he been so attentive to any conversation. The air between them hummed with anticipation.

"What we shared up until now was because we both gave in to our mutual attraction. After we are wed, I no longer have the choice to refuse. When we speak vows, anything between us will be obligation. To be frank, if I could share your bed without the unwanted legality of marriage, I do believe it would be…acceptable."

Wynbrook held his breath. He was not sure if she was truly saying what he thought she was saying. If it were anyone else, he would think it was some sort of perverse joke, but he knew Kate was incapable of such mean-spirited humor. "So you would like to share my bed, but only if we are not married. It is that what I'm hearing?"

Kate paused a moment and looked him square in the eye. "Yes, I suppose it is."

"So the natural conclusion is that we live together without the benefit of marriage." It was the most inter-esting conversation he'd ever had. In bed or otherwise.

"No, that is not possible. If nothing else, Robert would kill you."

Robert would kill him—besides, he had no intention of making Kate his mistress. He realized anticipating his wedding vows was not technically proper, but they would be married in a few hours, so what could it hurt?

"So what do you suggest? Is there any hope for us?" He reached out and stroked her hair, twisting a lock around one finger. He was playing with fire.

"Do you want there to be hope for us?" she asked breathlessly.

"Kate, I want to marry you. I want to take you to bed tonight and every night of my life. Any other lady would seem utterly dull and lifeless compared to you."

Kate's face, generally so firm and rigid, relaxed, and she gave him a true smile. "It is kind of you to say. I wish there was such a world in which we could be together, without obligations and contracts."

"We have tonight," he suggested softly.

"Would you be willing?" she asked in a small voice. "Would you be willing to spend the night with me?" She could not even look at him when she asked.

"The price is marriage. You must know that."

"Yes, but at least I would have one night when my body was my own."

He did not wait for her to change her mind but drew her into his arms to kiss her. She responded, wrapping her arms around him. This was one thing they did well. She was not the first woman he had kissed, but he was perfectly content with having her be the last.

She deepened the kiss, sparking fire within him. Despite it being a cold January night, he was burning hot. Excitement pulsed through his veins as she pressed herself closer to him, her softness melting into him.

"Admit it, you came here with the nefarious intent to ravish me senseless," he whispered in her ear when she at last allowed him to take a breath.

"Yes, I did." And she giggled—an occurrence so extraordinary, he had to pull back to make sure he was still holding Kate. Lady Katherine *never* giggled. But there she was, gazing at him with ethereal eyes and a naughty smile on her face.

"Well! I like you more and more each day!" He trailed kisses down her cheek to the hollow of her neck. "And especially more at night."

He slid a hand down her trim back to a rounded backside. He nearly groaned; he had wanted do to that for so long. He began pulling up the fabric around her, impatient to see her in all her naked glory.

"Wait, stop!" She pulled back, trembling.

He cursed himself for moving too fast. Stupid, stupid. "Forgive me. I…I was a little too eager."

"I do not blame you for wanting me." She looked at him slyly with glinting eyes. "But if this night is to be mine, I must have my way with you."

He had never been more turned on in his life. The bedclothes before him tented and *The Captain's Curse* fell to the floor.

❦

Kate's heart beat in her throat. She had thought she was shy. Apparently, she was not. She just wanted control.

John gave her a slow smile, as if reading her fevered mind. "I will lie back and let you do whatever you wish."

Slowly he pulled his nightshirt up over his head and dropped it over the side of the bed. He reclined back onto the pillows, a perfect model of masculinity. His tawny hair was mussed in an adorable manner. Stubble shadowed his square jaw. His chiseled chest rippled with muscles, just as it sent ripples of excitement down her spine. His green eyes beckoned her to come take a chance.

She moved forward and slid her hands up his chest, thrilling in the feel of him—warm, soft, yet solid and muscular. Truly, no man should be so attractive. But she was awfully glad he was. It should not make a difference to her what he looked like under his clothes, and certainly she did not like him because of it, but his chiseled physique was a delicious, sweet treat.

She ran her hands down his arms, enjoying the feel of his hardened muscles, which she suspected he was tensing just to give her a little show. No matter what he did, he was a glorious specimen of man. She pulled the covers down slowly, gradually unwrapping the present that was just for her.

The muscles of his lower abdomen and the little trail of hair leading down from his belly button made her heart pound. She was hot and sweaty in unmentionable places. She continued to pull down the covers until she revealed him in all his naked glory.

She had seen a naked man before. Even an aroused man. Living on board a naval vessel had left little to the imagination, but this was different. He was standing up proudly for her, only for her.

"You must like me a lot," she murmured.

"Immensely."

"I do not wish you to get a big head," she scolded.

"Too late!" He grinned at her.

She was not certain what to do next. He was naked before her. She was ready for more. She had a fairly decent idea of what more was, but how did one get from here to there?

"This is rather awkward," she confessed.

"We have a lifetime to practice," he said seductively, looking as comfortable lying naked before her as he did walking into a ballroom. "I do not suppose I could induce you to remove your wrap?"

Being a fair-minded person, she supposed she should afford him the same view. She unwrapped her dressing gown slowly, not because she was attempting to be seductive, but because she was unsure of what she was doing. Her wrapper fell around her on the bed, revealing a gauzy nightgown.

John parted his lips in anticipation. Gone was the suave, confident lover. He gazed at her with an intense longing that gave her pause. And made her continue. He looked like he wanted to devour her. Never in her life had she felt so desired. This might have been power, but it was terrifying.

She slowly pulled up her nightgown, bunching it in her hands. Was she truly going to do this? Nobody had seen her naked. Maybe the midwife who'd delivered her, but after that, no one.

She took a deep breath and pulled the nightgown up and over her head in one swift movement. His breath caught and he sat up in bed toward her. She trembled, whether from the cold or the intensity of his gaze she did not know.

"You are so beautiful." His voice was awed. It gave her hope. "And so small."

She was crushed. She crossed her arms over her breasts. She knew she did not have a mountainous bosom, but it was hardly chivalrous to mention her flaws when she was naked before him.

"No, I am not talking about your breasts, which are perfect by the way and I do hope you will allow me to pay them due homage. I speak of you. Your waist is tiny."

She was not sure if this was a good thing. "I have not a huge appetite."

"It is only that you are such a strong person, I am surprised to find all that power in a petite form." He held out his hands to her, beckoning her.

She allowed herself to be drawn into his embrace. It felt better with his arms around her. And warmer. He lay back down and she came with him, stretching herself out on top of him. He drew the blankets up around them, and that was a comfort too, keeping her warm and out of view.

"The candles?" she asked.

He pinched the wicks, heedless of the flames, casting them into complete darkness. This was better.

"May I touch you?" he whispered.

"My back," she relented and was rewarded with warm, powerful hands kneading up and down her back, massaging out the painful knots until she was like jelly on top of him. This she could get used to. Oh, yes, this was definitely something she wanted repeated. Often.

"My arms," she suggested, and he focused his attention on her arms, rubbing out the tension from her shoulders down to her hands. This was delightful.

"My neck." His strong hands moved to her neck, up to the back of her head. He seemed to know exactly where to touch her and how to touch her. She may have groaned a little.

"My…thighs." She had wanted to say something else but lost her nerve.

He coaxed her legs up so she was straddling him. His breath caught and he trembled beneath her. She felt open and very naughty. He massaged her thighs and heat built up inside her, yearning for release. It was good, but she wanted more, needed more.

"My backside." His hands were finally on her derrière, where she had wanted them since the night began, possibly since the night of their first kiss. This was heaven, but still she wanted more.

"More." It was the only word she had, and he knew what she wanted. He reached down to the place between them. She groaned again. She was ready to explode.

"Kate," his voice was raspy. "Kate, I cannot hold out much longer. Can we?"

"Yes, now!"

He rolled her over and they were joined. Pleasure and pain and then pure pleasure. The man knew what he was doing, and she surrendered willingly to the delicious tension he built within her. She could not hold back. She needed to trust him, wholly, fully, and she did. She cried out as her world exploded into sheer bliss. He shuddered and moaned and collapsed on top of her. Had she killed him?

He slid his full weight off of her but kept his arms around her, cradling her. "Incredible," he murmured.

"You liked it?" she asked tentatively. It was earth-shattering for her, but her experience was limited to a repertoire of one.

"Liked? My dear, sweet girl, I have never been more...or had such... Oh, I can't even form words right now. Suffice to say, if the rest of our married life will be celibate, I will still be satisfied."

"Oh, my dear, sweet man. Our marriage may be many things, but it will *not* be celibate." Of this she was certain.

"I am ecstatic to hear it."

"So...can we do it again?"

Thirty-seven

WYNBROOK AWOKE WITH THE SMILE STILL ON HIS face. He reached for her before remembering that he had escorted her back to her chamber in the early morning, before the house had awoken. They had whispered and giggled like guilty children stealing sticky treats. He rolled over in bed and breathed deeply. Her scent, an intoxicating mix of soap and lavender, still lingered on the pillows.

Kate's arrival the night before had been most unexpected. In truth, he had prepared himself for a long time of marital celibacy before Kate would be ready to share his bed. He had shoved aside his more amorous impulses, not wanting to frighten her away, particularly since she was overly skittish to begin with. But last night…last night was beyond anything he had allowed himself to dream.

He took a deep breath of the cool, early morning air. The fire had been lit in the grate, but the room was still chill and frost shone like sparkling diamonds on the windowpane. Today, he would marry Lady Katherine. Life was very good indeed.

Tristan had been good enough to bring John's valet, and with his help, Wynbrook was soon dressed in a light gray, double-breasted tailcoat with a striped gray-and-silver silk waistcoat. He wished to go speak to Kate at once, but he knew there would be a host of female objections to such a move, for it would be terribly bad luck to meet with the bride prior to the wedding. He wasn't sure how anticipating their vows the night before fell in the balance of good versus bad luck, but he hoped very much for a reprieve. They had endured enough difficulties. It was time to start afresh with something good in their lives.

"You look very well," said Anne when he walked into the drawing room. She looked him over with a critical eye and gave him a nod of approval.

"I am glad I am not a complete discredit to you. How is my bride-to-be this morning?"

Anne scowled at him. "She certainly has a mind of her own. But I sat her down for a discussion, and after a while, she came 'round to my point of view regarding her wedding clothes and specifically the veil," said his sister darkly.

Having been the recipient of several of his elder sister's "discussions," John felt no small measure of sympathy for Kate. He did not know the exact nature of the debate regarding wedding attire, but he was sure he would not wish to get in between those indomitable females in a head-to-head debate.

"I hope you have not badgered her to death."

His sister raised an eyebrow. "Not to death. Just until she complied."

"Poor Kate."

"Poor Kate? I'll have you know I was talking to her for at least two hours. You might have some sympathy for your sister."

"Yes, of course I do. And I appreciate your efforts to remedy the situation we find ourselves in. I do apologize if our hasty wedding has caused you any embarrassment or trouble."

His sister waved off the comment. "You did what had to be done. Darington was in trouble and you had to render assistance. I only wish you could have done so without taking Kate along."

"I wish I could have too. But she knew what the coach looked like and I did not. Besides, there was very little hope of convincing her not to go. I believe she felt more strongly about running after her brother than you do about wedding clothes."

"Well then, it would have been hopeless for you to try to discourage her," said his sister with a small smile. "In any case, I believe with the correct handling of the situation, we may be able to come out all right. I have been busy with my correspondence, telling the tale we need to distribute amongst our friends and relations, in the hope that it will be disseminated and believed."

"Perhaps you should let me know what the story is, that way I can be more ready to confirm."

"Yes, yes, that would be wise. I have told my friends that Darington was called back to service on an urgent matter and was on his way to Portsmouth to meet with his ship when he was attacked by robbers. He defended himself bravely, dispatching several and chasing off the rest, but in the process was shot. He lay at death's door, and missives were sent to his sister and best friend—that is you, my dear brother—to come as soon as may be to render aid and potentially hear his last words."

"Very dramatic. I do hope we arrived in time."

"A little drama does a lot in misdirecting attention," explained his sister. "Given the dire circumstances, Lady Kate and yourself, who had recently become engaged but had held off announcing it so as not to overshadow Jane's wedding, set out at once. You found Darington and nursed him back to health at the Darington family seat at Greystone Hall. Once he recovered, you were married in her local parish with his blessing. After spending the wedding night at Greystone Hall, you will travel to Brighton for the honeymoon before returning to London."

"Sounds like you have considered most everything." John was much impressed. "And Miss St. James?"

"I saw no need to mention her. Though we are most indebted for her assistance, it seems embroiling her in this particular adventure would in no way be of service to her."

"Yes, I agree. What are the possibilities of honeymooning in the Lake District instead of Brighton?"

Anne shrugged. "As you wish, but you must return to London as soon as possible and show yourselves to be man and wife."

"Yes, I suppose you're right."

"You suppose I am right? Of course I am right. Honestly, Brother, when will you learn to accept that I know all?" The last was spoken with a humorous twinkle in her eye.

John gave her leave to gloat. Considering how

much trouble they had brought themselves in this adventure, she had very neatly devised a story that accounted for their actions and would be satisfactory to all except for the true high sticklers, but they weren't very good company anyhow.

❧

Wynbrook stood at the front of the church, facing the local rector who looked even older than the ancient stone chapel. There were more people in the chapel than he'd expected. He had anticipated only his siblings and the household staff. Clearly, the elderly rector had let slip that a wedding of some magnitude was to be held, for many people from the sleepy fishing village had arrived to witness the public splendor of such an event. Even Kate's old housekeeper, Mrs. Hennings, along with her daughter, had managed to make an appearance.

Tristan stood next to him, and Anne acted as the matron of honor for Kate. Even Ellen made a rare public appearance in the front pew, the wheeled chair tucked out of sight for the proceedings. Despite the number of people in their Sunday best, it was a considerably smaller wedding than anything he had imagined he would have. He knew if Anne had had her way, he would have had a grand society wedding with hundreds of guests. To be able to marry in a small chapel with the lady who had stolen his heart was an unexpected blessing.

He knew the moment Kate entered the chapel. The air around him crackled and he ached to turn and look at her. Tradition, however, mandated that he remain looking at the rather ancient rector instead of turning to see his bride. It was agony to wait for her to walk up to him where she belonged. She had decided no one could take Robert's place, so she walked herself down the aisle.

"She's beautiful," whispered Tristan.

"I know."

"You haven't seen her today," returned his brother.

Yes, I have. But John kept that observation to himself. They may have anticipated their wedding vows, but he was well and truly married to her in his heart.

At last, Kate stood beside him. She was quite beautiful. He saw his sister's hand in the simple elegance of the silver dress with intricate beaded lace and the ancient lace veil that had graced the heads of many Lady Wynbrooks back through the generations. Anybody could look pretty in an expensive gown, but Kate had something more. There was a flash in her eyes when she looked at him, a spark that was only for him.

"Dearly beloved, we are gathered together here in the sight of God…" The rector began his traditional recitation of the order of marriage. He spoke in a monotone voice of deep reverence—or possibly boredom, having performed the office countless times.

John met Kate's eye. She was lovely. She was brilliant. And she was his.

"I love you," he whispered.

Kate's eyes opened wide. The rector continued on, clearly not hearing him.

"Truly?" breathed Kate.

"Truly. Thought you should know."

Kate said nothing more, but the light in her eyes

shone brighter as a smile grew on her lips. She was the happiest and most beautiful he had ever seen her. He returned her smile. He had spent so many years hiding behind a mask of cool detachment, but when she looked at him and smiled, there was no hope of pretending it did not shake him to his core. He had always hidden his insecurities at being thrust so quickly into the role of the earl after his father died. He feared he could never quite fill those shoes. But if Kate, his most vocal critic, could find in him something she liked, it gave him confidence to feel worthy of her and the title he had inherited.

"Therefore, if any man can show any just cause why they may not lawfully be joined together, let him now speak, or else hereafter forever hold his peace," intoned the rector. He paused the traditional few seconds. Wynbrook smiled at the true, honest smile Kate gave him. He turned to the rector to continue.

Instead, a voice rang out from the back of the church. "I know cause why these two cannot be wed."

Kate gasped. Everyone turned to the back of the chapel. The rector began to continue and then paused, his words trailing off. Clearly, he was unaccustomed to anyone interrupting him at that particular juncture.

A young man strode boldly forward into the chapel. He was dressed as a gentleman, with short, curly black hair and blue eyes. Beside him was a more burly man, dressed in a rough fashion.

"Forgive me for the interruption. I know it must be quite unwanted, but I have a paper you will want to see before you speak your vows." The young man and his companion strolled boldly down the aisle.

"State your name, sir, and your business," demanded Wynbrook, stepping in front of Kate to protect her.

"Forgive the intrusion, but I have just been informed that my father and the late Lord Darington had created a marriage contract between myself and Lady Katherine."

"*What?*" cried Kate, her happy face turned to anguish. John hated the man for that, hated him for ruining his bride's wedding day.

Everyone save Ellen were on their feet. People were talking in an excited manner. The rector tried to calm the overall din of the chapel. Wynbrook tried to find something to say. How could this be happening?

"May we see the document?" Wynbrook asked. The parchment was produced and Kate snatched it out of the man's hand and read it over.

"I cannot believe this. What was your association with our family?" demanded Kate.

"Apparently, our fathers made an accord long ago," stated the young man. "Perhaps we should withdraw from this public place and discuss it more privately."

John looked around at the church packed with eager townsfolk, whispering excitedly at the strange goings-on. "Yes, perhaps you are right." He did not wish to be a show for others, particularly because he knew how much Kate would hate it. They could read over the contract in detail when they were alone.

"I have my carriage outside, if it is convenient," suggested the man with a gallant air.

John was about to comply with the suggestion when he caught Ellen's urgent gesture. *Hobnail boots*, she mouthed to them.

Both he and Kate looked down at the footwear of the gentleman's companion. The man who stood a bit behind the young gentleman was wearing a pair of poorly constructed hobnail boots.

Kate leaned in quickly and whispered in his ear. "That is the man who kidnapped me."

Wynbrook fought the desire to shout to have the man arrested. He could not charge the villain with abducting Kate without revealing something they did not wish made public. He needed to remain impassive. "I beg your pardon. What did you say your name was?"

"Perhaps we should withdraw so as not to embarrass the lady further?" suggested the man in a polite undertone.

"Your name, sir, for in truth you look familiar to me. Have we met?" asked Wynbrook.

"No, no, I am certain we have not," said the man. "I am Captain Silas Bones, at your service." He gave a credible bow.

"The son of Dr. Bones?" Kate's words were like ice; her face had returned to the frozen mask she wore.

"Yes. He treated your father in his illness."

"He *killed* my father, you bastard!" shouted Kate.

Villagers gasped. One woman fainted to the floor and others rushed around her to fan her back to sensibility.

Captain Bones grew a shade paler, but his countenance did not change. "I understand sometimes families can blame the physician when their loved one departs this earth too soon—"

"No more lies, Captain Bones, in this holy place," said Wynbrook, struggling to maintain his civility and control. "The truth is your father poisoned the late Lord Darington."

"Poisoned? No, I assure you—" Bones backed down the church aisle, his man behind him.

"He poisoned my father out of revenge, because your father is none other than the traitor to the Crown, Captain Harcourt!"

The villagers again gasped in shock.

"Who told you that?" Bones asked, his eyes narrowing.

In the pews, Mrs. Hennings opened her mouth in an anguished, silent scream.

"The truth always comes to the fore," said Wynbrook in a cryptic manner. He would never betray the former housekeeper, nor would Kate.

The man's lips were tight, his eyes narrow. "Whatever the sins of my father, I think you will find the contract legal and binding. Do keep the papers. I have another copy. Of course I do not wish to break up such a happy couple, so all I ask is for you to follow the terms of the contract."

"The contract states if I do not wed you, you are entitled to my entire dowry," cried Kate.

Silas Bones shrugged. "I did not write the terms of the agreement. But it was signed by both our fathers."

"My father was blind in his last days," said Kate. "He had no idea what he was signing."

"So you say," returned Bones.

"'Tis true!" Mrs. Hennings rose shakily to her feet. "He was blind at the end and grievous ill."

Another gasp and titters arose from the villagers. Wynbrook considered it a shame they had not sold tickets for such a show. At least they were giving the village something to talk about for years to come.

"Thank you," said Kate to Mrs. Hennings, who held her head higher.

"You will find the contract was also signed by your legal guardian, General Roberts," said Captain Bones with an arrogant smirk. "There can be no question of it holding up in court. Good day to you all. I am staying at the Captain's Rest. I will expect you soon to discuss payment." He gave them a mocking bow and strolled out of the chapel to the hisses and boos of the villagers.

Wynbrook watched him walk away. There was something strangely familiar about him, but he could not quite place it. He turned to Kate to provide comfort, compassion, but any softness of her expression had been replaced by the steely eyes and rigid expression that had ruled her countenance when they first met.

His Kate was gone.

Thirty-eight

KATE WATCHED THE UNFOLDING DRAMA OF THE ruination of her wedding as if she was attending some tragic play. A cold numbness spread through her and all emotion slipped away. She retreated inside herself. Back where it was safe. She should never have tried to trust, never allowed her heart to feel such emotion—never allowed herself to hope. Was that not what Emma had said was produced by hardship? Hope, the worst of all emotions. It left one vulnerable and shaking when it all went wrong.

"Reverend, we must afford these two some privacy," said Anne in an undertone, taking command of a situation gone completely awry.

The rector ushered them out a side door and into the rectory, a comfortable cottage only a few feet away. Kate, Wynbrook, Anne, and Tristan carrying Ellen quickly followed, leaving the capable butler, Mr. Foster, to dispel the boisterous crowd.

Tea was offered and accepted, and the rector graciously left the family alone in the rectory drawing room to collect themselves in private. Kate sat on a low couch and wondered if her legs would have the strength to lift her up again. Ellen was deposited beside her and patted her shoulder in sympathy, her eyes moist. Anne sat by the tea service, staunchly pouring tea while Wynbrook and Tristan paced the room.

"So what if he has a marriage contract signed by your father and this General Roberts so many years ago?" said Wynbrook, striding back and forth. "It doesn't prevent us from getting married."

"If we wed now, he can sue us for breach of contract. He could be entitled to my entire dowry." Kate rubbed her temple; her head was starting to pound.

"So give him the dowry. I'm not marrying you for financial gain. All I want is you." Wynbrook knelt down and took both her hands in his. "Kate, all I want is you."

"That is easy for you to say," said Kate briskly, releasing his hands. "Considering you have nothing to lose. If I marry you now, I have nothing."

"Nothing?" Wynbrook turned silently and walked to the window. It was unusual for him to appear so somber and not to have a witty retort.

"We cannot marry if it means forfeiting my entire dowry," said Kate, addressing his back. "Only a fool would do that."

He turned to her, but his face was a distant mask she was unaccustomed to seeing on him. "Apparently, I am that fool." He stalked out of the room.

Everyone was silent. Ellen became fascinated with a piece of lint on her gown. Anne arranged the biscuits on a plate. Tristan just stared at the contract, which had been tossed on the table.

Now she truly had lost everything. Losing her

dowry was one thing, but the thought of losing John… She put a hand over her heart, for it hurt. She had heard the term "heartache" before but had not known that it actually hurt.

Ellen handed her a handkerchief with a look of empathetic concern that only made the ache worse.

"I am not inclined toward tears," said Kate, refusing the white cloth.

"Then you are leaking," Ellen said gently.

Kate took the handkerchief and blotted her eyes. She never cried. Never. She had the need to blot again. Strange.

"Thank you for alerting us to the danger. Whatever made you look at the man's shoes?" asked Kate, trying to focus on something other than her pain.

Ellen gave a small smile. "Force of habit. I always notice people's shoes, for I have none of my own. I suppose the habit was helpful today."

"Indeed it was!" said Kate with sincerity. "I was almost ready to go into his coach and put myself at his mercy. I do not wish to think what would have happened without you here."

Wynbrook entered the room once more. "May we have a moment alone?"

His family vanished like smoke—even Ellen, which was impressive.

"I'm sorry," said Kate. She was not exactly sure why, but she knew she had hurt him, pushed him away once too often.

"No, it is I who am sorry." John sat next to her and held her hand. It felt good, but there was a stiffness to his manner, a reserve to him that had not been there before.

"I simply cannot enter into a marriage without my dowry. Without any protection. Robert and I worked so hard to rebuild our lives. I cannot walk away with nothing."

"Of course not. What if I paid the amount? You keep your dowry."

"Give fifty thousand pounds to the son of the man who murdered my father? To the family who tricked my father into signing this marriage contract and then killed him? Unthinkable!"

"Unthinkable," John agreed with resignation.

"We shall just have to fight it in court," said Kate firmly. She looked up at him, a cloud coming over her eyes. "This is more drama than even your lurid novel could endure. I understand if you wish to walk away."

"You must know that is impossible." John squeezed her hand.

Kate sighed. "I would not blame you if you just called it off."

"I hope you know me better than that by this time. Besides, we could potentially have more than just ourselves to consider."

"You mean your family?"

"I mean after last night, we could be expecting an addition to the family," he said softly.

Kate thought there was nothing left that could surprise her. She was wrong. She had not considered the ramifications of the night before. Why should she? She was getting married.

"You do not think… It could not be possible that… No, I am certain I could not… Oh no, I could!"

"That's probably why the Bible says not to anticipate the wedding vows," said John wryly.

"But I intended to marry you!" she defended.

"I think it would be best if we marry as soon as may be," said John gently.

"Yes, but oh, the court case could go on for a while." What was she going to do?

"Perhaps we could be married and then fight the contract in court?"

"But we would have a stronger case before we are wed. And if we fail…I cannot wed without my dowry safe from that man!"

"Forgive me." Tristan rushed back in the room. "But this General Roberts who signed here. Do you think that could be Sir Antony Roberts?"

"Sir Antony?" John rose and stared at the parchment in Tristan's hand.

"Who is Sir Antony?" asked Kate.

"Friend of the family," answered John. "We could ask if he signed this and under what conditions."

"My godfather is an uncaring bastard," spat Kate.

"How do you know this?" asked John, suspicious.

Realization dawned. "The damn steward. He lied about everything else. Why not this too?" She rose to her feet, fresh anger an easier emotion to manage than sorrow.

"But did he not marry a Scot for a wife? They may be far off," said Tristan.

"No, he is wintering in Sussex," said Anne, entering the room.

John's eyebrows raised. "You truly do know all in society."

"Yes, and he was invited to Jane's wedding. Sent his regrets saying they were in Sussex, though I do not know the address."

"I do," said Kate, to the surprise of all. "He wrote me recently. In truth, I have received many letters from him throughout the years, but I could never forgive him for abandoning us when we needed him, so I never opened them."

"Sussex is not far," commented John.

"Care to go for a drive?" asked Kate.

A half hour later, they were packed in the coach, this time with a proper coachman and them on the inside with a large basket of goodies, intended for the wedding breakfast, and a warmer at their feet.

She had always thought of General Roberts as something of a villain, but now she very much hoped she was wrong. This had to work. They had to get this contract nullified and then they had to get married.

Wynbrook sat stiffly, looking out the window. Gone was the lively banter and playful manner. She needed to preserve her dowry, but what if the price was the man?

They drove on for hours. The roads were poor, but they had frequent changes of horses and made steady progress toward their object. Wynbrook was unusually quiet. He seemed content to stare out the window. Even when she suggested he look at his shocking novel, he only replied that he had experienced enough excitement for one day. He didn't even look at her when he said it.

It was time to get back to doing what she knew. She needed to make a list. Perhaps everything in her life had gone higgledy-piggledy because she had abandoned her practice of the cold comfort of making lists. She searched the pockets of her wool pelisse for a pencil and a notebook.

She found a stub of pencil and bit of paper. It would do. She went to work on her list for the day.

1. Nullify contract.
2. Restore dowry.
3. Send Silas Bones to perdition.
4. Marry the Earl of Wynbrook.
5. Get said earl to stop looking out the window and talk to me.

She observed the silent Wynbrook as they rattled along in the coach, being jostled to and fro as it bumped over the rough road. John had instructed the coachman to make haste, and the man was clearly following that instruction.

John was not happy. And he was quiet. She had not known he could be so silent. He had always been ready with lively discourse, but now, nothing.

She looked over the list again. Was she missing something? *Nullify contract.* That was important. *Restore dowry.* The same dowry she had been mad as fire her brother had given her. The dowry Wynbrook cared nothing for and was willing to marry her without.

Kate absently spun the pencil in her fingers. She had objected to a dowry when she had no intention of marrying. Now that her world had changed, to enter into the marriage without the dowry was to leave all security behind. It meant she would have to rely on another person, trust someone else to take care of her. The mere thought made her queasy with fear.

John said he loved her. *Loved* her. Truth was, she loved him back, and that was scarier than anything she had yet experienced. Would she sacrifice love on the altar of fear?

She glanced down and saw that on the other side of the paper was the verse Emma had given her. *All things are become new.*

Become new? That was a laugh. She was not new in the least. She would never be free of the past that haunted her.

And yet...John did not believe it. She also had begun to believe she could walk free of fear and doubt. She had thought she could never tolerate being vulnerable with a man, but last night had shattered that fear. She definitely had no problem with it. At least, not with John.

Lord, I know I have not prayed often. After everything that happened in her past, she had always assumed God was not particularly interested in her welfare. Or really didn't like her. Either way, it seemed best not to draw too much attention to herself.

But what if Emma was right? What if everything she had endured had given her the experience and drive to chase after Robert when he had been shot? And what if she had helped save his life? Was everything she had experienced, as miserable as it was, worth it if it meant saving her brother's life?

Lord, give me a sign. What shall I do?

Out the window on a little rise ahead of them stood a quaint, white church. A man, a curate by his cloth, walked outside the church and raised both hands to the sky.

"Stop the coach," said Kate, not even realizing she was speaking.

"I beg your pardon?" asked John.

"Stop the coach!"

He rapped on the ceiling with his cane and the coach slowed to a stop. He looked at her, questioning.

Kate took a deep breath. This was it. She was crossing a threshold from which she could not recover. She was doing a new thing.

"I just realized I love you." She gulped down fear.

He said nothing, but his face became alive once more and his eyes shone with emotion.

"I love you more than money. I'd rather be poor with you than rich and alone."

"Oh, Kate." He gathered her up into his arms and kissed her until her head swam and she wished they were back in bed once more. They definitely needed to get married now. "But, dear, I am not poor," he added.

"Apparently, I am. Would you be willing to marry me anyway?" She pointed to the little church.

He patted his breast pocket that contained the special license. "Anytime, anywhere." He beamed at her—the smile she had missed. It was worth her entire dowry.

Wynbrook hopped out of the coach and offered a hand to Kate. Together, they walked arm in arm to the little church. The wind rustled about in a fervent manner, ripping through the trees and tugging at her bonnet. The reverend was standing before the church with his back to them. When they drew nearer, it was clear he was praying.

"I've tried to follow you, Lord. I've tried to serve the needs of these people. How have I failed you? How could you let this happen?"

Wynbrook cleared his throat loudly to announce their presence.

The young man spun to face them. "Oh!" He was a wiry man of average build and height. He even had a rather average face, with brown hair and eyes, except for a white scar that slashed at an angle across his forehead.

"Forgive us for disturbing you," said Wynbrook calmly. "But we would like to be married."

"Yes, yes, of course," said the reverend, still recovering from his surprise at being caught praying aloud in a desperate manner. "Do come back tomorrow to the rectory. There will be a new rector installed soon and he will be able to help you set a date."

"We would like to be married now," explained Kate, holding her bonnet so the wind could not carry it off.

He motioned for them to step into the small church, limping as he went. "What is this, now?"

"Perhaps introductions are in order," said Wynbrook with his usual easy charm. Kate was relieved it had returned. "I am John Arlington, Earl of Wynbrook, and this is my fiancée, Lady Katherine."

"Tim Dawkins. Soon to be unemployed curate," said the morose man of the cloth.

"Forgive me, but we could not help overhear," said Kate. "You seem to be in some trouble. Can we help?"

The man sighed. "I have been the curate here under the rector for five years, waiting for the elderly rector to retire. The rectory was promised to me when it fell vacant, but when it came available, the living was given to another."

"Why?" asked Kate.

"Because of a riding accident. Got rolled by a horse and…" He lifted his trouser pant leg, revealing a wood and metal contraption instead of a leg. "Said I wasn't a full man before God."

"Outrageous!" cried Kate.

"Preposterous!" exclaimed Wynbrook.

The curate merely shrugged.

"I cannot believe anyone would be so shockingly prejudiced," continued Kate.

"Do you know where you will go?" asked Wynbrook.

"I can stay with some lads I met at Oxford for a while, until I can find a new situation."

Wynbrook handed the reverend his card. "Contact me if I can be of service to you."

Reverend Dawkins took the card with some surprise. "Thank you, my lord. Wish I could help you, but the banns would have to be read in your home parish."

"I do have a special license." Wynbrook produced it with a flourish.

A wry smile appeared on Reverend Dawkins's face. "I am still the curate for the remainder of the day. Let us have your wedding be the last office I perform!"

Kate smiled even as her heart beat in her throat. She was betting everything on the love of one man. One wonderful man. Her wonderful man.

A brief search for witnesses was commenced, and then they were ushered up to the front of the chapel. The Earl of Wynbrook was married to Lady Katherine Ashton by Reverend Dawkins in the presence of their coachman and a maid of all work.

Kate appreciated the soon-to-be-unemployed curate's style of speaking—straightforward and unapologetic. She held her breath when the curate asked if anyone had just cause why she could not wed John. This time all was silent. John released a breath and gave her a smile.

The ceremony was short but complete. A wave of relief washed over her when they were pronounced man and wife. They had done it. They were finally married. The curate was announcing them to the two other people in the church when Wynbrook swept her up and kissed her joyfully.

"I love you, Lady Wynbrook." John could not stop smiling. It made her smile right back. So far, her life of new things was not so bad.

After the appropriate papers had been signed, they walked arm in arm out of the church. "I wish there was something we could do to help our reverend friend," whispered Kate as they left. Everyone should be as happy as she. "I don't suppose you know of any situations? He seems a nice man."

John stopped short. "Actually, I need to find another rector at home." He said no more but led Kate back into the church.

"I think I may know a way to repay you for the service you provided us today," said Wynbrook to the good reverend. "Would you be interested in the rectory at Arlington Hall?"

The man dropped his prayer book. "Are you in jest?"

"No. The rectory serves my countryseat and—"

"Yes!" shouted the reverend. "Oh, bless the good Lord, yes!"

Thirty-nine

"WHAT WOULD YOU LIKE TO DO NOW, MY LOVE?" asked Wynbrook when they were back in the coach, celebrating their nuptials by eating from the basket of delicious meat pies and sweet treats packed by the cook.

"I did marry you for love, my dear, but would you mind ever so much if we try to nullify the marriage contract with the son of my father's murderer?"

"Not a usual activity for a honeymoon, but with you, I would expect nothing less."

She had a strong feeling he would deny her nothing. Marriage was making her feel stronger, not weak. Strange.

They continued their journey toward the country home of Sir Antony. This time, they enjoyed themselves, John reading aloud from *The Captain's Curse* while Kate whooped with laughter. She could not remember a time she had laughed so hard. In truth, she could not remember the last time she had laughed at all.

It had grown dark by the time they rolled up onto the drive of the country cottage. It was of stone construction and clearly more of a country retreat than the gentleman's countryseat. It had a cozy feel, with vines growing wild up one side of the cottage.

"This is the house?" asked Kate.

"Yes, I believe it to be." John helped her out of the coach. "I hope we will find Sir Antony amenable to unexpected guests."

"Perhaps General Roberts is not Sir Antony Roberts after all," commented Kate.

"Excuse me, my lord," said the coachman. "Seemed like someone was following us on horseback a while back, but I haven't seen the bloke for the past hour."

"Thank you," said Wynbrook. "After you see to the horses, go to the kitchen and get warm and something to eat. We have traveled long today, and I hope we will all receive a friendly welcome."

In a soft voice, Kate asked, "Do you think Silas Bones is following us?"

John shrugged. "Could be anyone."

"But given our luck, it's probably not." She glanced around, but there was no one in sight. It was a cold night—perhaps he had given up the chase.

She approached the front door with some dread. How were they to explain their arrival at such a late hour? John put his hand over hers and gave her gloved fingers a small squeeze. He always seemed to understand when she needed a little encouragement, and though she would have difficulty accepting such from most people, she was growing fond of his support.

"If General Roberts is Sir Antony, I am certain he will help us," said John with confidence.

"You know him well?"

"He was my father's friend more than mine, but he has a reputation as a fair and good man."

"I hope you are right," said Kate. She was beginning to believe Wynbrook could make anything right. Marriage must have gone to her head.

They stood at the door and John pulled the bell. In due time, the butler answered, looking a bit severe.

"Lord and Lady Wynbrook to see General Roberts," said Wynbrook in his most austere aristocratic manner. Kate bubbled with excitement to be so named Lady Wynbrook.

The butler was clearly surprised by such visitors but stayed true to his profession and invited them in with the utmost civility. He showed them to a nicely appointed sitting room, where they awaited their host. Wynbrook ensured Kate was warm by the fire before taking the seat opposite hers.

A middle-aged lady burst into the room with a swish of silk and a head full of ostrich feathers. "The Earl of Wynbrook?" asked the elegantly attired lady.

Wynbrook rose and gave her a nod.

She continued on before he had a chance to speak. "It's very nice to make your acquaintance, my lord. Have you brought your lovely wife too? Lady Kate, I believe?"

Kate was shocked for a moment that the woman knew her name before she recalled the gossip column. Everyone knew her name.

"To what do we owe the honor of your visit with us today?" Though she spoke with perfect diction, Kate could not fail but note a slight lilt to her tone, with a hint of something Scottish in the way she spoke.

"It is a matter of some delicacy. We are hoping to

speak with General Roberts," said Wynbrook pleasantly enough but not entirely inviting further conversation.

"You may say anything to me that you would say to him," said the lady, leaning rather close to Wynbrook. "I am his wife, Lady Roberts. So please feel at ease to speak as you wish. Do let us accommodate you for the night, for it is late and I would be greatly distressed if you were to leave us at such a time. If you are hungry, we can prepare something for you. I do like to think I keep a good table, but I am sure we can rouse the cook to produce such fare as you are accustomed to."

"Thank you but we have already eaten," said Wynbrook. "We are grateful for your hospitality."

"It is a great honor to meet you." Lady Roberts gave a handsome if unnecessarily low curtsy before them.

"This is a matter of some importance and I would very much like to speak with General Roberts," said Kate, wishing the woman would leave and send her husband instead.

The lady laughed. "General Roberts? Yes, I suppose he is, though we mostly call him Sir Antony. It has been a long while since he served his country in uniform."

"Though I did it with distinction." An elderly man with sparkling eyes entered the drawing room. He gave his wife a warm smile and she returned it prettily. "Lord Wynbrook? I am surprised to see you! Is everyone in the family well?"

"Yes, yes, my family is well. Do forgive this bold intrusion at such a late hour," said Wynbrook. "We come on a mission of some urgency. But please allow me to introduce you to my wife, Katherine, Lady Wynbrook."

"So tell me. Is it true? Did you run to Gretna Green?" asked Lady Roberts, leaning forward with anticipation. "I have been following your adventures in the papers."

"Have you been reading the society papers again?" chided Sir Antony with a twinkle in his eye.

"Oh yes, and if you did too, you would know of the great news Wynbrook has made running with the daughter of an earl." Lady Roberts laughed in a manner even Kate found a bit gauche.

"The rumors of our elopement have been much touted, but in truth, we left quickly because Darington was held up by bandits on the road and shot. Fortunately, he is doing well," Wynbrook said with unruffled calm.

"Lord Darington was shot?" exclaimed Lady Roberts, clearly delighting in this new piece of juicy gossip.

"Darington?" Sir Antony asked, clearly confused. "What is this about Darington?"

Kate stared at the kindly looking man before her. He did not look a villain. She took a deep breath. "Perhaps you knew my father, Lord Darington."

Sir Antony's face darkened. All was quiet in the room save the methodical ticking of a grandfather clock. "I was the best of friends with Darington. But is it really Lady Katherine? I have written many a letter to you and your brother, but I have never received an answer."

Kate produced his last letter from her reticule. "Was this one of your letters?"

Sir Antony took the letter. "Yes. But you never opened it?" He stared at her, questions in his eyes.

"Forgive me. I never opened any of them," Kate

confessed. The clock ticked on as everyone stared at each other in silence.

"Let us call for some hot rum punch," suggested Lady Roberts, breaking the awkward silence. "Please, everyone, do make yourselves comfortable. I am sure this problem will go down better with something warm."

It was the first thing Lady Roberts said that Kate agreed with. They sat in the cozy sitting room, and the ingredients for punch were brought. Wynbrook stood to do the honors of making the preparations.

"It has taken a long time to understand the nature of what happened," said Kate. She retold the story of Captain Harcourt's revenge in bankrupting their family and the death of her father succinctly, leaving out several aspects such that she didn't wish to have repeated, for Lady Roberts was clearly enjoying the tale.

"But this is infamy!" Sir Antony was on his feet and began to pace in an agitated manner. "Such things cannot happen. This is England!"

"I believe I said the same," said Wynbrook. "Here, do sit down and take some rum punch. It will do you good."

Sir Antony was tempted by the fragrant aroma wafting from the warm punch bowl Wynbrook was mixing. He accepted a cup and regained his seat.

"Directly after my father died, we returned to find our inheritance stolen and our estate deep in debt. We traveled to London to meet with you but were told you were too busy to be concerned with us, and we ended up in Fleet Prison."

"What?" roared Sir Antony, jumping to his feet once more. "Impossible!"

"I assure you it is possible. We managed to escape, but we thought you had abandoned us when we most needed it, so I was out of charity with you and refused ever to open your letters."

"My dear girl. My dear, sweet girl." Sir Antony buried his face in his hands. "Oh, I am so sorry. Darington was my dearest friend. He even named his son for me and made you your godfather."

"Oh," said Kate. "I never knew Robert was named for anyone."

"Please believe me when I say I never knew of this. I was injured in the war and it took a long time to recover. When I finally returned home, I learned of Darington's death. I was told in a letter from his steward that the children had gone to live with some relative of his wife's. I had no reason to disbelieve it, but I wish I had looked into the matter further."

"Indeed, you must not blame yourself," his wife chided. "For did you not come very close to death yourself? We have only been married a few months," she explained to Kate and Wynbrook and blushed as any new bride should do.

"I wish you great felicitations," said Wynbrook. "And you may also wish us happy, for we were wed just today."

"Today! Holy Saint Andrew! What are ye doing here now, luv?" cried Lady Roberts, letting her Scottish accent slip.

"Always welcome," said Sir Antony hurriedly. "But I wish I could have witnessed… Would have been honored to walk you down the aisle…but why are you here now?"

"Our ceremony was interrupted by a Captain Silas Bones who produced this paper." Wynbrook handed Sir Antony the contract. "It is a marriage agreement between Lady Kate and Bones. I must add that Silas Bones is the son of Dr. Bones, the alias used by Harcourt to gain entry into Greystone to kill Darington."

"That damn bastard son of a—Forgive me. Should not say in front of the ladies!" cried Sir Antony.

"The document appears to be signed by you," said Kate.

"What the—?" Sir Antony scanned the document with a scowl. "This is not my signature. I never saw this document before in my life. Besides, on the date of this paper, I was overseas getting shot in a disastrous campaign."

"And you would be willing to swear to it in court to have this contract invalidated?" asked Kate.

"Invalidated, repudiated, and utterly dismissed! Go to London myself tomorrow!"

Kate breathed easy for the first time in days. It was done. Settled. All was well.

Lady Roberts's attention was caught by a scratching at the window. She stood to look out the heavy drapes, commenting, "I do believe there was a man out there. I wonder who could be peeking in at our window at this time of night?"

Kate did not have to wonder at all. She looked over at Wynbrook.

"Silas Bones." They spoke as one.

Forty

KATE JUMPED UP, READY TO GIVE CHASE, BUT Wynbrook caught her arm. "Kate, please, for once, stay where it is safe and let us handle it."

"I am perfectly capable—"

"I know you are. But I am incapable of seeing you hurt, so as a wedding present to me, please stay by the fire, where I know you are safe." He held both her hands in his.

How could she deny him when he put it so prettily? "As you wish," she grumbled. "But stay safe yourself."

"Let us find your Captain Bones," said Sir Antony. "Always some excitement around Darington. I see his children are no different."

"I shall tell the housekeeper to ensure the doors and windows are locked," said Lady Roberts briskly. She followed the men out of the room, leaving Kate to sit by the fire.

"This is what being a lady is like," Kate said to herself. "What a dead bore." For the first time, she began to understand Emma's desire for adventure. Her upbringing, though unconventional, suited her better than the one generally afforded to gently born ladies.

Outside she could hear the men whacking the bushes and calling to each other as they searched the grounds around the house. If Silas Bones had any intelligence whatsoever, he would have made a run for it. She heard a horse galloping away followed by the shouts of men, and she knew Captain Bones had taken flight with the men in hot pursuit.

She was relieved that the contract had been proven invalid, but it was a discomfort to know Silas Bones was loose somewhere, waiting to cause mischief.

The door opened and a young chambermaid shuffled in, her eyes wide with fright. Something was wrong.

"What is it?" asked Kate, rising to her feet.

The girl opened and closed her mouth, no words forming. She continued to shuffle into the room followed by a figure wrapped in a black cloak. The cowl fell from his face, sending a ripple of fear through Kate.

Silas Bones stood in the doorway, a pistol pointed at the maid's head.

Kate's mind whirled, trying to keep up with the situation. So much for staying safe. "Captain Bones, you are becoming tiresome."

"I-I'm sorry, milady," stammered the terrified maid. "I was going to lock the cellar door like Lady Roberts told me when he g-grabbed me."

"Do not worry. This is not your fault," said Kate gently, trying to calm the maid.

"Since you have found a way to invalidate the marriage contract, I am forced to take a different course of action," said Captain Bones without emotion. "You owe me fifty thousand pounds, and I will not stop until this has been achieved. The number of people hurt in the process is up to you."

"You wish to hold me for ransom?" asked Kate. "Let the girl go. She has no part in this."

"She is to remind you to mind your manners." Silas touched the barrel of the pistol to the girl's head. "Take that knife you have tied to your ankle and drop it to the floor."

Kate froze a moment, surprised he knew so much about her. He must have gotten a report from the men who initially tried to abduct her. She had no choice while he held a gun to the girl's head. The knife fell to the ground with a clunk.

"Slide it to me," said Bones evenly.

Kate kicked it to him with the toe of her boot. "Why are you doing this? Your father made this accord and you know it to be false. I owe you nothing."

"You owe me everything," he hissed. "Where do you think your brother got his treasure? By raiding ships. My ship! I am just returning the favor."

"My brother only fought the enemies of England," cried Kate. "He would not have attacked your ship unless…unless you were sailing for France."

"After your father ruined my father's life, we had no choice but to serve as privateers for the French crown."

"Then you really are a traitor!" Kate seethed, her pulse pounding in her ears. "You will get nothing from me."

"I'll not be asking you. I'll be demanding it from that new husband of yours. If he wants you back, he'll pay. You just better hope he wants you back. Now tie up the maid." He grabbed the girl's jaw and held it close to his menacing face. "Say nothing of what you have seen or I will return and cut your throat."

"No need to scare the girl," Kate reprimanded, but she complied with his request. Between tying her up and shooting her, tying was the best option for the maid. "He will not harm you," she whispered to the frightened maid. Kate worked as slowly as she thought she could get away with and made the bonds loose.

"Good enough," snapped Silas. He motioned for Kate to step away and tightened the ropes while keeping his pistol and one eye on Kate. He walked up to her, his pistol leveled at her heart. Her pulse pounded loudly in her ears.

"Turn around and put your hands behind your back," he demanded. "Fight me and I shoot the girl."

She had no choice but to comply, and soon her hands were bound behind her.

"Now we are going to take a little trip. If you are well behaved, you shall return home in one piece."

Kate walked before him as he directed. He kept a hand on her shoulder and the pistol touching the back of her skull. It did not afford many opportunities for escape. Where were Wynbrook and Sir Antony now? Probably chasing some poor riderless horse around in the dark.

She wondered how he was going to get her out of the house without being seen, but instead of walking to the door, he pushed her toward the large bay window.

The large, leaded glass window was formed with smaller diamond panes, forming a crisscross pattern. He undid the latch and it swung open on side hinges. Since they were in a cottage, the first floor was the living quarters and the large window opened into a bit of garden.

"Step outside."

Kate did so, struggling a bit with the form-fitting silver gown, especially with her hands tied behind her. With an absurd sense of irony, she realized she was still wearing her wedding gown. The lace overlay tore as she climbed out the window and into a rhododendron. "Oh, Anne is going to kill you," she muttered.

"Would not that be the job of your new husband?" growled the man behind her.

"You don't know how strongly Lady Anne feels about lace."

She pushed past the shrub and out to the front of the house. She glanced about, hoping to catch sight of Wynbrook or Sir Antony or anyone. A bright moon hung low in the sky and all was quiet. She was running out of time.

Silas said nothing, but the firm hand on her shoulder and the cold pressure of the pistol to her head got her moving again. He led her around the side of the house. There, he had a curricle waiting.

"Get in."

A horrible screech pierced the night. "Heeeeeeeelp!" screamed Lady Roberts. "Sir Antony! Wynbrook! Lady Kate has been stolen!"

The scream momentarily startled him, and Kate used the distraction to fall to the ground and swing her legs around, knocking him over. She rolled to her feet and took off running back to the house. He was faster though, and she was tackled from behind.

Kate let out a scream and struggled against him as

best she could with her hands tied behind her. She was dragged up to standing and she screamed again, fighting him all the way.

"Unhand her." It was Wynbrook, not a hair out of place, immaculately attired in his gray, double-breasted tailcoat and silver-striped waistcoat.

Silas held her neck in a choke hold with one arm, the pistol to her head with the other hand. He was breathing heavily and smelled of mud and desperation.

She was happy to see Wynbrook, but she would have been happier to see him with a gun.

"This is simple," said Bones, breathing hard. "All I want is the dowry. Fifty thousand pounds and not a shilling less." He began to drag her back toward the curricle. "I get the money. You get the girl."

"You are holding my wife," noted Wynbrook. "I do not care for it."

Kate almost groaned. What was Wynbrook going to do? Talk him to death? She wanted him to get out of there before he got hurt.

"You know what to do to get her back," growled Silas.

"It has taken me a while to remember where we met. Eton, was it not? I knew you as Silas Harcourt."

Kate stared at her husband. He was slowly walking forward as if they were having polite conversation at Almack's.

Silas stopped dragging her backward. Maybe he was shocked by Wynbrook's manner as well. "I can no longer use that name. Her father made sure of that."

"I believe you were a few years ahead of me. Never went home. Spent all your holidays at Eton and then suddenly you were gone."

"Yes," said Silas bitterly. "I was in my last year at Eton when her father turned in mine as a traitor. I was shipped off before I even knew what was happening. And it is all their fault!" He began to drag her backward again with Wynbrook keeping pace, casually adjusting his sleeve.

"It was not fair for you to suffer because of something your father did," agreed Wynbrook. "You saved the life of David Turnbull."

Silas stopped again. Wynbrook drew closer, speaking in the same nonchalant manner. "He fell into the river and nearly drowned. It was December and bitter cold. You jumped in and saved him."

"Why are you talking about that?" Silas was confused enough to stop and listen.

"A truly bad seed would not have jumped into the frigid Thames to save the likes of Turnbull. He was in my class," Wynbrook explained to Kate. "And a complete arse."

"He was just a boy," muttered Silas.

"Bunch of boys on the bridge that day. The only one who jumped in was you."

Silas was silent, but his grip on her loosened and she could no longer feel the steel of the pistol pressed against her temple. Wynbrook *was* talking him to death.

"They rushed you both back to the house and began to strip the clothes off you," continued Wynbrook.

"Enough!" shouted Silas, his body tense.

Wynbrook regarded him coolly. "Your back was covered with scars. Truly horrible."

"I said enough," growled Silas.

"Your father was Captain Harcourt," said Wynbrook in a quiet voice. "That could not have been easy."

Silas's hand that held the pistol dropped to his side. "My father is a hard man. Made resentments easily and never forgave. If I disappointed him, it was the lash. As you saw, I was a huge disappointment."

"You didn't write the marriage contract. It was your father. You were not the traitor. It was him," continued Wynbrook.

"Darington ruined my life," said Silas, but his tone was not as sure.

"Darington did the only honorable thing he could by revealing treachery. All His Majesty's subjects are required to do the same. Even you."

Beside her, Silas was breathing hard. Wynbrook, in contrast, was as poised as ever. She was not sure if she was impressed or agitated by his unflappable calm.

"Your actions tonight are not like those of the lad I admired those many years ago," said Wynbrook. "What is this about, Silas?"

"Darington, Robert Ashton," clarified Silas, "raided my ship and took the cargo. I need to get back that prize. At first I tried to find where they had stashed my cargo by looking at the captain's log and ledgers. Failing that, I knew I needed to go for Lady Kate."

"Lady Wynbrook," corrected John.

"The cargo Darington took was my father's. I cannot return empty-handed."

"Then do not return at all," suggested Wynbrook.

Silas said nothing but released his hold on her. Kate slowly stepped away from him toward Wynbrook. She could not believe John had defeated him with nothing but his words.

A shot cracked through the night, and Wynbrook dove into her, pushing her down, covering her with his own body.

Silas dropped to the ground as well, shouting in pain. Sir Antony and Lady Roberts stepped out of the shadows, into the moonlight. John dashed forward, grabbing Silas's pistol, Kate's dagger, and another blade from Silas's boot before returning to Kate's side.

"Are you hurt?" asked John, checking her over.

"I shall survive," said Kate. "Though if you could cut these bonds..."

"Yes, dear!" John was quick to comply with her request. "I thought I was going to expire, seeing you with a gun to your head. Really, my dear, you must be more considerate to your husband. Such excitement cannot be good for the heart." He cut through the ropes and helped her to stand.

"You were wonderful." Kate leaned her head on his shoulder. "Simply amazing. You disarmed him with nothing but your wit!"

"I believe Sir Antony has helped us considerably," said Wynbrook, towering over the defeated Silas Harcourt, who, though alive, remained on the ground.

"Thank you, Sir Antony. That was an excellent shot," said Kate as he and his wife drew near.

"I know a crack shot when I see one," said Sir Antony, smiling at his wife. She smiled in return and shouldered the rifle.

"You mean...Lady Roberts fired the shot?" Kate stared at Lady Roberts, who gave her a serene smile.

"I confess I'm but a Highland lass at heart. Hunting is a wee bit of a passion."

"My lady is a true lady, but she is as fierce as any Highlander." Sir Antony gazed at his wife with obvious admiration.

Attention now turned to Silas, sitting on the ground, clutching his bloodied shoulder.

"What are we going to do with him?" asked Kate.

Sir Antony sighed. "Let's get him to the house."

Wynbrook and a burly groom helped to "escort" Silas Bones to the house. His face was pale with pain and the fight seemed to have left him. After a short debate, they took him to a small guest bedroom. With a groom and footman standing by as guards over the prisoner, Wynbrook helped Silas remove his coat, revealing a large, red stain on his white shirt. His cravat, collar, and waistcoat were soon removed, and finally, the shirt.

Blood ran from both the entrance and exit wounds, and the company was immediately consumed with stanching the flow. His back was covered in long scars with puckered, distorted flesh. It was difficult to view without wishing to turn away.

"What did your father do to you?" asked Kate, holding what used to be his cravat to his back to stop the flow of blood.

"Lashed me to the mast and whipped me," replied Silas through gritted teeth. To Wynbrook, he said, "I stayed at Eton over holidays not because I had to but because I wanted to."

"No child should be tortured in this manner," said Wynbrook.

"We have both been hurt by your father," Kate said quietly.

"When my father discovers I failed…" muttered Silas.

"Darington has gone after Harcourt," said Wynbrook.

"Hope he kills him," said Silas. "I know he's my father, but I cannot help but wish to be free of him. I am sorry for causing you pain."

Not long ago, she had wished him dead; now she just felt sorry for him. She was not much practiced in giving mercy—not for herself or anyone else—but maybe if she could find grace, so could the miserable man before her. Starting her marriage holding on to a grudge did not seem like a good beginning.

Kate nodded, accepting his apology. She breathed deep, experiencing a strange sense of relief that flooded through her. This man no longer had any power over her.

Lady Roberts compassionately poured Silas a dose of laudanum, which he took with a grimace. "I've called the surgeon," she added.

"Thanks for not killing me, I suppose," said Silas.

"If ye had no' dropped the pistol, I would have shot ye between the eyes. Feel better, dearie." She patted his hand.

They stepped out of the room to discuss whether a magistrate should be notified. There was agreement that Silas Harcourt had done some horrid things, but also that he'd felt he had little choice. The angry scars on his back were a testament to that.

"I do want to show some compassion for him," said Kate. "But I do not wish him to be at large in society."

"What about the military?" asked Sir Antony.

In the end, it was decided if he lived to give him a choice between jail and the Royal Navy. The surgeon arrived and Kate and Wynbrook retired to their guest room.

"I've had a hot bath drawn for you, dear," said Lady Roberts, her correct English diction restored. "I know I am not your godmother, but I am going to pretend to be."

"I would like that," said Kate honestly.

Ten minutes later, Kate sank into the hot water with a low groan. She began to rub lavender soap up and down her arms, washing off the dirt and mud from being knocked to the ground multiple times.

John poked his head into the room. "Can I be of service?"

"You can help wash the dirt out of my hair." He could help her do a few other things as well.

He entered wearing nothing but a dressing gown and a smile, locking the door behind him. "I was not sure now that we are married if I was to be barred from your bed and…well, bath."

"I do not recall ever mentioning I would ban you from the bath," said Kate with a slow smile.

"Ah, then I am on friendly ground. May I be permitted to join you?"

"By all means."

John joined her in the large tub, water sloshing over the sides. He settled in behind her and wrapped his arms around her. It was delicious.

"Remember when I said I did not think I could be intimate when married?" asked Kate, closing her eyes and leaning back against her husband's wonderfully muscular chest.

"Yes, I seem to recall something of that sort."

"Forget it. I was wrong. Bloomin' idiot."

He laughed, and she could feel it through her skin. He began washing her hair, slowly massaging her scalp. He then worked his way down, soothing and massaging everything along the way until she was desperate for him. She spun around and had her way with him, feeling more powerful, loved, protected, and alive than ever before.

By the time they climbed out of the tub, there was more water on the floor than in the bath.

"Lady Roberts will wonder what has happened here," said Kate, drying herself off.

"I think she might have a fair idea of what went on." John grinned at her. "We are newlyweds, after all."

"I am very glad I married you," said Kate. "I fear I have fallen quite in love with you."

His green eyes sparkled at her. "My heart beats for you alone. Though it has gotten a bit more use than usual and would like to request calm days ahead."

"But I thought you liked those exciting novels," said Kate with a laugh.

"To *read*, not to *live*," clarified John.

"My mistake," said Kate with a smile. "I shall become meek and mild-mannered. A perfect countess."

"Ha!" cried Wynbrook. "You'll do nothing of the sort or I'll be bored to distraction. I married you just as you are!"

Kate wrapped her arms around her husband again and sighed in contentment. He accepted her for who she was. And somehow, maybe, she did too.

Epilogue

KATE AND WYNBROOK RETURNED TO ARLINGTON Hall after a monthlong honeymoon of visiting many notable places, which she could not readily recall. What she did remember was seeing her new husband. A lot of him. Again. And again.

They returned amidst a general bustle of the staff welcoming home the master. Kate knew she would have the business of running the household and could not wait to begin the record keeping. Oh, and all the beautiful lists she could create. The sound of music and laughter greeted them as they walked toward the drawing room.

"Lady Jane is visiting Lady Ellen," explained the housekeeper. "And the new rector is making another visit. He has been quite attentive to Lady Ellen."

"Has he?" commented Wynbrook. "I'm glad Ellen has not been left all alone. Nice of him to show some compassion for a visit."

They entered the room and stopped short. Jane was at the pianoforte and Ellen was standing up in the arms of the rector. Kate blinked hard and looked again. Lady Ellen was on her feet! But how was that possible?

"What in the blue blazes is going on?" demanded Wynbrook.

"Why, Ellen, how are you standing up?" cried Kate.

"Tim—that is, Reverend Dawkins—made me new legs!" Ellen lifted her skirts a bit to reveal the wood and metal contraptions strapped to the stumps of her legs. "I am working on my balance. Is it not wonderful?"

"But…but…he has his arms around you!" stammered Wynbrook.

"It is the waltz. A common dance in Germany and France," Kate assured him.

"Reverend Dawkins says this is the best dance to start with because he can help keep my balance should I falter. Are you not pleased?" The excitement in Ellen's eyes waned.

"Of course we are pleased!" cried Kate. "Are we not, dear?" She gave her husband a quick nudge.

"Oh, yes, quite astounded. I never thought I'd see you dance."

"Nor I! I think, with more practice, I may be able to walk with a cane." Ellen beamed at them with bright, blue eyes.

Wynbrook gave her a warm but careful embrace for one on new legs. "I am so proud of you. It is truly a miracle."

"Thank you, Reverend Dawkins. We are deeply indebted," said Kate.

"Think nothing of it. Happy to help. I had to figure out how to be able to walk again after my accident, and I thought what I had constructed could help Lady

Ellen too. I was not sure she could do it, but she is an admirable lady." His eyes turned to the pleasing form of Lady Ellen.

"I would never wish harm on anyone," said Ellen most truthfully, "but I am very grateful Reverend Dawkins had the experience to be able to fashion legs for me!"

"*And we know that all things work together for good to them that love God, to them who are the called according to his purpose.* Romans 8:28," quoted Reverend Dawkins. "I never before knew it to be more true."

"Yes, indeed." Ellen held on to him for support and looked up at him in frank admiration.

Kate and Wynbrook exchanged glances.

"Maybe at some point, Reverend Dawkins, we can have a talk," said Wynbrook.

"Yes, I would like that, for there is something I must ask you."

Ellen and Jane exchanged significant looks and giggles.

"I think you may soon marry off yet another sister," Kate whispered to John.

"Inconceivable," he murmured, but the smile had returned to his face. "Shall we dance?"

"I do not dance," said Kate automatically.

"I said I would get you to dance someday. Besides, you have found you enjoy many things you once thought you would not," John whispered suggestively.

Kate couldn't squelch the smile.

"Strike up that waltz, Jane," said John. "Can't have Ellen beat me to the dance floor."

Jane struck up her tune, John put his arms around Kate, and they began to dance. They spun around the room, most likely making a horrible muddle of the waltz, but Kate felt alive and free and oh so happy.

The butler interrupted their revelry to announce a visitor. "Lord and Lady Darington," he intoned.

"My brother has returned!" Kate exclaimed. She ran toward the doorway, pulling John along with her. She got halfway across the room before she stopped short. "Wait, *Lady* Darington? Either my mother has risen from the dead or my brother has gotten married!"

Acknowledgments

No book is written without considerable help and support, and this one in particular needed encouragement throughout. Thank you to my agent, Barbara Poelle, and my editor, Deb Werksman, who are always there to make me shine. I greatly appreciate my beta reader, Laurie Maus, who didn't think I was crazy when I had to change my ending to the book because the villain wouldn't let me kill him. Special thanks to my husband, who helps and encourages me in so many ways. Everything I know about a true hero, I learned from him.

About the Author

Amanda Forester holds a PhD in psychology and worked many years in academia before discovering that writing historical romance was way more fun. Whether in the rugged Highlands of medieval Scotland or the decadent ballrooms of Regency England, her novels offer fast-paced adventures filled with wit, intrigue, and romance. You can visit her at www.amandaforester.com.